I0661546

Sarah Orne Jewett

Human Documents

Portraits and biographies of eminent men

Sarah Orne Jewett

Human Documents
Portraits and biographies of eminent men

ISBN/EAN: 9783337370510

Printed in Europe, USA, Canada, Australia, Japan

Cover: Foto ©Raphael Reischuk / pixelio.de

More available books at **www.hansebooks.com**

HUMAN DOCUMENTS

PORTRAITS AND BIOGRAPHIES

OF EMINENT MEN

ARTICLES BY ROBERT LOUIS STEVENSON, HERBERT
SPENCER, PROFESSOR DRUMMOND, EDWARD EVER-
ETT HALE, H. H. BOYESEN, GEN. HORACE PORTER,
HAMLIN GARLAND, ROBERT BARR AND OTHERS

WITH 275 ILLUSTRATIONS

NEW YORK

S. S. McCLURE, Limited

30 Lafayette Place

1895

COPYRIGHT, 1893, BY
S. S. McCLURE, LIMITED

COPYRIGHT, 1894, BY
S. S. McCLURE, LIMITED

COPYRIGHT, 1895, BY
S. S. McCLURE, LIMITED

INTRODUCTION.

By Sarah Orne Jewett.

TO give to the world a collection of the successive portraits of a man is to tell his affairs openly, and so betray intimate personalities. We are often found quarreling with the tone of the public press, because it yields to what is called the public demand to be told both the private affairs of noteworthy persons and the trivial details and circumstances of those who are insignificant. Some one has said that a sincere man willingly answers any questions, however personal, that are asked out of interest, but instantly resents those that have their impulse in curiosity; and that one's instinct always detects the difference. This I take to be a wise rule of conduct; but beyond lies the wider subject of our right to possess ourselves of personal information, although we have a vague remembrance, even in these days, of the belief of old-fashioned and decorous people, that subjects, not persons, are fitting material for conversation.

But there is an honest interest, which is as noble a thing as curiosity is contemptible; and it is in recognition of this, that Lowell writes in the largest way in his "Essay on Rousseau and the Sentimentalists."

"Yet our love of minute biographical details," he says, "our desire to make ourselves spies upon the men of the past, seems so much of an instinct in us, that we must look for the spring of it in human nature, and that somewhat deeper than mere curiosity or love of gossip." And more emphatically in another paragraph: "The moment he undertakes to establish . . . a rule of conduct, we ask at once how far are his own life and deed in accordance with what he preaches?"

This I believe to be at the bottom of even our insatiate modern eagerness to know the best and the worst of our contemporaries; it is simply to find out how far their behavior squares with their words and position. We seldom stop to get the best point of view, either in friendly talk or in a sober effort, to notice the growth of character, or, in the widest way, to comprehend the traits and influence of a man whose life in any way affects our own.

Now and then, in an old picture gallery, one comes upon the grouped portraits of a great soldier, or man of letters, or some fine lady whose character still lifts itself into view above the dead level of feminine conformity which prevailed in her time. The blurred pastel, the cracked and dingy canvas, the delicate brightness of a miniature which bears touching signs of wear—from these we piece together a whole life's history. Here are the impersonal baby face; the domineering glance of the schoolboy, lord of his dog and gun; the wan-visaged student who was just beginning to confront the serried ranks of those successes which conspired to hinder him from his duty and the fulfilment of his dreams; here is the mature man, with grave reticence of look and a proud sense of achievement; and at last the older and vaguer face, blurred and pitifully conscious of fast waning powers. As they hang in a row they seem to bear mute witness to all the successes and failures of a life.

This very day, perhaps, you chanced to open a drawer and take in your hand, for amusement's sake, some old family daguerreotypes. It is easy enough to laugh at the stiff positions and droll costumes; but suddenly you find an old likeness of yourself, and walk away with it, self-consciously, to the window, with a pretence of seeking a better light on the quick-reflecting, faintly impressed plate. Your earlier, half-forgotten self confronts you seriously; the youth whose hopes you have disappointed, or whose dreams you have turned into realities. You search the young face; perhaps you even look deep into the eyes of your own babyhood to discover your dawning consciousness; to answer back to yourself, as it were, from the known and discovered countries of that baby's future. There is a fascination in reading character backwards. You may or may not be able easily to revive early thoughts and impressions, but with an early portrait in your hand they do revive again in spite of you; they seem to be living in the pictured face to applaud or condemn you. In these old pictures exist our former selves. They wear a mystical expression. They are still ourselves, but with unfathomable eyes staring back to us out of the strange remoteness of our outgrown youth.

> " Surely I have known before
> Phantoms of the shapes ye be —
> Haunters of another shore
> 'Leaguered by another sea."

It is somehow far simpler and less startling to examine a series of portraits of some other face and figure than one's own. Perhaps it is most interesting to take those of some person whom the whole world knows, and whose traits and experiences are somewhat comprehended. You say to yourself, " This was Nelson before ever he fought one of his great sea battles ; this was Washington, with only the faintest trace of his soldiering and the leisurely undemanding aspect of a country gentleman ! " *Human Documents* the phrase is Daudet's, and tells its own story, with no need of additional attempts of suggestiveness.

It would seem to be such an inevitable subject for sermon writing, that no one need be unfamiliar with warnings, lest our weakness and wickedness leave traces upon the countenance—awful, ineffaceable hieroglyphics, that belong to the one universal primitive language of mankind. Who cannot read faces? The merest savage, who comprehends no written language, glances at you to know if he may expect friendliness or enmity, with a quicker intelligence than your own.

The lines that are written slowly and certainly by the pen of character, the deep mark that sorrow once left, or the light sign-manual of an unfading joy, there they are and will remain ; it is at length the aspect of the spiritual body itself, and belongs to the unfolding and existence of life. We have never formulated a science like palmistry on the larger scale that this character-reading from the face would need ; but to say that we make our own faces, and, having made them, have made pieces of immortality, is to say what seems trite enough. A child turns with quick impatience and incredulity from the dull admonitions of his teachers, about goodness and good looks. To say, " Be good and you will be beautiful," is like giving him a stone for a lantern. Beauty seems an accident rather than an achievement, and a cause

instead of an effect ; but when childhood has passed, one of the things we are sure to have learned, is to read the sign-language of faces, and to take the messages they bring. Recognition of these things is sure to come to us more and more by living ; there is no such thing as turning our faces into unbetraying masks. A series of portraits is a veritable Human Document, and the merest glance may discover the progress of the man, the dwindled or developed personality, the history of a character.

These sentences are written merely as suggestions, and from the point of view of morals ; there is also the point of view of heredity, and the curious resemblance between those who belong to certain professions. Just what it is that makes us almost certain to recognize a doctor or a priest at first glance is too subtle a question for discussion here. Some one has said that we usually arrive, in time, at the opposite extreme to those preferences and opinions which we hold in early life. The man who breaks away from conventionalities, ends by returning to them, or out of narrow prejudices and restrictions grows towards a late and serene liberty. These changes show themselves in the face with amazing clearness, and it would seem also, that even individuality sways us only for a time ; that if we live far into the autumnal period of life we lose much of our individuality of looks, and become more emphatically members of the family from which we spring. A man like Charles the First was already less himself than he was a Stuart ; we should not fail in instances of this sort, nor seek far afield. The return to the type compels us steadily ; at last it has its way. Very old persons, and those who are dangerously ill, are often noticed to be curiously like their nearest of kin, and to have almost visibly ceased to be themselves.

All time has been getting our lives ready to be lived, to be shaped as far as may be by our own wills, and furthered by that conscious freedom that gives us to be ourselves. You may read all these in any Human Document—the look of race, the look of family, the look that is set like a seal by a man's occupation, the look of the spirit's free or hindered life, and success or failure in the pursuit of goodness—they are all plain to see. If we could read one human face aright, the history not only of the man, but of humanity itself, is written there.

NOTE.—The above paper originally introduced series of portraits published in McCLURE'S MAGAZINE. As these portraits form a large part of the contents of the present volume, the paper may very aptly introduce it too, although the author, in writing, did not have in contemplation the biographical studies with which the portraits are here combined.—EDITOR.

TABLE OF CONTENTS.

TABLE OF CONTENTS.

The articles and pictures in this volume are reproduced, for the most part, from numbers of MCCLURE'S MAGAZINE between June, 1893, and May, 1895.

MR. GLADSTONE IN 1861. AGE 52.

Mr. Gladstone is standing in the Gothic porchway of Sir Arthur Hayter's house at Tintagel, Cornwall. From a
photograph by Frederick Argall, Truro, Cornwall.

HUMAN DOCUMENTS.

A DAY WITH GLADSTONE.

FROM THE MORNING AT HAWARDEN TO THE EVENING AT THE HOUSE OF COMMONS.

BY H. W. MASSINGHAM OF THE "LONDON CHRONICLE."

I AM often asked what is the secret of Mr. Gladstone's extraordinary length of days and of the perfection of his unvarying health. It may be partly attributed to the remarkable longevity of the Gladstone family, a hardy Scottish stock with fewer weak shoots and branches than perhaps any of the ruling families of England. But it has depended mainly on Mr. Gladstone himself and on the undeviating regularity of his habits. Most English statesmen have been either free livers or with a touch of the *bon vivant* in them. Pitt and Fox were men of the first character ; Melbourne, Palmerston, and Lord Beaconsfield were of the last. But Mr. Gladstone is a man who has been guilty of no excesses, save perhaps in work. He rises at the same hour every day, uses the same fairly generous, but always carefully regulated, diet, goes to bed about the same hour, pursues the same round of work and intellectual and social pleasure. An extraordinarily varied life is accompanied by a certain rigidity of personal habit I have never seen surpassed. The only change old age has witnessed has been that the House of Commons work has been curtailed, and that Mr. Gladstone has not of late years been seen

MRS. W. E. GLADSTONE.
From a photograph by Barraud, London.

This paper, written when Mr. Gladstone, still Prime Minister of England, was in the very hottest of the battle for Home Rule for Ireland, describes the round of his daily life at what is the most significant and dramatic moment of all his long career.—EDITOR.

in the House after the dinner hour, which lasts from eight till ten, except on nights when crucial divisions are expected. With the approach of winter and its accompanying chills, to which he is extremely susceptible, he seeks the blue skies and dry air of the Mediterranean coasts and of his beloved Italy. With this exception his life goes on in its pleasant monotony. At Hawarden, of course, it is simpler and more private than in London. In town to-day Mr. Gladstone avoids all large parties and great crushes and gatherings where he may be expected to be either mobbed or bored or detained beyond his usual bed-time.

HIS PERSONALITY.

Personally Mr. Gladstone is an example of the most winning, the most delicate, and the most minute courtesy. He is a gentleman of the elder English school, and his manners are grand and urbane, always stately, never condescending, and genuinely modest. He affects even the dress of the old school, and I have seen him in the morning wearing an old black evening coat such as Professor Jowett still affects. The humblest passer-by in Piccadilly, raising his hat to Mr. Gladstone, is sure to get a sweeping salute in return. This courtliness is all the more remarkable because it accompanies and adorns a very strong temper, a will of iron, and a habit of being regarded for the greater part of his lifetime as a personal force of unequalled magnitude. Yet the most foolish, and perhaps one may add the most impertinent, of Mr. Gladstone's dinner-table questioners is sure of an elaborate reply, delivered with the air of a student in deferential talk with his master. To the cloth Mr. Gladstone shows a reverence that occasionally woos the observer to a smile. The callowest curate is sure of a respectful listener in the foremost Englishman of the day. On the other hand, in private conversation the premier does not often brook contradiction. His temper is high, and though, as George Russell has said, it is under vigilant control, there are subjects on which it is easy to arouse the old lion. Then the grand eyes flash, the torrent of brilliant monologue flows with more rapid sweep, and the dinner table is breathless at the spectacle of Mr. Glad-

stone angry. As to his relations with his family, they are very charming. It is a pleasure to hear Herbert Gladstone—his youngest, and possibly his favorite son—speak of "my father." All of them, sons and daughters, are absolutely devoted to his cause, wrapped up in his personality, and enthusiastic as to every side of his character. Of children Mr. Gladstone has always been fond, and he has more than one favorite among his grandchildren.

MR. GLADSTONE SETTING OUT ON HIS MORNING WALK HOME FROM CHURCH AT HAWARDEN.

MR. GLADSTONE'S MORNING.

Mr. Gladstone's day begins about 7:30, after seven hours and a half of sound, dreamless sleep, which no disturbing crisis in public affairs was ever known to spoil. At Hawarden it usually opens with a morning walk to church, with which no kind of weather—hail, rain, snow, or frost—is ever allowed to interfere. In his rough slouch hat and gray Inverness cape, the old man plods sturdily to his devotions. To the

THE LIBRARY AT HAWARDEN.

forenoon, for when he is in the country he has practically no other continuous and regular work-time. Yet into this space he has to condense his enormous correspondence— for which, when no private secretary is available, he seeks the help of his sons and daughters—his political work, and his varied literary pursuits. The explanation of this extreme orderliness of mind is probably to be found in his unequalled habit of concentration on

rain, the danger of sitting in wet clothes, and small troubles of this kind, he is absolutely impervious, and Mrs. Gladstone's solicitude has never availed to change his lifelong custom in this respect. Breakfast over, working time commences. I am often astonished at the manner in which Mr. Gladstone manages to crowd his almost endlessly varied occupations into the business before him. As in matters of policy, so in all his private habits, Mr. Gladstone thinks of one thing and of one thing only at a time. When Home Rule was up, he had no eyes or ears for any subject but Ireland, of course except ing his favorite excursions into the twin subjects of Homer and Christian theology Enter the room when Mr. Gladstone is

THE GLADSTONE FAMILY.

reading a book : you may move noisily about the chamber, ransack the books on the shelves, stir the furniture, but never for one moment will the reader be conscious of your presence. At Downing Street, during his earlier ministries, these hours of study were often, I might say usually, preceded by the famous breakfast at which the celebrated actor or actress, the rising poet, the well-known artist, the diplomatist halting on his way from one station of the kingdom to another, were welcome guests. Madame Bernhardt, Miss Ellen Terry,

ever, Sir Andrew Clark, Mr. Gladstone's favorite physician and intimate friend, has recommended that tree-felling be given over ; and now Mr. Gladstone's recreation, in addition to long walks, in which he still delights, is that of lopping branches off veterans whose trunks have fallen to younger arms.

AS A READER.

Between the afternoon tea and dinner the statesman usually retires again, and

LUNCH AT HAWARDEN.

Henry Irving, Madame Modjeska, have all assisted at these pleasant feasts.

HIS AFTERNOON.

Lunch with Mr. Gladstone is a very simple meal, which neither at Hawarden nor Downing Street admits of much form or publicity. The afternoon which follows is a very much broken and less regular period. At Hawarden a portion of it is usually spent out of doors. In the old days it was devoted to the felling of some giant of the woods. Within the last few years, how-

gets through some of the lighter and more agreeable of his intellectual tasks. He reads rapidly, and I think I should say that, especially of late years, he does a good deal of skipping. If a book does not interest him, he does not trouble to read it through. He uses a rough kind of *memoria technica* to enable him to mark passages with which he agrees, from which he dissents, which he desires to qualify, or which he reserves for future reference. I should say the books he reads most of are those dealing with theology, always the first and favorite topic, and the history of Ire-

MR. GLADSTONE ON HIS WAY TO THE HOUSE OF COMMONS.

select or really first-rate collection. It comprises an undue proportion of theological literature, of which he is a large and not over-discriminating buyer. I doubt, indeed, whether there is any larger private bookbuyer in England. All the booksellers send him their catalogues, especially those of rare and curious books. I have seen many of these lists, with a brief order in Mr. Gladstone's own handwriting on the flyleaf, with his tick against twenty or thirty volumes which he desires to buy. These usually range round classical works, archæology, special periods of English history, and, above all, works reconciling the Biblical record with science.

THE LIBRARY AT HAWARDEN—MR. GLADSTONE AS A BUYER OF BOOKS.

Of late, as is fairly well known, Mr. Gladstone has built himself an octagonal iron house in Hawarden village, a mile and a half from the castle, for the storage of his specially valuable books and a collection of private papers which traverse a good many of the state secrets of the greater land before and after the Act of Union. Indeed, everything dealing with that memorable period is greatly treasured. I remember one hasty glance over Mr. Gladstone's book table in his own house. In addition to the liberal weekly, "The Speaker," and a few political pamphlets, there were, I should say, fifteen or twenty works on theology, none of them, so far as I could see, of first-rate importance. Of science Mr. Gladstone knows little, and it cannot be said that his interest in it is keen. He belongs, in a word, to the old-fashioned Oxford ecclesiastical school, using the controversial weapons which are to be found in the works of Pusey and of Hurrell Froude. In his reading, when a question of more minute and out-of-the-way scholarship arises, he appeals to his constant friend and assistant, Lord Acton, to whose profound learning he bows with a deference which is very touching to note.

Mr. Gladstone's library is not what can be called a

THE STAIRCASE, HAWARDEN CASTLE,
From a photograph by G. W. Webster, Chester, England.

part of the century. The importance of these is great, and the chances are that before Mr. Gladstone dies they will all be grouped and indexed in his upright, a little crabbed, but perfectly plain handwriting. By the way, a great many statements have been made about Mr. Gladstone's library, sand or so are now distributed be the little iron house to which I ha ferred, and the Hawarden library. riously enough, Mr. Gladstone is worshipper of books for the sake of outward adornments. He loves the what is inside rather than outside.

and I may as well give the facts, which have never before been made public. His original library consisted of about twenty-four thousand volumes. In the seventies, however, he parted with his entire collection of political works, amounting to some eight thousand volumes, to the late Lord Wolverton. The remaining fifteen thou- even occasionally sells extremely rar costly editions for which he has no s use. In all money matters, indeed, thrifty, orderly Scotchman. He has been rich, though his affairs have g improved since the time when in hi premiership he had to sell his valuabl lection of china.

AT THE DINNER TABLE.

Dinner with Mr. Gladstone is the stately ceremonial meal which it has become to healthy appetite of a man of thirty. A glass of champagne is agreeable to him, and if he does not take his glass or two of port at dinner, he makes it up by two or three glasses of claret, which he considers

HAWARDEN CASTLE.

the upper-middle-class Englishman. Mr. Gladstone invariably dresses for it, wearing the high crest collar which Harry Furniss has immortalized, and a cutaway coat which strikes one as of a slightly old-fashioned pattern. His digestion never fails him, and he eats and drinks with the an equivalent. Oysters he never could endure; but, like Schopenhauer and Goethe and many another great man, he is a consistently hearty and unfastidious eater. He talks much in animated monologue, though the common complaint that he monopolizes the conversation is not a just

MR. GLADSTONE'S BEDROOM AT HAWARDEN CASTLE.

From a photograph by G. W. Webster, Chester, England.

one. You cannot easily turn Mr. Gladstone into a train of ideas which does not
interest him, but he is a courteous and even
eager listener ; and if the subject is of
general interest, he does not bear in it any
more than the commanding part which the
rest of the company invariably allows him.
His speaking voice is a little gruffer and
less musical than his oratorical notes,
which, in spite of the invading hoarseness,
still at times ring out with their old clearness. As a rule he does not talk on politics. On ecclesiastical matters he is a
can meet an old friend or two, and see a
young face which he may be interested in
seeing. One habit of his is quite unvarying. He likes to walk home, and to walk
home alone. He declines escort, and slips
away for his quiet stroll under the stars, or
even through the fog and mist, on a London winter's night. Midnight usually
brings his busy, happy day to a close.
With sleeplessness he has never been at all
bothered, and at eighty-three his nights
are as dreamless and untroubled as those
of a boy of ten.

THE MORNING-ROOM AT HAWARDEN CASTLE.

From a photograph by G. W. Webster, Chester, England.

never wearied disputant. Poetry has also
a singular charm for him, and no modern
topic has interested him more keenly than
the discussion as to Tennyson's successor
to the laureateship. I remember that at a
small dinner at which I recently met him,
the conversation ran almost entirely on the
two subjects of old English hymns and
young English poets. His favorite religious poet is, I should say, Cardinal Newman, and his favorite hymn, Toplady's
"Rock of Ages," of which his Latin rendering is to my mind far stronger and
purer than the original English. When he
is in town, he dines out almost every day,
though, as I have said, he eschews formal
and mixed gatherings, and affects the
small and early dinner party at which he

IN THE HOUSE.

His afternoons when in town and during
the season are, of course, given up pretty
exclusively to public business and the
House of Commons, which he usually
reaches about four o'clock. He goes by a
side door straight to his private room,
where he receives his colleagues, and hears
of endless questions and motions, which
fall like leaves in Vallombrosa around the
head of a prime minister. Probably steps
will be taken to remove much of this irk-
some and somewhat petty burden from the
shoulders of the aged minister. But leader
Mr. Gladstone must and will be at eighty-
three, quite as fully as he was at sixty. Indeed, the complaint of him always has been

that he does too much, both for his own health and the smooth manipulation of the great machine which, as was once remarked, creaks and moves rather lumberingly under his masterful but over-minute guidance. During the last two or three years it has been customary for the Whigs to so arrange that Mr. Gladstone speaks early in the evening. He is not always able to do this while the Home Rule Bill is under discussion, but I do not think he will ever again find it necessary to follow the entire course of a Parliamentary debate. He never needed to do as much listening from the Treasury Bench as he was wont to do in his first and second ministries. I do not think that any prime minister ever spent half as much time in the House of Commons as did Mr. Gladstone; certainly no one ever made one-tenth part as many speeches. Indeed, it requires all Mrs. Gladstone's vigilance to avert the physical strain consequent upon overwork. With this purpose she invariably watches him in the House of Commons, from a corner seat in the right hand of the Ladies' Gallery, which is always reserved for her and which I have never known her to miss occupying on any occasion of the slightest importance.

SPEECH-MAKING.

I have before me two or three examples of notes of Mr. Gladstone's speeches; one of them refers to one of the most important of his addresses on the customs question. It was a long speech, extending, if I remember rightly, to considerably over an hour. Yet the memoranda consist purely of four or five sentences of two or three words apiece, written on a single sheet of note paper, and no hint of the course of the oration is given. Occasionally, no doubt, especially in the case of the speech on the introduction of the Home Rule Bill, which was to my mind the finest Mr. Gladstone has ever delivered, the notes were rather more extensive than this, but as a rule they are extremely brief. When Mr. Gladstone addresses a great public meeting, the most elaborate pains are taken to insure his comfort. He can now only read the very largest print, and careful and delicate arrangements are made to provide him with lamps throwing the light on the desk or table near which he stands. Sir Andrew Clark observes the most jealous watchfulness over his patient. A curious instance of this occurred at Newcastle, when Mr. Gladstone was delivering his address to the great liberal caucus which assembles as the annual meeting of the National Liberal Federation. Sir Andrew had insisted that the orator should confine himself to a speech lasting only an hour. Fearing that his charge would forget all about his promise in the excitement of speaking, the physician slipped onto the platform and timed Mr. Gladstone, watch in hand. The hour passed, but there was no pause in the torrent of words. Sir Andrew was in despair. At last he pencilled a note to Mr. Morley, beseeching him to insist upon the speech coming to an end. But Mr. Morley would not undertake the responsibility of cutting a great oration, and the result was that Mr. Gladstone stole another half hour from time and his physician. The next day a friend of mine went breathlessly up to Sir Andrew, and asked how the statesman had borne the additional strain. "He did not turn a hair," was the reply. Practically the only sign of physical failure which is apparent in recent speeches has been that the voice tends to break and die away after about an hour's exercise, and for a moment the sound of the curiously veiled notes and a glance at the marble pallor of the face gives one the impression that after all Mr. Gladstone is a very, very old man. But there is never anything like a total breakdown. And no one is aware of the enormous stores of physical energy on which the prime minister can draw, who has not sat quite close to him, and measured the wonderful breadth of his shoulders and heard his voice coming straight from his chest in great *bouffées* of sound. Then you forget all about the heavy wrinkles in the white face, the scanty silver hair, and the patriarchal look of the figure before you.

PORTRAITS OF GLADSTONE.

MR. GLADSTONE was born at Liverpool, December 29, 1809. He has been a member of the House of Commons almost continuously since 1832; and when he resigned the office of prime minister last year, on account of his advanced age, he was serving in it for the fourth time. His first premiership extended from December, 1868, to February, 1874; the second, from April, 1880, to June, 1885; the third, from February to August, 1886; and the fourth, from August, 1892, to March, 1894. Here are nearly thirteen years; and as a prime minister retires the moment the country is not with him, they tell in a word what a power Mr. Gladstone has been.

It would be strange if, in a political career of upwards of sixty years, Mr. Gladstone had shown no changes of opinion. To several of the measures with which his name is particularly identified, as, for example, Home Rule for Ireland, he has come by slow and cautious degrees and with almost a complete turn on himself. He entered Parliament, indeed, as a Conservative, and the first prime minister under whom he held office was Sir Robert Peel. It was not until 1851 that he parted company completely with the Conservatives. The next year, 1852, he achieved one of the most brilliant oratorical triumphs of his whole career. Parliament was debating a budget presented by Mr. Disraeli, and Disraeli made in defence of his measure a speech of such cleverness and power that friend and foe alike thought it to be unanswerable. At two o'clock in the morning Mr. Gladstone began a reply. Long before he finished he had completely dissipated the impression left by Disraeli and had captured the House.

GLADSTONE AT THREE YEARS OF AGE, WITH HIS SISTER.
From a miniature.

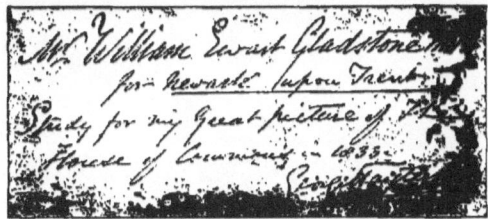

From a painting by George Hayter, reproduced by the kind permission of Sir John Gladstone, Bart. This year Mr. Gladstone had just entered Lincoln's Inn as a student of law, and was serving his first months in Parliament, having received his first election in December, 1832.

MR. GLADSTONE IN 1839.   AGE 29.

From a life portrait by Bradley. At this time Mr. Gladstone was of the Opposition in the House of Commons, and acting under the leadership of Sir Robert Peel.

MR. GLADSTONE IN 1841. AGE 31.

From a photograph, by Fradelle & Young, London, of a chalk drawing by W. B. Richmond. In 1841 Mr. Gladstone entered the cabinet as Vice-President of the Board of Trade and Master of the Mint.

MR. GLADSTONE IN 1852. AGE 42.

From a photograph by Samuel A. Walker, London. In 1852 Mr. Gladstone became for the first time Chancellor of the Exchequer, an office for which he has many times proved unequalled fitness.

MR. GLADSTONE IN 1859. AGE 49.

From a photograph by Samuel A. Walker, London. This year, under Lord Palmerston, Mr. Gladstone became a second time Chancellor of the Exchequer.

MR. GLADSTONE IN 1865. AGE 55.

From a photograph by Samuel A. Walker, London.

MR. GLADSTONE IN 1865.   AGE 55.

From a photograph by Frederick Hollyer, London, of a portrait painted by Sir G. F. Watts.   It was the latter part of 1865, on the death of Lord Palmerston, that Mr. Gladstone first became leader of the House of Commons

MR. GLADSTONE IN 1866. AGE 56.

From a photograph by Samuel A. Walker, London. June 18, 1866, Mr. Gladstone, then in his first experience as leader of the House of Commons, suffered defeat on a reform bill, by the Tories under Disraeli.

MR. GLADSTONE IN 1868. AGE 58.

From a photograph by Samuel A. Walker, London. In 1868 Mr. Gladstone secured the defeat of the Disraeli ministry on the disestablishment of the Irish Church, and himself became prime minister for the first time.

MR. GLADSTONE IN 1880. AGE 70.

From a photograph by Samuel A. Walker, London. This year the Liberals recovered a lost majority in Parliament, Mr. Gladstone himself making a famous campaign, and securing election by a famous majority, in Midlothian. Disraeli (now Lord Beaconsfield) and his cabinet resigned, and Mr. Gladstone again became prime minister.

MR. GLADSTONE AND HIS GRANDSON (SON OF HIS ELDEST SON, THE LATE W. H. GLADSTONE). 1890. AGE 80.

From a portrait painted by McClure Hamilton, and presented by the ladies of England, Scotland, Wales, and Ireland to Mrs. Gladstone as a souvenir of hers and Mr. Gladstone's golden wedding, celebrated the year before (1889).

MR. GLADSTONE IN 1890. AGE 80.

After a painting by John Colin Forbes, R. C. A.   Reproduced by the kind permission of Henry Graves & Co., London.

, WITH H   GREAT-GRANDCHILDREN.

From a photograph by Valentine & Sons, Dundee, taken at Hawarden (Mr. Gladstone's country house),
October 1 ... . At this time Parliament was adjourned for a month or two after long and excited debates
on the subject of Home Rule for Ireland.

MR. GLADSTONE, HAWARDEN, OCTOBER 13, 1893. AGE 83.

From a photograph by Valentine & Sons, Dundee.

Mr. GLADSTONE, HAWARDEN, AUGUST, 1896. VOL. 74.
From a photograph by Robinson & Thompson, Liverpool and Birkenhead.

PORTRAITS OF BISMARCK.

PRINCE OTTO EDWARD LEOPOLD VON BISMARCK was born April 1, 1815, of a very old and sturdy German family. He was put early to school, attended several universities, and served his term in the army. His political life began in 1846, when he was elected a member of the diet of his province, Saxony. The next year he went to Berlin as a representative in the General Diet, and immediately attracted attention by the force and boldness of his speeches. In 1851 he began his diplomatic career as secretary to the Prussian member of the representative Assembly of German Sovereigns at Frankfort. He has been described at this time as " of very tall, stalwart, and imposing mien, with blue gray, penetrating, fearless eyes; of a bright, fresh countenance, with blond hair and beard." In 1859 he was sent as ambassador to Russia. In 1862 he was transferred to Paris; but a few months later he was made minister of foreign affairs. He inaugurated his ministry by the summary dissolution of the Prussian Chamber of Deputies, because it refused to pass the budget proposed by the throne, curtly informing the body that the king's government would be obliged to do without its sanction. Five times the deputies were dismissed in this fashion. Bismarck was denounced on all sides; but as his profound project, already conceived, of uniting the German states into a compact empire, with Prussia at the head, advanced, by one brilliant stroke of statesmanship after another, toward fulfilment, the early distrust was forgotten, and he became, in spite of his apparent contempt for popular rights, a popular idol. The short, sharp war of 1866, terminating Austrian dominance in Germany, began a national progress, under Bismarck's sagacious and strong direction, which came to its consummation at the close of the war with France, when, on January 18, 1871, in the palace of the French kings, at Versailles, William I., King of Prussia, was proclaimed Emperor of united Germany. In 1890, differences with the present Emperor, William II., led to Bismarck's retirement from public life.

BISMARCK IN 1834. AGE 19.

Student in the University of Göttingen.

3

1851. AGE 36.

Diplomatist at Frankfort. From a photograph by A. Bockmann, Strasburg.

1854.   AGE 39.   STILL SERVING AT FRANKFORT.

1866, THE YEAR OF THE WAR WITH AUSTRIA.   AGE 51.

BISMARCK IN 1871. AGE 56.

From a photograph by Loescher & Petsch, Berlin. On January 18, 1871, the war with France having been brought to a triumphant close, Bismarck had the satisfaction of seeing King William of Prussia crowned Emperor of united Germany in the palace of the French kings, at Versailles, himself becoming at the same time Chancellor of the German Empire. The formal treaty of peace with France was signed a month later.

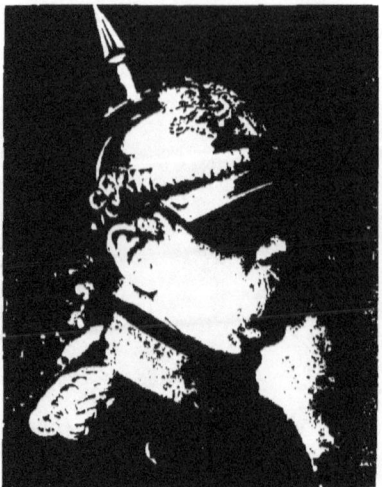

BISMARCK IN 1871. AGE 56.

PROCLAIMING WILLIAM I, EMPEROR. VERSAILLES, JANUARY 18, 1871. BISMARCK, IN WHITE UNIFORM, STANDS JUST BEFORE THE THRONE. FROM A PHOTOGRAPH BY THE BERLIN PHOTOGRAPH COMPANY.

BISMARCK IN 1877.   AGE 62.

On the eve of the Congress of Berlin, wherein the European powers, largely under Bismarck's guidance, fixed the relations of Turkey.   From a photograph by Loescher & Petsch, Berlin.

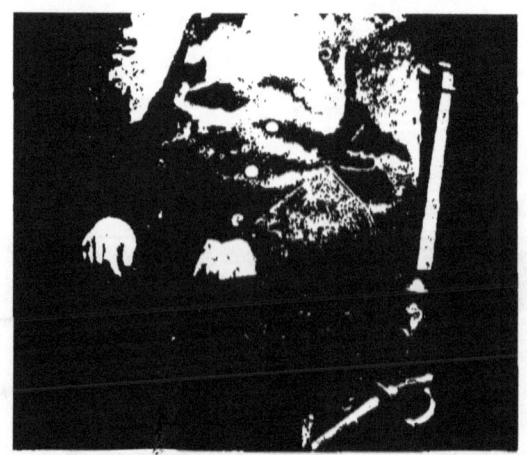

BISMARCK IN 1880.   AGE 65.
From a photograph by Ad. Braun & Co., Paris.

1883.   AGE 68.

1885.   AGE 70.

From a photograph by Loescher and Petsch, Berlin.

From a photograph by Loescher and Petsch, Berlin.

BISMARCK IN 1885.   AGE 70.

From a photograph by Loescher & Petsch, Berlin.   Bismarck's seventieth birthday was celebrated as a great national event in Germany, as have been his succeeding birthdays.

BISMARCK IN 1886. AGE 71.
From a photograph taken at Friedrichsruh by A. Bockmann, Strasburg.

BISMARCK IN 1886. AGE 71.
From a photograph by A. Bockmann, Lübeck

BISMARCK IN 1887. AGE 72.
From a photograph by M. Ziesler, Berlin.

EMPEROR WILLIAM II. AND PRINCE BISMARCK, 1888.
From a photograph by M. Fiesler, Berlin.

1889, AGE 74.
From a photograph by M. Fiesler, Berlin.

1889, AGE 74.
From a photograph by Jul. Braatz, Berlin

BISMARCK IN 1890. AGE 75.

In the spring of this year Bismarck's differences with William II. culminated in a retirement from office, which was practically a dismissal, after a continuous cabinet service of nearly thirty years. This portrait was taken at Friedrichsruh two months after his resignation. From a photograph by A. Bockmann, Strasburg.

BISMARCK IN 1890. AGE 75.
From a copyright photograph owned by Strumper & Co., Hamburg.

BISMARCK IN 1891. AGE 76.
Greeted by a body of students at Kissingen. From a photograph by Pilartz, Kissingen

BISMARCK IN 1894.   AGE 79.

From a photograph by Karl Hahn, Munich

PERSONAL TRAITS OF GENERAL GRANT.

By GENERAL HORACE PORTER.

[General Horace Porter served on General Grant's staff from the time Grant took command of the army in the East until the close of the war. He was also Grant's Assistant Secretary of War, and, through Grant's first term as President, his private secretary.—EDITOR.]

THE recurrence of General Grant's birthday never fails to recall to the minds of those who were associated with him the many admirable traits of his character. A number of these traits, if not absolutely peculiar to him, were more thoroughly developed in his nature than in the natures of other men.

His personal characteristics were always a source of interest to those who served with him, although he never seemed to be conscious of them himself. He had so little egotism in his nature that he never took into consideration any of his own peculiarities, and never seemed to feel that he possessed any qualities different from those common to all men. He always shrank from speaking of matters personal to himself, and evidently never analyzed his own mental powers. In his intercourse he did not appear to study to be reticent regarding himself ; he appeared rather to be unconscious of self. He was always calm and unemotional, yet deeply earnest in every work in which he engaged. While his mental qualities and the means by which he accomplished his purposes have been something of a puzzle to philosophers, he was always natural in his manners and intensely human in everything he did.

Among the many personal traits which might be mentioned, he possessed five attributes which were pronounced and conspicuous, and stand out as salient points in his character. They were Truth, Courage, Modesty, Generosity, and Loyalty.

He was, without exception, the most absolutely truthful man I ever encountered in

General J. A. Rawlins,   General Grant.   Colonel Bowers.
Chief of Staff.   Assistant Adjutant-General.

TAKEN AT CITY POINT HEADQUARTERS EARLY IN 1865.

From a photograph by Pach Brothers.

public or private life. This trait may be recognized in the frankness and honesty of expression in all his correspondence. He was not only truthful himself, but he had a horror of untruth in others. One day while sitting in his bedroom in the White House, where he had retired to write a message to Congress, a card was brought in by a servant. An officer on duty at the time, seeing that the President did not want to be disturbed, remarked to the servant, "Say the President is not in." General Grant overheard the remark, turned around suddenly in his chair, and cried out to the servant, "Tell him no such thing. I don't lie myself, and I don't want any one to lie for me."

When the President had before him for his action the famous Inflation Bill, a member of Congress urged him persistently to sign it. When he had vetoed it, and it was found that the press and public everywhere justified his action, the Congressman came out in a speech reciting how materially he had assisted in bringing about the veto. When the President read the report of the speech in the newspapers, he said, "How can So-and-so state publicly such an untruth! I do not see how he can ever look me in the face again." He had a contempt for the man ever after. Even in ordinary conversation he would relate a simple incident which happened in one of his walks upon the street, with all the accuracy of a translator of the new version of the Scriptures ; and if in telling the story he had said mistakenly, for instance, that he had met a man on the south side of the avenue, he would return to the subject hours afterward to correct the error and state with great particularity that it was on the *north* side of the avenue that the encounter had taken place. These corrections and constant efforts to be accurate in every statement he made once led a gentleman to say of him that he was "tediously" truthful. It has often been a question of ethics in warfare whether an officer is justifiable in putting his signature to a false report or a deceptive letter for the purpose of having it fall into the hands of the enemy, with a view to misleading him. It is very certain that General Grant would never have resorted to such a subterfuge, however important might have been the results to be attained.

General Grant possessed a rare and con-

MASSAPONAX CHURCH, VIRGINIA.   GRANT'S HEADQUARTERS IN MAY, 1864.
PHOTOGRAPH BY BRADY.

spicuous Courage, which, seen under all circumstances, appeared never to vary. It was not a courage inspired by excitement; it was a steady and patient courage in all the scenes in which it was displayed. It might be called, more appropriately, an unconsciousness of danger. He seemed never to be aware of any danger to himself or to any person about him. His physical and moral courage were both of the same high order. To use an Americanism, he was "clean grit." This characteristic early displayed itself in the nerve he exhibited, as a cadet at West Point, in breaking fractious horses in the riding-hall. His courage was conspicuous in all the battles in Mexico in which he was engaged, particularly in leading an attack against one of the gates of the

GRANT'S HEADQUARTERS AT CITY POINT EARLY IN 1905.

Photograph by Brady.

City of Mexico, at the head of a dozen men whom he had called on to volunteer for the purpose. It showed itself at Belmont, in the gallant manner in which he led his troops, and in his remaining on shore in the retreat until he had seen all his men aboard the steamboats. At Donelson and Shiloh, and in many of the fights in the Virginia campaign, while he never posed for effect, or indulged in mock heroics, his exposure to danger when necessary, and his habitual indifference under fire, were constantly noticeable. He was one of the few men who never displayed the slightest nervousness in battle. Dodging bullets is by no means proof of a lack of courage. It proceeds from a nervousness which is often purely physical, and is no more significant as a test of courage than the act of winking when something is thrown suddenly in one's face. It is entirely involuntary. Many a brave officer has been known to indulge in "jack-knifing" under fire, as it is called; that is, bending low or doubling up, when bullets were whistling by. In my own experience I can recall only two persons who, throughout a rattling musketry fire, could sit in their saddles without moving a muscle or even winking an eye. One was a bugler in the regular cavalry, and the other was General Grant.

The day the outer lines of Petersburg were carried, and the troops were closing up upon the inner lines, the General halted near a house on a piece of elevated ground which overlooked the field. The position was under fire, and the enemy's batteries seemed to pay particular attention to the spot, noticing, perhaps, the group of officers collected there, and believing that some of the Union commanders were among them. The General was engaged in writing some despatches, and paid no attention whatever to the shots falling about him. Members of the staff remarked that the place was becoming a target, and suggested that he move to a less conspicuous position, but he seemed to pay no attention to the advice given. After he had finished his despatches, and taken another view of the enemy's works, he quietly mounted his horse and rode slowly to another part of the field, remarking to the officers about him, with a jocose twinkle in his eye, " Well, they do seem to have the range on us."

During one of the fights in front of Petersburg the telegraph-poles had been thrown down, and the twisted wires were scattered about upon the ground. While our troops were falling back before a vigorous attack made by the enemy, the General's horse caught his foot in a loop of the wire, and in the animal's efforts to free himself the coil became twisted still tighter. The enemy

THE McLEAN HOUSE IN APPOMATTOX, VIRGINIA, WHERE GRANT AND LEE MET AND FIXED THE TERMS OF LEE'S
SURRENDER, APRIL 9, 1865.

was moving up rapidly, delivering a heavy fire, and there was no time to be lost. The staff officers began to wear anxious looks upon their faces, and became very apprehensive for the General's safety. He sat quietly in his saddle, giving directions to an orderly, and afterward to an officer who had dismounted, as they were struggling nervously to uncoil the wire, and kept cautioning them in a low, calm tone of voice not to hurt the horse's leg. Finally the foot was released ; but none too quickly, as the enemy a few minutes later had gained possession of that part of the field.

His moral courage was manifested in many instances. He took a grave responsibility in paroling the officers and men captured at Vicksburg and sending them home, and persons who did not understand the situation subjected him to severe criticism. But he shouldered the entire responsibility, and subsequent events proved that he was entirely correct in the action he had taken.

It was supposed at Appomattox that the terms he gave to Lee and his men might not be approved by the authorities at Washington. But without consulting them, General Grant assumed the entire responsibility. There was not a moment's hesitation.

Even in trivial matters he never seemed to shrink from any act which he set out to

perform. The following incident, though trifling in itself, illustrates this trait in his character. When we were in the heat of the political campaign in which he was a candidate for the Presidency a second time, and when there was the utmost violence in campaign meetings, and unparalleled abuse exchanged between members of the contesting parties, the President made many trips by rail in New Jersey, where he was residing at his summer home at Elberon. He always travelled in an ordinary passenger-car, and mingled freely with all classes of people. On one of these trips he said to me : "I think I will go forward into the smoking-car and have a smoke." The car was filled with a rough class of men, several of them under the influence of liquor. The President sat down in a seat next to one of the passengers. He was immediately recognized, and his neighbor, evidently for the purpose of "showing off," proceeded to make himself objectionably familiar. He took out a cigar, and turning to the President cried : "I say, give us a light, neighbor," and reached out his hand, expecting the President to pass him the cigar which he was smoking. The President looked him in the eye calmly for a few seconds, and then pulled out a match-box, struck a match, and handed it to him. Those who had been looking on applauded the act, and the smoker was silenced, and afterward became very respectful.

Even the valor of his martial deeds was surpassed by the superb courage displayed in the painful illness which preceded his death. Though suffering untold torture, he held death at arm's length with one hand, while with the other he penned the most brilliant chapter in American history. His fortune had disappeared, his family was without support, and summoning to his aid all of his old-time fortitude, he sat through months of excruciating agony, laboring to finish the book which would be the means of saving those he loved best from want. He seemed to live entirely upon his will-power until the last lines were finished, and then yielded to the first foe to whom he had ever surrendered—Death.

His extreme Modesty attracts attention in all of his speeches and letters, and especially in his " Memoirs." A distinguished literary critic once remarked that that book was the only autobiography he had ever read which was totally devoid of egotism. The General not only abstains from vaunting himself, but seems to take pains to enumerate all the good qualities in which

he is lacking ; and, while he describes in eulogistic terms the persons who were associated with him, he records nothing which would seem to be in commendation of himself. Although his mind was a great storehouse of useful information, the result of constant reading and a retentive memory, he laid no claim to any knowledge he did not possess. He agreed with Addison that " pedantry in learning is like hypocrisy in religion, a form of knowledge without the power of it." He had a particular aversion to egotists and braggarts. Though fond of telling stories, and at times a most interesting *raconteur*, he never related an anecdote which was at all off color, or which could be construed as an offence against modesty. His stories possessed the true geometrical requisiton of excellence ; they were never too long and never too broad.

His unbounded generosity was at all times displayed towards both friends and foes. His unselfishness towards those who served with him is one of the chief secrets of their attachment to him, and the unqualified praise he gave them for their work was one of the main incentives to the efforts which they put forth. After the successes

Colonel Ely S. Parker   Colonel Badeau.   General Grant.   Colonel Babcock.   Colonel Porter.

FROM A PHOTOGRAPH TAKEN IN 1865 AT BOSTON, WHEN GRANT WAS RECEIVING PUBLIC WELCOMES THROUGHOUT THE NORTH AFTER THE CLOSE OF THE WAR.

4

in the West, in writing to Sherman, he said : "What I want is to express my thanks to you and McPherson as the men to whom above all others I feel indebted for whatever I have had of success. How far your advice and assistance have been of help to me, you know. How far your execution of whatever has been given you to do entitles you to the reward I am receiving, you cannot know as well as I."

After Sherman's successful march to the sea there was a rumor that Congress intended to create a lieutenant-generalship for him and give him the same grade as that of Grant. By this means he would have become eligible to the command of the army. Sherman wrote at once to his commander, saying that he had no part in the movement, and should certainly decline such a commission if offered to him. General Grant wrote him in reply one of the most manly letters ever penned, which contained the following words : "No one would be more pleased with your advancement than I ; and if you should be placed in my position, and I put subordinate, it would not change our relations in the least. I would make the same exertions to support you that you have ever done to support me, and I would do all in my power to make our cause win."

When Sherman granted terms of surrender to General Joe Johnston's army which the government repudiated, and when Stanton denounced Sherman's conduct unsparingly, and Grant was ordered to Sherman's headquarters by the President to conduct further operations there in person, the General-in-chief went only as far as Raleigh. He remained there in the background instead of going out to the front, so as not to appear to share the credit of receiving Johnston's final surrender upon terms approved by the government. He left that honor solely to Sherman. He stood by him manfully when his motives were questioned and his patriotism unjustly assailed. After Sheridan had won his great victories, some one spoke in General Grant's presence in a manner which sought to belittle Sheridan and make it appear that he was only a hard

hitter in battle and not an officer of brains. General Grant resented this with great warmth, and immediately took up the cudgels in Sheridan's favor. He said : "While Sheridan has a magnetic influence possessed by few men in an engagement, and is seen to best advantage in battle, he does as much beforehand to contribute to victory as any living commander. His plans are always well matured, and in every movement he strikes with a definite purpose in view. No man is better fitted to command all the armies in the field."

General Grant's generosity to his foes will be remembered as long as the world con-

GRANT'S HORSE "JEFF DAVIS," CAPTURED ON DAVIS'S PLANTATION IN MISSISSIPPI.

Photograph by Brady.

tinues to honor manly qualities. After the surrender at Vicksburg he issued a field order saying : "The paroled prisoners will be sent out of here to-morrow. Instruct the commands to be orderly and quiet as the prisoners pass, and to make no offensive remarks."

In his correspondence with General Lee. looking to the surrender of the Army of Northern Virginia, he said : "I will meet you, or designate officers to meet any officers you may name, for the purpose of arranging definitely terms upon which the surrender of the Army of Northern Virginia will be received." He thus took pains to relieve General Lee from the humiliation of making the surrender in person, in case that commander chose to designate another officer for the purpose. In this General Grant showed the same delicacy of feeling as that which actuated Washington when he spared Cornwallis from the necessity of surrendering his army in person at Yorktown.

After the surrender at Appomattox our troops began to fire salutes. General Grant sent orders at once to have them stopped, using the following words: "The war is over, the rebels are our countrymen again, and the best sign of rejoicing after the

GRANT'S HORSE "EGYPT," A THOROUGHBRED FROM SOUTHERN ILLINOIS.

Photograph by Brady.

victory will be to abstain from all demonstrations in the field."

When, two months after the close of the war, Lee made application in writing to have the privileges included in the President's amnesty proclamation extended to him, General Grant promptly indorsed his letter as follows : " Respectfully forwarded through the Secretary of War to the President, with the earnest recommendation that the application of General Robert E. Lee for amnesty and pardon may be granted him." Andrew Johnson was, however, at that time bent upon having all ex-Confederate officers indicted for the crime of treason, whether they kept their paroles or not, and a number of indictments had

already been found against them. In this emergency General Lee applied by letter to General Grant for protection, and he knew that such an application would not be in vain. General Grant put the most emphatic indorsement upon this letter, which contained the following language : " In my opinion the officers and men paroled at Appomattox Court House, and since upon the same terms given Lee, cannot be tried for treason so long as they observe the terms of their parole. . . . The action of Judge Underwood in Norfolk has already had an injurious effect, and I would ask that he be ordered to quash all indictments found against paroled prisoners of war, and to desist from further prosecution of them." It must be remembered that this action was taken when the country was still greatly excited by the events of the war and the assassination of President Lincoln, and it required no little courage on the part of General Grant to take so decided a stand in these matters.

Perhaps the most pronounced t r a i t in General Grant's character was that of unqualified Loyalty. He was loyal to every work and cause in which he was engaged : loyal to his friends, loyal to his family, loyal to his country, and loyal to his God. This characteristic produced a reciprocal effect in those who served with him, and was one of the chief reasons why men became so loyally attached to him. It so dominated his entire nature that it sometimes led him into error, and caused him to stand by friends who were no longer worthy of his friendship, and to trust those in whom his faith should not have been reposed. Yet it is a trait so noble that we do not stop to count the errors which may have resulted from it. It showed that he was proof against the influence of malicious aspersions and slanders aimed at worthy men, and that he had the courage to stand as a barrier between them and their unworthy detractors, and to let generous sentiments have a voice in an age in which the heart plays so small a part in public life.

It has been well said that "the best

GENERAL GRANT'S FATHER AND MOTHER.

teachers of humanity are the lives of great will afford a liberal education to American men." A close study of the traits which youth in the virtues which should adorn the were most conspicuous in General Grant character of a man in public life.

AS BREVET SECOND LIEUTENANT, AGE 21.

Taken in Cincinnati in 1843, just after graduation from West Point.

AS CAPTAIN WHILE STATIONED AT SACKETT'S HARBOR, NEW YORK, 1849. AGE 27.

From a very small miniature.

GENERAL GRANT IN THE AUTUMN OF 1861. AGE 39.

From a photograph loaned by Colonel Frederick D. Grant.

GENERAL GRANT IN 1864, DURING THE CAMPAIGN OF THE WILDERNESS. AGE 42.

Photograph by Brady.

TAKEN IN 1862 BEFORE VICKSBURG, ÆT 41.
From a defective negative.

AGE 42. TAKEN AT HEADQUARTERS IN THE WILDERNESS.

Brady, photographer.

EARLY IN 1865, NEAR THE CLOSE OF THE WAR. AGE 43.

From a spoiled negative.

NO. 13. TAKEN BY GUTEKUNST, PHILADELPHIA, ON GRANT'S FIRST TRIP NORTH AFTER THE WAR.

1868. AGE 46. NOT LONG BEFORE GRANT'S FIRST ELECTION AS PRESIDENT.

1869. AGE 47. SOON AFTER GRANT'S FIRST INAUGURATION AS PRESIDENT.

ABOUT 1870.   AGE 48.

ABOUT 1872.   AGE 50.

Kurtz, photographer, New York.

1876. AGE 51. AT THE BEGINNING OF GRANT'S SECOND TERM AS PRESIDENT.
Brady, photographer.

1876. AGE 54.

GRATIN — "LI HUNG CHANG."

From a photograph taken at the viceroy's palace at Tien-Tsin, China, June, 1879, on General Grant's trip around the world.

GENERAL GRANT, MRS. GRANT, AND THEIR ELDEST SON COLONEL FREDERICK D. GRANT.

Taken by Taber at San Francisco on Grant's landing from the voyage around the world, September 22, 1879.

1881.   AGE 59.   WHEN GRANT TOOK UP HIS RESIDENCE IN NEW YORK.   W. KURTZ, PHOTOGRAPHER.

1882.   AGE 60.

Fredricks, photographer, New York.

GENERAL SHERMAN WHEN IN COMMAND OF THE MILITARY DIVISION OF THE MISSISSIPPI, 1866. AGE 46.

SOME PERSONAL RECOLLECTIONS OF GENERAL SHERMAN.

By S. H. M. Byers.

HOW well I recall now the first time I ever heard the voice of General Sherman. It was night, in the woods by the banks of the Tennessee River. On looking over my half-faded war diary, I find this entry :

"November 23, 1863. It has rained all the day. The men have few rations, the animals no food at all. Thousands of horses and mules are lying dead in the muddy roads and in the woods. We are a few miles below Chattanooga, close to the river. The Rebels are on the other side. Everybody here expects a great battle. Since noon our colonel got orders for us to be ready to ferry over the river at midnight—no baggage."

It was very dark that night in the woods when our division slipped down to the water's edge and commenced entering the pontoons.

"Be as quiet as possible, and step into the boats rapidly," I heard a voice say.

The speaker was a tall man, wearing a long waterproof coat that covered him to his heels. He stood close beside me as he spoke, and one of the boys said in a low voice : "That is Sherman."

It was the first time I had ever heard

him speak. Though a great commander, at that moment leading many troops, still he was down there in the dark, personally attending to every detail of getting us over the river. Shortly our rude boat, with thirty people aboard, pushed out into the dark water, and we were whirled around by the eddies, while expecting every moment a blaze of musketry in our faces from the other shore. But, somehow, we felt confident that all was well, for was not our great general himself close by, watching the movement?

In the battle that followed, our troops were successful. Sherman was everywhere along the front, personally directing every movement. He was sharing every danger, and the soldier's fear was that his general might be killed, and the battle lost in consequence.

In the charge of the "Tunnel," I, with many comrades, fell into the enemy's hands, and was taken to Libby Prison. Few of those captured with me ever got back North alive, and those who did are nearly all long since dead.

Fifteen months of terrible experience in the prisons of the South passed. More than once I had escaped, only to be retaken. At last, though, I did get away, and when

Sherman's army, marching north through the Carolinas, captured Columbia, they found me secreted in the garret of a negro's cabin in the town.

It happened that, while I was a prisoner, I had written some verses in praise of the great campaign from Chattanooga to the ocean. The song found favor with my prison comrades. It also soon reached the soldiers in the North, and, before I knew it, it was being sung everywhere. It was "Sherman's March to the Sea," and the song soon gave its name to the campaign itself.

As Sherman entered Columbia at noon that 17th of February, 1865, riding at the head of his sixty thousand victorious veterans, a soldier ran up to him, and told him the author of the song had escaped from prison, and was standing near by, on the steps of a house. He halted the whole column, while he motioned to me to come out, and warmly shook my hand.

"Tell all the prisoners who have escaped," said he, "to come to me at camp to-night. I want to do something for all of them. They must be made comfortable."

The bands played, and the vast column again moved on amidst cheers for "Billy" Sherman, "Johnny" Logan, and other heroes of the line. I looked at the battle-worn flags of the regiments. I had not seen loyal colors for about sixteen months. Perhaps I was weak, but I am sure I felt my eyes moisten and my heart bound when I looked upon the very flag I had seen in the hot charge that day at Missionary Ridge.

I did not go to the General's headquarters that night. I was ashamed to go in all my rags. But I walked the streets and saw the city burned to ashes. But Sherman had not done this. Long before the Union troops entered, I saw Hampton's Confederate cavalry firing thousands of bales of cotton to prevent its falling into Union hands. A fearful wind raged towards morning, and the flakes of burning cotton soon set the city on fire. That night I heard with my own ears South Carolinians condemn Wade Hampton and Jefferson Davis.

"They are those who brought all this on the people of the South," cried one old man as he saw his home devoured by the flames, and thought of his sons dead on useless battlefields.

Later, Wade Hampton was foolish enough to publicly attack Sherman for inhumanity during his "March."

"His paper is for home consumption," the General wrote to me; "but if he attempts to enlarge his sphere I will give him a blast of the truth as you and hundreds know it."

I went to friends in my old brigade the next day after the burning of the city, but to my surprise General Sherman sent an officer to hunt me up and bring me to headquarters.

"You must go," said the officer, in answer to my expressed reluctance. "You must; it is an order."

Our meeting, unimportant in itself, showed the simplicity and character of Sherman. It was in the woods. The columns had halted for the night, and the tent of the General was pitched at a lone spot away from the roadside. As was usual at army headquarters, an enormous flag was suspended between two trees. Near by the horses of the bodyguard were picketed to long ropes, while the men either lay about on the grass or busied themselves preparing their supper. Not far away, in the woods and at roadsides, were the bivouacs of the tired army. I was but a stripling officer, and was not a little abashed at the idea of appearing before the commander of the army. I found him sitting on a camp-stool by a low rail fire. He was looking over some papers.

"This is Adjutant Byers," said the officer.

The General dropped his papers, stepped right over the fire with his long legs, and seized me by the hand.

"I want to thank you for your song," he said, "and I want you to tell me how you, there in prison, got hold of all that I was doing. You hit it splendidly. I have little for you to do here at headquarters. There is little for anybody to do," he said after awhile (I think he meant he did it all himself); "but I want to give you a place on my staff. You must take your meals with me."

Now, for a prisoner of war, just getting out of a horrible pen, a place on the commander's staff, with the privilege of eating at his table, was like getting into paradise.

"Later you will get a horse and all you need," he went on.

That moment the cook, a great ebony-faced negro, came up, bowed very low, and announced supper. The General pushed me into the supper tent ahead of him. The well-uniformed staff officers were already there, assembled about a long rude table of boards. Every one of them held up his fork and stared at me. The General introduced me, adding some complimentary things.

"And I want you all to know him," he said, "and after supper you must hunt him up some clothes."

"I have an extra coat," said Surgeon Moore. "And I a pair of trousers," said another.

My wardrobe was to be renewed in no time. The bare anticipation of the fact restored my confidence. The General seated me at his right hand, and bade me make no ceremony about proceeding to whatever was before me. The meal was simple. It was the ordinary army rations,

that Sherman never could march or swim an army through the lower part of North Carolina in midwinter, but he was a commander who never stopped at such obstacles as rivers and swamps when marching for a desired object. Here were rivers swollen into a dozen channels, dark swamps that seemed interminable, miles of roads that were lately bottomless, or often under three feet of ice-cold water. The bridges were destroyed everywhere. The narrow causeways, called roads by courtesy, if not submerged, were defended by the enemy's batteries. It rained almost constantly day and night, and the only

SHERMAN BEFORE ATLANTA, 1864. AGE 44.

with a chicken or two added, which the cook had foraged that day on the march. I ventured to relate something of my experiences in prison. The General listened with the closest attention, and it seemed to me that from that moment he was my friend. It was the commencement of an attachment that lasted until his death, twenty-five years.

During the rest of that famous marching and wading through the Carolinas I was constantly at headquarters until we reached the Cape Fear River. And what a campaign that was, through swamps and woods and over bridgeless streams! Joe Johnston's engineers had told their chief

protection the army had was the little rubber blankets or shelter tents they carried on their backs in addition to their knapsacks and several days' rations. There were not a half dozen complete tents in the army. Sherman himself oftenest slept under a tent "fly," under trees, or else in stray country churches.

Through all the mud, swamp, forest, and water, the troops dragged two thousand wagons, besides ambulances and batteries. The horses and mules often floundered in the bottomless roads, became discouraged, gave out, and died. Then the men took their places, and dragged wagons and cannon for miles. Whole brigades worked sometimes day and night making temporary roadbeds from trees felled in the swamps. The men were glad to sleep anywhere—in the mud, in the woods, in the rain, at the roadside—anywhere, if only they could lie down without being shot at. There is official record that one division of the troops on this terrible march waded through swamps and forded thirty-five rivers where the ice-cold water often reached to the men's waists. The same division, while floundering through the swamps, constructed fifteen miles of corduroy wagon road and one hundred and twenty-two miles of side road for the troops. There were no quartermaster's trains, so the troops were nearly destitute of clothing. Thousands of the army were shoeless before the campaign was half over.

One night Sherman and his staff lodged in a little deserted church they found in the woods. I recall how the General himself would not sleep on the bit of carpet on the pulpit platform.

"Keep that for some of you young fellows who are not well," he said laughingly, as he stretched himself out on a long hard bench till morning.

He shared all the privations and hardships of the common soldier. He slept in his uniform every night of the whole campaign. Sometimes we did not get into a camp till midnight. I think every man in the army knew the General's face, and thousands spoke with him personally. The familiarity of the troops at times was amusing.

"Don't ride too fast, General," they would cry out, seeing his horse plunging along in the mire at the roadside, as he tried to pass some division. "Pretty slippery going, Uncle Billy; pretty slippery going." Or, "Say, General, kin you tell us is this the road to Richmond?"

Every soldier of his army had taken on the enthusiasm of the General himself. They would go anywhere that he might point to. Often as he approached some regiment, a wild huzza would be given, and taken up and repeated by the troops a mile ahead. Instinct seemed to tell the boys, when there was any loud shouting anywhere whatever, that Uncle Billy was coming, and they joined in the cheers till the woods rang. It was a common thing for the General to stop his horse and speak words of encouragement or praise to some subordinate officer or private soldier struggling at the roadside. He seemed to know the faces and even the names of hundreds of his troops. Even the foragers, whose cleverness and fleetness fed the army, and who left the regiments at daylight every morning on foot, and at the close of each day returned to camp on horseback and muleback, laden with supplies, he knew often by name. Along with perfect discipline, every day showed some proof of his sympathy with the common soldiers. He had his humorous side with them too. When the army reached Goldsborough, half the men were in rags. One day a division was ordered to march past him in review. The men were bare-legged and ragged, some of them almost hatless.

"Only look at the poor fellows with their bare legs," said an officer at the General's side, sympathizingly.

"Splendid legs," cried the General, with a twinkle in his eye, "splendid legs. Would give both of mine for any one of them."

On the march and in the camp Sherman's life was simplicity itself. He had few brilliantly uniformed and useless aids about him. The simple tent "fly" was his usual headquarters, and under it all his military family ate together. His despatches he wrote mostly with his own hand. He had little use for clerks. But Dayton, his adjutant-general, was better than a regiment of clerks. When we halted somewhere in the woods for the night, the General was the busiest man in the army. While others slept, his little camp-fire was burning, and often in the long vigils of the night I have seen a tall form walking up and down by that fire. Sometimes we got a little behind the army with our night camp, or too far in front, and then the staff officers and the orderlies would buckle on their pistols, and we remained awake all night. Sherman himself slept but little. He did not seem to need sleep, and I have known him to stay but two hours in bed many a night. In later years a slight asthma made much sleep impossible for him. After the war, when I was at his home in St. Louis, he seldom retired till twelve or one o'clock. It was often as late, too, on this march.

It was a singularly impressive sight to see this solitary figure walking there by the flickering camp-fire while the army slept. If a gun went off somewhere in the distance, or if an unusual noise were heard, he would instantly call one of us to go and find out what it meant. He paid small attention to appearances; to dress almost none.

"There is going to be a battle to-day, sure," said Colonel Audenreid, of the staff, one morning before daylight.

GENERAL SHERMAN IN 1865. AGE 45.
From a photograph by Brady.

" How do you know?" asked a comrade.
" Why, don't you see? The General's up there by the fire putting on a clean collar. The sign's dead sure."

A battle did take place that day, and Cheraw, with forty cannon, fell into our hands. It was more a run than a battle.

Daylight usually saw us all ready for the saddle. When noon came we dismounted at the roadside, sat down on a log or on the grass, and had a simple lunch, washed down with water from the swamp, or something stronger from a flask that was ever the General's companion ; for he was a soldier, and was living a soldier's life.

When we reached the Cape Fear River, in the Carolinas, we found there (at Fayetteville) a splendid arsenal, built in former times by the United States. Now it was used for making arms to destroy the Government. Sherman burned it to the ground; but first he took me all through the building and explained its complicated machinery and apparatus. I was astonished that any one but a mechanical engineer could know all about such things.

"Why, of course, one must learn everything," he said to me. "I picked this thing up at leisure hours. One must never let a chance to learn something be lost. I say this to young men always," he continued. "No matter if the thing don't seem to be of much use at the time. Who knows how soon it may be wanted? No matter how far away from one's calling it may seem, all knowledge, however gained, is of use; sometimes of great use. Why," he went on, "once when I captured a town in Alabama, I found the telegraph wire in perfect order. The enemy had forgotten it or had run away too quick to cut it. My operator was not with me. I called to know if any soldier in the bodyguard could work an instrument.

"'I can,' said a beardless private.

"He had picked up a knowledge of the thing, 'just for fun,' he said. I set him at work. Important news was going over the wire from Lee. That boy caught the message. I had it signalled back of my lines to be repeated to General Grant in Virginia. Perhaps it helped to save a battle. Anyway, that young man won promotion. Learning a little thing once when chance offered, afterward gave him the opportunity of his life.

"When I was a young man stationed in Georgia," he continued, "my comrades at the military post spent their Sundays playing cards and visiting. I spent mine in riding or walking over the hills of the neighborhood. I learned the topography of the country. It was no use to me then. Later, I led an army through that region, and the knowledge of the country I had gained there as a young fellow helped me to win a dozen victories."

We went from the arsenal back to the breakfast table in an adjoining house.

"This arsenal has cost a mint of money," he said, "but it must burn. It is time to commence hurting these fellows. They must find out that war is war; and the more terrible it is made, the sooner it is over."

I told him what Stonewall Jackson said as to not taking prisoners.

"Perhaps he was right," said the General. "It seems cruel; but if there were no quarter given, most men would keep out of war. Rebellions would be few and short."

While we were eating, a whistle blew. It was from a little tugboat that had steamed its way up the swollen and dangerous river from Wilmington. It passed the enemy hidden on either bank. It was the first sound from the North heard since the army left the ocean. No one in all the North knew where Sherman's army was. Rumors brought from the South said it was "floundering and perishing in the swamps of the Carolinas." That day the General directed me to board this tugboat, run down the river in the night, and carry despatches to General Grant in front of Richmond, and to President Lincoln at Washington.

"Don't say much about how we are doing down here," said the General, as he put his arm about me and said farewell that evening down at the river bank. "Don't tell them in the North we are cutting any great swath here. Just say we are taking care of whatever is getting in front of us. And be careful your boat don't get knocked to the bottom of the river before daylight."

Our little craft was covered nearly all over with cotton bales. The river was very wide and out of its banks everywhere; the night was dark. Whatever the enemy may have thought of the little puffs of steam far out on the dark, rapid water, we got down to the sea unharmed. A fleet ocean steamer at once carried me to Virginia. Grant was in a little log cabin at City Point, and when an officer was announced with despatches from Sherman, he was delighted. He took me into a back room, read the letters I ripped out of my clothing, and asked me many questions. Then General Ord entered.

"Look here," said General Grant, delighted as a child. "Look here, Ord, at the news from Sherman. He has beaten even the swamps of the Carolinas."

"I am so glad," said Ord, rattling his big spurs; "I am so glad. I was getting a little uneasy."

"I not a bit," said Grant. "I knew Sherman. I knew my man. I knew my man," he gravely continued, almost to himself.

Rawlins, the adjutant-general, was called in to rejoice with the others. Then a

GENERAL SHERMAN IN 1865. AGE 40.
From a photograph by Brady.

leave of absence was made out for me to go North to my home, where I had been but eight days during the whole war, and now my months of painful imprisonment had undermined my health.

When next I saw General Sherman it was at my own house in Switzerland, after the war had closed. He was making his grand tour of Europe, and came out of his way to visit me. I was then a consul at Zurich. For days we talked the old times over. All the military men in Switzerland wanted to see the great American captain. A company of them were invited to an excursion up the lake. Then it was learned that nearly all of them had been students of Sherman's campaigns for months. It was a novel sight to see them under the awning of the steamer, surrounding Sherman, while with pencil and maps in hand he traced for them all the strategic lines of "The March to the Sea." A high officer begged as a souvenir the map that Sherman's hand had traced.

"It shall be an heirloom in my family," he declared.

The lake pleased the General. "Still," said he, "it is no prettier than the lakes at Madison, Wisconsin. It looks like them, but they are our own; they are American."

He appreciated beautiful scenes and dwelt upon them almost with the love of a poet. "I am glad you saw San Remo," he wrote me. "Vividly I recall the ride to Genoa, the gorgeous scenery of the sea and shore, of sheltered vales and olive-

far up the lake, at the time of his visit. It was two miles from the boat landing at the village, and I could get no fit carriage to take him up.

"Let me walk," said he. "Don't rob me of the only opportunity I have had to use my feet in Europe."

All the villagers hung out flags, and the peasants, who knew from the town papers that he was coming, stood at the roadsides with bared heads. Then a company of village cadets marched up hill to our house to do him honor. He spoke to them in English. They did not understand a word, but gave a grand hurrah, and then marched down again.

When Sherman went to live in Wash-

GENERAL SHERMAN IN 1876, AGE 56.
From a photograph by Mora.

clad hills, with the snow-capped Apennines behind. Washington," he said, "is to my mind the handsomest city in the world, not excepting Paris; and the Potomac, when walled in and its shores in grass-plots, may some day approximate to the Rhine in loveliness."

It rained a little the morning he was starting from Zurich to the St. Gothard Pass for Italy, and threatened storm. My wife tried to induce him to wait for better weather.

"No, that I never do," said he. "If it is raining when I start, it is sure to clear up on the way; and that's when we like the weather to be good. No, I would rather start in a storm than not."

We lived in Bocken, a country house

ington it seemed as if every soldier who came there felt bound to call on him. Every man of them was received as an old friend and companion. Day in, day out, the bell would ring, and, "It's a soldier," the maid would announce.

"Let him in," the General would answer.

No matter what he was engaged upon, or who was in the room, the worthy and the unworthy alike went off with his blessing, and, if need be, his aid. He kept open accounts at shoe-stores, where every needy soldier calling on him could get shoes at his expense. One of his beneficiaries, at least, did not withhold due expressions of gratitude. A young colored man, who wore a big scarlet necktie and twirled in one hand a silk hat and in the other a fancy cane, calling, said :

"Yes, Mr. Sherman, I wants to thank you very much for the place you done got for me in the department. I likes the place. Yes, Mr. Sherman. And I wants to thank God for you very much, and I hopes you'll get to heaven just sure. Fact is, I just know you will."

"That's all right," said the General, glancing over the top of the newspaper he was reading, "only you look out that you don't get to the other place."

Sherman loved young people—associated with them all his life. There was no frolic he could not take part in with them. Boys, not less than girls, liked him and his happy ways. He made the sun shine for them. If he kissed the girls, the girls kissed him.

Once I saw him at Berne when he was boarding the train for Paris. Every American girl who happened to be in the town came to see him off. Not one of them had ever seen him before, but every one of them kissed him ; so did some of their mothers. Women like real heroes in this world.

In 1874 he moved up town to Fifteenth Street, and almost next door to Mr. Blaine. Sometimes in the hot summer evenings the two sat on the stone walk out in front of Sherman's house till late in the night, talking about everything except politics. I was often an interested listener. Sherman called Blaine the "Great Premier."

"He has a great genius for running things," said he, "and parties ; likes to make friends, and has got lots of them ; knows how to make enemies too. Can't keep all his promises—makes too many ; forgets them. That's politics. He is a great man, though, a statesman, spite of shortcomings."

Speaking of Blaine's bitter enemies, he once said : "All successful men are hated by somebody."

Sometimes those hot summer evenings, in Fifteenth Street, he held quasi-receptions out in front of the house, so many people came to see him. Everybody felt at liberty to call, or, if he saw friends passing under the gaslight, he bade them sit down and chat. Inside the house his hospitality was boundless. There was never any end to guests. He kept open house, as it were. The table was always spread, and unexpected guests sat down daily. I wondered at the time how his salary, though large, ever paid his expenses.

His private office was a little room down in the basement. Who in Washington can ever forget the little tin sign on the window below, bearing the simple words :

"OFFICE OF GENERAL SHERMAN."

"Not the *great* Sherman !" many a passer-by has exclaimed, as he halted and looked down at the window, hoping possibly for a single glimpse of the man himself. He always chose these modest basements for his own office, whether in Washington, St. Louis, or New York. The furnishing was no less modest. A plain desk, his familiar chair, seats for a few friends by the little open fireplace, a fine engraving of General Grant, an occasional battle scene, a big photograph of Sheridan, and some cases and shelves filled with his books, war maps, and valuable correspondence. Simple as it seemed, all was systematized. The Government allowed him one clerk, Mr. Barrett, whose whole time was spent in classifying and indexing papers and letters as valuable as any in all America. Sherman had for twenty-five years corresponded with many notable people—Lincoln, Chase, Grant, Sheridan, all the heroes of the war times, civil or military, besides hundreds of private individuals. It is in these latter letters, scattered among friends everywhere, that is best seen the spark of nature's fire that, next to his deeds, most marks Sherman as a man of genius. He wrote as he talked, sometimes at random, but always brilliantly. Often late in the night, as he walked up and down the little room among the letters of the great men he had known, it seemed as if he might be in communion with their spirits. They were nearly all dead ; he had outlived most of the heroes of the war North or South, and seemed at times like one who had been in the world, seen its glories and its follies, and was ready himself to depart.

"Some night as I come home from the theatre or a dinner," he once said, "a chill will catch me. I will have a cold, be unwell a day, and then——"

It all happened, at last, just as his imagination had foreseen it.

After he removed to St. Louis, where he had a quiet house at 912 Garrison Avenue, the office was in the simple basement as before. The same tin sign was on the window. All seemed as before ; nothing changed. Almost every night, after other friends had left, we sat in his room and talked or read. I had been invited to his house at this time for the purpose of editing certain of his letters for the " North American Review."

" Here are my keys," he said one night, throwing them on my desk. " There are all my papers and letters. You will find things there that will interest people."

And I did ; but I did not regard it as right, nor myself at liberty, to print many of the letters at the time.

" Before you moved out of Atlanta, General," I once asked, " what did you think would be the effect of your marching that army down to the ocean ? "

" I thought it would end the war," he answered quickly. " It was to put me behind Lee's army so soon as I should turn north to the Carolinas. You have the letter there that Lee once wrote, saying it was easy for him to see that unless my plans were interrupted he would be compelled to leave Richmond. I had scarcely reached the Roanoke River when he commenced slipping out of Richmond, and the whole Confederacy suddenly came to an end."

General Grant realized to the full the tremendous importance of Sherman's last movements.

" That was a campaign," said he, " the like of which is not read of in the past history."

I looked over hundreds of Sherman's papers. When I found anything that specially interested me, I mentioned it to him. Then he dropped his book, and talked by the hour, relating to me the incidents, and speaking of noted men whom he had known. These were the times when it was most worth while to hear Sherman talk.

While I busied myself with the letters, he was deep in Walter Scott, or Dickens, or Robert Burns. A copy of Burns lay on his desk constantly. Certain of Dickens's novels he read once every year. I have forgotten which they were. He was a constant reader of good books, and I think he knew Burns almost by heart. He was also fond of music, and went much to the opera. Army songs always pleased him, and there was one commencing, " Old fellow, you've played out your time," he could not hear too often.

" It is the whole and true history of a soldier's life and sorrows," he would say.

He hated the newspapers, yet through necessity, almost, he read them every morning, making running comments on what they said. If there were funny things in them, or spicy, he read them aloud, for he was a lover of a good joke.

" But there's none of it true," he would say. " I almost think it impossible for an editor to tell the truth. If this country is ever given over to socialism, communism, and the devil, the newspapers will be to blame for it. The chief trouble of my life has been in dealing with newspapers. They want sensations—something that will sell. If they make sad a hundred or a thousand hearts, it is of no concern to them."

For professional politicians he had as little regard as for the newspapers.

" But there are newspapers and newspapers," said he ; " politicians and politicians ; but statesmen are scarce as hens' teeth. No American can help interesting himself in politics. That belongs to a republic. Every man's a ruler here whether he knows anything about it or not ; and all parties are about alike."

But he had every confidence in our government.

" Thanks to the Union soldiers," said he, " the Ship of State is in port, and it don't matter much who's President. But parties are necessary. No single man can run this government without a united party to help him. Again," he said," our national strength is tested by the political hurricanes which pass over us every four years, and by such transitions as took place when the government passed from Garfield to Arthur. Next week the Democrats will meet and nominate Jeff Davis, Cleveland, or some other fellow ; but it don't matter who is captain—the ship's in. Anyway, our best Presidents are usually accidents."

Sherman's own name was always being proposed for President, but he had no desire for the office.

" My consent never will be obtained," said he. " It is entirely out of the question. I don't want the Presidency and will not have it. I recall too well the experiences of Jackson, Harrison, Taylor, Grant, Hayes, Garfield—all soldiers—to be tempted by the siren voice of flattery."

When in 1884 it was insisted that he should run, and he was told it was a duty, and that " no man dare refuse a call of the people," he answered sternly : " No political party convention is the keeper of the United States ; and if really nominated I would decline in such language as would do both the convention and myself harm."

No matter how early the General was out of bed those mornings in St. Louis, it was hard to get him to breakfast if once he had commenced reading or writing down in the basement. To remedy this, his wife had the newspapers put on the breakfast table. Mrs. Sherman always called him " Cump."

That was his name with her before he was eminent, and I am sure he liked it, with all the love and familiarity it conveyed, far more than any of the titles given him by Presidents and legislatures. In fact, he gave little regard to titles alone.

"Lieutenant A—— is again off looking up his ancestors," he once said to me, "just as if ancestors or titles made a man. I suppose I had some military talent to start with, but it was work, not ancestors,

instantly pulled the metal badge from his own breast and pinned it on my coat.

That badge is on my desk while I write these recollections.

Once he took me to see "Buffalo Bill" at the fair grounds. A crippled soldier we met on the way begged for help, and he so nearly emptied his pocket-book to the man, he had to borrow money to get us into the show. The show delighted him as it might have delighted a little child. He called for

GENERAL SHERMAN IN 1888.   AGE 68.

From a photograph by Sarony.

and study, and forever work, that brought me my success."

His nature was generous and unselfish in the extreme. One night at St. Louis he was invited to speak at the presentation of a new flag to Ransom Post. When I came down stairs to accompany him, he stood in the parlor dressed and waiting.

"Where's your badge?" he said to me.

"Why, General, I have none here."

"Have none? Take this," he said, and

Colonel Cody ("Buffalo Bill") to be brought to him that he might shake hands with him. He had known him many years before.

"That man's a genius," said he, when Cody went back to the ring. "He puts his life into his show, and Cody believes in himself."

Not every warrior can shed a tear. Sherman's heart was as tender as a child's. I have seen those thin, compressed lips tremble, and the brown eyes moisten, at the recital of a wrong. He had two sides to his nature. In war he had all the elements of the stern soldier; he could be resolute, but not pitiless. Gallantry and chivalry were parts of his nature. In peace he was a student, a gracious gentleman; the man whom women and children loved. His kindness simply knew no bounds. For a companion-in-arms, no matter what his rank, he had abiding regard.

"Sherman recommends everybody for place," said a department chief to me one day. "Now which one can he want appointed?"

"He wants them all appointed," I replied.

His tall form, his genial manners, but above all the story of his great deeds, made him a constantly noticeable figure wherever he went. His face was as familiar to Americans as the face of Washington or Lincoln. He always seemed to me younger than he really was. He had to the last a buoyancy of spirits that usually belongs only to youth. I never saw him speak to a young person without smiling; and as to his ways toward women, he was a Bayard of the Bayards. The term chivalrous belonged to him by birthright.

I recall how, after a noon dinner party at Berne once, a lady, not a young or a beautiful one, had started up the stairs alone. A dozen young fellows loitering there allowed her to go unnoticed. The General, at the *salon* door, got a glimpse of her half way up to the landing. In long strides he bounded instantly up the stairs, and had her arm before she knew it. Her smile repaid him as it rebuked the rest. Despite reports to the contrary, he was as chivalrous toward women and children in the South as he was toward his own people, and protected them as fully. I recall vividly how once on the march in the Carolinas he caused a young staff officer to be led out before the troops, his sword broken in two and his shoulder-straps cut from his shoulders, because he

had permitted some of his men to rob a Southern woman of her jewelry.

"I am a thief," were the words he placarded over the head of another soldier, who had stolen a woman's finger-ring. With this inscription above his head, the culprit stood on top of a barrel by a bridge while the whole army filed past him.

He was always making little speeches. He had to; it was demanded of him. He was no orator, but he said original things. His words were crisp, to the point, and never to be forgotten.

When the family were preparing to remove from St. Louis to New York, Sherman said: "I must see people; I must talk."

He loved St. Louis, but there was only one New York. I begged a trifle from his little room before he went—that room in which I had so often, late into the night, sat alone with him and listened to the magic of his talk. He took a bronze paper-weight from his desk.

"It is the image of America's greatest captain," he said, and gave me a little figure of General Grant that had been on his desk for many years.

General Sherman's appreciation of Grant knew no bounds.

"He was the one level-headed man among us all," he said one night.

In New York I was with him again from time to time. Again his office was in the basement. The same furniture, the same pictures, the little open fireplace, the same man, the same talk. Advancing years changed his features a little, but not his spirits. His hair was gray, but his eyes were bright as ever.

Then came a day when I went into the little basement in Seventy-first Street only to find the chair of the Great Captain forever vacant. His body lay in its coffin in a darkened room up-stairs. It was clad in the full uniform of a commanding general. The commander of an opposing army helped bear it to the tomb; and never was the grief of a nation more sincere.

PROFESSOR JOHN TYNDALL.

By Herbert Spencer.

JOHN TYNDALL, LL.D., F.R.S. 1865. AGE 45.

AMONG the various penalties entailed by ill-health, a not infrequent one is the inability to pay the last honors to a valued friend; and sometimes another is the undue postponement of such tribute to his memory as remains possible. Of both these evils I have just had experience.

It was, I think, in 1852 that Professor Tyndall gave at the Royal Institution the lecture by which he won his spurs: proving, as he then did, to Faraday himself, that he had been wrong in denying diamagnetic polarity. I was present at that lecture; and when introduced to him very shortly after it, there commenced one of those friendships which enter into the fabric of life and leave their marks. Though both had pronounced opinions about most things, and though neither had much reticence, the forty years which have elapsed since we first met witnessed no interruption of our cordial relations. Indeed, during recent years of invalid life suffered by both of us, the warmth of nature characteristic of him has had increased opportunity for manifesting itself. A letter from him, dated November 25th, inquiring my impressions concerning the climate of this place (St. Leonard's), raised the hope that something more than intercourse by correspondence would follow; but before I received a response to my reply there came the news of the sad catastrophe.

I need not dwell on the more conspicuous of Professor Tyndall's intellectual traits, for these are familiar to multitudes of readers. His copiousness of illustration, his closeness of reasoning, and his lucidity of statement have been sufficiently emphasized by others. Here I will remark only on certain powers of thought, not quite so obvious, which have had much to do with his successes. Of these the chief is "the scientific use of the imagination." He has himself insisted upon the need for this, and his own career exemplifies it. There prevail, almost universally, very erroneous ideas concerning the nature of imagination. Superstitious peoples, whose folk-lore is full of tales of fairies and the like, are said to be imaginative; while nobody ascribes imagination to the inventor of a new machine. Were this conception of imagination the true one, it would imply that, whereas children and savages are largely endowed with it, and whereas it is displayed in a high degree by poets of the first order, it is deficient in those having intermediate types of mind. But, as rightly conceived, imagination is the power of mental representation, and is measured by the vividness and truth of this representation. So conceived, it is seen to distinguish not poets only, but men of science; for in them, too, "imagination bodies forth the forms [and actions] of things unknown." It does this in an equal, and sometimes even in a higher degree; for, strange as the assertion will seem to most, it is nevertheless true that the mathematician who discloses to us some previously unknown order of space-relations, does so by a greater effort of imagination than is implied by any poetic creation. The difference lies in the fact that, whereas the imagination of the poet is exercised upon objects of human interest and his ideas glow with emotion, the imagination of the mathematician is exercised upon things utterly remote from human interest, and which excite no emotion: the contrasted appreciations of their respective powers being due to the circumstance that whereas people at large can follow, to a greater or less extent, the imaginations of the poet, the imaginations of the mathematician lie in a field inacces-

PROFESSOR TYNDALL IN 1872, DURING HIS VISIT TO AMERICA.
AGE 52.
From a photograph by Mora, Broadway, New York.

PROFESSOR TYNDALL IN 1885. AGE 65.
From a photograph by Kingsbury & Notcutt, London.

sible to them, and practically non-exist-
ent.

This constructive imagination (for we
are not concerned with mere reminiscent
imagination), here resulting in the creations of the poet and there in the discoveries of the man of science, is the highest of human faculties. With this faculty
Professor Tyndall was largely endowed.
In common with successful investigators
in general, he displayed it in forming true
conceptions of physical processes previously misinterpreted or uninterpreted;
and, again, in conceiving modes by which
the actual relations of the phenomena
could be demonstrated; and, again, in
devising fit appliances to this end. But to
a much greater extent than usual, he displayed constructive imagination in other
fields. He was an excellent expositor;
and good exposition implies much constructive imagination. A prerequisite is
the forming of true ideas of the mental
states of those who are to be taught; and
a further prerequisite is the imagining of
methods by which, beginning with conceptions they possess, there may be built up
in their minds the conceptions they do not
possess. Of constructive imagination as
displayed in this sphere, men at large appear to be almost devoid; as witness the
absurd systems of teaching which in past
times, and in large measure at present,
have stupefied, and still stupefy, children
by presenting abstract ideas before they

have any concrete ideas from which they
can be drawn. Whether as lecturer or
writer, Professor Tyndall carefully avoided
this vicious practice.

In one further way was his constructive
imagination exemplified. When at Queen-
wood College he not only took care to set
forth truths in such ways and in such
order that the comprehension of them developed naturally in the minds of those he
taught—he did more: he practised those
minds themselves in constructive imagination. He so presented his problems as to
exercise their powers of investigation. He
did not, like most teachers, make his pupils
mere passive recipients, but made them
active explorers.

As these facts imply, Professor Tyndall's
thoughts were not limited to physics and
allied sciences, but passed into psychology; and though this was not one of
his topics, it was a subject of interest to
him. Led as he was to make excursions
into the science of mind, he was led also
into that indeterminate region through
which this science passes into the science
of being; if we can call that a science of
which the issue is nescience. He was
much more conscious than physicists
usually are that every physical inquiry,
pursued to the end, brings us down to
metaphysics, and leaves us face to face with
an insoluble problem. Sundry proposi-
tions which physicists include as lying within their domain do not belong to physics

at all, but are concerned with our cognitions of matter and force—a fact clearly shown by the controversy at present going on about the fundamentals of dynamics. But in him the consciousness that here there exists a door which, though open, science cannot pass through, if not always present, was ever ready to emerge. Not improbably his early familiarity with theological questions, given him by the controversy between Catholicism and Protestantism, which occupied his mind much during youth, may have had to do with this. But whatever its cause, the fact, as proved by various spoken and written words, was a belief that the known is surrounded by an unknown, which he recognized as something more than a negation. Men of science may be divided into two classes, of which the one, well exemplified in Faraday, keeping their science and their religion absolutely separate, are untroubled by any incongruities between them ; and the other of which, occupying themselves exclusively with the facts of science, never ask what implications they have. Be it trilobite or be it double star, their thought

about it is much like the thought of Peter Bell about the primrose. Tyndall did not belong to either class ; and of the last I have heard him speak with implied scorn.

Being thus not simply a specialist but in considerable measure a generalist, willingly giving some attention to the organic sciences, if not largely acquainted with them, and awake to "the humanities," if not in the collegiate sense, yet in a wider sense—Tyndall was an interesting companion ; beneficially interesting to those with brains in a normal state, but to me injuriously interesting, as being too exciting. Twice I had experience of this. When, after an injury received while bathing in a Swiss mountain stream, he was laid up for some time and, on getting back to England, remained at Folkestone, I went down to spend a few days with him. "Do you believe in matter?" was a question which he propounded just as we were about to bid one another good-night after a day's continuous talking. Ever since a nervous breakdown in 1855, over my second book, talking has told upon me just as much as working, and has had to be kept within narrow limits ; so that persistence in this kind of thing was out of the question, and I had to abridge my stay. Once more the like happened when, after the meeting of the British Association at Liverpool, we adjourned to the Lakes. Gossip, which may be carried on without much intellectual tax, formed but a small element in our conversation. There was almost unceasing discussion as we rambled along the shores of Windermere, or walked up to Rydal Mount (leaving our names in the visitors' book), or as we were being rowed along Grasmere, or when climbing Loughrig on our way back. Tyndall's intellectual vivacity gave me no rest ; and after two utterly sleepless nights I had to fly.

I do not think that on these occasions, or on any occasion, politics formed one of our topics. Whether this abstention resulted by accident or whether from perception that we should disagree, I cannot say—possibly the last. Our respective leanings may be in part inferred from our respective attitudes towards Carlyle. To me, profoundly averse to autocracy, Carlyle's political doctrines had

PROFESSOR TYNDALL, IN 1890. AGE 70.

From a photograph by Fradelle & Young, London.

ever been repugnant. Much as I did, and still do, admire his marvelous style and the vigor, if not the truth, of his thought—so much so that I always enjoy any writing of his, however much I disagree with it —intercourse with him soon proved impracticable. Twice or thrice, in 1851-52, I was taken to see him by Mr. G. H. Lewes; but I soon found that the alternatives were—listening in silence to his dogmas, sometimes absurd, or getting into a hot argument with him, which ended in our glaring at one another; and as I

HINDHEAD HOUSE, PROFESSOR TYNDALL'S ENGLISH HOME, WHERE HE DIED.

did not like either alternative I ceased to go. With Tyndall, however, the case seems to have been different—possibly because of greater tolerance of his political creed and his advocacy of personal government. The rule of the strong hand was not, I fancy, as repellant to Tyndall as to me; and, indeed, I suspect that, had occasion offered, he would not have been reluctant to exercise such rule himself. Though his sympathies were such as made him anxious for others' welfare, they did not take the direction of anxiety for others' freedom as the means to their welfare; and hence he was, I suppose, not in pronounced antagonism with Carlyle on these matters. But divergent as our beliefs and sentiments were in earlier days, there has been in recent days mutual approximation. A conversation with him some years since made it manifest that personal experience had greatly shaken the faith he previously had in public administrations, and made him look with more favor on the view of state functions held by me. On the other hand, my faith in free institutions, originally strong (though always joined with the belief that the maintenance and success of them is a question of popular character), has in these later years been greatly decreased by the conviction that the fit character is not possessed by any people, nor is likely to be possessed for ages to come. A nation of which the legislators vote as they are bid and of which the workers surrender their rights of selling their labor as they please, has neither the ideas nor the sentiments needed for the maintenance of

liberty. Lacking them, we are on the way back to the rule of the strong hand in the shape of the bureaucratic despotism of a socialist organization, and then of the military despotism which must follow it; if, indeed, some social crash does not bring this last upon us more quickly. Had we recently compared notes, I fancy that Tyndall and I should have found ourselves differing but little in our views concerning the proximate social state, if not of the ultimate social state.

In the sketch he has recently given of our late friend, who was one of the small group known as the "X Club," Professor Huxley has given some account of that body. Further particulars may not unfitly be added; one of which may come better from me than from him. The impression that the club exercised influence in the scientific world (not wholly without basis, I think) was naturally produced by such knowledge as there eventually arose of its composition. For it contained four presidents of the British Association, three presidents of the Royal Society, and among its members who had not filled these highest posts there were presidents of the College of Surgeons, the Mathematical Society, the Chemical Society, etc. Out of the nine I was the only one who was fellow of no society and had presided over nothing. I speak in the past tense, for now, unhappily, the number of members is reduced to five, and of these only three are in good health. There has been no meeting for the past year, and it seems scarcely likely that there will ever be another. But the detail of most interest which Professor Huxley has not given, concerns a certain supplementary meeting which, for many years, took place after the close of our session. This lasted from October in each year to June in the next; and toward the close of June we had a gathering in the country to which the married members brought their wives, raising the number on some occasions to fifteen. Our programme was to leave town early on Saturday afternoon, in time for a ramble or a boating excursion before dinner; to have on the Sunday a picnic in some picturesque place adjacent to our temporary quarters; and, after dinner that evening, for some to return to town, while those with less pressing engagements remained until the Monday morning. Two of our picnics were held under Burnham Beeches, one or more on St. George's Hill, Weybridge, and another in Windsor Forest. As our spirits in those days had not been subdued by years, and as we had the added pleasure of ladies' society, these gatherings were extremely enjoyable. If Tyndall did not add to the life of our party by his wit, he did by his hilarity. But my special motive for naming these rural meetings of the "X" is that I may mention a fact which, to not a few, will be surprising and perhaps instructive. We sometimes carried with us to our picnic a volume of verse, which was duly utilized after the repast. On one occasion, while we reclined under the trees of Windsor Forest, Huxley read to us Tennyson's "Œnone," and on another occasion we listened to Tyndall's reading of Mrs. Browning's poem, "Lady Geraldine's Courtship." The vast majority of people suppose that science and poetry are antagonistic. Here is a fact which may, perhaps, cause some of them to revise their opinions.

From the impressions of Tyndall which these facts indirectly yield, let me return to impressions more directly yielded. Though it is scarcely needful to say anything about his sincerity, yet it cannot properly be passed over, since it was a leading trait in his nature. It has been conspicuous to all, alike in his acts and his words. The Belfast address to the British Association exhibited his entire thought on questions which most men of science pass over from prudential considerations. But in him there was no spirit of compromise. It never occurred to him to ask what it was politic to say, but simply to ask what was true. The like has of late years been shown in his utterances concerning political matters—shown, it may be, with too great an outspokenness. This outspokenness was displayed, also, in private, and sometimes perhaps too much displayed; but every one must have the defects of his qualities, and where absolute sincerity exists, it is certain now and then to cause an expression of a feeling or opinion not adequately restrained. But the contrast in genuineness between him and the average citizen was very conspicuous. In a community of Tyndalls (to make a wild supposition) there would be none of that flabbiness characterizing current thought and action—no throwing overboard of principles elaborated by painful experience in the past, and adoption of a hand-to-mouth policy unguided by any principle. He was not the kind of man who would have voted for a bill or a clause which he secretly believed would be injuri-

THE HALL IN HINDHEAD HOUSE.

PROFESSOR TYNDALL'S STUDY, HINDHEAD HOUSE.

ous, out of what is euphemistically called "party loyalty," or would have endeavored to bribe each section of the electorate by *ad captandum* measures, or would have hesitated to protect life and property for fear of losing votes. What he saw right to do he would have done, regardless of proximate consequences.

The ordinary tests of generosity are very defective. As rightly measured, generosity is great in proportion to the amount of self-denial entailed ; and where ample means are possessed large gifts often entail no self-denial. Far more self-denial may be involved in the performance, on another's behalf, of some act which requires time and labor. In addition to generosity under its ordinary form, which Professor Tyndall displayed in unusual degree, he displayed it under a less common form. He was ready to take much trouble to help friends. I have had personal experience of this. Though he had always in hand some investigation of great interest to him, and though, as I have heard him say, when he had bent his mind to a subject he could not with any facility break off and resume it again, yet, when I have sought his scientific aid—information or critical opinion—I never found the slightest reluctance to give me his undivided attention. Much more markedly, however, was this kind of generosity shown in another direction. Many men, while they are eager for appre-

ciation, manifest little or no appreciation of others, and still less go out of their way to express it. With Tyndall it was not thus : he was eager to recognize achievement. Notably in the case of Faraday, and less notably, though still conspicuously, in many cases, he has bestowed much labor and sacrificed many weeks in setting forth others' merits. It was evidently a pleasure to him to dilate on the claims of fellow-workers.

But there was a derivative form of this generosity calling for still greater eulogy. He was not content with expressing appreciation of those whose merits were recognized, but he spent energy unsparingly in drawing public attention to those whose merits were unrecognized ; and time after time, in championing the causes of such, he was regardless of the antagonisms he aroused and the evils he brought on himself. This chivalrous defence of the neglected and the ill-used has been, I think, by few, if any, so often repeated. I have myself more than once benefited by his determination, quite spontaneously shown, that justice should be done in the apportionment of credit ; and I have with admiration watched like actions of his in other cases—cases in which no consideration of nationality or of creed interfered in the least with his insistence on equitable distribution of honors.

In thus undertaking to fight for those

who were unfairly dealt with, he displayed in another direction that very conspicuous trait which, as displayed in his Alpine feats, has made him to many persons chiefly known—I mean courage, passing very often into daring. And here let me, in closing this sketch, indicate certain mischiefs which this trait brought upon him. Courage grows by success. The demonstrated ability to deal with dangers produces readiness to meet more dangers, and is self-justifying where the muscular power and the nerve habitually prove adequate. But the resulting habit of mind is apt to influence conduct in other spheres, where muscular power and nerve are of no avail —is apt to cause the daring of dangers which are not to be met by strength of limb or by skill. Nature as externally presented in precipices, ice-slopes, and crevasses may be dared by one adequately endowed; but Nature as internally presented in the form of physical constitution, may not be thus dared with impunity. Prompted by high motives, Tyndall tended too much to disregard the protests of his body. Over-application in Germany caused at one time absolute sleeplessness for, I think he told me, more than a week; and this, with kindred transgressions, brought on that insomnia by which his after-life was troubled, and by which his powers of work were diminished; for, as I have heard him say, a sound night's sleep was followed by marked exaltation of faculty. And then, in later life, came the daring which, by its results, brought his active career to a close. He conscientiously desired to fulfil an engagement to lecture at the Royal Institution, and was not to be deterred by fear of consequences. He gave the lecture, notwithstanding the protest which for days before his system had been making. The result was a serious illness, threatening, as he thought at one time, a fatal result; and, notwithstanding a year's furlough for the recovery of health, he was eventually obliged to resign his position. But for this defiance of nature there might have been many more years of scientific exploration, pleasurable to himself and beneficial to others; and he might have escaped that invalid life which for a long time past he had to bear.

In his case, however, the penalties of invalid life had great mitigations—mitigations such as fall to the lot of but few. It is conceivable that the physical discomforts and mental weariness which ill-health brings, may be almost compensated, if not even quite compensated, by the pleasurable emotions caused by unflagging attentions and sympathetic companionship. If this ever happens, it happened in his case. All who have known the household during these years of nursing are aware of the

PROFESSOR TYNDALL'S COTTAGE IN THE ALPS.

unmeasured kindness he has received without ceasing. I happen to have had special evidence of this devotion on the one side and gratitude on the other, which I do not think I am called upon to keep to myself, but rather to do the contrary. In a letter I received from him some half-dozen years ago, referring, among other things, to Mrs. Tyndall's self-sacrificing care of him, he wrote: "She has raised my ideal of the possibilities of human nature."

CHARLES A. DANA IN HIS OFFICE AT "THE SUN."

(Drawn from life by Corwin Knapp Linson.)

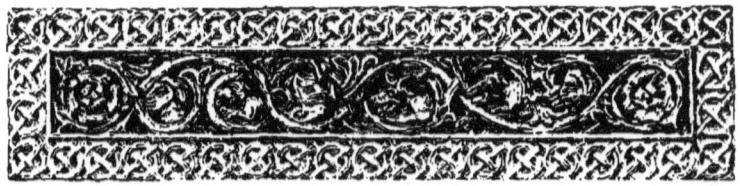

MR. DANA OF "THE SUN."

By Edward P. Mitchell.

KINGLAKE'S picture of a great editor —the most famous, if not the greatest, editor that English journalism has known— represents a man wrapped in midnight mystery. He is surrounded by sentinels, and perpetually absorbed during business hours in highly responsible thought. Part of the description of John T. Delane at work making the next morning's "Times" is worth quoting here, for it does not lack unconscious humor :

"From the moment of his entering the editor's room until four or five o'clock in the morning, the strain he had to put on his faculties must have been always great, and in stirring times almost prodigious. There were hours of night when he often had to decide—to decide, of course, with great swiftness—between two or more courses of action momentously different ; when, besides, he must judge the appeals brought up to the paramount arbiter from all kinds of men, from all sorts of earthly tribunals ; when despatches of moment, when telegrams fraught with grave tidings, when notes hastily scribbled in the Lords or Commons, were from time to time coming in to confirm or disturb, perhaps even to annul, former reckonings ; and these, besides, were the hours when, on questions newly obtruding, yet so closely, so importunately present that they would have to be met before sunrise, he somehow must cause to spring up sudden essays, invectives, and arguments which only strong power of brain, with even much toil, could supply. For the delicate task any other than he would require to be in a state of tranquillity ; would require to have ample time. But for him there are no such indulgences ; he sees the hand of the clock growing more and more peremptory, and the time drawing nearer and nearer when his paper must, *must* be made up."

No trait is more characteristic of Mr. Dana than his intolerance of anything like humbug about his professional labors or methods. For almost fifty years he has managed to keep easily ahead of the clock, and to meet, without much personal consciousness of effort, all sorts of new and suddenly developed situations requiring swift decision as between courses of action momentously different. Mr. Dana's own imagination has never decorated with mystic importance this power to dispose rapidly and accurately of any newspaper question that comes up at any hour of the day or night. It has never seemed remarkable to him that he should be able to get out his paper morning after morning, and year after year, without any sense on his part of high pressure or extraordinary intellectual strain. He works hard, and, at the same time, it is quite true that he works easily ; for he works with absolute tranquillity, undisturbed by that most common and most wearing attendant of mental effort, the mind's constant recognition of its own attitude towards the labor in which it is at the time engaged. Thus Mr. Dana has always been the master, and not the slave, of the immediate task. The external features of his journalism are simplicity, directness, common sense, and the entire absence of affectation. He would no more think of attempting to live up to Mr. Kinglake's ideal of a great, mysterious, and thought-burdened editor, than of putting on a conical hat and a black robe spangled with suns, moons, and stars, when about to receive a visitor to his editorial office in Nassau Street.

I.

THE rather naked little corner room in the "Sun" Building in which Mr. Dana has sat almost daily for twenty-five years, is a surprise to many persons who see it for the first time. His genuine love of beautiful things, his disposition to acquire them if possible, and the extraordinary range and accuracy of his æsthetic appreciations, are so widely known that it is quite natural for those who do not understand him to expect to find his tastes reflected in his accustomed place of work. The room might be even barer than it is and yet serve Mr. Dana's purpose as well as if it were the Gallery of Apollo. On the other hand, if his chair and desk were established in the middle of the vastest and most sumptuous presence-chamber to be found anywhere, and amid a throng of curious and noisy onlookers, Mr. Dana would work on with the same tranquil efficiency, providing his pen did not splutter and the capacious waste-basket at his feet were emptied from time to time. The processes of his mind are neither stimulated nor intimidated by the surroundings. The accessories of luxurious professional habits are absent because they are superfluous to Mr. Dana; if he thought they would help him to make a better newspaper, they would all be there.

In the middle of the small room a desk-table of black walnut, of the Fulton Street style and the period of the first administration of Grant; a shabby little round table at the window, where Mr. Dana sits when the day is dark; one leather-covered chair, which does duty at either post, and two wooden chairs, both rickety, for visitors on errands of business or ceremony; on the desk a revolving case with a few dozen books of reference; an ink-pot and pen, not much used except in correcting manuscript or proofs, for Mr. Dana talks off to a stenographer his editorial articles and his correspondence, sometimes spending on the revision of the former twice as much time as was required for the dictation; a window-seat filled with exchanges, marked here and there in blue pencil for the editor's eyes; a big pair of shears, and two or three extra pairs of spectacles in cache against an emergency: these few items constitute what is practically the whole objective equipment of the editor of "The Sun." The shears are probably the newest article of furniture in the list. They replaced, three or four years ago, another pair of unknown antiquity, besought and obtained by Eugene Field, and now occupying, alongside of Mr.

Gladstone's axe, the place of honor in that poet's celebrated collection of edged instruments.

For the non-essentials, the little trapezoid-shaped room contains a third table, holding a file of the newspaper for a few weeks back, and a heap of new books which have passed review; an iron umbrella rack; on the floor a cheap Turkish rug; and a lounge covered with horse-hide, upon which Mr. Dana descends for a five minutes' nap perhaps five times a year. The adornments of the room are mostly accidental and insignificant. Ages ago somebody presented to Mr. Dana, with symbolic intent, a large stuffed owl. The bird of wisdom remains by inertia on top of the revolving book-case, just as it would have remained there had it been a stuffed cat or a statuette of Folly. Unnoticed and probably long ago forgotten by its proprietor, the owl solemnly boxes the compass as Mr. Dana swings the case, reaching in quick succession for his Bible, his Portuguese dictionary, his compendium of botanical terms, or his copy of the Democratic National Platform of 1892. On the mantelpiece is an ugly, feather-haired little totem figure from Alaska, which likewise keeps its place solely by possession. It stands between a photograph of Chester A. Arthur, whom Mr. Dana liked and admired as a man of the world, and the japanned calendar case which has shown him the time of year for the last quarter of a century. A dingy chromo-lithograph of Prince von Bismarck stands shoulder to shoulder with George, the Count Joannes.

The same mingling of sentiment and pure accident marks the rest of Mr. Dana's picture gallery. There is a large and excellent photograph of Horace Greeley, who is held in half-affectionate, half-humorous remembrance by his old associate in the management of "The Tribune." Another is of the late Justice Blatchford of the United States Supreme Court; it is the strong face of the fearless judge whose decision from the Federal bench in New York twenty years ago blocked the attempt to drag Mr. Dana before a servile little court in Washington, to be tried without a jury on a charge of criminal libel, at the time when "The Sun" was demolishing the District ring. Over the mantel is Abraham Lincoln. There are pictures of the four Harper brothers and of the five Appletons. Andrew Jackson is there twice, once in black and white, once in vivid colors. An inexpensive Thomas Jefferson faces the livelier Jackson. A framed diploma certifies that Mr. Dana was one of several gentlemen who presented to the State

CITY HALL PARK AND PRINTING HOUSE SQUARE.

a portrait in oils of Samuel J. Tilden. On different sides of the room are William T. Coleman, the organizer of the San Francisco Vigilantes, and a crude colored print of the Haifa colony at the foot of Mount Carmel, in Syria. Strangest of all in this singular collection is a photograph of a tall, lank, and superior-looking New England mill girl, issued as an advertisement by some Connecticut concern engaged in the manufacture of spool cotton. For a good many years the most available wall space in Mr. Dana's office was occupied by a huge pasteboard chart, showing elaborately, in deadly parallel columns, the differences in the laws of the several States of the Union respecting divorce. It was put there, and it remained there, serving no earthly purpose except to illustrate the editor's indifference as to his immediate surroundings, until it disappeared as mysteriously as it had come. Mr. Dana's divorce chart may have been stolen, but Superintendent Byrnes was not consulted.

Thus far in deference to Mr. McClure's respect for objective detail, as throwing light on character. After this hasty but approximately complete catalogue, it is needless to remark that the scheme of decoration carried out in the workroom of the foremost personage and most interesting figure in American journalism would indicate to nobody that the occupant of the room knew Manet from Monet, or old Persian lustre from Gubbio.

From the windows of his room in the dwarf "Sun" Building, the old Tammany Hall in Park Row, Mr. Dana can look out and up to the sky-high edifices built all around him by his esteemed contemporaries during recent years. He is perfectly content to work on, as he has worked in this same block between Spruce Street and Frankfort almost continuously since February, 1846, in the old-fashioned way, as far as externals are concerned. The absence of ostentation that distinguishes his professional methods and habits extends to the whole establishment. While the "Sun" Building, as a workshop, lacks no modern appliance or mechanical improvement that contributes to the production of a great daily newspaper, there are few journals less impressively housed, even in the smaller cities of the United States.

II.

INTO the corner room described, there swings nearly every morning in the year a man of seventy-five, looking fifteen years younger: largely built, square-framed, with a step as firm as a sea captain's; vigorous, sometimes to abruptness, in his bodily movements, but deliberate and gentle in his speech; dressed always in such a way that his clothes seem to belong to him and not he to them; with strong brown hands, rather large, which do not tremble as they hold book or paper; and a countenance, familiar to most Americans through portraits or caricatures, whose marked features the caricaturists distort in various whimsical ways without ever succeeding in making the face seem either ridiculous or ignoble. Mr. Dana's full beard is trimmed more closely than in former years. It ranks as snow white only by courtesy; the last strongholds of the pigment are not yet conquered.

The impression which Mr. Dana makes upon those who come into contact with him personally, for the first time or the fortieth, is that of vigorous and sympathetic good will, both desirous and capable of pleasing. He is frank and engaging in conversation, and the wonderful range of his intellectual interests makes him equally ready to learn or to communicate. Men who seek him merely to measure their wits against his for a purpose, often go away charmed with their reception and well satisfied with results until they begin to reckon at a distance what has actually been accomplished by the interview. If shrewd kindness beams on the stranger through one of the two lenses of his gold-bowed spectacles, kind shrewdness is alert behind the other glass. He has learned how to say No when necessary, and even to say it in italics; but he has never learned how to say an inconsiderate thing.

A very observant Frenchman once remarked about Mr. Dana: "He is one of the few men over sixty I have known who remember the way to blush. The only times I have seen Mr. Dana blush have been when something discourteous was said or done in his presence, too trivial to call for direct rebuke."

The physical vitality which has served Mr. Dana so well through life that he has never experienced a single hour of serious illness, and which brings him to his desk now at seventy-five with as keen a joy for the day's work and the day's fun as that of any youth under his command, is the most obvious and the least important factor. It accounts, perhaps, for the occasional blush which the French gentleman noted, for the heartiness of his hand-grasp, and in a measure for the general cheerfulness of the view he habitually takes of life; but inveterate health is by no means a possession peculiar to the editor of "The Sun." Nor is the analysis which goes into the questions of a man's diet and hours of sleep, in order to ascertain the secret of his genius, likely to be rewarding in its results. Mr. Dana uses no tobacco, but that is not the reason why he is superior to petulance and never frets himself under any circumstances, whatever his mood. He knows wine, and respects it and himself; but that is not the reason why he knows at a glance good poetry from bad, even if the good be disguised in cramped handwriting and words misspelled, while the bad is displayed in typography beautiful to see. He prefers the mushroom to mush and milk, being both a connoisseur and a cultivator of the former; but that is not the reason why, as a journalist, his perception of the interesting, the unexpected, the refreshing, has not been dulled by fifty years' exercise. First, a natural, God-given faculty for the acquisition, the discrimination, and the dissemination of facts and ideas; secondly, a life uncommonly rich and varied in its acquaintance with men and its experience of affairs: these are the lines of inquiry to be pursued by any one who is curious for an explanation of the success of Mr. Dana's career, and the incalculable influence of his mind upon the general progress and special methods of American journalism during the long period of his activity in that profession.

Mr. Dana was born with a voracious intellectual appetite, which has remained healthy and insatiate all of his life. He shrinks at nothing short of actual dulness, or literary deformity so marked as to be repulsive. He is a tireless reader of books, magazines, and journals in many languages. Whether print or manuscript comes under his eyes, he takes in the ideas seemingly by whole paragraphs, rather than by words, lines, or even sentences. Unlike most other very rapid readers that I have known, he does not merely sample the page or the chapter or the book. A glance through his glasses seems to establish a circuit which at once puts his brain in possession not only of the essential facts, but also of any refinement of style that may be there, or any novel or felicitous verbal formula, no matter how inconspicuous. When he closes the book or throws aside the newspaper, the probability is small that he has missed anything worth having. This process of acquisition has been going on without a break and with constantly increasing speed ever since his early boyhood. It is supported by a memory which selects with discrimination and then retains with tenacity.

III.

MR. DANA was two years old when he left the town of his birth, Hinsdale, New Hampshire. His childhood was spent at Gaines, on the Erie Canal, in Orleans County, New York State, in Buffalo, and at Guildhall, Vermont. One of his earliest recollections is of running away from home in Buffalo at the age of three, and going down to the lake to see the first steamboat come in. He got himself very muddy, and on his return his mother tied him to the well-post with her garter.

At Gaines he attended the district school during two winter sessions, and picked up what he could find, openly or by stratagem, in the limited literature within his reach. "The first book I remember reading," he says, "was Miss Porter's 'Thaddeus of Warsaw.' That romance made an extraordinary impression on my mind. I must have been five years old, certainly not more than six. 'Thaddeus' was not considered as a suitable book for me; it was kept stowed away in a drawer of my mother's bureau. I discovered it there, and read it on foot from beginning to end in short installments, standing over the open book in the open drawer, crying hard at the pathetic passages, but always ready to push the drawer to and run if I heard anybody coming. It seemed to me to be a great story."

The favorite books of Mr. Dana's boyhood were "Pilgrim's Progress," "Robinson Crusoe," and, later, "Ivanhoe." He read them over and over again until he almost knew them by heart. When he was eleven he returned to Buffalo to be a clerk in his uncle's dry goods and notions store. "I was pretty good," he says, "at selling stuff, and quick at figures and in making change." For seven years he clerked it, occupying his scant leisure with miscellaneous reading, but touching no school books until he was almost nineteen. His uncle failed in business in 1837, and the future of Mr. Dana's mercantile career became clouded. He remained in Buffalo for two years longer, helping to settle up the affairs of the establishment, and meanwhile preparing himself for college. "I was just about nineteen when I tackled the Latin grammar and *musa, musæ, musæ, musam.* I found the utmost difficulty in remembering the paradigms. Nothing but the steadiest determination kept my nose to that book."

Two winter terms in a country district school and two years in college consti-

THE APPROACH TO DOSORIS ISLAND, MR. DANA'S SUMMER HOME.

tuted the whole of Mr. Dana's experience of any system of education in which he himself was not master as well as pupil. He entered Harvard in 1839 at the age of twenty. His eyesight was seriously affected by too close application, and he was obliged to leave his class at the end of the sophomore year. Mr. Dana would have been graduated in 1843. Although he was prevented from completing the course, the university afterward gave him his degree. His name appears in the triennial catalogue, and last year he met his old classmates in Boston to celebrate the fiftieth anniversary of the class of 1843.

While at Cambridge Mr. Dana was a hard student. He so far overcame the first repugnance with which paradigms of declension or conjugation inspired him, as to conceive a marked and genuine fondness for the acquisition of other languages than English, living and dead. No year has passed during his busy life without adding to his stock of languages, or increasing his familiarity with some of those which he has already partially acquired. Most spoken languages except the Slavonic and the Oriental are at his command ; and he has but just now started on Russian. He is restless so long as something which he really wants to know remains behind a curtain of words which he does not comprehend. An accidental circumstance, a chance reference, impatience with an obviously imperfect translation, may direct his attention to some tongue or some dialect which he has not yet checked off. Then he turns to with grammar and dictionary, and is not satisfied until his mastery of that particular medium of thought is sufficient for practical purposes. Many visitors to the "Sun" office have found Mr. Dana bending over text-book and lexicon, and working away with the energy of a freshman who has only half an hour before Greek recitation. Such visitors have seen the editor in some of his happiest moments.

Curiosity concerning the Norwegian-Icelandic literature led Mr. Dana, years ago, to a systematic and persistent study of the old Norse. That and its surviving Scandinavian kindred have long been a favorite occupation with him. He reads the Sagas and Henrik Ibsen's last play with equal readiness, although not with equal reverence. In the whole range of classic literature, next to the Bible, for which his admiration is profound and unaffected, the "Divine Comedy" perhaps holds the first place in his esteem. He began to read Dante in the original in 1862, taking it up for the benefit of his eldest daughter, and afterward accompanying his other children in turn through the incomparable poem. His Dante classes have included some very distinguished men, and have given him great pleasure. Mr. Dana's study of Dante has been almost continuous for thirty years. He has accumulated an extensive and valuable Dante library. One could scarcely quote a line in the "Divine Comedy" which Mr. Dana would not immediately place. When the editor of "The Sun" met Pope Leo XIII, a few years ago in the Vatican Palace, two most accomplished Dante scholars came together, and they exchanged ideas on doubtful readings upon equal terms and with mutual satisfaction.

IV.

AFTER leaving Harvard the need of out-of-door life and the prospect of intellectual companionship, at a time when books were forbidden to him by the oculists, turned Mr. Dana to the Brook Farm Association for Agriculture and Education, then recently established in West Roxbury. In that remarkable attempt to combine high ideals of thought and conduct with the manipulation of fertilizers and the cultivation of vegetables, Mr. Dana was associated with Nathaniel Hawthorne, Margaret Fuller, George William Curtis, A. Bronson Alcott, William Henry Channing, George and Sophia Ripley, and others. Theodore Parker, as pastor of the Unitarian Church in West Roxbury, was in close touch with the community. Mr. Dana's share in the division of labor was the management of the fruit department.

The history of the Brook Farm experiment, notable because of its relation to the intellectual movement in New England at that time, as well as for the distinction subsequently attained by most of those who held hoes or milked cows in its service, is not likely to be written by any one directly informed. Nearly all of the Associates have passed away without recording their reminiscences of Brook Farm. Hawthorne's tale is avowedly a fanciful picture. In the preface to the "Blithedale Romance" he appealed to Mr. Dana to preserve for the public both the outward narrative and the inner truth and spirit of the whole affair. That was in 1852 ; there has been no response yet, and I do not think Mr. Dana will ever find time to chronicle Brook Farm. A gentleman now living in the West, who as a boy was placed by his parents under the tutelage of the philosophers of the community, once told me that he remembered Dana as the sole person connected with the enterprise who showed any real talent for farming, or manifested much practical sagacity in affairs generally.

In one way Brook Farm determined Mr. Dana's career; for while a member of that celebrated community he had a part in the management of a publication called "The Harbinger," devoted to · social reform, transcendental philosophy, and general literature. In 1844, when the condition of his eyesight permitted him to go to work in earnest, he obtained a place under Elizur Wright on "The Boston Chronotype," a daily newspaper; and from that time, just fifty years ago, his connection with daily journalism has been unbroken, except during the period of the Civil War.

Elizur Wright, better remembered in Boston as an insurance actuary than as a newspaper editor, used to tell one story about the youth whom he hired to help him run "The Chronotype." It was an orthodox newspaper, and a great favorite with the

A GATEWAY AT DOSORIS.

Congregational ministers of Massachusetts and the adjoining States. Mr. Wright went away for a few days, leaving his assistant in control. "During my absence," said Wright, "'The Chronotype' came out mighty strong editorially against hell, to the astonishment of the subscribers and the consternation of the responsible editor. When I got back I was obliged to write a personal letter to every Congregational minister in the State, and to many deacons, explaining that the paper had been left in charge of a young man without mellow journalistic experience. Dana always had a weakness for giving people with fixed convictions something new to think about."

"On 'The Chronotype,' " says Mr. Dana himself, "I wrote editorials on all sorts of subjects, read the exchanges, edited the news, did almost everything, and drew five dollars a week. Then I left Boston to better myself, and came on to New York, where 'The Tribune' gave me ten dollars as city editor. That was in February, 1847. Along in the autumn I struck, and Greeley made it fourteen dollars. So it went on until the French Revolution of 1848. I went to Greeley and told him I wanted to go to Europe for the newspaper. He said: 'Dana, that's no use. You don't know anything about European matters. You would have to get your education before your correspondence was worth your expenses.' Then I asked him how much he would pay me for a letter a week. 'Ten dollars,' he said. I went across and wrote one letter a week to 'The Tribune' for ten; one to McMichael's Philadelphia 'North American' for ten; one to 'The Commercial Advertiser' in New York for ten; and to 'The Harbinger' and 'The Chronotype' one apiece for five. That gave me forty dollars a week for five letters, until 'The Chronotype' went up, and then I had thirty-five. On this I lived in Europe eight months, went everywhere, saw plenty of revolutions, supported myself there and my family here in New York, and came home only sixty-three dollars out for the whole trip." Mr. Dana had married, in 1846, Miss Eunice Macdaniel, who then lived in Walker Street, New York.

"On returning from Europe," Mr. Dana went on, continuing the narrative of his early journalism in the financial aspect personal to himself, "I went back to 'The Tribune' at twenty dollars a week. That and twenty-five dollars were the figures for a long time; in fact, until another newspaper offered me one hundred. I went to 'The Tribune' people and told them I couldn't afford to stay at twenty-five. They reminded me gently that Mr. Greeley drew only fifty dollars; it clearly wouldn't do for me to get more than he had. So they gave me fifty, the same as Horace had, and that was the highest salary I ever received on 'The Tribune.' I worked for fifty until I went into the War Department with Stanton."

V.

In the "Tribune" establishment, during the exciting ten years that prepared for and ushered in the Civil War, Mr. Dana supplied the journalistic qualities which Mr. Greeley lacked. Every newspaper man understands that while Horace Greeley was a great genius, with a power of writing that drove thought home with a force and a piquancy unsurpassed, he was not a great editor in the proper sense of the word. Dana, with his wider range of intellectual interest, his more accurate sense of news perspective, his saner and steadier judgment of men and events, and his vastly superior executive ability, impressed his own personality upon the journal of which he was one of the proprietors, and more than nominally the managing editor.

The brilliant staff which Mr. Greeley and Mr. Dana gathered around them during the long fight against the extension of slavery, and for the organization of that sentiment in the North which gave birth to the Republican party, included among other writers Bayard Taylor, George Ripley, William Henry Fry, Richard Hildreth the historian, the Count Adam Gurowski, and James S. Pike. The private letters from Greeley and Dana published by Mr. Pike some years before his death, in a volume entitled "First Blows of the Civil War," and those letters of Greeley to Dana which have found their way into print, sketch the inner workings of the "Tribune" office during this most interesting period. The "Tribune" men were dead in earnest, working both for a great principle and for newspaper fortune. Greeley, uneven in temperament, is seen alternating between enthusiasm and despondency; sometimes putting in the heaviest licks, sometimes dispirited almost to hopelessness in face of the South, and harassed by the cranks and impracticables at the North. "At the outset," writes the Hon. Henry Wilson in his "Rise and Fall of the "Slave Power, "Mr. Greeley seemed disinclined to enter the contest. He told his associates that he would not restrain them, but, as for himself, he had no heart for the strife."

Dana, the central figure in the activity of the establishment, overflowing with vitality, enterprise, and pertinacious cheerfulness, lived ten lives in the ten years that carried him from thirty to forty. We see him prodding the sluggards and holding back the over-hasty; taking the whole responsibility on his shoulders during Gree-

MR. DANA'S HOUSE ON DOSORIS ISLAND AS SEEN FROM THE DRIVEWAY.

ley's protracted vacations in Europe ; rushing off to the stump for some favorite Free Soil candidate ; laying plans to gratify his chief's tacit but unconquerable desire for public office ; arranging newspaper combinations in New York, and sending "The Weekly Tribune" up to two hundred and eighty thousand among the farmers of the Northern States ; finding fun in every new phase of politics, while keeping the paper straight on its course as the leading organ of anti-slavery sentiment, and working night and day with as serious a purpose as ever animated any journalist ; and in brief intervals of leisure running down to his family at Westport, and writing thence such descriptions of tranquil domesticity as this :

"I have been busy with my children, driving them about in old Bradley's one-horse wagon, rowing and sailing with them on the bay and Sound, gathering shells on the shore with them, picking cherries, lounging on the grass, gazing into the sky with the whole tribe about me. Who'd think of paying notes under such circumstances? There's no delight like that in a pack of young children—of your own. Love is selfish, friendship is exacting, but this other affection gives all and asks nothing. The man who hasn't half a dozen young children about him must have a very mean conception of life. Besides, there ought always to be a baby in every house. A house without a baby is inhuman."

It was during these crowded years just before the war that Mr. Dana found time to project and produce, in connection with Mr. Ripley, the "American Cyclopedia," an undertaking that involved on his part an amount of editorial labor that would have seemed formidable to any other man. While this tremendous job was still in hand, he prepared and published the first edition of his "Household Book of Poetry," one of the best anthologies in existence, shaped by a catholic taste and a genuine love of poetry. Few books have gone into more American homes, or counted more for sound education and continuing pleasure.

In the last year of Mr. Dana's fifteen years' connection with "The Tribune," he made an unsuccessful effort to put Horace Greeley in the place wherein that sage fancied he would be most useful to his country ; that is to say, in the Senate of the United States. The most important consequence of the estrangement which had brought about the dissolution of the political firm of Seward, Weed and Greeley, had been the defeat of Seward at Chicago, and the nomination of Abraham Lincoln ;

a fortunate event largely, if not principally, due to the attitude of the "Tribune" men towards Seward. Early in the spring of 1860, Greeley was privately offering to bet twenty dollars against Seward's nomination, and was defining his own position in this philosophic, if somewhat profane, fashion :

"I don't care what is done about the nomination. I know what ought to be done ; and having set that forth, am content. I stand in the position of the rich old fellow who, having built a church entirely out of his own means, addressed his townsmen thus :

> "'I've built you a meeting-house,
> And bought you a bell ;
> Now go to meeting,
> Or go to h—!'"

The next year the New York Legislature had to elect a senator to succeed Mr. Seward, then already chosen by Mr. Lincoln to be his Secretary of State. Mr. Dana went to Albany in Greeley's interest, and managed a campaign which nearly resulted in his nomination by the Republican caucus. The vote was almost equally divided between Mr. Greeley's friends and those of Mr. William Maxwell Evarts ; while a few legislators, pledged to Judge Ira Harris, held the balance of power. Thurlow Weed defeated Greeley by procuring the transfer of the entire Evarts vote to Judge Harris, an achievement which partially squared the Chicago account, and which is interesting as the last incident of a famous political quarrel.

Mr. Dana withdrew from "The Tribune" on April 1, 1862. His resignation as managing editor was due to a radical disagreement between Mr. Greeley and himself as to the newspaper's policy with regard to the conduct of the war. Mr. Dana was immediately asked by Secretary Stanton to go to Cairo to examine and settle the accounts of the Quartermaster's Department. The job involved the investigation of tangled and disputed claims against the Government, amounting to between one and two millions of dollars. By far the larger part of the claims were found to be unsound, and were rejected. This work, and other special work of importance to which Stanton at once assigned Mr. Dana, led to his appointment as Assistant Secretary of War, an office which he held until the end of hostilities.

VI.

Mr. Dana's services as Assistant Secretary of War are matters of public history,

and need be related here only so far as they illustrate the character of the man, or help to describe the perimeter of his many-sided experience.

Mr. Lincoln once defined one of Mr. Dana's functions during the war period by styling him "the eyes of the Government at the front." For perhaps a third of the whole time between his appointment as Assistant Secretary of War and the fall of Richmond, Mr. Dana represented the Department at the scene of operations. He was with Grant before and behind and around Vicksburg for four months. He saw the Chattanooga campaign from beginning to end. He went with Sherman to the relief of Burnside in Knoxville. He was in the Wilderness, and at Spottsylvania, and everywhere with the army throughout the tremendous fighting in the spring of 1864. He was with Sheridan in the Shenandoah Valley in the autumn of that year ; and he travelled with Grant back to Washington from Richmond, after the surrender of Lee and the death of the Confederacy. For months at a time he was at the front, in the saddle, on the march, on the field when there was fighting, living at army headquarters as the official representative of the civil authority, in close personal relations with the commanding generals, fully posted as to their intended movements and largest plans, and sending back to Washington, over General Eckert's wires, daily, and often hourly, despatches for the information of the Secretary of War and the President. Dana's reports to Stanton, when they were of importance, as they generally were, went straight to the White House as soon as they had been translated from the cipher.

These despatches, distinguished by common sense, clear perception, direct and fearless statement, and utter lack of respect for foolish or unnecessary routine, constitute what is unquestionably the most important work of reporting ever done by any newspaper man. The same qualities which make Mr. Dana a great journalist, made him a consummate reporter of military events. Lincoln saw from the first that he had committed no mistake in his choice of a pair of eyes. He wanted, most of all, the absolute truth of the situation—the broad truth freed from unessential details—as it appeared to a swift and accurate intelligence and a keen judge of human character. He got it, and more, in Dana's despatches and letters to Stanton. In the routine reports of the military service, tardy in arrival, and in construction hampered by all of the conventions, the leaders and lesser officers upon whose personal qualities depended, in the last analysis, the fate of the Union cause, figured merely as names, with hardly more individuality than so many algebraic symbols. In the Assistant Secretary's reports the men in the field jump into life in from two to half a dozen lines of rapid portraiture. They stood before Lincoln in his study in the White House as if they were there in person, with all of their virtues and imperfections. A few words of incidental characterization, a half humorous reference to some small incident, gave the President a better understanding of the remote instru-

relied, as it has always been his habit to rely, with full confidence upon the soundness of his own electric intuitions. He represented the facts about men and affairs at the front precisely as he himself saw them, without fear or favor, and without terror of precedent. His sole purpose at any time was to give the Government at Washington the information of which it had need at that time. In the whirl and din of the front he sometimes made mistakes of fact, and was quick to correct them. He misjudged men occasionally, and at the earliest opportunity put them right again. He kept his head at times when camp sentiment and even headquarters

MR. DANA'S HOUSE ON DOSORIS ISLAND AS IT FRONTS LONG ISLAND SOUND.

ments through which he was working to suppress the Rebellion than he could have derived by any other medium short of his own personal observation of the men themselves. Miles of the customary military reports were worth less to Lincoln, for his purposes, than half a dozen of Dana's vivid sentences.

It is quite obvious that in most hands this would be a dangerous and misleading method of reporting military events. Few men in Mr. Dana's place would have had the courage to disregard so entirely the conventional formulas of official communication; few men in Mr. Lincoln's place would have been so quick to recognize and appreciate the value of the service. Mr. Dana treated his subject in the only way possible to his mind and pen. He

were in the delirium of false hope, or in the indigo depths of unnecessary discouragement.

Upon the steadiness of Dana's judgment, the justice of his observations, and the singleness of his patriotic purpose, Abraham Lincoln came to depend more and more during the last two years of the war. It is impossible to look over the Assistant Secretary's telegrams and letters from the front, either those already printed in the voluminous collection of war documents issuing from the Government Press, or the equally important papers that still belong to unpublished history, without wondering at the discernment shown in his early estimates of leaders then almost unknown; at the sureness with which he distinguished the stuffed heroes from the real ones, recog-

A CORNER OF THE LIBRARY AT DOSORIS.

nized latent military genius, and detected the bogus article under no matter what pretentiousness of pomp and circumstance; or at the extent to which his observations and suggestions from the field influenced the military policy of the Administration, and helped to determine the career of generals, the achievements of armies, and the destiny of the national cause.

From the hundreds of character sketches swiftly drawn at first sight for the information of Stanton and Lincoln, take, for example, this estimate of John A. Logan, then not very conspicuous among the volunteer generals for the Western States: "This is a man of remarkable qualities and peculiar character. Heroic and brilliant, he is sometimes unsteady. Inspiring his men with his own enthusiasm on the field of battle, he is splendid in all its crash and commotion; but before it begins he is doubtful of the result, and after it is over he is fearful we may yet be beaten. A man of instinct, and not of reflection, his judgments are often absurd, but his extemporaneous opinions are very apt to be right. Deficient in education; deficient, too, in a nice and elevated moral sense, he is full of generous attachments and sincere animosities. On the whole, few can serve the cause of the country more effectively than he, and none will serve it more faithfully."

Mentioning Sherman at the time when that commander's name was scarcely known in the East, except for his failure to take Vicksburg in the December previous to Grant's success at that point, Dana writes nothing but admiration and praise: "Sherman tolerates no idlers, and finds something for everybody to do. The Chief of Artillery [in the Fifteenth Corps staff], Major Taylor, directed by Sherman's omnipresent eye and quick judgment, is an officer of great value, although under another general he might not be worth so much. On the whole, General Sherman has a very small and a very efficient staff, but the efficiency comes mainly from him. What a splendid soldier he is!"

Long afterwards, when Sherman was about to start on his march to the sea, it became Mr. Dana's official duty to rebuke that commander, gently and indirectly, for his lack of one of the prime qualities of good generalship, namely, tightness of mouth concerning his own military plans. Grant had been annoyed by the publication in certain Western newspapers of authentic intelligence concerning Sherman's intended movements. The silent general complained of this to Stanton, implying that the leakage was in the War Department. There was a prompt investigation, and it proved that one of Sherman's paymasters was communicating to his friends the general's plans as stated by Sherman himself. Stanton got hold of a letter written by a member of Sherman's staff to somebody in Washington, also giving full details of projects which it was better the enemy should not know.

" If Sherman cannot keep from telling his plans to paymasters," wrote Stanton angrily to Grant, " and his staff are permitted to send them broadcast over the land, the Department cannot prevent their publication."

Dana thereupon politely notified Sherman that correct information was escaping from headquarters at Atlanta and getting into the public prints ; and he received this cheerful, if somewhat irresponsible, reply :

" To Hon. C. A. Dana, Assistant Secretary of War : If indiscreet newspaper men publish information too near the truth, counteract its effect by publishing other paragraphs calculated to mislead the enemy, such as, ' Sherman's army has been much reënforced lately, especially in the cavalry, and he will soon move by several columns in circuit, so as to catch Hood's army ;' or, ' Sherman's destination is not Charleston, but Selma, where he will meet an army from the Gulf.' "

VII.

EARLY in September, 1864, Mr. Dana went to Rosecrans's headquarters at Chattanooga to accompany the Army of the Cumberland in the great movement which was then expected to be the finishing blow of the war. On his way down through Tennessee he had a long interview with Andrew Johnson on the political future of that almost reconquered State. When he reached headquarters at Stevens's Gap, Rosecrans received him with proper courtesy, but at once began a long tirade against Stanton.

" General," said Mr. Dana, " I am not here to report your opinion of Mr. Stanton. If there's anything your army needs, or that you want done by the Department, tell me, and you shall have it."

The Assistant Secretary had not been many weeks with this estimable gentleman, but most unfortunate soldier, before he saw clearly that what the army needed above all things was another commander. The disastrous day of Chickamauga came, with its casualty list on the Union side of sixteen hundred killed, nine thousand wounded, and five thousand prisoners or missing, and its blunder of generalship rendering useless this awful sacrifice. Dana witnessed the rout of Sheridan's and Davis's divisions, and was swept off that part of the field in the panic which seemed

like another Bull Run. The first news which he sends to Stanton and Lincoln is disheartening, but he is able to modify it a few hours later, when he gets from General Garfield the story of Thomas's heroic stand at the left of the long line. Rosecrans withdraws the entire army into Chattanooga, and begins to waver between plans for resistance and plans for further and final retreat. He follows up the great blunder of the Chickamauga day with the almost equally expensive mistake of withdrawing the Union forces which held Lookout Mountain, and abandoning that position to Bragg's army.

This much of history is necessary in order to understand the full significance of Mr. Dana's despatch to Stanton on September 24th, two days after the retreat into Chattanooga, recommending the removal of Rosecrans and the substitution of " some Western general of high rank and great prestige, like Grant."

Six days later, after a long and frank talk with Garfield, then Rosecrans's chief of staff, Mr. Dana repeated urgently his recommendation that Rosecrans should be removed ; and he suggested that Thomas, " the rock of Chickamauga," be put in command. " He is certainly," wrote Dana, " an officer of the very highest qualities, soldierly and personal."

An incident very creditable to Thomas then occurred. On the strength of the camp gossip, Brigadier-General Rousseau, who was briefly described by Dana to Stanton as a person " regarded throughout this army as an ass of eminent gifts," went on his own account to Thomas, and informed him that the War Department was inquiring how the army would like to have him in the chief command. Thomas at once sent a confidential friend to Dana to say that while ready to answer any other call to duty, he could not consent to become the successor of Rosecrans, because he would not do anything to countenance the suspicion that he had intrigued against his commander.

Meanwhile, with Thomas holding to this attitude on the question of his own promotion, affairs at Chattanooga went from bad to worse. The army had lost both confidence in its commander and spirit for the work ahead. At headquarters incapacity ruled, with fluctuating designs, fussiness over details, procrastination on frivolous pretexts, and seeming indifference to the perils that were gathering about the army as the autumn grew older. Dana telegraphed again on October 12 :

"I have never seen a public man possessing talent with less administrative power, less steadiness and clearness in difficulty, and greater practical incapacity than General Rosecrans. He has invention, fertility, and knowledge, but he has no strength of will and no concentration of purpose. His mind scatters; there is no system in the use of his busy days and restless nights; no courage against individuals, in his composition; and, with great love of command, he is a feeble commander. He is conscientious and honest, just as he is imperious and disputatious; always with a stray vein of caprice, and an overweening passion for the approbation of his personal friends and the public outside. I consider the army to be very unsafe in his hands, but know of no man except Thomas who could now be safely put in his place."

The sequel is well known. A week later Mr. Dana went to Nashville, returning to Chattanooga the next day in company with General Grant; the train narrowly escaping wreck on a high embankment, where a railroad tie had been planted on the track by rebel sympathizers for the destruction of the Union commander. Two days later Rosecrans had been practically superseded by both Grant and Thomas, through a military reorganization by which the former took the command of the military departments of the Tennessee, Ohio, and Cumberland, and the latter the command of the old Army of the Cumberland, increased by the addition of the Eleventh and Twelfth Corps. Then followed the splendid actions around Chattanooga, Orchard Knob, Lookout Mountain, Missionary Ridge, with their momentous results. Mr. Dana saw the storming of the Ridge, perhaps the most glorious and picturesque exploit of the whole war. He telegraphed to Stanton:

"Glory to God! the day is decisively ours. Missionary Ridge has just been carried by a magnificent charge of Thomas's troops, and the rebels routed." And afterwards: "The storming of the Ridge was one of the greatest miracles in military history. No man who climbs the ascent by any of the roads that wind along its front can believe that eighteen thousand men were moved up its broken and crumbling face, unless it was his fortune to witness the deed. It seems as awful as a visible interposition of God. Neither Grant nor Thomas intended it. Their orders were to carry the rifle-pits along the base of the Ridge and capture their occupants; but, when this was done, the unaccountable spirit of the troops bore them bodily up these impracticable steeps, over the bristling rifle-pits on the crest and the thirty cannon enfilading every gully. The order to storm appears to have been given simultaneously by Generals Sheridan and Wood, because the men were not to be held back, dangerous as the attempt appeared to military prudence. Besides, the generals had caught the inspiration of the men, and were themselves ready to undertake impossibilities."

In the middle of December Mr. Dana went back to Washington, at Grant's request, to explain that general's wishes in regard to the winter campaign.

VIII.

MR. DANA'S relations with Grant, from his first acquaintance with him at Vicksburg until the end of the war, were of a peculiarly interesting character. There is no doubt that Grant's military and personal fortunes were at a critical stage when Dana went down to Vicksburg from the War Department early in the spring of 1863. The long delay in capturing the rebel stronghold had started up all the grumblers and growlers at the North. Amazing reports were current, and generally credited, as to personal habits which unfitted the general for high or continuous responsibility. McClernand hoped to regain the command of the expedition, and it was notorious that he and his friends were intriguing against Grant. Other enemies were raising a clamor in the newspapers, and demanding Grant's removal. General Sherman has testified that at this time even Mr. Lincoln and General Halleck seemed to be losing confidence in Grant. His local successes had been brilliant, but the true measure of his military ability and his capacity for larger enterprises were as yet unknown quantities. Mr. Dana's firm belief in Grant's staying powers and certain future usefulness to the country, was based on close and accurate observation of his character. His letters and despatches from Vicksburg, urging the retention of the general as strongly as he afterwards urged the removal of Rosecrans, for the sake of the Union cause, effectually silenced Grant's enemies at Washington, and unquestionably deterred the Administration from a colossal mistake which, as everybody can now see, would have changed the whole course of history.

The Assistant Secretary was in camp with Grant frequently during the rest of

the war. The general liked to have Dana
at headquarters, and that was likewise the
case with the other commanders with whom
his missions to the front brought him into personal association. Whatever there
might be of military jealousy of civilian
supervision, yielded to the charm of his
companionship and the tact with which he
performed his delicate duties. The commanders quickly discovered that he was
there not in any sense as a watch over, or
check upon, their operations, but to help
them along with all of the aid the Department and the Administration could render.
The generals were invariably Mr. Dana's
friends.

When the fighting began in the Wilderness, in May, 1864, the bloodiest month of
the whole war, Dana was summoned to the
War Department late one night, when he
was at a party. He hurried over to the
Department in his evening dress. The
President was there, talking very soberly
with Stanton.

"Dana," said Mr. Lincoln, "you know
we have been in the dark for two days
since Grant moved. We are very much
troubled, and have concluded to send you
down there. How soon can you start?"

"In half an hour," replied Dana.

In about that time he had an engine
fired up at Alexandria, a cavalry escort
awaiting him there, and with his own horse
was aboard the train at Maryland Avenue
that was to take him to Alexandria. His
only baggage was a toothbrush. He was
just starting, when an orderly galloped
with word that the President wished to see
him. Dana rode back to the Department
in hot haste. Mr. Lincoln was sitting in
the same place.

"Well, Dana," said he, looking up,
"since you went away I've been thinking
about it. I don't like to send you down
there."

"Why not, Mr. President?" asked Dana,
a little surprised.

"You can't tell," continued the President, "just where Lee is, or what he
is doing; and Jeb Stuart is rampaging
around pretty lively in between the Rappahannock and the Rapidan. It's a considerable risk, and I don't like to expose you
to it."

"Mr. President," said Dana, "I have a
cavalry guard ready and a good horse myself. If it comes to the worst, we are
equipped to run. It's getting late, and I

A VIEW OF THE PARLORS AT DOSORIS.

want to get down to the Rappahannock by daylight. I think I'll start."

"Well now, Dana," said the President, with a little twinkle in his eyes, "if you feel that way, I rather wish you would. Good night, and God bless you."

He reached the scene of action on May 7th, without encountering the redoubtable Jeb Stuart, who was mortally wounded five days later in an engagement with Sheridan's cavalry. Dana saw all of the fighting of the next two months, and rode with Grant to the James and to the front of Petersburg. From Cold Harbor, on June 7th, Grant telegraphs to Stanton that Mr. Dana's full despatches render unnecessary frequent or extended despatches from himself. Read continuously, these Virginia despatches of Mr. Dana's afford a panorama of that tremendous campaign as powerfully drawn and as vivid in color as his story of the three months at Chattanooga.

Here is an interesting request from Grant to the War Department, as forwarded by Mr. Dana the day before the assault on Petersburg: "General Grant wishes that you would send him five hundred thousand dollars in Confederate money for use in a cavalry expedition in which he prefers to pay for everything taken."

The conscientious raid contemplated in this financial arrangement was probably the same expedition, led by General James Harrison Wilson, which gives us incidentally in Dana's despatches, a fortnight later, a flashlight view of General Meade. Wilson was one of the youngest, as well as one of the best and bravest soldiers in the Union army, and he distinguished himself in a thousand ways besides his capture of Jefferson Davis. He was accused by the Richmond "Examiner" of stealing, while on this raid, not only negroes and horses, but also silver plate and clothing. On the young general's return, Meade summons him to headquarters, and, "taking the 'Examiner's' statement for truth, reads him a lecture and demands an explanation. Wilson gravely denies the charge of robbing women and churches, and hopes that Meade will not be ready to condemn his command because its operations have excited the ire of the enemy."

A picture of Lincoln, on his visit to the front in June, 1864: "The President arrived here about noon, and has just returned from visiting the lines before Petersburg. As he came back, he passed through the division of colored troops under General Hinks, which so greatly distinguished itself on Wednesday last. They were drawn up in double lines on each side of the road, and welcomed him with hearty shouts. It was a memorable thing to behold the President, whose fortune it is to represent the principles of emancipation, passing bare-headed through the en-

A CORNER OF THE PARLOR.

thusiastic ranks of those negroes armed to defend the integrity of the American Nation."

IX.

At his desk in the War Department in Washington Mr. Dana was the same man as at his desk in the "Tribune" office or in the "Sun" office. The visitor, whatever his business, met with a courteous reception, was listened to attentively and without any signs of undue haste, and then got a very prompt and decisive answer. Mr. Dana's remarkable capacity for disposing of questions and of persons swiftly, justly, and, in rightful cases, satisfactorily to the applicant, soon attracted Lincoln's attention, and he made good use of it. It was the President's habit, during the last two years of his life, to send over from the White House to the Assistant Secretary's office all sorts of people, from war governors to soldiers' sweethearts, bearing little cards like this :

Will Assistant Sec. of War Dana pleen ser & hear this lady? A Lincoln

Sep. 2d 1864

The Assistant Secretary's numberless functions when not at the front gave full employment to his energy. He conducted a good part of the more important official correspondence of the Department. His despatches to Grant and other commanders kept them informed of whatever it was necessary to know of the progress of events outside of their own immediate field. At one time he is in the Northwest untangling the red tape with which the governors of some of the States tied up at home troops which the Government badly needed for service. At another time he is looking after the plots of the rebel conspirators across the Canadian frontier. He receives reports, sends orders, investigates abuses, adjusts controversies, attends to multifarious details of routine, and runs the Department in Mr. Stanton's absence.

Only once, as far as I am aware, did any general attempt to obtain a reversal of one of Mr. Dana's decisions. It was a small matter, but the incident now seems rather amusing.

The Union Ladies' Committee of Baltimore proposed to provide a Thanksgiving dinner for the wounded in the hospitals there, and permission was asked by friends of the wounded Confederate prisoners to feed them likewise. Mr. Dana promptly granted it, seeing no great peril to the Union cause in turkey and cranberry sauce. Thereupon General Lew Wallace, in command at Baltimore, telegraphed to Stanton, through the Adjutant-General's office, this ringing and rhetorical protest :

"I hope the permission given by Hon. Mr. Dana, Assistant Secretary of War, to feast the rebel prisoners in hospital, will

be withdrawn. I was not consulted. Had I been, I would have objected to the making of such a request. The permission will be construed as a license to make manifest once more the disloyalty, now completely cowed in this city. I beg the sleeping fiend may be let alone."

Stanton's reply was a short lesson in common sense. "The Secretary sees no objection to supplies for Thanksgiving being received and distributed to rebel prisoners by our Union Committee, provided our own men receive an equal share." The poor rebel wounded got their Thanksgiving dinner, and the sleeping fiend slept the better for being fed.

X.

MR. DANA'S duties brought him into personal contact, and often into intimate acquaintance, with nearly every conspicuous figure of the period, in civil or military life. With Stanton and with Lincoln, of course, his relations were particularly close. For both of those remarkable men his memory cherishes profound admiration and warm affection. Between Lincoln and Dana there was a bond in their common and equally strong perception of the humorous. The quality was lacking in Stanton ; and when Lincoln, on the night of the Presidential election of 1864, sat in the War Department awaiting the nation's verdict upon his administration, and sought to relieve the intense strain of the hour by reading aloud some of the nonsense of Petroleum V. Nasby and commenting upon the same, it was to the Assistant Secretary and not to the Secretary that the extraordinary lecture was addressed. Stanton listened with amazement. He could scarcely control his disgust and indignation at what seemed to him the unaccountable frivolity of such a performance at such a time.

Mr. Dana first saw Mr. Lincoln soon after his inauguration in March, 1861. He went to the White House with a party of New York Republicans on a political errand. The interview was in progress, and the President was explaining his views as to the New York patronage, when a door opened, and a tall and lank employee stuck in his head and made this announcement :

"She wants you !"

"Yes, yes," said Mr. Lincoln, visibly annoyed, and he went on with the explanation of his views.

Presently the door opened again, and the messenger returned :

" I say she wants you ! "

Four years afterwards Mr. Dana came up to Washington from Richmond with Grant after the final victory of the Union army. He reached the capital on April 13th. On the afternoon of the 14th he received a despatch from Portland, Maine, reporting that Jacob Thompson was expected to pass through that town in disguise, on his way from Canada to England. Stanton was for arresting the rebel Commissioner, but he sent Dana over to the White House to see the President about it. Lincoln was in the little closet just off his office, in his shirt-sleeves, washing his large hands.

" Halloa, Dana," he said ; "what is it now ? "

Dana explained that Mr. Stanton had an opportunity to arrest Thompson, and thought it ought to be done.

" Well," drawled Lincoln, "I think not. When you have an elephant on hand and he wants to run away, better let him run."

A few hours later Abraham Lincoln lay unconscious in the little bedroom in the Petersen house, opposite Ford's Theatre. Dana was with Stanton until two o'clock in the room adjoining the death-chamber. Then he went home to sleep. He was awakened in the morning by a knock at his door. It was Colonel Pelouze, one of the assistant adjutant-generals.

" Mr. Dana," said Colonel Pelouze, " Mr. Lincoln is dead, and Mr. Stanton directs you to arrest Jacob Thompson."

I have dwelt, perhaps, beyond the limits of due proportion upon the two years spent by Mr. Dana in the only public office he ever held, and constituting the only interruption to his continuous professional career of half a century. He talks much less than one would expect about his experiences during the war period, and has shown no signs of a disposition to put in permanent form the unequalled material afforded by his personal recollections of that period. Indeed, an almost curious indifference to past history, especially as concerning his own performances, is a noticeable trait of his character. With the keenest sense of news perspective in the matter of recording contemporaneous history, and with insatiable avidity for its facts of all sorts, he is inclined to regard as " old " things back of day before yesterday, or at least back of week before last. Possibly it is not natural that the

historical impulse and the journalistic instinct, each in the highest form, should coexist. But Mr. Dana is always glad to see his friends of the war time, and he smiles when some veteran whom he last met it may be at Milliken's Bend, or Crawfish Springs, or New Bethesda Meeting House, persists in addressing him as General Dana, a military title which is not his by right.

XI.

The failure of the Chicago " Republican " enterprise, in which Mr. Dana engaged after the Civil War was over, is still a mystery to those who know the man, but do not know the facts. The active promoter was a Mr. Mack, and the concern was organized with a capital of five hundred thousand dollars on paper. Only a very small part of this, perhaps sixty or eighty thousand dollars, was ever paid up, a large block of the stock being set aside as a bonus to induce some eminent man to become the editor. Mack went to Mr. Dana soon after Lee's surrender, and brought the influence of the Hon. Lyman Trumbull and others to bear in order to persuade him to accept the place. Mr. Dana went out to Chicago, and was welcomed with a banquet. On his part, and on the part of his friends in Chicago, there was complete ignorance of the true state of the concern's finances. Mack tried to build up a newspaper without cash. Mr. Dana took his stock, and became nominally editor-in-chief at a nominal salary of seven thousand or ten thousand dollars, he doesn't remember which, on a five years' or eight years' contract. A little later, when the emergencies of the concern compelled an assessment, he paid his notes to the amount of ten thousand dollars in good faith. He did not discover till afterwards that his was the sole response to the assessment. The business part of the establishment got in so bad a way on account of the lack of money, that, to disentangle himself, Mr. Dana offered to relinquish all of his stock, to release the company from its contract with him, and to quit, for ten thousand dollars in cash. That was paid to him, and he got out about square. Afterwards, by advice of counsel, he declined to pay the notes given by him at the time of the peculiar assessment already spoken of. Suit was brought against him, but after occupying the Illinois courts for ten or a dozen years, the case was decided in Mr. Dana's favor. Under such circumstances, he was editor of the Chicago " Republican "

THE BILLIARD HOUSE AT DOSORIS.

for about a year, and during that time it was a bright, spunky newspaper.

Then Mr. Dana came to New York, and, under conditions very different from those of the Chicago undertaking, acquired with his friends the old " Sun " establishment, which had been owned for thirty years by the Beach family. He took possession of the property at the beginning of 1868, and soon afterwards moved into the little corner room already described. From that time until this Mr. Dana has been the editor of " The Sun " in the full sense of the word. He is, and always has been, in sole charge. The prosperity of " The Sun," its achievements, and its position among the journals of the country, express Mr. Dana's absolute control over its every department. But this is not the story of a newspaper. It is only a necessarily imperfect sketch of the man who edits that newspaper ; whose personality, however, perhaps to a greater extent than in the case of any other conspicuous journalist, is identified with the newspaper he edits.

XII.

WHAT are Mr. Dana's theories of journalism ? At the bottom of my heart, I don't believe he ever stopped to think ; that is to say, to formulate anything of the kind, apart from his general ideas of human interest, common sense, and the inborn knowhow. He has always been much more concerned about the practical question of making for to-morrow morning a paper which its purchasers will be sure to read. Mr. Dana has lectured more than once on journalism, and his audiences and the readers of his published remarks have been delighted with his presentation of the subject ; but his experience is too ripe and his wisdom far too alert to attempt a code of specific directions for the making of a great newspaper. The range of a newspaper depends first of all upon the breadth of its editor's sympathy with human affairs, and the diversity of things in which he takes a personal interest. If he is genuine, its qualities are his ; and nothing that is in him, or that he can procure, is too good to go into its ephemeral pages.

What Mr. Dana himself writes, in " The Sun " or elsewhere, has that indefinable piquant quality of style which holds your interest and makes you read on without conscious effort, instead of laboring on with admiration—the flavor that is in Charles Reade, but not in George Meredith or George Eliot ; in Saint-Simon and Sainte-Beuve, but not in Ruskin or Gibbon ; in field strawberries, but not in California peaches.

When he was a very young man, Mr. Dana wrote poetry. Among his earliest contributions to periodical literature were from half a dozen to a dozen sonnets, usually of sixteen lines, published between 1841 and 1844 in various numbers of " The Dial," the remarkable magazine which Margaret Fuller, Ralph Waldo Emerson, and George Ripley edited for the benefit of a small but earnest group of men and women. " The Dial " was printed quarterly for about four years, and among Mr. Dana's fellow contributors during that period were Emerson, Thoreau, Channing, Christopher P. Cranch, James Russell Lowell, and Jones Very.

Perhaps one of Dana's poems, written fifty-one years ago, will have now the same interest as a " human document," as would the daguerreotype of him in early manhood which the editor of this magazine has not been lucky enough to find :

VIA SACRA.

Slowly along the crowded street I go,
Marking with reverent look each passer's face,
Seeking, and not in vain, in each to trace
That primal soul whereof he is the show.
For here still move, by many eyes unseen,
The blessed gods that erst Olympus kept ;
Through every guise these lofty forms serene
Declare the all-holding Life hath never slept ;
But known each thrill that in Man's heart hath
       been,
And every tear that his sad eyes have wept.
Alas for us ! the heavenly visitants,——
We greet them still as most unwelcome guests,
Answering their smile with hateful looks askance,
Their sacred speech with foolish, bitter jests ;
But oh ! what is it to imperial Jove
That this poor world refuses all his love !

That was in 1843. During the half century since then, Mr. Dana has read more poetry and written less than any other man on earth in whom the love of verse is genuine and strong.

In judging and using the prose or poetry of others, he is hospitable to almost any respectable style or method, no matter how different from his own, as long as the writer has something to say. His tastes are very catholic. He can tolerate either a style approaching barrenness in its simplicity, or rhetoric that is florid and ornate in the extreme, providing it conveys ideas that are not rubbish. He is continually reaching out for fresh vigor, unconventional modes, originality of thought and phrase. If all of Mr. Dana's staff of writers should happen to be cast in one mould, or should gradually assimilate themselves to a single type, so that there was monotony of expression in his newspaper, he would become uneasy. The first thing that would probably occur to him to do would be to send out for a blacksmith, or perhaps the second mate of a tramp steamship, or what not, to write for "The Sun" in the interest of virility and variety. If the man had good ideas, all right : Mr. Dana himself would attend to the syntax.

Imagination is a quality for which he has the highest respect, but it must go with sincerity. Dulness he cannot stand. He is

as impatient of wishy-washy writing as of cant. He pities a fool and can be kind to him, but he hates a sham ; and this hatred, seated in the profoundest depths of his nature, is the key to much that has puzzled some observers of Mr. Dana's professional career.

He communicates his individuality and methods to those around him unconsciously and by personal force, rather than by any attempt at didactics. No office is less a school of journalism in the sense of formal instruction, or even of systematic suggestion, than the " Sun " office.

In all of his relations with his subordinates and assistants in every department, Mr. Dana is a model chief. He is true to his helpers, reasonable in his requirements, constant in a good opinion once formed. His eyes are on every part of the paper every day, and they are not less sharp for points of defect than for points of excellence, but his tongue is ten times quicker to praise than to blame. Generous and prompt recognition of good service of any sort, or of honest, although only partially successful, effort, is habitual with him. His condemnation can be particularly emphatic, if there is occasion for emphasis : small literary sins and venial infractions of discipline provoke him to humorous commiseration, rather than to anger. He never fusses, never is overbearing, never quarrels with what can't be helped.

Mr. Augustin Daly tells a story about a visit of his to Mr. Dana's office to remonstrate upon what the manager regarded as too severe criticism of Miss Ada Rehan's performance in a certain part. The present publisher of " The Sun " was at that time its dramatic critic.

" I found no difficulty," says Mr. Daly, " in getting an audience with Mr. Dana. He glanced up from his work and asked, cheerily, ' What can I do for you to-day ?'

" ' Mr. Dana,' I began with great firmness, ' I have called to try to convince you that you should discharge your dramatic editor. He has——'

" ' Yes, I see,' he interrupted, all suavity and smiles. ' Well, Mr. Daly, I will speak to Mr. Laffan about this matter, and if he thinks that he really deserves to be discharged, I will most certainly do it.' "

There is an apocryphal tradition, probably with some slight foundation of fact, which will do as well as if it were entirely true to illustrate Mr. Dana's indifference to disturbing elements, except as they may be useful for newspaper purposes. One night, in the early times of " The Sun," the city editor rushed in from the outside room. "The Sun's" editorial office then consisted of four rooms, all small.

"Mr. Dana," exclaimed the city editor, "there's a man out there with a cocked revolver. He is very much excited. He insists on seeing the editor-in-chief."

"Is he very much excited?" replied Mr. Dana, turning back to his pile of proofs. "If you think it worth the space, ask Amos Cummings if he will kindly see the gentleman and write him up."

His judgment of the merits of articles submitted to him is, to an extent rarely equalled, independent of the writer's literary reputation. A famous name is no passport to his admiration. I think that Mr. Dana would write "Respectfully declined," or even "Nothing in it!" on a scrap of paper, and fold the same around a manuscript from Mr. Gladstone, providing it did not seem useful to him, with as little hesitation as across a poem on "Spring" from a schoolma'am in the backwoods of Maine or Georgia. If he were prejudiced either way, it would be in favor of the unknown schoolma'am struggling to find an outlet for her poetic sentiment. It is a source of great satisfaction to him to discover in out-of-the-way corners genius that has not been recognized, and to help it out of obscurity. This benevolent weakness has cost him, in the aggregate, thousands of hours of valuable time spent in the personal attempt to make a poor thing presentable, or in imparting advice and kind but frank criticism to persons unknown to him.

Once a clergyman of considerable eminence and sensational proclivity volunteered to write anonymously for "The Sun." His first article came. He had made the amazing blunder of trying to adapt himself to what he supposed to be the worldly and reckless tone proper to a Sunday newspaper. Mr. Dana chuckled quietly as he sent the manuscript back, indorsed in blue pencil, "This is too damned wicked!"

A clerk in the New York Post-Office, several years ago, copied out in his own handwriting the Rev. Edward Everett Hale's story, "The Man Without a Country," and offered it to "The Sun" as original matter for ten dollars. He had evidently found the story in a loose copy of the magazine where it was first published, and supposed it to be forgotten literature. Somebody proposed to publish the impostor's name.

"No," said Mr. Dana. "Mark the manuscript 'Respectfully declined,' and mail it to him. He has been honest enough to inclose postage stamps."

XIII.

MR. DANA looks upon the daily newspaper as something more than a bulletin of the world's events, or a vehicle for contemporaneous literature. He has steadily resisted the modern tendency to subordinate the editorial page, or to render it a mere reflection of public or partisan sentiment as understood by the newspaper's managers.

"The place of the newspaper press in education," he wrote not long ago in reply to a question from the State Department of Public Instruction, "is like that of the pulpit. It is incidental, not essential." But with Mr. Dana, as with every journalist who is influenced by his brilliant example, the place of the editorial page in the daily newspaper is essential, and not merely incidental. A newspaper without positive, independent, aggressive convictions, generated inside and not outside of the office, and without the habit of uttering them fearlessly, is easy enough to imagine; but it would be a newspaper without Mr. Dana.

He does not think it necessary to check off every piece of news, or even every important piece of news, with a corresponding paragraph of comment. That is not his idea of an editorial page.

"A man at the dinner table, or anywhere else," he said one day to a new writer, "who insists on giving you his opinion about everything on earth, is a bore. So is the newspaper."

He has no hard and fast rules to go by in the selection of topics for editorial treatment. You can never tell what subjects Mr. Dana will discuss, or what subjects he will pass over, in to-morrow's "Sun." His inclination is always towards the specific, rather than the abstract; towards the novel, the fresh, the unexpected, rather than the matter-of-course. He would leave over an article any day on "The State of the Union," in favor of one on "The Market for Poetry," or "The Vitality of Islam," or "The Sorrows of Rich Men," or "How Engaged Couples Should Act;" providing the latter were the more meritorious production, and seemed to him likely to be read with more interest by more people.

He has always believed in iteration as an agent in the process of planting ideas. "If you say a true and important thing once, in the most striking way, people read it, and say to themselves, 'That is very likely so,' and forget it. If you keep on saying it, over and over again, even with less felicity of expression, you'll hammer it into their heads so firmly that they'll say, 'It *is* so ;' and they'll remember forever it is so."

The characteristics of the man are in "The Sun." His broad sense of news interest, persistent, inquisitive, sympathetic, and appreciative in a thousand different directions, and as keen with respect to sons whom he is supposed to regard with unconditional disapproval.

The strongest and steadiest impulse in Mr. Dana's mind as an editor, is the American sentiment. It lies deeper than his partisanship, and it shapes his politics. His political philosophy may be Jeffersonian in its conception of the functions and limitations of the Federal Government in ordinary times, but back of that are not only the patriotism that is natural to his temperament, but also that broader idea of the

DOSORIS BLUFF, OVERLOOKING LONG ISLAND SOUND.

small things as to great, shapes every part of the paper, and dominates every department. His editorial page is himself. It reflects his independence of thought, his self-reliance, his humor and philosophy, and his marked partiality, ethical considerations being equal, or nearly so, for the cause of the under dog in the fight. No matter how the crowd shouts, he follows his own judgment. He follows it unhesitatingly, and without worrying about questions of expediency as affecting himself. He is loyal beyond most men in his friendships, and positive, although less persistent, and rather impersonal, in his dislikes. Nothing is more common than to hear him speaking kindly, and with just appreciation of their good qualities, of per- nation's might and destiny which was bred in him by the events of the years when he was with Lincoln and Stanton, and with the armies in the field.

XIV.

THE revolution which his genius and invention have wrought in the methods of practical journalism in America during the past twenty-five years can be estimated only by newspaper makers. His mind, always original, and unblunted and unwearied at seventy-five, has been a prolific source of new ideas in the art of gathering, presenting, and discussing attractively the news of the world. He is a radical and unterrified innovator, caring not a copper for tradition or precedent when a change of method promises a real improvement. Restlessness like his, without his genius, discrimination, and honesty of purpose, scatters and loses itself in mere whimsicalities or pettinesses ; or else it deliberately degrades the newspaper upon which it is exercised. To Mr. Dana's personal invention are due many, if not most, of the broad changes which within a quarter of a century have transformed journalism in this country. From his individual perception of the true philosophy of human interest, more than from any other single source, have come the now general repudiation of the old conventional standards of news importance ; the modern newspaper's appreciation of the news value of the sentiment and humor of the daily life around us ; the recognition of the principle that a small incident, interesting in itself and well told, may be worth a column's space, when a large dull fact is hardly worth a stickful's ; the surprising extension of the daily newspaper's province so as to cover every department of general literature, and to take in the world's fancies and imaginings, as well as its actual events. The word "news" has an entirely different significance from what it possessed twenty-five or thirty years ago under the ancient common law of journalism as derived from England ; and in the production of this immense change, greatly in the interest of mankind and of the cheerfulness of daily life, it would be difficult to exaggerate the direct and indirect influence of Mr. Dana's alert, scholarly, and widely sympathetic perceptions.

The idea of the newspaper syndicate system, extensively and successfully applied during the past ten years, and with such marked effect upon the character of the miscellaneous literature furnished to the public through the daily press, originated with Mr. Dana. The first story syndicated by him, if I am not mistaken, was one by Mr. Bret Harte, in 1877 or 1878. Soon after that he purchased a number of short stories from some of the most eminent of living writers, "The Sun" sharing the expense and the right to publish the series with half a dozen selected journals in different parts of the United States. One of these stories was a tale called "Georgina's Reasons," by Mr. Henry James, Jr. A circumstance that seemed highly humorous to Mr. Dana, and particularly so in view of Mr. James's fastidious ideas of literary form, was that one of the Western journals in the syndicate should have lent distinction to the narra-

tive by means of the following scheme of headlines in large, bold type :

GEORGINA'S REASONS !

HENRY JAMES'S LATEST STORY !

A WOMAN WHO COMMITS BIGAMY AND ENFORCES SILENCE ON HER HUSBAND ! TWO OTHER LIVES MADE MISERABLE BY HER HEARTLESS ACTION !

XV.

MR. DANA's life outside of his work is his own property, and is to be touched here with reserve. From late in the autumn until early in the spring he occupies his town house at the northwest corner of Madison Avenue and Sixtieth Street. His summer home, Dosoris, two or three miles from the village of Glen Cove, is an island of about fifty acres, in the Sound, close to the Long Island shore, and connected therewith by a short bridge. The estate gets its name from the circumstance that the island was once a wife's dowry, *dos uxoris.* Mr. Dana bought the place soon after his return from Chicago to New York, and extended and modernized the interior of the homely, comfortable mansion, which is just visible, through the foliage, from the passing steamboats in the Sound. One of the greatest enjoyments of his life has been found in the beautifying of Dosoris Island. Its trees and fruits and flowers are famous. Its proprietor is an accomplished botanist, a zealous and scientific cultivator, and an artist who might have been a distinguished landscape gardener if he had not been a great editor. He has made Dosoris a wonderful and celebrated arboretum ; but to most visitors it is first of all a lovely spot.

An eminent painter who travelled in Cuba with Mr. Dana several years ago, was somewhat puzzled at the gratification which his companion manifested after a hot and tiresome excursion in the hills of the Vuelta Abajo. He did not learn the cause until dinner-time. Mr. Dana had satisfied himself by personal observation that the *pinus Elliotti,* or some other special *pinus* which had been troubling his mind, did grow in that region. He regarded the day as a perfect success.

Mr. Dana is fond of horses, of cattle, of dogs, even of pigs and feathered bipeds. He likes to have life, in all of its amiable forms, animal and vegetable, going on healthily and happily around him.

He is as constant in his tastes as in his friendships. An intellectual or æsthetic pursuit once begun by him becomes a lasting occupation and resource. Whether he takes up orchids, or Norse literature, or early Persian ceramics, his interest in the subject never shades back into indifference. His collection of Chinese porcelain of the best period is noted among connoisseurs for the rarity and beauty of its specimens, and the knowledge governing his selections. In pictorial art, his special fondness is for some of the painters of the Barbizon school, as shown by his purchases; but he is appreciative of all good art. He has never formed a large library, and is nothing of a bibliomaniac. He owns some rare volumes, but, as a rule, books are with him tools rather than treasures. He cares nothing for acquisition for the sake of display. He is fond of showing his pictures, or his china, or his trees, to those who can share his own unaffected enjoyment of them.

He is a companionable man, and he likes to gather entertaining people around him. His circle of personal acquaintance is remarkably large and various. He can be happy in the society of any refined person able to interest him, but he is happiest with his own family, his children and grandchildren. For twenty years his most intimate friend and most constant companion has been his son and principal professional assistant, Mr. Paul Dana.

A few weeks ago, just two days before he was seventy-five years old, Mr. Dana climbed to the top of Croydon Mountain in New Hampshire, leading a party of much younger men who came toiling and puffing after him. In his editorial office he is hard at work six days in the week, putting in like a boy of fifty, and still setting the pace for the profession which acknowledges him as its leader. To his own mind there is nothing extraordinary in this.

1852. AGE 33.

1865. AGE 46.

1857. AGE 38.

1867. AGE 48.   1882. AGE 63.

MR. DANA BEFORE GRANT'S HEADQUARTERS AT SPOTTSYLVANIA, 1864.   AGE 44.

1870.   AGE 71.

1854. AGE 75. FROM A PHOTOGRAPH BY ANDERSON, NEW YORK.

MR. DANA AT THE PRESENT DAY. FROM A PHOTOGRAPH TAKEN BY HIS SON, MR. PAUL DANA.

MY FIRST BOOK—"TREASURE ISLAND."

By Robert Louis Stevenson.

IT was far, indeed, from being my first book, for I am not a novelist alone. But I am well aware that my paymaster, the great public, regards what else I have written with indifference, if not aversion. If it call upon me at all, it calls on me in the familiar and indelible character ; and when I am asked to talk of my first book, no question in the world but what is meant is my first novel.

Sooner or later, somehow, anyhow, I was bound I was to write a novel. It seems vain to ask why. Men are born with various manias : from my earliest childhood it was mine to make a plaything of imaginary series of events ; and as soon as I was able to write, I became a good friend to the paper-makers. Reams upon reams must have gone to the making of "Rathillet," the "Pentland Rising,"* the "King's Pardon" (otherwise "Park Whitehead"), "Edward Darren," "A Country Dance," and a "Vendetta in the West ;" and it is consolatory to remember that these reams are now all ashes, and have been received again into the soil. I have named but a few of my ill-fated efforts : only such, indeed, as came to a fair bulk ere they were desisted from ; and even so, they cover a long vista of years. "Rathillet" was attempted before fifteen, the "Vendetta" at twenty-nine, and the succession of defeats lasted unbroken till i was thirty-one. By that time I had written little books and little essays and short stories, and had got patted on the back and paid for them—though not enough to live upon. I had quite a reputation. I was the successful man. I passed my days in toil, the futility of which would sometimes make my cheek to burn,—that I should spend a man's energy upon this business, and yet could not earn a livelihood ; and still there shone ahead of me an unattained ideal. Although I had attempted the thing with vigor not less than ten or twelve times, I had not yet written a novel. All—all my pretty ones—had gone for a little, and then stopped inexorably, like a schoolboy's watch.

* *Ne pas confondre.* Not the slim green pamphlet with the imprint of Andrew Elliott, for which (as I see with amazement from the booklists) the gentlemen of England are willing to pay fancy prices ; but its predecessor, a bulky historical romance without a spark of merit, and now deleted from the world.

I might be compared to a cricketer of many years' standing who should never have made a run. Anybody can write a short story—a bad one, I mean—who has industry and paper and time enough ; but not every one may hope to write even a bad novel. It is the length that kills. The accepted novelist may take his novel up and put it down, spend days upon it in vain, and write not any more than he makes haste to blot. Not so the beginner. Human nature has certain rights ; instinct—the instinct of self-preservation—forbids that any man (cheered and supported by the consciousness of no previous victory) should endure the miseries of unsuccessful literary toil beyond a period to be measured in weeks. There must be something for hope to feed upon. The beginner must have a slant of wind, a lucky vein must be running, he must be in one of those hours when the words come and the phrases balance of themselves—*even to begin.* And having begun, what a dread looking

LLOYD OSBOURNE, THE "SCHOOLBOY IN THE LATE MISS MCGREGOR'S COTTAGE."

THE STEVENSON FAMILY COTTAGE ABOVE PITLOCHRY

PITLOCHRY, A VILLAGE NEAR THE STEVENSON COTTAGE.
From a photograph by G. W. Wilson & Co., Aberdeen.

SPITTAL OF GLENSHEE.

forward is that until the book shall be accomplished! For so long a time the slant is to continue unchanged, the vein to keep running; for so long a time you must hold at command the same quality of style; for so long a time your puppets are to be always vital, always consistent, always vigorous. I remember I used to look, in those days, upon every three-volume novel with a sort of veneration, as a feat—not possibly of literature—but at least of physical and moral endurance and the courage of Ajax.

In the fated year I came to live with my father and mother at Kinnaird, above Pitlochry. There I walked on the red moors and by the side of the golden burn. The rude, pure air of our mountains inspirited, if it did not inspire us; and my wife and I projected a joint volume of bogie stories, for which she wrote "The Shadow on the Bed," and I turned out "Thrawn Janet," and a first draft of the "Merry Men." I love my native air, but it does not love me; and the end of this delightful period was a cold, a fly blister, and a migration, by Strathairdle and Glenshee, to the Castleton of Braemar. There it blew a good deal and rained in proportion. My native air was more unkind than man's ingratitude; and I must consent to pass a good deal of my time between four walls in a house lugubriously known as "the late Miss McGregor's cottage." And now admire the finger of predestination. There was a schoolboy in the late Miss McGregor's cottage, home for the holidays, and much in want of "something craggy to break his mind upon." He had no thought of literature; it was the art of Raphael that received his fleeting suffrages, and with the aid of pen and ink, and a shilling box of water-colors, he had soon turned one of the rooms into a picture gallery. My more immediate duty towards the gallery was to be showman; but I would sometimes unbend a little, join the artist (so to speak) at the easel, and pass the afternoon with him in a generous emulation, making colored drawings. On one of these occasions I made the map of an island; it was elaborately and (I thought) beautifully colored; the shape of it took my fancy beyond expression; it contained harbors that pleased me like sonnets; and, with the unconsciousness of the predestined, I ticketed my performance "Treasure Island." I am told there are people who do not care for maps, and find it hard to believe. The names, the shapes of the woodlands, the courses of the roads and rivers, the prehistoric footsteps of man still distinctly trace-

ROBERT LOUIS STEVENSON.
From a photograph by Sir Percy Shelley.

MRS. ROBERT LOUIS STEVENSON.

able up hill and down dale, the mills and the ruins, the ponds and the ferries, perhaps the " Standing Stone " or the " Druidic Circle " on the heath—here is an inexhaustible fund of interest for any man with eyes to see, or twopence worth of imagination to understand with. No child but must remember laying his head in the grass, staring into the infinitesimal forest, and seeing it grow populous with fairy armies. Somewhat in this way, as I pored upon my map of " Treasure Island," the future characters of the book began to appear there visibly among imaginary woods; and their brown faces and bright weapons peeped out upon me from unexpected quarters, as they passed to and fro, fighting and hunting treasure, on these few square inches of a flat projection. The next thing I knew, I had some paper before me and was writing out a list of chapters. How often have I done so, and the thing gone no farther! But there seemed elements of success about this enterprise. It was to be a story for boys; no need of psychology or fine writing; and I had a boy at hand to be a touchstone. Women were excluded. I was unable to handle a brig (which the " Hispaniola " should have been), but I thought I could make shift to sail her as a schooner without public shame. And then I had an idea for John Silver from which I promised myself funds of entertainment : to take an

admired friend of mine (whom the reader very likely knows and admires as much as I do), to deprive him of all his finer qualities and higher graces of temperament, to leave him with nothing but his strength, his courage, his quickness, and his magnificent geniality, and to try to express these in terms of the culture of a raw tarpaulin. Such psychical surgery is, I think, a common way of " making character ; " perhaps it is, indeed, the only way. We can put in the quaint figure that spoke a hundred words with us yesterday by the wayside ; but do we know him ? Our friend, with his infinite variety and flexibility, we know—but can we put him in? Upon the first we must engraft secondary and imaginary qualities, possibly all wrong ; from the second, knife in hand, we must cut away and deduct the needless arborescence of his nature ; but the trunk and the few branches that remain we may at least be fairly sure of.

On a chill September morning, by the cheek of a brisk fire, and the rain drumming on the window, I began the " Sea Cook," for that was the original title. I have begun (and finished) a number of other books, but I cannot remember to have sat down to one of them with more complacency. It is not to be wondered at, for stolen waters are proverbially sweet. I am now upon a painful chapter. No doubt the parrot once belonged to Robin-

CASTLETON OF BRAEMAR, FROM MORRONE.

Photograph by G. W. Wilson & Co., Aberdeen.

" THE LATE MISS McGREGOR'S COTTAGE," BRAEMAR.

son Crusoe. No doubt the skeleton is conveyed from Poe. I think little of these, they are trifles and details; and no man can hope to have a monopoly of skeletons or make a corner in talking-birds. The stockade, I am told, is from "Masterman Ready." It may be—I care not a jot. These useful writers had fulfilled the poet's saying: departing, they had left behind them

    " Footprints on the sands of time ;
    Footprints that perhaps another——"

and I was the other! It is my debt to Washington Irving that exercises my conscience, and justly so, for I believe plagiarism was rarely carried farther. I chanced to pick up the " Tales of a Traveller " some years ago, with a view to an anthology of prose narrative, and the book flew up and struck me : Billy Bones, his chest, the company in the parlor, the whole inner spirit and a good deal of the material detail of my first chapters—all were there, all were the property of Washington Irving. But I had no guess of it then as I sat writing by the fireside, in what seemed the springtides of a somewhat pedestrian inspiration ; nor yet day by day, after lunch, as I read aloud my morning's work to the family. It seemed to me original as sin ; it seemed to belong to me like my right eye. I had counted on one boy ; I found I had two in my audience. My father caught fire at once with all the romance and childishness of his original nature. His own stories, that every night of his life he put himself to sleep with, dealt perpetually with ships, roadside inns, robbers, old sailors, and commercial travellers before the era of steam. He never finished one of these romances : the lucky man did not require to ! But in "Treasure Island" he recognized something kindred to his own imagination ; it was *his* kind of picturesque ; and he not only heard with delight the daily chapter, but set himself actively to collaborate. When the time came for Billy Bones's chest to be ransacked, he must have passed the better part of a day preparing, on the back of a legal envelope, an inventory of its contents, which I exactly followed ; and

BRAEMAR, FROM CRAIG COYNACH,
Photograph by G. W. Wilson & Co., Aberdeen.

the name of "Flint's old ship," the "Walrus," was given at his particular request. And now, who should come dropping in, *ex machina*, but Dr. Jaap, like the disguised prince who is to bring down the curtain upon peace and happiness in the last act, for he carried in his pocket not a horn or a talisman, but a publisher—had, in fact, been charged by my old friend Mr. Henderson to unearth new writers for "Young Folks." Even the ruthlessness of a united family recoiled before the extreme measure of inflicting on our guest the mutilated members of the "Sea Cook;" at the same time we would by no means stop our readings, and accordingly the tale was begun again at the beginning, and solemnly redelivered for the benefit of Dr. Jaap. From that moment on I have thought highly of his critical faculty; for when he left us, he carried away the manuscript in his portmanteau.

Here, then, was everything to keep me up—sympathy, help, and now a positive engagement. I had chosen besides a very easy style. Compare it with the almost contemporary "Merry Men;" one may prefer the one style, one the other—'tis an affair of character, perhaps of mood; but no expert can fail to see that the one is much more difficult, and the other much easier, to maintain. It seems as though a full-grown, experienced man of letters might

engage to turn out "Treasure Island" at so many pages a day, and keep his pipe alight. But alas! this was not my case. Fifteen days I stuck to it, and turned out fifteen chapters; and then, in the early paragraphs of the sixteenth, ignominiously lost hold. My mouth was empty; there was not one word more of "Treasure Island" in my bosom; and here were the proofs of the beginning already waiting me at the "Hand and Spear"! There I corrected them, living for the most part alone, walking on the heath at Weybridge in dewy autumn mornings, a good deal pleased with what I had done, and more appalled than I can depict to you in words at what remained for me to do. I was thirty-one; I was the head of a family; I had lost my health; I had never yet paid my way, had never yet made two hundreds pounds a year; my father had quite recently bought back and cancelled a book that was judged a failure: was this to be another and last fiasco? I was indeed very close on despair; but I shut my mouth hard, and during the journey to Davos, where I was to pass the winter, had the resolution to think of other things, and bury myself in the novels of M. du Boisgobey. Arrived at my destination, down I sat one morning to the unfinished tale, and behold! it flowed from me like small talk; and in a second tide of delighted industry, and again at the rate of a chapter a day, I finished "Treasure Island." It had to be transacted almost secretly. My wife was ill, the schoolboy remained alone of the faithful, and John Addington Symonds (to whom I timidly mentioned what I was engaged on) looked at me askance. He was at that time very eager I should write on the "Characters" of Theophrastus, so far out may be the judgments of the wisest men. But Symonds (to be sure) was scarce the confidant to go to for sympathy in a boy's story. He was large-minded; "a full man," if there ever was one; but the very name of my enterprise would suggest to him only capitulations of sincerity and solecisms of style. Well, he was not far wrong.

"Treasure Island"— it was Mr. Henderson who deleted the first title, "The Sea Cook" —appeared duly in the story paper, where it figured in the ignoble midst without woodcuts, and attracted not the least attention. I did not care. I liked the tale myself, for much the same reason as my father liked the beginning: it was my kind of picturesque. I was not a little proud of John Silver also, and to this day rather admire that smooth and formidable adventurer. What was infinitely more exhilarating, I had passed a landmark; I had finished a tale, and written "The End" upon my manuscript, as I had not done since the "Pentland Rising," when I was a boy of sixteen, not yet at college. In truth it was so by a set of lucky accidents: had not Dr.

Jaap come on his visit, had not the tale flowed from me with singular ease, it must have been laid aside like its predecessors, and found a circuitous and unlamented way to the fire. Purists may suggest it would have been better so. I am not of that mind. The tale seems to have given much pleasure, and it brought (or was the means of bringing) fire and food and wine to a deserving family in which I took an interest. I need scarce say I mean my own.

But the adventures of "Treasure Island" are not yet quite at an end. I had written it up to the map. The map was the chief part of my plot. For instance, I had called an islet "Skeleton Island," not knowing what I meant, seeking only for the immediate picturesque; and it was to justify this name that I broke into the gallery of Mr. Poe and stole Flint's pointer. And in the same way, it was because I had made two harbors that the "Hispaniola" was sent on her wanderings with Israel Hands. The time came when it was decided to republish, and I sent in my manuscript and the map along with it to Messrs. Cassell. The proofs came, they were corrected, but I heard nothing of the map. I wrote and asked; was told it had never been received, and sat aghast. It is one thing to draw a map at random, set a scale in one corner of it at a venture, and write up a story to the measurements. It is quite another to have to examine a whole book, make an

MOULIN, ANOTHER VILLAGE NEAR THE STEVENSON COTTAGE. THIS VIEW IS FROM THE SOUTH.

STEVENSON IN 1893.
From a photograph taken in Australia.

inventory of all the allusions contained in it, and with a pair of compasses painfully design a map to suit the data. I did it, and the map was drawn again in my father's office, with embellishments of blowing whales and sailing ships ; and my father himself brought into service a knack he had of various writing, and elaborately *forged* the signature of Captain Flint and the sailing directions of Billy Bones. But somehow it was never " Treasure Island " to me.

I have said it was the most of the plot. I might almost say it was the whole. A few reminiscences of Poe, Defoe, and Washington Irving, a copy of Johnson's "Buccaneers," the name of the Dead Man's Chest from Kingsley's "At Last," some recollections of canoeing on the high seas, a cruise in a fifteen-ton schooner yacht, and the map itself with its infinite, eloquent suggestion, made up the whole of my materials. It is perhaps not often that a map figures so largely in a tale ; yet it is always important. The author must know his countryside, whether real or imaginary, like his hand ; the distances, the points of the compass, the place of the sun's rising, the behavior of the moon, should all be beyond cavil. And how troublesome the moon is ! I have come to grief over the moon in

"Prince Otto;" and, so soon as that was pointed out to me, adopted a precaution which I recommend to other men—I never write now without an almanac. With an almanac, and the map of the country and the plan of every house, either actually plotted on paper or clearly and immediately apprehended in the mind, a man may hope to avoid some of the grossest possible blunders. With the map before him, he will scarce allow the sun to set in the east, as it does in the "Antiquary." With the almanac at hand, he will scarce allow two horsemen, journeying on the most urgent affair, to employ six days, from three of the Monday morning till late in the Saturday night, upon a journey of, say, ninety or a hundred miles; and before the week is out, and still on the same nags, to cover fifty in one day, as he may read at length in the inimitable novel of "Rob Roy."

And it is certainly well, though far from necessary, to avoid such *croppers*. But it is my contention—my superstition, if you like—that he who is faithful to his map, and consults it, and draws from it his inspiration, daily and hourly, gains positive support, and not mere negative immunity from accident. The tale has a root there; it grows in that soil; it has a spine of its own behind the words. Better if the country be real, and he has walked every foot of it and knows every milestone. But, even with imaginary places, he will do well in the beginning to provide a map. As he studies it, relations will appear that he had not thought upon. He will discover obvious though unsuspected shortcuts and footpaths for his messengers; and even when a map is not all the plot, as it was in "Treasure Island," it will be found to be a mine of suggestion.

"VAILIMA," STEVENSON'S HOUSE NEAR APIA, SAMOA.

9

PORTRAITS OF ROBERT LOUIS STEVENSON.

Born November 13, 1850; died December 3, 1894.

AGE 20 MONTHS, 1852.

AGE 6. 1857.

AGE 14. 1865.

AGE 19. 1870.

AGE 21. 1872.

AGE 24. 1875.

AGE 42. AUSTRALIA, 1893.

AGE 44. AUSTRALIA, 1875. THESE FOUR PORTRAITS ARE ALL OF ONE TIME.

AN AFTERNOON WITH OLIVER WENDELL HOLMES.

By Edward Everett Hale.

DOROTHY Q.
From the portrait in Dr. Holmes's study.

MY first recollection of Dr. Holmes is seeing him standing on a bench at a college dinner when I was a boy, in the year 1836. He was full of life and fun, and was delivering—I do not say reading—one of his little college poems. He always writes them with joy, and recites them—if that is the word—with a spirit not to be described. For he is a born orator, with what people call a sympathetic voice, wholly under his own command, and entirely free from any of the tricks of elocution. It seems to me that no one really knows his poems to the very best who has not had the good fortune to hear him read some of them.

But I had known all about him before that. As little boys, we had by heart, in those days, the song which saved " Old Ironsides " from destruction. That was the pet name of the frigate "Constitution," which was a pet Boston ship, because she had been built at a Boston shipyard, had been sailed with Yankee crews, and, more than once, had brought her prizes into Boston Harbor.

We used to spout at school :

> " Nail to the mast her holy flag,
> Spread every threadbare sail,
> And give her to the god of storms,
> The lightning and the gale ! "

Ah me ! There had been a Phi Beta anniversary not long before, where Holmes had delivered a poem. You may read " Poetry, a Metrical Essay," in the volumes now. But you will look in vain for the covert allusions to Julia and Susan and Elizabeth and the rest, which, to those who knew, meant the choicest belles of our little company. Have the queens of to-day any such honors ?

Nobody is more accessible than Dr. Holmes. I doubt if any doorbell in Boston is more rung than his. And nowhere is the visitor made more kindly at home. His own work-room takes in all the width of a large house in Beacon Street ; a wide window commands the sweep of the mouth of Charles River ; in summer the gulls are hovering above it, in winter you may see them chaffing together on bits of floating ice, which is on its way to the sea. Across that water, by stealthy rowing, the boats of the English squadron carried the men who were to die at Concord the next day, at Concord Bridge. Beyond is Bunker Hill Monument ; and just this side of the monument Paul Revere crossed the same river to say that that English army was coming.

For me, I had to deliver on Emerson's ninetieth birthday an address on my memories of him and his life. Holmes used to meet him, from college days down, in a thousand ways, and has written a charming memoir of his life. I went round there one day, therefore, to ask some questions, which might put my own memories of Emerson in better light, and afterwards I obtained his leave to make this sketch of the talk of half an hour. When we think of it here, if we ever fall to talking about such things, every one would say that Holmes is the best talker we have or know. But when you are with him, you do not think whether he is or is not. You are under the spell of his kindness and genius. Still no minute passes in which you do not say to yourself : " I hope I shall remember those very words always."

Thinking of it after I come home. I am reminded of the flow and fun of the Autocrat. But you never say so to yourself when you are sitting in his room.

I had arranged with my friend Mr. Sample that he should carry his camera to the house, and it was in gaps in this very conversation that the picture of both of us was taken. I told Dr. Holmes how pleased I was at this chance of going to posterity under his escort.

I told him of the paper on Emerson which I had in hand, and thanked him, as well as I could, in a few words, for his really marvellous study of Emerson in the series of American Authors. I said I really wanted

NOTE.—This article was written in May, 1893. Dr. Holmes died October 7, 1894.—EDITOR.

O. W. HOLMES'S BIRTH-PLACE AT CAMBRIDGE, MASSACHUSETTS, ERECTED IN 1725.

From a photograph by Wilfrid A. French.

to bring him my paper to read. What I was trying to do, was to show that the great idealist was always in touch with his time, and eager to know what, at the moment, were the real facts of American life.

I. I remember where Emerson stopped me on State Street once, to cross-question me about some details of Irish emigration.

Holmes. Yes, he was eager for all practical information. I used to meet him very often on Saturday evenings at the Saturday Club; and I can see him now, as he bent forward eagerly at the table, if any one were making an interesting observation, with his face like a hawk as he took in what was said. You felt how the hawk would be flying overhead and looking down on your thought at the next minute. I remember that I once spoke of "the three great prefaces," and quick as light Emerson said, "What are the three great prefaces?" and I had to tell him.

I. I am sure I do not know what they are. What are they?

Holmes. They are Calvin's to his "Institutes," Thuanus's to his history, and Polybius's to his.

I. And I have never read one of them!

Holmes. And I had then never read but one of them. It was a mere piece of encyclopædia learning of mine.

I. What I shall try to do in my address is to show that Emerson would not have touched all sorts of people as he did, but for this matter-of-fact interest in his daily surroundings—if he had not gone to town-meetings, for instance. Was it you or Lowell who called him the Yankee Plato?

Holmes. Not I. It was probably Lowell, in the "Fable for Critics." I called him

GARDEN DOOR OF THE CAMBRIDGE HOUSE.

"a wingèd Franklin," and I stand by that. Matthew Arnold quoted that afterwards, and I was glad I had said it.

I. I do not remember where you said it. How was it?

Dr. Holmes at once rose, went to the turning book-stand, and took down volume three of his own poems, and read me with great spirit the passage. I do not know how I had forgotten it.

" Where in the realm of thought, whose air is song,
Does he, the Buddha of the West, belong?
He seems a wingèd Franklin, sweetly wise,
Born to unlock the secrets of the skies;
And which the nobler calling,—if 'tis fair
Terrestrial with celestial to compare,—
To guide the storm-cloud's elemental flame,
Or walk the chambers whence the lightning came,
Amidst the sources of its subtile fire,
And steal their effluence for his lips and lyre?"

Here he said, with great fun, " One great good of writing poetry is to furnish you with your own quotations." And afterwards, when I had made him read to me some other verses from his own poems, he said, " Oh, yes, as a reservoir of the best quotations in the language, there is nothing like a book of your own poems."

I said that there was no greater nonsense than the talk of Emerson's time, that he introduced German philosophy here, and I asked Holmes if he thought that Emerson had borrowed anything in the philosophical line from the German. He agreed with me that his philosophy was thoroughly home-bred, and wrought out in the experience of his own home-life. He said that he was disposed to believe that that would be true of Emerson which he knew was true of himself. He knew Emerson went over a great many books, but he did not really believe that he often really read a book through. I remember one of his phrases was, that he thought that Emerson "tasted

THE HOUSE IN RUE MONSIEUR LE PRINCE WHERE DR. HOLMES LIVED FOR TWO YEARS WHEN STUDYING MEDICINE IN PARIS.

books;" and he cited a bright lady from Philadelphia, whom he had met the day before, who had said that she thought men of genius did not rely much upon their reading, and had complimented him by asking if he did so. Holmes said:

" I told her—I had to tell her—that in reading my mind is always active. I do not follow the author steadily or implicitly, but my thought runs off to right and left. It runs off in every direction, and I find I am not so much taking his book as I am thinking my own thoughts upon his subject."

I. I want to thank you for your contrast between Emerson and Carlyle: " The hatred of unreality was uppermost in Carlyle; the love of what is real and genuine, with Emerson." Is it not perhaps possible that Carlyle would not have been Carlyle but for Emerson? Emerson found him discouraged, and as he supposed alone, and at the very beginning led him out of his darkest places.

I think it was on this that Dr. Holmes spoke with a good deal of feeling about the value of appreciation. He was ready to go back to tell of the pleasure he had received from persons who had written to him, even though he did not know them, to say of how much use some particular line of his had been. Among others he said that Lothrop Motley had told him that, when he was all worn out in his work in a country where he had not many friends, and among stupid old manuscript archives, two lines of Holmes's braced him up and helped him through:

" Stick to your aim: the mongrel's hold will slip,
But only crowbars loose the bulldog's grip."

He was very funny about flattery. " That is the trouble of having so many friends, everybody flatters you. I do not mean to let them hurt me if I can help it, and flattery is not necessarily untrue. But you have to be on your guard when everybody is as kind to you as everybody is to me."

He said, in passing, that Emerson once quoted two lines of his, and quoted them horribly. They are from the poem called "The Steamboat:"

" The beating of her rest-
        less heart,
    Still sounding through
        the storm."

Emerson quoted them thus :

" The pulses of her
        iron heart
    Go beating through
        the storm."

I was curious to know about Dr. Holmes's experience of country life, he knows all nature's processes so well. So he told me how it happened that he went to Pittsfield. It seems that, a century and a half ago, his ancestor, Jacob

O. W. HOLMES'S RESIDENCE IN BEACON STREET, BOSTON.

and poetical composition which come from being in the open air and living in the country. He wrote, at the request of the neighborhood, his poem of "The Ploughman," to be read at a cattle-show in Pittsfield. "And when I came to read it afterwards I said, 'Here it is! Here is open air life, here is what breathing the mountain air and living in the midst of nature does for a man!' And I want to read you now a piece of that poem, because it contained a prophecy." And while he was looking for the verses, he said, in the vein of the Autocrat, "Nobody knows but a man's self how many good things he has done."

So we found the first volume of the poems, and there is "The Plough-

Wendell, had a royal grant for the whole township there, with some small exception, perhaps. The place was at first called Pontoosoc, then Wendelltown, and only afterward got the name of Pittsfield from William Pitt. One part of the Wendell property descended to Dr. Holmes's mother. When he had once seen it he was struck with its beauty and fitness for a country home, and asked her that he might have it for his own. It was there that he built a house in which he lived for eight or nine years. He said that the Housatonic winds backwards and forwards through it, so that to go from one end of his estate to the other in a straight line required the crossing it seven times. Here his children grew up, and he and they were enlivened anew every year by long summer days there.

He was most interesting and animated as he spoke of the vigor of life and work

man," written, observe, as early as 1849.

" O gracious Mother, whose benignant breast
    Wakes us to life, and lulls us all to rest,
    How thy sweet features, kind to every clime,
    Mock with their smile the wrinkled front of
        time !
    We stain thy flowers,—they blossom o'er the dead ;
    We rend thy bosom, and it gives us bread ;
    O'er the red field that trampling strife has torn,
    Waves the green plumage of thy tasselled corn ;
    Our maddening conflicts scar thy fairest plain,
    Still thy soft answer is the growing grain.
    Yet, O our Mother, while uncounted charms
    Steal round our hearts in thine embracing arms,
    Let not our virtues in thy love decay,
    And thy fond sweetness waste away our strength away.

No ! by these hills, whose banners now displayed
    In blazing cohorts Autumn has arrayed ;
    By yon twin summits, on whose splintery crests
    The tossing hemlocks hold the eagles' nests ;
    By these fair plains the mountain circle screens,
    And feeds with streamlets from its dark ravines,—
    True to their home, these faithful arms shall toil
    To crown with peace their own untainted soil ;

THE BAY WINDOW IN DR. HOLMES'S STUDY.

And, true to God, to freedom, to mankind,
If her chained bandogs Faction shall unbind,
These stately forms, that bending even now
Bowed their strong manhood to the humble
    plough,
Shall rise erect, the guardians of the land,
The same stern iron in the same right hand,
Till o'er the hills the shouts of triumph run,
The sword has rescued what the ploughshare
    won ! "

Now in 1849, I, who remember, can tell you, every-day people did not much think that Faction was going to unbind her bandogs and set the country at war; and it was only a prophet-poet who saw that there was a chance that men might forge their ploughshares into swords again. But you see from the poem that Holmes was such a prophet-poet, and now, forty-four years after, it was a pleasure to hear him read these lines.

I asked him of his reminiscences of Emerson's famous Phi Beta Kappa oration at Cambridge, which he has described, as so many others have, as the era of independence in American literature. We both talked of the day, which we remembered, and of the Phi Beta dinner which followed it, when Mr. Everett presided, and bore touching tribute to Charles Emerson, who had just died. Holmes said : "You cannot make the people of this generation understand the effect of Everett's oratory. I have never felt the fascination of speech as I did in hearing him. Did it ever occur to you,—did I say to you the other day,

—that when a man has such a voice as he had, our slight nasal resonance is an advantage and not a disadvantage?"

I was fresher than he from his own book on Emerson, and remembered that he had said there somewhat the same thing. His

A CORNER IN DR. HOLMES'S STUDY.

words are : "It is with delight that one who remembers Everett in his robes of rhetorical splendor ; who recalls his full-blown, high-colored, double-flowered periods ; the rich, resonant, grave, far-reaching music of his speech, with just enough of nasal vibration to give the vocal sounding-board its proper value in the harmonies of utterance,—it is with delight that such a one recalls the glowing words of Emerson whenever he refers to Edward Everett. It is enough if he himself caught enthusiasm from those eloquent lips. But many a listener has had his youthful enthusiasm fired by that great master of academic oratory." I knew, when I read this, that Holmes referred to himself as the "youthful listener," and was glad that within twenty-four hours he should say so to me.

So we fell to talking of his own Phi Beta poem. A good Phi Beta poem is an impossibility ; but it is the business of genius to work the miracles, and Holmes's is one of the few successful Phi Beta poems in the dreary catalogue of more than a century. The custom of having "*the* poem," as people used to say, as if it were always the same, is now almost abandoned.

Fortunately for us both, a tap was heard at the door, and Mr. John Holmes appeared, his brother. Mr. John Holmes has not chosen to publish the bright things which he has undoubtedly written, but in all circles where he favors people with his presence he is known as one of the most agreeable of men. Everybody is glad to set him on the lines of reminiscences. The two brothers, with great good humor, began telling of a dinner party which Dr. Holmes had given within a few days to a number of gentlemen whose average ages, according to them, exceeded eighty. One has to make allowance for the exaggeration of their fun, but I think, from the facts which they dropped, that the average must have been maintained. One would have given a good deal to be old enough to be permitted to be at that dinner. This led to talk of the Harvard class of 1829, for whose meetings Holmes has written so many of his charming poems. He said that they are now to have a dinner within a few days, and named the gentlemen who were to be there. Among them, of course, is Dr. Samuel F. Smith, the author of "America." I noticed that Dr. Holmes always called him " My country 'tis of thee," and so did all of us. And then these two critics began analyzing that magnificent song. "It will not do to laugh at it. People show that they do not know what they are talk-

DOROTHY Q's HOUSE IN QUINCY, MASSACHUSETTS.*

* Also called the Peter Butler house. Sewall in his diary speaks of it as Mr. Quincy's new house (1680–85). There Dorothy was born and married.

DR. O. W. HOLMES DELIVERING HIS FAREWELL ADDRESS AS PARKMAN PROFESSOR OF ANATOMY IN THE MEDICAL SCHOOL OF HARVARD UNIVERSITY, NOVEMBER 28, 1882.

From a proof print in the possession of Dr. James R. Chadwick.

ing about when they speak lightly of it. Did you ever think how much is gained by making the first verse begin with the singular number? Not *our* country, but '*My* country,' '*I* sing of thee'? There is not an American citizen but can make it his own, and does make it his own, as he sings it. And it rises to a Psalm-like grandeur at the end. It is a magnificent hold to have upon fame to have sixty million people sing the verses that you have written." John Holmes said : " How good 'templed hills' is, and that is not alone in the poem." Both John Holmes and I pleaded to be permitted to come to the class dinner, but Dr. Holmes was very funny. He pooh-poohed us both ; we were only children, and we were not to be present at so rare a solemnity. For me, I already felt that I had been wicked in wasting so much of his time. But he has the gift of making you think that you are the only person in the world, and that he is only living for your pleasure. Still I knew, as a matter of fact, that this was

not so, and very unwillingly I took myself away.

———

As I walked home I meditated on the fate of a first-rate book in our time. Holmes had expressed unaffected surprise that I spoke with the gratitude which I felt about his "Life of Emerson." The book must have cost him the hard work of a year. It is as remarkable a study as one poet ever made of another. Yet I think he said to me that no one had seemed to understand the care and effort which he had given to it.

Here is the position in the United States now about the criticism of such work. At about the time that the " North American Review" ceased to review books, there came, as if by general consent, an end to all elaborate criticism of new books here.

I think myself that this is a thing very much to be regretted. In old times, whoever wrote a good book was tolerably sure that at least one competent person would study it and write down what he thought

O. W. HOLMES AND L. L. HALE.

From a photograph taken in Dr. Holmes's study, May 22, 1866.

about it; and, from at least one point of view, an author had a prospect of knowing how his book struck other people. Now we have nothing but the hasty sketches, sometimes very good, which are written for the daily or weekly press.

So it happens that I, for one, have never seen any fit recognition of the gift which Dr. Holmes made to our time and to the next generation when he made his study of Emerson's life for the "American Men of Letters" series. Apparently he had not. Just think of it! Here is a poet, the head of our "Academy," so far as there is any such Academy, who is willing to devote a year of his life to telling you and me what Emerson was, from his own personal recollections of a near friend, whom he met as often as once a week, and talked with perhaps for hours at a time, and with whom he talked on literary and philosophical subjects. More than this, this poet has been willing to go through Emerson's books again, to re-read them as he had originally read them when they came out, and to make for you and me a careful analysis of all these books. He is one of

five people in the country who are competent to tell what effect these books produced on the country as they appeared from time to time. And, being competent, he takes the time to tell us this thing. That is a sort of good fortune which, so far as I remember, has happened to nobody excepting Emerson. When John Milton died, there was nobody left who could have done such a thing; certainly nobody did do it, or tried to do it. I must say, I think it is rather hard that, when such a gift as that has been given to the people of any country, that people, while boasting of its seventy millions of numbers and its thousands of billions of acres, should not have one critical journal of which it is the business to say at length, and in detail, whether Dr. Holmes has done his duty well by the prophet, or whether, indeed, he has done it at all.

When we left Dr. Holmes, he and his household were looking forward to the annual escape to Beverly. Somebody once wrote him a letter dated from "Manchester-by-the-Sea," and Holmes wrote his reply under the date "Beverly-by-the-Depot."

And here let me stop to tell one of those jokes for which the English language and Dr. Holmes were made. A few years ago, in a fit of economy, our famous Massachusetts Historical Society screwed up its library and other offices by some fifteen feet, built in the space underneath, and rented it to the city of Boston. This was all very well for the treasurer; but for those of us who had passed sixty years, and had to climb up some twenty more iron stairs whenever we wanted to look at an old pamphlet in the library, it was not so great a benefaction. When Holmes went up, for the first time, to see the new quarters of the Society, he left his card with the words, "O. W. Holmes. High-story-call Society." We understood then why the councils of the Society had been over-ruled by the powers which manage this world, to take this flight towards heaven.

I ought to have given a hint above of his connection and mine with the society of "People who Think we are Going to Know More about Some Things By and By." This society was really formed by my mother, who for some time, I think, was the only member. But one day Dr. Holmes and I met in the "Old Corner Bookstore," when the "corner" had been moved to the corner of Hamilton Place, and he was telling me one of the extraordinary coincidences which he collects with such zeal. I ventured to trump his story with another; and, in the language of the ungodly, I thought I went one better than he. This led to a talk about coincidences, and I said that my mother had long since

said that she meant to have a society of the people who believed that some time we should know more about such curious coincidences. Dr. Holmes was delighted with the idea, and we "organized" the society then and there; he was to be president, I was to be secretary, and my mother was to be treasurer. There were to be no other members, no entrance fees, no constitution, and no assessments. We seldom meet now that we do not authorize a meeting of this society and challenge each other to produce the remarkable coincidences which have passed since we met before.

There is an awful story of his about the last time a glove was thrown down in an English court-room. It is a story in which Holmes is all mixed up with a marvellous series of impossibilities, such as would make Mr. Clemens's hair grow gray, and add a new chapter to his studies of telepathy. I will not enter on it now, with the detail of the book that fell from the ninth shelf of a book-case, and opened at the exact passage where the challenge story was to be described.

As for the story of his hearing Dr. Phinney at Rome, and the other story of Mr. Emerson's hearing Dr. Phinney at Rome, I never tell that excepting to confidential friends who know that I cannot tell a lie. For if I tell it to any one else, he looks at me with a quizzical air, as much as to say, "This is as bad as the story of the 'Man Without a Country;' and I do not know how much to believe, and how much to disbelieve."

O. W. HOLMES'S SUMMER RESIDENCE AT BEVERLY FARMS.

PORTRAITS OF OLIVER WENDELL HOLMES.

OLIVER WENDELL HOLMES was the son of a clergyman, eminent in his day, and the author of a book well known to students of American history, "Annals of America." He was born in Cambridge, Massachusetts, August 29, 1809, the third in a family of five children. He prepared for college at Phillips Andover Academy, and graduated from Harvard in 1829. He then began the study of the law, but later turned to medicine, and passed three years in study in Europe—chiefly in Paris. He received his degree in 1836. In 1839 he became professor of anatomy and physiology at Dartmouth College. He resigned the position after a year or two, and took up the practice of his profession in Boston. In 1847 he became professor of anatomy and physiology at Harvard ; and in this office he served continuously until near the close of 1882, when he discontinued his lectures and instructions on account of his age. Thenceforward until his death, October 7, 1894, he led a life of comparative leisure and retirement.

Such in outline was Dr. Holmes's career. The literary employments which are the source of his fame were in the main diversions. The business of his life was the teaching and practice of medicine. Yet he began to write as a school-boy, and continued with unabated vigor almost to the very last of his days. As a student at Harvard he contributed to the college periodicals, and delivered a poem at commencement ; and the year after his graduation, when he was but twenty-one years old, he wrote the famous poem "Old Ironsides," which helped to save the frigate "Constitution" from irreverent destruction. One of six frigates which Congress had ordered constructed in 1794, the "Constitution" had played a brilliant part, as Commodore Preble's flagship, in the war against Tripoli, between 1801 and 1805. Then, under Captain Isaac Hull, she had fought the first naval battle of the war of 1812, capturing the British frigate "Guerrière," and had followed this with other notable victories over the British. So when, in 1830, it was thriftily proposed to break her up, because no longer fit for service, Holmes, to adopt his own phrase on the matter, "mocked the spoilers with his school-boy scorn." Not alone as a school-boy, though, was he outspoken against the spoilers. His muse never grew too mature or dignified to speak a warm, strong word for any good human cause.

Holmes's great literary opportunity and inspiration came in 1857, when the "Atlantic Monthly" was founded. He provided the name for the new magazine, shared in the preliminary conferences, and by his contributions did more than any one else to secure it immediate popularity. Lowell accepted the editorship—with some misgivings, as it should seem, for he said, "I will take the place, as you all seem to think I should ; but, if success is achieved, we shall owe it mainly to the doctor" (meaning Holmes).

The opulent fulfilment of this expectation was "The Autocrat of the Breakfast-Table." In beginning his famous talks, the "Autocrat," it will be remembered, remarks : "I was just going to say, when I was interrupted ;" and in "The Autocrat's autobiography," which prefaces the volume, it is explained that the interruption referred to was "just a quarter of a century in duration." Two articles entitled "The Autocrat of the Breakfast-Table" had been published, one in November, 1831, and one in February, 1832, in the "New England Magazine" of that day ; and twenty-five years later, when asked to contribute to the "Atlantic," "the recollection," Dr. Holmes says, "of these crude products of his uncombed literary boyhood suggested the thought that it would be a curious experiment to shake the same bough again, and see if the ripe fruit were better or worse than the early windfalls."

The experiment proved so acceptable that Dr. Holmes recurred to the "Autocratic" form again and again. "The Professor at the Breakfast-Table" followed the "Autocrat ;" then, though many years later, "The Poet at the Breakfast-Table ;" and finally, three years before the author's death, came to complete the series, "Over the Teacups." But in addition to these Dr. Holmes produced several books of poems, three novels ("Elsie Venner," 1861 ; "The Guardian Angel," 1868 ; and "A Mortal Antipathy," 1885), several biographies, and numerous medical works and papers—a large list for a man with whom writing was never the main business of his life.

ALL FROM DAGUERREOTYPES—THE TWO LAST ONES, BETWEEN 1845 AND 1855. THE FIRST IS THE EARLIEST PICTURE OF DOCTOR HOLMES, AND HE IS UNABLE TO PLACE A DATE UPON IT.

MARCH, 1862. AGE 49.

AUGUST, 1874. AGE 63.

ABOUT 1882. AGE 73.

NOVEMBER, 1891. AGE 82.

Oliver Wendell Holmes

Boston. May 24th 1893.

HOWELLS AND BOYESEN.

A CONVERSATION BETWEEN W. D. HOWELLS AND PROFESSOR H. H. BOYESEN.

RECORDED BY PROFESSOR BOYESEN.

WHEN I was requested to furnish a dramatic biography of Mr. Howells, I was confronted with what seemed an insuperable difficulty. The more I thought of William Dean Howells, the less dramatic did he seem to me. The only way that occurred to me of introducing a dramatic element into our proposed interview was for me to assault him with tongue or pen, in the hope that he might take energetic measures to resent my intrusion; but as, notwithstanding his unvarying kindness to me, and many unforgotten benefits, I cherished only the friendliest feelings for him, I could not persuade myself to procure dramatic interest at such a price.

My second objection, I am bound to confess, arose from my own sense of dignity, which rebelled against the *rôle* of an interviewer, and it was not until my conscience was made easy on this point that I agreed to undertake the present article. I was reminded that it was an ancient and highly dignified form of literature I was about to revive; and that my precedent was to be sought not in the modern newspaper interview, but in the Platonic dialogue. By the friction of two kindred minds, sparks of thought may flash forth which owe their origin solely to the friendly collision. We have a far more vivid portrait of Socrates in the beautiful conversational turns of "The Symposium" and the first book of "The Republic" than in the purely objective account of Xenophon in his "Memorabilia." And Howells, though he may not know it, has this trait in common with Socrates, that he can portray himself, unconsciously, better than I or anybody else could do it for him.

If I needed any further encouragement, I found it in the assurance that what I was expected to furnish was to be in the nature of "an exchange of confidences between two friends with a view to publication." It was understood, of course, that Mr. Howells was to be more confiding than myself, and that his reminiscences were to predominate; for an author, however unheroic he may appear to his own modesty, is bound to be the hero of his biography. What made the subject so alluring to me, apart from the personal charm which inheres in the man and all that appertains to him, was the consciousness that our friendship was of twenty-two years' standing, and that during all that time not a single jarring note had been introduced to mar the harmony of our relation.

Equipped, accordingly, with a good conscience and a lead pencil (which remained undisturbed in my breast-pocket), I set out to "exchange confidences" with the author of "Silas Lapham" and "A Modern Instance." I reached the enormous human hive on Fifty-ninth Street where my subject, for the present, occupies a dozen most comfortable and ornamental cells, and was promptly hoisted up to the fourth floor

know. I am aware, for instance, that you were born at Martin's Ferry, Ohio, March 11, 1837; that you removed thence to Dayton, and a few years later to Jefferson, Ashtabula County; that your father edited, published, and printed a country newspaper of Republican complexion, and that you spent a good part of your early years in the printing office. Nevertheless, I have some difficulty in realizing the environment of your boyhood."

Howells. If you have read my "Boy's Town," which is in all essentials autobiographical, you know as much as I could tell you. The environment of my early life was exactly as there described.

Boyesen. Your father, I should judge, then, was not a strict disciplinarian?

Howells. No. He was the gentlest of men—a friend and companion to his sons. He guided us in an unobtrusive way without our suspecting it. He was continually putting books into my hands, and they were always good books; many of them

PROFESSOR BOYESEN IN HIS STUDY AT COLUMBIA COLLEGE.

and deposited in front of his door. It is a house full of electric wires and tubes—literally honeycombed with modern conveniences. But in spite of all these, I made my way triumphantly to Mr. Howells's den, and after a proper prelude began the novel task assigned to me.

"I am afraid," I remarked quite *en passant*, "that I shall be embarrassed not by my ignorance, but by my knowledge concerning your life. For it is difficult to ask with good grace about what you already

became events in my life. I had no end of such literary passions during my boyhood. Among the first was Goldsmith, then came Cervantes and Irving.

Boyesen. Then there was a good deal of literary atmosphere about your childhood?

Howells. Yes. I can scarcely remember the time when books did not play a great part in my life. Father was, by his culture and his interests, rather isolated from the community in which we lived, and this made him and all of us rejoice the more in a new author, in whose world we would live for weeks and months, and who colored our thoughts and conversation.

Boyesen. It has always been a matter of wonder to me that, with so little regular schooling, you stepped full-fledged into literature with such an exquisite and wholly individual style.

Howells. If you accuse me of that kind of thing, I must leave you to account for it. I had always a passion for literature, and to a boy with a mind and a desire to learn, a printing office is not a bad school.

Boyesen. How old were you when you left Jefferson and went to Columbus?

Howells. I was nineteen years old when I went to the capital and wrote legislative reports for Cincinnati and Cleveland papers; afterwards I became one of the editors of the "Ohio State Journal." My duties gradually took a wide range, and I edited the literary column and wrote many of the leading articles. I was then in the midst of my enthusiasm for Heine, and was so impregnated with his spirit that a poem which I sent to the "Atlantic Monthly" was mistaken by Mr. Lowell for a translation from the German poet. When he had satisfied himself, however, that it was not a translation, he accepted and printed it.

Boyesen. Tell me how you happened to publish your first volume, "Poems by Two Friends," in partnership with John J. Piatt.

Howells. I had known Piatt as a young printer; afterwards when he began to write poems, I read them and was delighted with them. When he came to Columbus I made his acquaintance, and we became friends. By this time we were both contributors to the "Atlantic Monthly." I may as well tell you that his contributions to our joint volume were far superior to mine.

Boyesen. Did Lowell share that opinion?

Howells. That I don't know. He wrote me a very charming letter, in which he said many encouraging things, and he briefly reviewed the book in the "Atlantic."

Boyesen. What was the condition of society in Columbus during those days?

Howells. There were many delightful and cultivated people there, and society was charming; the North and South were both represented, and their characteristics united in a kind of informal Western hospitality, warm and cordial in its tone, which gave of its very best without stint. Salmon P. Chase, later Secretary of the Treasury, and Chief Justice of the United States, was then Governor of Ohio. He had a charming family, and made us young editors welcome at his house. All winter long there was a round of parties at the different houses; the houses were large and we always danced. These parties were brilliant affairs, socially, but besides, we young people had many informal gayeties. The Old Starling Medical College, which was defunct as an educational institution, except for some vivisection and experiments on hapless cats and dogs that went on in some out-of-the-way corners, was used as a boarding-house; and there was a large circular room in which we often improvised dances. We young fellows who lodged in the place were half

MR. HOWELLS AT THE TIME OF WRITING "ANNIE KILBURN," 1857.

a dozen journalists, lawyers, and law students; one was, like myself, a writer for the "Atlantic," and we saw life with joyous eyes. We read the new books, and talked them over with the young ladies whom we seem to have been always calling upon. I remember those years in Columbus as among the happiest years of my life.

Boyesen. From Columbus you went as consul to Venice, did not you?

Howells. Yes. You remember I had written a campaign "Life of Lincoln." I was, like my father, an ardent anti-slavery man. I went myself to Washington soon after President Lincoln's inauguration. I was first offered the consulate to Rome; but as it depended entirely upon perquisites, which amounted only to three or four hundred dollars a year, I declined it, and they gave me Venice. The salary was raised to fifteen hundred dollars, which seemed to me quite beyond the dreams of avarice.

Boyesen. Do not you regard that Venetian experience as a very valuable one?

Howells. Oh, of course. In the first place, it gave me four years of almost uninterrupted leisure for study and literary work. There was, to be sure, occasionally an invoice to be verified, but that did not take much time. Secondly, it gave me a wider outlook upon the world than I had hitherto had. Without much study of a systematic kind, I had acquired a notion of English, French, German, and Spanish literature. I had been an eager and constant reader, always guided in my choice of books by my own inclination. I had learned German. Now, my first task was to learn Italian; and one of my early teachers was a Venetian priest, whom I read Dante with. This priest in certain ways suggested Don Ippolito in "A Foregone Conclusion."

Boyesen. Then he took snuff, and had a supernumerary calico handkerchief?

Howells. Yes. But what interested me most about him was his religious skepticism. He used to say, "The saints are the gods baptized." Then he was a kind of baffled inventor; though whether his inventions had the least merit I was unable to determine.

Boyesen. But his love story?

Howells. That was wholly fictitious.

Boyesen. I remember you gave me, in 1874, a letter of introduction to a Venetian

THE BIRTHPLACE OF W. D. HOWELLS AT MARTIN'S FERRY, OHIO.

friend of yours, named Brunetta, whom I failed to find.

Howells. Yes, Brunetta was the first friend I had in Venice. He was a distinctly Latin character—sober, well regulated, and probity itself.

Boyesen. Do you call that the Latin character?

Howells. It is not our conventional idea of it; but it is fully as characteristic, if not more so, than the light, mercurial, pleasure-loving type which somehow in literature has displaced the other. Brunetta and I promptly made the discovery that we were congenial. Then we became daily companions. I had a number of other Italian friends too, full of beautiful *bonhomie* and Southern sweetness of temperament.

Boyesen. You must have acquired Italian in a very short time?

Howells. Yes; being domesticated in that way in the very heart of that Italy which was then *Italia irridente*, I could not help steeping myself in its atmosphere and breathing in the language, with the rest of its very composite flavors.

Boyesen. Yes; and whatever I know of Italian literature I owe largely to the completeness of that soaking process of yours. Your book on the Italian poets is one of the most charmingly sympathetic and illuminative bits of criticism that I know.

Howells. I am glad you think so; but the book was never a popular success. Of all the Italian authors, the one I delighted in the most was Goldoni. His exquisite realism fascinated me. It was the sort of thing which I felt I ought not to like ; but for all that I liked it immensely.

Boyesen. How do you mean that you ought not to like it ?

Howells. Why, I was an idealist in those days. I was only twenty-four or twenty-five years old, and I knew the world chiefly through literature. I was all the time trying to see things as others had seen them, and I had a notion that, in literature, persons and things should be nobler and better than they are in the sordid reality ; and this romantic glamour veiled the world to me, and kept me from seeing things as they are. But in the lanes and alleys of Venice I found Goldoni everywhere. Scenes from his plays were enacted before my eyes, with all the charming Southern vividness of speech and gesture, and I seemed at every turn to have stepped unawares into one of his comedies. I believe this was the beginning of my revolt. But it was a good while yet before I found my own bearings.

THE GIUSTINIANI PALACE. HOWELLS'S HOME IN VENICE.

Boyesen. But permit me to say that it was an exquisitely delicate set of fresh Western senses you brought with you to Venice. When I was in Venice in 1878, I could not get away from you, however much I tried. I saw your old Venetian senator, in his august rags, roasting coffee ; and I promenaded about for days in the chapters of your " Venetian Life," like the Knight Huldbrand in the Enchanted Forest in " Undine," and I could not find my way out. Of course, I know that, being what you were, you could not have helped writing that book, but what was the immediate cause of your writing it ?

Howells. From the day I arrived in Venice I kept a journal in which I noted down my impressions. I found a young pleasure in registering my sensations at the sight of notable things, and literary reminiscences usually shimmered through my observations. Then I received an offer from the " Boston Daily Advertiser " to write weekly or bi-weekly letters, for which they paid me five dollars, in greenbacks, a column, nonpareil. By the time this sum reached Venice, shaven and shorn by discounts for exchange in gold premium, it had usually shrunk to half its size or less. Still I was glad enough to get even that, and I kept on writing joyously. So the book grew in my hands until, at the time I resigned, in 1865, I was trying to have it published. I offered it successively to a number of English publishers ; but they all declined it.

At last Mr. Trübner agreed to take it, if I could guarantee the sale of five hundred copies in the United States, or induce an American publisher to buy that number of copies in sheets. I happened to cross the ocean with Mr. Hurd of the New York firm of Hurd & Houghton, and repeated Mr. Trübner's proposition to him. He refused to commit himself ; but some weeks after my arrival in New York he told me that the risk was practically nothing at all, and that his firm would agree to take the five hundred copies. The book was an instant success. I don't know how many editions of it have been printed, but I should say that its sale has been upward of forty thousand copies, and it still continues. The English weeklies gave me long complimentary notices, which I carried about for months in my pocket like love-letters, and read surreptitiously at odd moments. I thought it was curious that other people to whom I showed the reviews did not seem much interested.

Boyesen. After returning to this country, did not you settle down in New York ?

Howells. Yes; I was for a while a free lance in literature. I did whatever came in my way, and sold my articles to the newspapers, going about from office to office, but I was finally offered a place on "The Nation," where I obtained a fixed position at a salary. I had at times a sense that, by going abroad, I had fallen out of the American procession of progress; and, though I was elbowing my way energetically through the crowd, I seemed to have a tremendous difficulty in recovering my lost place on my native soil, and asserting my full right to it. So, when young men beg me to recommend them for consulships, I always feel in duty bound to impress on them this great danger of falling out of the procession, and asking them whether they have confidence in their ability to reconquer the place they have deserted; for while they are away it will be pretty sure to be filled by somebody else. A man returning from a residence of several years abroad has a sense of superfluity in his own country— he has become a mere supernumerary whose presence or absence makes no particular difference.

Boyesen. What year did you leave "The Nation" and assume the editorship of "The Atlantic"?

Howells. I took the editorship in 1872, but went to live in Cambridge six or seven years before. I was first assistant editor under James T. Fields, who was uniformly kind and considerate, and with whom I got

W. D. HOWELLS, AFTER HIS RETURN
FROM VENICE.

along perfectly. It was a place that he could have made odious to me, but he made it delightful. I have the tenderest regard and the brightest respect for his memory.

Boyesen. I need scarcely ask you if your association with Lowell was agreeable?

Howells. It was in every way charming. He was twenty years my senior, but he always treated me as an equal and a contemporary. And you know the difference between thirty and fifty is far greater than between forty and sixty, or fifty and

seventy. I dined with him every week, and he showed the friendliest appreciation of the work I was trying to do. We took long walks together; and you know what a rare talker he was. Somehow I got much nearer to him than to Longfellow. As a man Longfellow was flawless. He was full of noble friendliness and encouragement to all literary workers in whom he believed.

Boyesen. Do you remember you once said to me that he was a most inveterate praiser?

Howells. I may have said that; for in the kindness of his heart, and his constitutional reluctance to give pain, he did undoubtedly often strain a point or two in speaking well of things. But that was part of his beautiful kindliness of soul and admirable urbanity. Lowell, you know, confessed to being "a tory in his nerves;" but Longfellow, with all his stateliness of manner, was nobly and perfectly democratic. He was ideally good; I think he was without a fault.

Boyesen. I have never known a man who was more completely free from snobbishness and pretence of all kinds. It delighted him to go out of his way to do a man a favor. There was, however, a little touch of Puritan pallor in his temperament, a slight lack of robustness; that is, if his brother's biography can be trusted. What I mean to say is, that he appears there a trifle too perfect: too bloodlessly and almost frostily, statuesque. I have always had a little diminutive grudge against the Rev. Samuel Longfellow for not using a single one of those beautiful anecdotes I sent him illustrative of the warmer and more genial side of the poet's character. He evidently wanted to portray a Plutarchian man of heroic size, and he therefore had to exclude all that was subtly individualizing.

Howells. Well, there is always room for another biography of Longfellow.

Boyesen. At the time when I made your acquaintance, in 1871, you were writing

W. D. HOWELLS.

From a photograph taken at Cambridge in 1868.

"Their Wedding Journey." Do you remember the glorious talks we had together, while the hours of the night slipped away unnoticed? We have no more of those splendid conversational rages nowadays. How eloquent we were, to be sure; and with what delight you read those chapters on "Niagara," "Quebec," and "The St. Lawrence;" and with what rapture I listened! I can never read them without supplying the cadence of your voice, and seeing you seated, twenty-two years younger than now, in that cosey little library in Berkeley Street.

Howells. Yes; and do you mind our sudden attacks of hunger, when we would start on a foraging expedition into the cellar, in the middle of the night, and return, you with a cheese and crackers, and I with a watermelon and a bottle of champagne? What jolly meals we improvised! Only it is a wonder to me that we survived them.

Boyesen. You will never suspect what an influence you exerted upon my fate by your friendliness and sympathy in those never-to-be-forgotten days. You Americanized me. I had been an alien, and felt alien in every fibre of my soul, until I met you. Then I became domesticated. I found a kindred spirit, who understood me, and whom I understood; and that is the first and indispensable condition of happiness. It was at your house, at a luncheon, I think, that I met Henry James.

Howells. Yes; James and I were constant companions, we took daily walks together; and his father, the elder Henry James,

was an incomparably delightful and interesting man.

Boyesen. Yes; I remember him well. I doubt if I ever heard a more brilliant talker.

Howells. No; he was one of the best talkers in America. And didn't the immortal Ralph Keeler appear upon the scene during the summer of '71 or '72?

Boyesen. Yes; your small son "Bua" insisted upon calling him "Big Man Keeler," in spite of his small size.

Howells. Yes, Bua was the only one who ever saw Keeler life-size.

Boyesen. I remember how he sat in your library and told stories of his negro minstrel days and his wild adventures in many climes, and did not care whether you laughed with him or at him, but would join you from sheer sympathy; and how we all laughed in chorus until our sides ached!

Howells. Poor Keeler! He was a sort of migratory, nomadic survival; but he had fine qualities, and was well equipped for a sort of fiction. If he had lived he might have written the great American novel. Who knows?

Boyesen. Was not it at Cambridge that Björnstjerne Björnson visited you?

Howells. No; that was in 1881, at Belmont, where we went in order to be in the country, and give the children the benefit of country air. When I met Björnson before we had always talked Italian; but

MR. HOWELLS'S STUDY IN CAMBRIDGE.

W. D. HOWELLS'S SUMMER HOME AT BELMONT IN 1878.

the first thing he said to me at Belmont was: "Now we will speak English." And when he had got into the house he picked up a book and said, in his abrupt way: "We do not put enough in;" meaning, thereby, that we ignored too much of life in our fiction—excluded it out of regard for propriety. But when I met him, some years later, in Paris, he had changed his mind about that, for he detested the French naturalism, and could find nothing to praise in Zola.

Boyesen. I am going to ask you one of the interviewer's stock questions, but you need not answer, you know: Which of your books do you regard as the greatest?

Howells. I have always taken the most satisfaction in "A Modern Instance." I have there come closest to American life, as I know it.

Boyesen. But in "Silas Lapham" it seems to me that you have got a still firmer grip on American reality.

Howells. Perhaps. Still, I prefer "A Modern Instance." "Silas Lapham" is the most successful novel I have published, except "A Hazard of New Fortunes," which has sold nearly twice as many copies as any of the rest.

Boyesen. What do you attribute that to?

Howells. Possibly to the fact that the scene is laid in New York; the public throughout the country is far more interested in New York than in Boston. New York, as Lowell once said, is a huge pudding, and every town and village has been helped to a slice, or wants to be.

Boyesen. I rejoice that New York has found such a subtly appreciative and faithful chronicler as you show yourself to be in "A Hazard of New Fortunes." To the equipment of a great city—a world-city, as the Germans say—belongs a great novelist; that is to say, at least one. And even though your modesty may rebel, I shall persist in regarding you henceforth as *the* novelist *par excellence* of New York.

Howells. Ah, you don't expect me to live up to *that* bit of taffy!

NOTE.—On October 4, 1895, as this book was going through the press, Professor Boyesen died suddenly, in the very prime of his life, being but forty-seven years old. Writing of the event, one who knew him intimately says: "The death of Hjalmar Hjorth Boyesen takes from the world not the scholarly professor and eminent author only; it removes from our midst a large-hearted, generous, public-spirited gentleman, and this is the loss which we feel first. The value of his educational labors and his fame as a writer are known to all; the active part he has taken in the various movements to purify our political life is known to many; but only those who came into personal contact with the man know how large was his generosity, how helpful his advice." The same writer speaks of Professor Boyesen's gifts as a lecturer, and referring particularly to a series of lectures on the modern novel, he says: "In these the personal element was strong; Professor Boyesen had been on terms of friendship and even intimacy with the leading novelists of many lands. His lectures attracted thousands; the large hall at Columbia College was filled to overflowing, often an hour before the time announced. . . . 'It was all due to the personal element,' he said."—EDITOR.

PORTRAITS OF W. D. HOWELLS.

AGE 18. 1855. RESIDENCE, JEFFERSON, OHIO.

AGE 23. 1860. NEWS EDITOR OF "OHIO STATE JOURNAL."

AGE 28. MAY, 1865. VENICE, "VENETIAN LIFE."

AGE 25. 1862. CONSUL AT VENICE.

AGE 32. 1869. CAMBRIDGE, MASS. "SUBURBAN SKETCHES."

AGE 41. 1878. BELMONT, MASS. "THE LADY OF THE AROOSTOOK."

AGE 47. 1884. BOSTON, MASS. "THE RISE OF SILAS LAPHAM."

AGE 50. 1887. BOSTON. "APRIL HOPES."

AGE   1893. BOSTON. "THE SHADOW OF A DREAM."

PORTRAITS OF PROFESSOR H. H. BOYESEN.

Born in Frederiksvarn, Norway, September 23, 1848; died in New York, October 4, 1895.

AGE 17. 1865. STUDENT, CHRISTIANIA, NORWAY.

AGE 19. 1867. STUDENT, UNIVERSITY OF CHRISTIANIA.

AGE 21, 1869. CHICAGO. EDITOR OF "FREMAD."

AGE 27, 1875. PROFESSOR OF GERMAN AT CORNELL UNIVERSITY, ITHACA, NEW YORK. "TALES OF TWO HEMISPHERES."

AGE 34, 1882. PROFESSOR OF MODERN LANGUAGES, COLUMBIA COLLEGE, NEW YORK CITY. "DAUGHTER OF THE PHILISTINES."

1893. THE AUTHOR OF "SOCIAL STRUGGLERS."

JAMES WHITCOMB RILEY.

A CONVERSATION BETWEEN THE "HOOSIER" POET AND HAMLIN GARLAND.

RECORDED BY MR. GARLAND.

RILEY'S country, like most of the State of Indiana, has been won from the original forest by incredible toil. Three generations of men have laid their bones beneath the soil that now blooms into gold and lavender harvests of wheat and corn.

The traveller to-day can read this record of struggle in the fringes of mighty elms and oaks and sycamores which form the grim background of every pleasant stretch of stubble or corn land.

Greenfield, lying twenty miles east of Indianapolis, is to-day an agricultural town, but in the days when Whitcomb Riley lived here it was only a half-remove from the farm and the wood-lot; and the fact that he was brought up so near to the farm, and yet not deadened and soured by its toil, accounts, in great measure at least, for his work.

But Greenfield as it stands to-day, modernized and refined somewhat, is apparently the most unpromising field for literature, especially for poetry. It has no hills and no river nor lake. Nothing but vast and radiant sky, and blue vistas of fields between noble trees.

It has the customary main street with stores fronting upon it; the usual small shops, and also its bar-rooms, swarming with loungers. It has its court-house in the square, half-hid by great trees—a grim and bare building, with its portal defaced and grimy. The people, as they pass you in the street, speak in the soft, high-keyed nasal drawl which is the basis of the Hoosier dialect. It looks to be, as it is, halfway between the New England village and the Western town.

The life, like that of all small towns in America, is apparently slow-moving, purposeless, and uninteresting; and yet from this town, and other similar towns, has Whitcomb Riley drawn the sweetest honey of poesy—honey with a native delicious tang, as of buckwheat and basswood bloom,

JAMES WHITCOMB RILEY.
From a photograph by Barraud, London.

"GRIGGSBY'S STATION," THE OLD RILEY HOUSE AND PRESENT SUMMER RESIDENCE, GREENFIELD, INDIANA.

> " Le's go a-visitin' back to Griggsby's Station—
> Back where the latch-string's a-hangin' from the door,
> And ever' neighbor round the place is dear as a relation—
> Back where we ust to be so happy and so pore ! "

with hints of the mullein and the thistle of dry pastures.

I found Mr. Riley sitting on the porch of the old homestead, which has been in alien hands for a long time, but which he has lately bought back. In this house his childhood was passed, at a time when the street was hardly more than a lane in the woods. He bought it because of old-time associations.

"I am living here," he wrote me, "with two married sisters keeping house for me during the summer; that is to say, I ply spasmodically between here and Indianapolis."

I was determined to see the poet here, in the midst of his native surroundings, rather than at a hotel in Indianapolis. I was very glad to find him at home, for it gave me opportunity to study both the poet and his material.

It is an unpretentious house of the usual village sort, with a large garden ; and his two charming sisters with their families (summering here) give him something more of a home atmosphere than he has had since he entered the lecturer's profession. Two or three children—nephews and nieces—companion him also.

After a few minutes' chat Riley said, with a comical side glance at me : " Come up into my library." I knew what sort of a library to expect. It was a pleasant little upper room, with a bed and a small table in it, and about a dozen books.

Mr. Riley threw out his hand in a comprehensive gesture, and said : " This is as sumptuous a room as I ever get. I live most o' my time in a Pullman car or a hotel, and you know how blamed luxurious an ordinary hotel room is."

I refused to be drawn off into side discussions, and called for writing paper. Riley took an easy position on the bed, while I sharpened pencils, and studied him closely, with a view to letting my readers know how he looks.

He is a short man, with square shoulders and a large head. He has a very dignified manner—at times. His face is smoothly shaven, and, though he is not bald, the light color of his hair makes him seem so. His eyes are gray and round, and generally solemn, and sometimes stern. His face is the face of a great actor—in rest, grim and inscrutable ; in action, full of the most elusive expressions, capable of humor and pathos. Like most humorists, he is sad in repose. His language, when he chooses to have it so, is wonderfully concise and penetrating and beautiful. He drops often into dialect, but always with a look on his face which shows he is aware of what he is doing. In other words, he is master of both forms of speech. His mouth is his wonderful feature: wide, flexible, clean-cut. His lips are capable of the grimmest and the merriest lines. When he reads they pout like a child's, or draw down into a straight, grim line like a New England deacon's, or close at one side, and uncover his white and even teeth at the other, in the sly smile of "Benjamin F. Johnson," the humble humorist and philosopher. In his own proper person he is full of quaint and beautiful philosophy. He is wise rather than learned—wise with the quality that is in proverbs, almost always touched with humor.

His eyes are near-sighted and his nose prominent. His head is of the "tack-hammer" variety, as he calls it. The public insists that there is an element of resemblance between Mr. Riley, Eugene Field, and Bill Nye. He is about forty years of age and a bachelor—presumably from choice. He is a man of marked neatness of dress and delicacy of manner. I began business by asking if he remembered where we met last.

"Certainly — Kipling's. Great story-teller, Kipling. I like to hear him tell about animals. Remember his story of the two elephants that lambasted the one that went 'must'?"

"I *guess* I do. I have a suspicion, however, that Kipling was drawing a long bow for our benefit, especially in that story of the elephant that chewed a stalk of cane into a swab to wind in the clothing of his keeper, in order to get him within reach. That struck me as bearing down pretty hard on a couple of simple Western boys like us."

"Waive the difference for genius. He made it a good story, anyway; and, aside from his great gifts, I consider Kipling a lovely fellow. I like him because he's natively interested in the common man."

I nodded my assent, and Riley went on:

"Kipling had the good fortune to get started early, and he's kept busy right along. A man who is great has no time for anything else," he added, in that peculiarity of phrase and solemnity of utterance which made me despair of ever dramatizing him.

"He's going to do better," I replied.

"The best story in that book is 'His Private Honor.' That's as good as anybody does. What makes Kipling great is his fidelity to his own convictions and to his own conditions, his writing what he knows about. And, by the way, the Norwegians and Swedes at the World's Fair have read us a good lesson on that score. They've put certain phases of their life and landscape before us with immense vim and truth, while our American artists have mainly gone hunting for themes—Breton peasants and Japanese dancing-girls."

Riley sternly roused up to interrupt: "And ignoring the best material in the world. Material just out o' God's hand, lying around thick"—then quick as light he was Old Man Johnson again:

"'Thick as clods in the fields and lanes
Er these-ere little hop-toads when it rains!'"

"American artists and poets have always known too much," I went on. "We've been so afraid the world would find us lacking in scholarship, that we've allowed it to find us lacking in creative work. We've been so very correct, that we've imitated. Now, if you'd had four or five years of Latin, Riley, you'd be writing Latin odes or translations."

Riley looked grave. "I don't know but you're right. Still, you can't tell. Sometimes I feel that I am handicapped by ignorance of history and rhetoric and languages."

"Well, of course, I ought not to discuss a thing like this in your presence, but I think the whole thing has worked out beautifully for the glory of Indiana and Western literature.".

There came a comical light into his eyes, and his lips twisted up into a sly grin at the side, as he dropped into dialect: "I don't take no credit for my ignorance. Jest born thataway," and he added a moment later, with a characteristic swift change to deep earnestness: "My work did itself."

As he lay, with that introspective look in his eyes, I took refuge in one of the questions I had noted down: "Did you ever actually live on a farm?"

"No. All I got of farm life I picked up right from this distance—this town—this old homestead. Of course, Greenfield was nothing but a farmer town then, and besides, father had a farm just on the edge of town, and in corn-plantin' times he used to press us boys into service, and we went very loathfully, at least I did. I got hold of farm life some way—all ways, in fact.

I might not have made use of it if I had been closer to it than this."

"Yes, there's something in that. You would have failed, probably, in your perspective. The actual work on a farm doesn't make poets. Work is a good thing in the retrospect, or when you can regulate the amount of it. Yes, I guess you had just the kind of a life to give you a hold on the salient facts of farm life. Anyhow, you've done it, that's settled."

Riley was thinking about something which amused him, and he roused up to dramatize a little scene. "Sometimes some kins with for feed, and I get the smell of the fodder and the cattle, so that it brings up the right picture in the mind of the reader. I don't know how I do it. It ain't me."

His voice took on a deeper note, and his face shone with a strange sort of mysticism which often comes out in his earnest moments. He put his fingers to his lips in a descriptive gesture, as if he held a trumpet. "I'm only the 'willer' through which the whistle comes."

"The basis of all art is spontaneous observation," I said, referring back a little.

"MILROY'S GROVE" AND OLD NATIONAL ROAD BRIDGE, BRANDYWINE.

" Where the dusky turtle lies basking on the gravel
Of the sunny sand-bar in the middle tide,
And the ghostly dragonfly pauses in his travel
To rest like a blossom where the water-lily died."

—*Babyhood.*

real country boy gives me the round turn on some farm points. For instance, here comes one stepping up to me : 'You never lived on a farm,' he says. ' Why not ? ' says I. 'Well,' he says, 'a turkey-cock gobbles,' but he don't ky-ouck as your poetry says.' He had me right there. It's the turkey-hen that ky-oucks. ' Well, you'll never hear another turkey-cock of mine ky-ouckin',' says I."

While I laughed, Riley became serious again. "But generally I hit on the right symbols. I get the frost on the pumpkin and the fodder in the shock ; and I see the frost on the old axe they split the pump-

"If a man is to work out an individual utterance with the subtlety and suggestion of life, he can't go diggin' around among the bones of buried prophets. I take it you didn't go to school much."

"No, and when I did I was a failure in everything—except reading, maybe. I liked to read. We had McGuffey's Series, you know, and there was some good stuff there. There was Irving and Bryant and Cooper and Dickens——"

"And ' Lochiel's Warning '——"

He accepted the interruption. "And ' The Battle of Waterloo,' and ' The Death of Little Nell '——"

I rubbed my knees with glee as I again interrupted: "And there was 'Marco Bozzaris,' you know, and 'Rienzi.' You recollect that speech of Rienzi's—'I come not here to talk,' etc.? I used to count the class to see if 'Rouse, ye Slaves,' would come to me. It was capitalized, you remember. It always scared me nearly to death to read those capitalized passages."

Riley mused. "Pathos seems to be the worst with me. I used to run away when we were to read 'Little Nell.' I knew I couldn't read it without crying, and I knew they'd all laugh at me and make the whole thing ridiculous. I couldn't stand that. My teacher, Lee O. Harris, was a friend to me and helped me in many ways. He got to understand me beautifully. He knew I couldn't learn arithmetic. There wasn't any gray matter in that part of my head. Perfectly empty! But I can't remember when I wasn't a declaimer. I always took natively to anything theatrical. History I took a dislike to, as a thing without juice, and so I'm not particularly well stocked in dates and events of the past."

"Well, that's a good thing, too, I guess," I said, pushing my point again. "It has thrown you upon the present, and kept you dealing with your own people. Of course, I don't mean to argue that perfect ignorance is a thing to be desired, but there is no distinction in the historical poem or novel, to my mind. Everybody's done that."

Riley continued: "Harris, in addition to being a scholar and a teacher, was, and is, a poet. He was also a playwright, and made me a success in a comedy part which he wrote for me, in our home theatricals."

"Well, now, that makes me think. It was your power to recite that carried you into the patent-medicine cart, wasn't it? And how about that sign-painting? Which came first?"

"The sign-painting. I was a boy in my teens when I took up sign-painting."

"Did you serve a regular apprenticeship?"

"Yes, learned my trade of an old Dutchman here, by the name of Keefer, who was an artist in his way. I had a natural faculty for drawing. I suppose I could have illustrated my books if I had given time to it. It's rather curious, but I hadn't been with the old fellow much more than a week before I went to him and asked him why he didn't make his own letters. I couldn't see why he copied from the same old forms all the time. I hated to copy anything."

"Well, now, I want to know about that patent-medicine peddling."

Something in my tone made him reply quickly:

"That has been distorted. It was really a very simple matter, and followed the sign-painting naturally. After the 'trade' episode I had tried to read law with my father, but I didn't seem to get anywhere. Forgot as diligently as I read. So far as school equipment was concerned, I was an advertised idiot; so what was the use? I had a trade, but it was hardly what I wanted to do always, and my health was bad—very bad—bad as I was!

"A doctor here in Greenfield advised me to travel. But how in the world was I to travel without money? It was just at this time that the patent-medicine man came along. He needed a man, and I argued this way: 'This man is a doctor, and if I must travel, better travel with a doctor.' He had a fine team, and a nice-looking lot of fellows with him; so I plucked up courage to ask if I couldn't go along and paint his advertisements for him."

Riley smiled with retrospective amusement. "I rode out of town behind those horses without saying good-by to any one. And though my patron wasn't a diploma'd doctor, as I found out, he was a mighty fine man, and kind to his horses, which was a recommendation. He was a man of good habits, and the whole company was made up of good straight boys."

"How long were you with them?"

"About a year. Went home with him, and was made same as one of his own lovely family. He lived at Lima, Ohio. My experience with him put an idea in my head—a business idea, for a wonder—and the next year I went down to Anderson and went into partnership with a young fellow to travel, organizing a scheme of advertising with paint, which we called 'The Graphic Company.' We had five or six young fellows, all musicians as well as handy painters, and we used to capture the towns with our music. One fellow could whistle like a nightingale, another sang like an angel, and another played the banjo. I scuffled with the violin and guitar."

"I thought so, from that poem on 'The Fiddle' in 'The Old Swimmin' Hole.'"

"Our only dissipation was clothes. We dressed loud. You could hear our clothes an incalculable distance. We had an idea it helped business. Our plan was to take one firm of each business in a town, paint-

"THE OLD SWIMMIN'-HOLE" AS IT NOW APPEARS.

" Childish voices, farther on,
  Where the truant stream has gone,
Vex the echoes of the wood
Till no word is understood—
Save that we are well aware
Happiness is hiding there :—
There, in leafy coverts, nude
Little bodies poise and leap,
Spattering the solitude

" And the silence everywhere—
  Mimic monsters of the deep !—
Wallowing in sandy shoals—
Plunging headlong out of sight,
And, with spurtings of delight,
Clutching hands and slippery soles,
Climbing up the treacherous steep
Over which the spring-board spurns
Each again as he returns."
                              —*In Swimming-Time.*

ing its advertisements on every road leading into the town : 'Go to Mooney's,' and things like that, you understand. We made a good thing at it."

"How long did you do business?"

"Three or four years, and we had more fun than anybody." He turned another comical look on me over his pinch-nose eyeglasses. "You've heard this story about my travelling all over the State as a blind sign-painter? Well, that started this way. One day we were in a small town somewhere, and a great crowd watching us in breathless wonder and curiosity; and one of our party said : 'Riley, let me introduce you as a blind sign-painter.' So just for mischief I put on a crazy look in the eyes and pretended to be blind. They led me carefully to the ladder, and handed me my brush and paints. It was great fun. I'd hear them saying as I worked, 'That feller ain't blind.' 'Yes, he is; see his eyes.' 'No, he ain't, I tell you; he's playin' off.' 'I tell you he *is* blind. Didn't you see him fall over a box there and spill all his paints?'"

Riley rose here and laughingly reënacted the scene, and I don't wonder that the villagers were deceived, so perfect was his assumption of the patient, weary look of a blind person.

I laughed at the joke. It was like the tricks boys play at college.

Riley went on. "Now, that's all there was to it. I was a blind sign-painter one day, and forgot it the next. We were all boys, and jokers, naturally enough, but not lawless. All were good fellows. All had nice homes and good people."

"Were you writing any at this time?"

"Oh, yes, I was always writing for purposes of recitation. I couldn't find printed poetry that was natural enough to speak. From a child I had always flinched at false rhymes and inversions. I liked John G. Saxe because he had a jaunty trick of rhyming artlessly; made the *sense* demand the rhyme—like

" Young Peter Pyramus—I call him Peter,
Not for the sake of the rhyme or the metre,
But merely to make the name completer.'

"I liked those classic travesties, too—he poked fun at the tedious old themes, and that always pleased me." Riley's voice grew stern, as he said : "I'm against the fellows who celebrate the old to the neglect of our own kith and kin. So I was always trying to write of the kind of people I *knew*, and especially to write verse that I could

read just as if it were being spoken for the first time."

"I saw in a newspaper the other day that you began your journalistic work in Anderson."

"That's right. When I got back from my last trip with 'The Graphic Company,' young Will M. Croan offered me a place on a paper he was just connecting himself with. He had heard that I could write, and took it for granted I would be a valuable man in the local and advertising departments. I was. I inaugurated at once a feature of free doggerel advertising, for our regular advertisers. I wrote reams and miles of stuff like this :

" ' O Yawcob Stein,
Dot frent of mine,
He got dot Cloding down so fine
Dot effer'body bin a-buyin'
Fon goot old Yawcob Stein.' "

"I'd like to see some of those old papers. I suppose they're all down there on file."

"I'm afraid they are. It's all there. Whole hemorrhages of it."

"Did you go from there to Indianapolis?"

He nodded.

"How did you come to go? Did you go on the venture?"

"No, it came about in this way. I had a lot of real stuff, as I fancied, quite different from the doggerel I've just quoted ; and when I found something pleased the people, as I'd hold 'em up and *read* it to 'em, I'd send it off to a magazine, and it would come back quite promptly by return mail. Still I believed in it. I had a friend on the opposition paper who was always laughing at my pretensions as a poet, and I was anxious to show him I could write poetry just as good as that which he praised of other writers ; and it was for his benefit I concocted that scheme of imitating Poe. You've heard of that?"

"Not from any reliable source."

"Well, it was just this way. I determined to write a poem in imitation of some well-known poet, to see if I couldn't trap my hypercritical friend. I had no idea of doing anything more than that. So I coined and wrote and sent 'Leonainie' to a paper in a neighboring county, in order that I might attack it myself in my own paper and so throw my friend completely off the track. The whole thing was a boy's fool trick. I didn't suppose it would go out of the State exchanges. I was appalled at the result. The whole country

RAILROAD BRIDGE, BRANDYWINE.

" Through the viny, shady-shiny
  Interspaces, shot with tiny
Flying motes that fleck the winy
  Wave-engraven sycamores."
          —*A Dream of Autumn.*

took it up, and pitched into me unjustifiably."

"Couldn't you explain?"

"They wouldn't *let* me explain. I lost my position on the paper, because I had let a rival paper have 'the discovery'! Everybody insisted I was trying to attract attention, but that wasn't true. I simply wanted to make my critic acknowledge, by the ruse, that I *could* write *perfect* verse, so far as *his* critical (?) judgment comprehended. The whole matter began as a thoughtless joke, and ended in being one of the most unpleasant experiences of my life."

"Well, you carried your point, anyway. There's a melancholy sort of pleasure in doing that."

Riley didn't seem to take even that pleasure in it.

"In this dark time, just when I didn't know which way to turn—friends all dropping away—I got a letter from Judge Martindale of the 'Indianapolis Journal,' saying, 'Come over and take a regular place on the "Journal," and get pay for your work.'"

"That was a timely piece of kindness on his part."

"It put me really on my feet. And just about this time, too, I got a letter from Longfellow, concerning some verses that I had the 'nerve' to ask him to examine, in which he said the verses showed 'the true poetic faculty and insight.' This was high praise to me then, and I went on writing with more confidence and ambition ever after."

"What did you send to him?"

"I don't remember exactly—some of my serious work. Yes, one of the things was 'The Iron Horse.'" He quoted this:

    "No song is mine of Arab steed—
    My courser is of nobler blood
    And cleaner limb and fleeter speed
    And greater strength and hardihood
    Than ever cantered wild and free
    Across the plains of Araby."

"How did Judge Martindale come to make that generous offer? Had you been contributing to the 'Journal'?"

"Oh, yes, for quite a while. One of the things I had just sent him was the Christmas story, 'The Boss Girl,' a newsboy's story. He didn't know, of course, that I was in trouble when he made the offer, but he stood by me afterwards, and all came right."

"What did you do on the 'Journal'?"

"I was a sort o' free-lance—could do anything I wanted to. Just about this time I began a series of 'Benjamin F. Johnson' poems. They all appeared with editorial comment, as if they came from an old Hoosier farmer of Boone County. They were so well received that I gathered them together in a little parchment volume, which I called 'The Old Swimmin' Hole and 'Leven More Poems,' my first book."

"I suppose you put forth that volume with great timidity?"

"Well, I argued it couldn't break me, so I printed a thousand copies—hired 'em done, of course, at my own expense."

"Did you sell 'em?"

"They sold themselves. I had the ten-bushel box of 'em down in the 'Journal' office, and it bothered me nearly to death to attend to the mailing of them. So when Bowen & Merrill agreed to take the book off my hands, I gladly consented, and that's the way I began with them."

"It was that little book that first made me acquainted with your name," I said. "My friend and your friend, Charles E. Hurd, of the 'Boston Transcript,' one day read me the poem 'William Leachman,' which he liked exceedingly, and ended by giving me a copy of the book. I saw at once you had taken up the rural life, and carried it beyond Whittier and Lowell in respect of making it dramatic. You gave the farmer's point of view."

"I've tried to. But people oughtn't to get twisted up on my things the way they do. I've written dialect in two ways. One, as the modern man, bringing all the art he can to represent the way some other fellow thinks and speaks; but the 'Johnson' poems are intended to be like the old man's *written* poems, because he is supposed to have sent them in to the paper himself. They are representations of written dialect, while the others are representations of dialect as manipulated by the artist. But, in either case, it's the other fellow doin' it. I don't try to treat of people as they *ought* to think and speak, but as they do think and speak. In other words, I do not undertake to edit nature, either physical or human."

"I see your point, but I don't know that I would have done so without having read 'The Old Swimmin' Hole,' and the 'Tale of the Airly Days.'"

I quoted here those lines I always found so meaningful:

    "Tell of the things just like they was,
    They don't need no excuse.
    Don't tech 'em up as the poets does,
    Till they're all too fine for use!"

BEREAVED.

Let me come in where you sit weeping—aye,
Let me, who have not any child to die,
Weep with you for the little one whose love
        I have known nothing of.

The little arms that slowly, slowly loosed
Their pressure round your neck;—the hands you used
To kiss.—Such arms—such hands I never knew.
        May I not weep with you?

Fain would I be of service—say some thing,
Between the tears, that would be comforting,—
But ah! so sadder than yourselves am I,
        Who have no child to die.

        —James Whitcomb Riley.

Indpls. Aug. 7:
—1893—

FACSIMILE OF AN AUTOGRAPH POEM BY MR. RILEY.

Riley rose to his feet, and walked about the room. "I don't believe in dressing up nature. Nature is good enough for God, it's good enough for me. I see Old Man Johnson, a living figure. I know what the old feller has read. I'd like to have his picture drawn, because I love the old codger, but I can't get artists to see that I'm not making fun of him. They seem to think that if a man is out o' plumb in his language he must be likewise in his morals."

I flung my hand-grenade: "That's a relic of the old school, the school of caricature—a school that assumes that if a man has a bulbous nose he necessarily has a bulbous intellect; which doesn't follow. I've known men with bulbous noses who were neither hard drinkers nor queer in any other particular, having a fine, dignified speech and clear, candid eyes."

"Now, old Benjamin looks queer, I'll admit. His clothes don't fit him. He's bent and awkward. But that don't prevent him from having a fine head and deep and tender eyes, and a soul in him you can recommend."

Riley paused, and looked down at me with a strange smile. "I tell you, the crude man is generally moral, for Nature has just let go his hand. She's just been leading him through the dead leaves and the daisies. When I deal with such a man I give him credit for every virtue; but what he does, and the way he does it, is his action and not mine."

He read at this point, with that quaint arching of one eyebrow, and the twist at the side of the mouth with which he always represents "Benjamin F. Johnson":

      " ' My Religen is to jest
        Do by all my level best,
        Feelin' God'll do the rest.—
      Facts is, fur as *I* can see,
      The *good* Bein', makin' me,
      'Ll make me what I *ort* to be.'—

And that's the lovely Old Man Johnson talkin', and not *me*—but I'm *listenin'*
to him, understand, yes, and keepin'
still ! ' "

The tender side of the poet came out
here, and I said : " I had a talk with your
father yesterday, and I find that we're in
harmony on a good many reform topics.
He's a Populist and a Greenbacker. Do
you have any reform leanings ? "

" Father is a thinker, and ain't afraid
of his thinkin' machine. I'm turned away
from reform because it's no use. We've
got to *conform*, not *reform*, in our attitude
with the world and man. Try reformin',
and sooner or later you've got to quit,
because it's always a question of politics.
You start off with a reform idea, that is, a
moral proposition. You end up by doing
something politic. It's in the nature of
things. You can, possibly, reform just
one individual, but you can't reform the
world at large. It won't work."

" All reforms, in your mind, are apparently hopeless, and yet, as a matter of
fact, the great aggregate conforms to a
few men every quarter of a century."

This staggered Riley, and he looked at
me rather helplessly. " Well, it's an unpleasant thing, anyhow, and I keep away
from it. I'm no fighter. In my own kind
of work I can do good, and make life
pleasant."

He was speaking from the heart. I
changed the subject by looking about the
room. " You don't read much, I imagine ? "

He turned another quizzical look on
me. " I'm afraid to read much, I'm so
blamed imitative. But I read a good
deal of chop-feed fiction, and browse with
relish through the short stories and poems
of to-day. But I have no place to put
books. Have to do my own things where
I catch time and opportunity."

" Well, if you'd had a library, you
wouldn't have got so many *people* into
your poems. You remind me of Whit-
man's poet, you tramp a perpetual journey.
Where do you think you get your verse-
writing from ? "

" Mainly from my mother's family, the
Marines. A characteristic of the whole
family is their ability to write rhymes, but
all unambitiously. They write rhymed

letters to each other, and joke and jim-
crow with the Muses."

" Riley, I want to ask you. Your father
is Irish, is he not ? "

" Both yes and no. *His* characteristics
are strongly Irish, but he was born a Pennsylvania Dutchman, and spoke the German dialect before he spoke English. It
has been held that the name Riley probably comes from ' Ryland,' but there's an
' O'Reilly ' theory I muse over very pleasantly."

I saw he was getting tired of indoors,
so I rose. " Well, now, where's the old
swimmin' hole ? "

His face lighted up with a charming,
almost boyish, smile. " The old swimmin' hole is right down here on Brandywine—the old ' crick,' just at the edge of
town."

" Put on your hat, and let's go down and
find it."

We took our way down the main street
and the immensely dusty road towards the
east. The locusts quavered in duo and
trio in the ironweeds, and were answered
by others in the high sycamores. Large
yellow and black butterflies flapped about
from weed to weed. The gentle wind
came over the orchards and cornfields,
filled with the fragrance of gardens and
groves. The road took a little dip towards the creek, which was low, and almost
hidden among the weeds.

Riley paused. " I haven't been to the
old swimmin' hole for sixteen years. We
used to go across there through the grass,
all except the feller with the busted toe-
nail. He had to go round." He pointed
at the print of bare, graceful feet in the
dust, and said :

" We could tell, by the dent of the heel and the sole,
   There was lots of fun on hand at the old swimmin'
     hole."

As we looked out on the hot midsum-
mer landscape, Riley quoted again, from
a poem in his then forthcoming book—a
poem which he regards as one of his best :

" The air and the sun and the shadows
    Were wedded and made as one,
  And the winds ran o'er the meadows
    As little children run :

" And the wind flowed over the meadows,
    And along the willowy way
  The river ran, with its ripples shod
    With the sunshine of the day :

" O, the winds poured over the meadows
    In a tide of eddies and calms,
  And the bared brow felt the touch of it
    As a sweetheart's tender palms.

" And up through the rifted tree-tops
  That signalled the wayward breeze
I saw the hulk of the hawk becalmed
  Far out on the azure seas."

Riley recited this with great beauty of tone and rhythm—such as audiences never hear from him, hearing only his dialect.

As we walked on we heard shouts, and I plucked Riley's sleeve : " Hear that ? If that isn't the cry of a swimming boy, then my experiences are of no value. A boy has a shout which he uses only when splashing about in a pond."

Riley's face glowed. " That's right, they're there—just as we used to be."

After climbing innumerable fences, we came upon the boys under the shade of the giant sycamore and green thorn-trees. The boys jiggled themselves into their clothes, and ran off in alarm at the two staid and dignified men, who none the less had for them a tender and reminiscent sympathy.

All about splendid elm-trees stood, and stately green thorn-trees flung their delicate, fern-like foliage athwart the gray and white spotted boles of tall, leaning sycamores. But the creek was very low, by reason of the dry weather.

We threaded our way about, seeking out old paths and stumps and tree trunks,

which sixteen years of absence had not entirely swept from the poet's mind. Then, at last, we turned homeward over the railroad track, through the dusty little town. People were seated in their little backyards here and there eating watermelon, and Neighbor Johnson's poem on the " Wortermelon " came up :

" Oh, wortermelon time is a-comin' 'round agin,
  And they ain't no feller livin' any tickleder'n me."

We passed by the old court-house, where Captain Riley, the poet's father, has practised law for fifty years. The captain lives near, in an odd-looking house of brick, its turret showing above the trees. On the main street groups of men of all ranks and stations were sitting or standing and they all greeted the poet as he passed by with an off-hand : " How are ye, Jim?" to which the poet replied : " How are you, Tom ?" or " How are you, Jack ? How's the folks ?" Personally, his townsmen like him. They begin to respect him also in another way, so successful has he become in a way measurable to them all.

Back at the house, we sat at lunch of cake and watermelon, the sisters, Mrs. Payne and Mrs. Eitels, serving as hostesses most delightfully. They had left

MR. GARLAND TAKES NOTES WHILE THE "HOOSIER" POET TALKS.

their own homes in Indianapolis for the summer, to give this added pleasure to their poet brother. They both have much of his felicity of phrase, and much the same gentleness and sweetness of bearing. The hour was a pleasant one, and brought out the simple, domestic side of the man's nature. The sisters, while they showed their admiration and love for him, addressed him without a particle of affectation.

There is no mysterious abyss between Mr. Riley and his family. They are well-to-do, middle-conditioned Americans, with unusual intellectual power and marked poetic sensibility. Mr. Riley is a logical result of a union of two gifted families, a product of hereditary power, coöperating with the power of an ordinary Western town. Born of a gentle and naturally poetic mother, and a fearless, unconventional father (lawyer and orator), he has lived the life common to boys of villages from Pennsylvania to Dakota, and upon this were added the experiences he has herein related.

It is impossible to represent his talk that night. For two hours he ran on—he the talker, the rest of us the irritating cause.

The most quaintly wise sentences fell from his lips in words no other could have used; scraps of verse, poetic images, humorous assumptions of character, daring figures of speech—I gave up in despair of ever getting him down on paper. He read, at my request, some of his most beautiful things. He talked on religion, and his voice grew deep and earnest.

"I believe a man prays when he does well," he said. "I believe he worships God when his work is on a high plane; when his attitude towards his fellow-men is right, I guess God is pleased with him."

I said good-night, and went off down the street, musing upon the man and his work. Genius, as we call it, defies conditions. It knows no barriers. It finds in things close at hand the most inexhaustible storehouse. All depends upon the poet, not upon materials. It is his love for the thing, his interest in the fact, his distribution of values, his selection of details, which makes his work irresistibly comic or tender or pathetic.

No poet in the United States has the same hold upon the minds of the people as Riley. He is the poet of the plain

VIEW OF GREENFIELD FROM "IRVING'S SPRING," BRANDYWINE.

" Whilse the old town, fur away
'Crost the hazy pastur-land,
Dozed-like in the heat o' day
Peaceful as a hired hand."
     —*Up and Down Old Brandywine.*

American. They bought thirty thousand dollars' worth of his verse last year ; and he is also one of the most successful lecturers on the platform. He gives the lie to the old saying, for he *is* a prophet in his own country. The people of Indiana are justly proud of him, for he has written " Poems Here at Home." He is read by people who never before read poetry in their lives, and he appeals equally well to the man who is heart-sick of the hollow conventional verse in imitation of some classic.

He is absolutely American in every line he writes. His schooling has been in the school of realities. He takes things at first-hand. He considers his success to be due to the fact that he is one of the people, and has written of the things he liked and they liked. The time will come when his work will be seen to be something more than the fancies of a humorist.

As I walked on down the street, it all came upon me with great power—this production of an American poet. Everything was familiar to me. All this life, the broad streets laid off in squares, the little cottages, the weedy gardens, the dusty fruit-trees, the young people sauntering in couples up and down the sidewalk, the snapping of jack-knives, and the low hum of talk from scattered groups. This was Riley's school. This was his material, apparently barren, dry, utterly hopeless in the eyes of the romantic writers of the East, and yet capable of becoming world-famous when dominated and mastered and transformed as it has been mastered and transformed by this poet of the people.

In my estimation, this man is the most remarkable exemplification of the power of genius to transmute plain clods into gold that we have seen since the time of Burns. He has dominated stern and unyielding conditions with equal success, and reflected the life of his kind with greater fidelity than Burns.

This material, so apparently grim and barren of light and shade, waited only for a creative mind and a sympathetic intelligence ; then it grew beautiful and musical, and radiant with color and light and life.

Therein is the magnificent lesson to be drawn from the life and work of the " Hoosier poet."

A MORNING WITH BRET HARTE.

By HENRY J. W. DAM.

" IF I had been an artist I should have painted them," he says, referring to John Oakhurst and M'liss and Tennessee's Partner and all the other denizens of that strange literary land which he was the first to discover and describe to all the world. " If I had been an artist " is his phrase, and it sounds strange from his lips, for a more artistic personality, in thought, speech, sympathies, and methods, was never numbered among the creators of character or the observers of nature than that of the historian of the Golden Age of California, Mr Bret Harte.

It is one of those winter mornings in London when upon parks and lawns and all the architectural distances the cold gray mist lies heavily. The sun, a preposterous ruby set in fog, looms red and high. Through the study window its radiance comes balefully, as if fleeing the dreariness of streets that stretch silent and deserted under London's Sabbath spell. Within the room, however, all is cheerfulness and warmth. The heaped-up coals make flickering traceries of shadow over walls covered with the originals of pictures and engravings which all the world has seen in certain famous books. Some of these originals will be found among the illustrations of this article, and are interesting exhibitions of the manner in which the English imagination endeavors to conceive the unfamiliar California types. The sides of the room are given up to high book-shelves. Bric-a-brac meets the eye in all directions, the mantel being covered with pretty souvenirs of continental watering-places, those guide-posts on the highway of memory by which charming acquaintances are recalled and favorite spots revisited.

BRET HARTE IN PERSON.

At the desk, surrounded by an incalculable visitation of Christmas cards, sits Bret Harte, the Bret Harte of actuality, a

BRET HARTE, FROM A PAINTING BY JOHN PETTIE, R.A. REPRODUCED BY THE KIND PERMISSION
OF THE FINE ARTS SOCIETY, LONDON. PHOTOGRAPHED BY FRADELLE & YOUNG, LONDON.

gentleman as far removed from the Bret Harte of popular fancy as is the St. James Club from Mount Shasta, or a Savoy Hotel supper from the cinder cuisine of a mining camp in the glorious days of '49. Instead of being, as the reader usually conceives, one of the long-bearded, loose-jointed heroes of his Western Walhalla, he is a polished gentleman of medium height, with a curling gray mustache. In lieu of the recklessness of Western methods in dress, his attire exhibits a nicety of detail which, in a man whose dignity and sincerity were less impressive, would seem foppish. This quality, like his handwriting and other characteristic trifles, perceptibly assists one in grasping the main elements of a personality which is as harmonious as it is peculiar, and as unconventional as it is sensitive to fine shades, of whatever kind they be. Over his cigar, with a gentle play of humor and a variety of unconscious gestures which are always graceful and never twice the same, he touches upon this very subject—the impressions made upon him by his first sight of gold-hunting in

BRET HARTE IN 1869, WHILE EDITOR OF THE "OVERLAND MONTHLY." FROM A PHOTOGRAPH LOANED BY THE PRESENT PUBLISHERS OF THE "OVERLAND MONTHLY."

California, and the eye and mind which he brought to bear upon the novel scene.

BRET HARTE'S STORY OF HIS LIFE IN CALIFORNIA.

"I left New York for California," says Mr. Harte, "when I was scarcely more than a boy, with no better equipment, I fear, than an imagination which had been expanded by reading Froissart's 'Chronicles of the Middle Ages,' 'Don Quixote,' the story of the Argonauts, and other books from the shelves of my father, who was a tutor of Greek. I went by way of Panama, and was at work for a few months in San Francisco in the spring of 1853, but felt no satisfaction with my surroundings until I reached the gold country, my particular choice being Sonora, in Calaveras County.

" Here I was thrown among the strangest social conditions that the latter-day world has perhaps seen. The setting was itself heroic. The great mountains of the Sierra Nevada lifted majestic snow-capped peaks against a sky of purest blue. Magnificent pine forests of trees which were themselves enormous, gave to the landscape a sense of largeness and greatness. It was a land of rugged cañons, sharp declivities, and magnificent distances. Amid rushing wa-

ters and wild-wood freedom, an army of strong men in red shirts and top boots were feverishly in search of the buried gold of earth. Nobody shaved, and hair, mustaches, and beards were untouched by shears or razor. Weaklings and old men were unknown. It took a stout heart and a strong frame to dare the venture, to brave the journey of three thousand miles, and battle for life in the wilds. It was a civilization composed entirely of young men, for on one occasion, I remember, an elderly man—he was fifty, perhaps, but he had a gray beard—was pointed out as a curiosity in the city, and men turned in the street to look at him as they would have looked at any other unfamiliar object.

" These men, generally speaking, were highly civilized, many of them being cultured and professionally trained. They were in strange and strong contrast with their surroundings, for all the trammels and conventionalities of settled civilization had been left thousands of miles behind. It was a land of perfect freedom, limited only by the instinct and the habit of law which prevailed in the mass. All its forms were original, rude, and picturesque. Woman was almost unknown, and enjoyed the high estimation of a rarity. The chiv-

BRET HARTE IN 1871. FROM A PHOTOGRAPH TAKEN BY SARONY, NEW YORK, SHORTLY AFTER THE PUBLICATION OF "THE HEATHEN CHINEE."

alry natural to manhood invested her with ideal value when respect could supplement it, and with exceptional value even when it could not. Strong passions brought quick climaxes, all the better and worse forces of manhood being in unbridled play. To me it was like a strange, ever-varying panorama, so novel that it was difficult to grasp comprehensively. In fact, it was not till years afterwards that the great mass of primary impressions on my mind became sufficiently clarified for literary use.

"The changes of scene were constant and unexpected. Here is one that I remember very well. Clothing was hard to get in the early days, and everything that could serve was made use of. Our valley, in its ordinary aspect, had as many 'spring styles for gentlemen' as there were
men to be seen.
One hot summer
morning, how-
ever, the old order
changed. A large
consignment of
condemned navy
outfits, purchased
by a local store-
keeper, had found
ready sale, and the
result was that the
valley was filled
with men, hard at
work over their
claims, and all
dressed in white
'jumpers,' white
duck trousers, and
top boots. On
their heads were
yellow straw hats,
and around their
shoulders gaudy
bandanna hand-
kerchiefs of yel-
low, blue, red, and
green patterns.
Perspiration was
so profuse in the
hot weather that a
handkerchief was
as necessary to a
miner as a whiskey
flask or a revol-
ver. They wore
them clung loose-
ly around their
necks and falling
over their chests,
like the collar of

some extraordinary order, and each man as he worked would now and then dab his forehead with the handkerchief and push it a little farther round. The white clothes and bright handkerchiefs against the wild background made a very novel picture, and I said something to this effect to a miner by my side. He took a look down the valley, the standpoint being one that had not occurred to him, and said : 'It does look kinder nice. Didn't know we gave ourselves away like that,' and sham-bled down the trail with a chuckle. Every day brought new scenes and new experiences, though I did not commit them to paper till many years afterward."

MINER, EXPRESS MESSENGER, SCHOOLMASTER, EDITOR.

ELT HARTE IN 1876. FROM A PHOTOGRAPH BY SARONY, NEW YORK.

"And were you taking notes for future literary work at this period?"

"Not at all. I had not the least idea at this time that any portion of literary fame awaited me. I lived their life, un-thinking. I took my pick and shov-el, and asked where I might dig. They said 'Any-where,' and it was true that you could get 'color,' that is, a few grains of gold, from any of the surface earth with which you chose to fill your pan. In an ordinary day's work you got enough to live on, or, as it was called, 'grub wages.' I was not a success as a gold-digger, and it was conceived that I would an-swer for a Wells Fargo messenger. A Wells Fargo messenger was a person who sat beside the driver on the box-seat of a stage-coach, in charge of the letters and 'treasure' which the Wells Fargo Express Company took from a mining camp to the nearest town or city. Stage robbers were plentiful. My predecessor in the position had been shot through the arm, and my successor was killed. I held the post for some months, and then gave it up to become the schoolmaster near Sonora—Sonora having by immigration attained the size and population which called for a school. For several years after this I wandered about California from city to camp, and camp to city, without any special purpose. I became an editor, and learned to set type, the ability to earn my own living as a printer being a source of great satisfaction to me, for, strange to say, I had no confidence, until long after that period, in literature as a means of livelihood. I have never in my life had an article refused publication, and yet I never had any of that confidence which, in the case of many others, does not seem to have been impaired by repeated refusals. Nearly all my life I have held some political or editorial post, upon which I relied for an income. This has, no doubt, affected my work, since it gave me more liberty to write as pleased myself, instead of endeavoring to write for a purpose, or in accordance with the views of somebody else.

"A great part of this distrust of literature as a profession arose, I think," continues Mr. Harte, and he smiles at the reminiscence, "from my first literary effort. It was a poem called 'Autumn Musings.' It was written at the mature age of eleven. It was satirical in character, and cast upon the fading year the cynical light of my repressed dissatisfaction with things in general. I addressed the envelope to the New York 'Sunday Atlas,' at that time a journal of some literary repute in New York, where I was then living. I was not quite certain how the family would regard this venture on my part, and I posted the missive with the utmost secrecy. After that I waited for over a week in a state of suspense that entirely absorbed me. Sunday came, and with it the newspapers. These were displayed on a stand in the street near our house, and held in their places—I shall never forget them—with stones. With an unmoved face, but a beating heart, I scanned the topmost copy of the 'Atlas.' To my dying day I shall remember the thrill that came from seeing 'Autumn Musings,' a poem, on the first page. I don't know that the headline type was any longer than usual, but to me it was colossal. It had something of the tremendousness of a three-sheet poster. I bought the paper and took it home. I exhibited it to the family by slow and cautious stages. My hopes sank lower and lower. At last I realized the enormity of my offence. The lamentation was general. It was unanimously conceded that I was lost, and I fully believed it. My idea of a poet—it was the family's idea also—was the Hogarthian one, born of a book of Hogarth's drawings belonging to my father. In the lean and miserable and helpless guise of 'The Distressed Poet,' as therein pictured, I saw, aided by the family, my probable future. It was a terrible experience. I sometimes wonder that I ever wrote another line of verse."

His natural tendency in that direction was too strong to be crushed, however. He has always, he says, had a weakness for humorous verse, and in that particular direction his pen is as playful as ever. All of which digression leads naturally to the "Heathen Chinee," concerning which he has several new facts to make public.

BRET HARTE. FROM A PHOTOGRAPH BY THOMAS FALL, LONDON.

BRET HARTE AT THE PRESENT TIME.   FROM A PHOTOGRAPH BY ELLIOTT AND FRY, LONDON.

SOME NEW FACTS ABOUT THE "HEATHEN CHINEE."

" I was always fond of satiric verse, and the instinct of parody has always possessed me. The 'Heathen Chinee' is an instance of this, though I don't think I have told anybody, except a well-known English poet, who observed and taxed me with the fact, the story of its metrical origin. The 'Heathen Chinee' was for a time the best known of any of my writings. It was written for the 'Overland Monthly,' of which I was editor, with a satirical political purpose, but with no thought of aught else than its local effect. It was born of a somewhat absurd state of things which appealed to the humorous eye. The thrifty Oriental, who was invading California in large numbers, was as imitative as a monkey. He did as the Caucasian did in all respects, and, being more patient and frugal, did it a little better. From placer mining to card playing he industriously followed the example set him by his superiors, and took cheating at cards quite seriously, as a valuable addition to the interesting game. He cheated admirably, but, instead of winning praises for it, found himself, when caught at it, abused, contemned, and occasionally mobbed by his teachers in a way that had not been dreamt of in his philosophy. This point I put into verse. I heard nothing of it for some time, until a friend told me it was making the rounds of the Eastern press. He himself had heard a New York brakeman repeating :

Yet he played it that day upon William and me in a way I despise.'

Soon afterwards I began to hear from it frequently in a similar way. The lines were popular. The points seemed to catch.

the ear and hold the memory. I never intended it as a contribution to contemporary poetry, but I doubt, from the evidence I received, if I ever wrote anything more catching. The verses had, however, the dignity of a high example. I have told you of the English poet who was first to question me regarding the metre, and appreciate its Greek source. Do you remember the threnody in Swinburne's 'Atalanta in Calydon'? It occurred to me that the grand and beautiful sweep of that chorus was just the kind of thing which Truthful James would be the last man in the world to adopt in expressing his views. Therefore I used it. Listen," and he quotes, marking the accents with an amused smile :

" 'Atalanta, the fairest of women, whose name is a
blessing to speak—

Yet he played it that day upon William and me
in a way I despise.

The narrowing Symplegades whitened the straits
of Propontis with spray—

And we found on his nails, which were taper,
what's frequent in tapers, that's wax.' "

He laughs over the parody in metre and goes on quoting ; and as he talks of his verse and his work in general, it is evident that the humorous is one of his most fully developed literary characteristics. He still takes delight in the "Condensed Novels," and is as much in the mood for writing them to-day, at fifty-three, as he was twenty years ago. They belonged, it seems, to a kind of chrysalis period in his development, when, living in San Francisco, he wrote variously for a number of local literary periodicals, the most widely known of which was the "Golden Era." These writings, and the position which he won through them, led to the editorship of the "Californian Weekly," and finally of a magazine, the "Overland Monthly." The latter was the inducing cause of the first of that series of stories which carried his name all over the world. At the start he was most bitterly opposed. The first step was the one that cost, with him as with others. His narrative is full of interest, as a matter both of personal and of literary history.

EDITORIAL CAUTION AND "THE LUCK OF ROARING CAMP."

"I was eventually offered the editorship of a new magazine, the 'Overland Monthly,' which was about to make its first issue, and it was through the acceptance of this post that my career, generally speaking, began. As the editor of this magazine, I received for its initial number many contributions in the way of stories. After looking these over, it impressed me as a strange thing that not one of the writers had felt inspired to treat the fresh subjects which lay ready to his hand in California. All the stories were conventional, the kind of thing that would have been offered to an editor in the Atlantic States, stories of those localities and of Europe, in the customary form. I talked the matter over with Mr. Roman, the proprietor, and then wrote a story whose sole object was to give the first number a certain amount of local coloring. It was called 'The Luck of Roaring Camp.' It was a

BRET HARTE IN HIS STUDY.

BRET HARTE'S "M'LISS," FROM A PAINTING BY EDWIN LONG. REPRODUCED BY KIND PERMISSION OF MESSRS. BROOKS AND SONS, LONDON. PHOTOGRAPHED BY FRADELLE & YOUNG, LONDON.

single picture out of the panorama which had impressed me years before. It was put into type. The proof-reader and printer declared it was immoral and indecent. I read it over again in proof, at the request of the publisher, and was touched, I am afraid, only with my own pathos. I read it to my wife—I had married in the meantime—and it made her cry also. I am told that Mr. Roman also read it to his wife, with the same diabolically illogical result. Nevertheless, the opposition was unshaken.

"I had a serious talk with an intimate friend of mine, then the editor of the 'Alta California.' He was not personally opposed to the story, but felt that that sort of thing might be injudicious and unfavorably affect immigration. I was without a sympathizer or defender. Even Mr. Roman felt that it might imperil the prospects of the magazine. I read the story again, thought the matter over, and told Mr. Roman that if 'The Luck of Roaring Camp' was not a good and suitable story I was not a good and suitable editor for his magazine. I said that the chief value of an editor lay in the correctness of his judgment, and if his view was the true one, my judgment was clearly at fault. I am quite sure that if the decision had been left to San Francisco, the series of mining pictures that followed the first would not have been written—at least, not in that city. But the editor remained, and the story appeared. It was received harshly. The religious papers were unanimous in declaring it immoral, and they published columns in its disfavor. The local press, reflecting the pride of a young and new community, could not see why stories should be printed by their representative magazine which put the community into such unfavorable contrast with the effete civilization of the East. They would have none of it!

"A month later, however, by return of mail from Boston, there came an important letter. It was from Fields & Osgood, the publishers, and was addressed to me as editor. It requested me to hand the enclosed note to the author of 'The Luck of Roaring Camp.' The note was their offer to publish anything he chose to write, upon his own terms. This became known, and it turned the tide of criticism. Since Boston indorsed the story, San Francisco was properly proud of it. Thenceforth I had my own way without interruption. Other stories, the mining tales with which you are familiar, followed in quick succession. The numberless impressions of the earlier days were all vividly fixed in my mind, waiting to be worked up, and their success was made apparent to me in very substantial ways, though the religious press continued to suffer from the most painful doubts, and certain local critics who had torn my first story to pieces, fell into a quiet routine of stating that each succeeding story was the worst thing that had yet appeared from my pen."

"A PHYLLIS OF THE SIERRAS." FROM A PHOTOGRAPH BY FRADELLE & YOUNG, LONDON, OF A
DRAWING BY CATON WOODVILLE.

BRET HARTE'S FIRST MEETING WITH MARK TWAIN.

"Local color having been placed, through the dictum of the Atlantic States, at a premium," Mr. Harte continues, "the 'Overland' became what it should have been from the start, truly Californian in tone. Other writers followed my 'trail,' and the freshness and vivid life of the country found a literary expression. At that time I held a political office, the secretaryship of the San Francisco Mint. The Mint was but a few steps from the leading newspaper establishments, and as I had previously been the editor of 'The Californian,' a literary weekly, my office was a rendezvous for contributors and would-be contributors to the magazine.

"Some months before the 'Overland' appeared, George Barnes, a well-known journalist and an intimate friend of mine, walked into my office one morning with a young man

whose appearance was unmistakably interesting. His head was striking. He had the curly hair, the aquiline nose, and even the aquiline *eye*—an eye so eagle-like that a second lid would not have surprised me —of an unusual and dominant nature. His eyebrows were very thick and bushy. His dress was careless, and his general manner one of supreme indifference to surroundings and circumstances. Barnes introduced him as Mr. Sam Clemens, and remarked that he had shown a very original talent in a number of newspaper contributions over the signature of 'Mark Twain.' We talked on different topics, and about a month afterwards Clemens dropped in upon me again.

"He had been away in the mining district on some newspaper assignment in the meantime. In the course of conversation he remarked that the unearthly laziness that prevailed in the town he had been visiting was beyond anything in his previous experience. He said the men did nothing all day long but sit around the barroom stove, spit, and 'swop lies.' He spoke in a slow, rather satirical, drawl which was in itself irresistible. He went on to tell one of those extravagant stories, and half unconsciously dropped into the lazy tone and manner of the original narra-

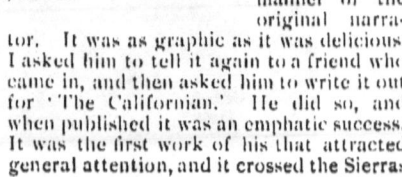

THE ISLAND OF YERBA BUENA. PAINTED BY G. MONTBARD TO ILLUSTRATE BRET HARTE'S STORY, "A WARD OF THE GOLDEN GATE." PHOTOGRAPHED BY TRABELLE & YOUNG, LONDON.

tor. It was as graphic as it was delicious. I asked him to tell it again to a friend who came in, and then asked him to write it out for 'The Californian.' He did so, and when published it was an emphatic success. It was the first work of his that attracted general attention, and it crossed the Sierras for an Eastern hearing. From that point his success was steady. The story was 'The Jumping Frog of Calaveras.' It is now known and laughed over, I suppose, wherever the English language is spoken ; but it will never be as funny to anybody in print as it was to me, told for the first time by the unknown Twain himself, on that morning in the San Francisco Mint.''

HOW MUCH IS REAL IN BRET HARTE'S TALES.

Whether or not there ever really existed an innocent frog, wickedly filled with bird shot, for speculative purposes, by a designing man, it now appears that there certainly did exist a John Oakhurst, and that all the Bret Harte characters and incidents were drawn from life to a greater or less extent.

"'Greater or less' is perhaps the best way to answer the question,'' says their creator, thoughtfully, and this statement, like every other expression of opinion from him, is very emphatic, but very polite, in fact, almost deferential in tone. He is firm in his own conclusions, but as gentle in differing with you as an oriental potentate, who might beg you with tears in his

BRET HARTE'S DAUGHTERS, JESSAMY AND ETHEL. FROM A PHOTOGRAPH TAKEN SEVERAL YEARS AGO IN PLAINFIELD, N. J.

eyes to agree with him, and complacently drown you if you didn't.

"I may say with perfect truth," he adds, "that there were never any natural phenomena made use of in my novels of which I had not been personally cognizant, except one, and that was the bursting of the reservoir, in 'Gabriel Conroy.' But not a year had elapsed after the publication of the book before I received a letter from a man in Shasta County, California, asking how I happened to know so much about the flood that had occurred there, and stating that I had described many of its incidents to the very life. I have been credited with great powers of observation, and not a few discoveries in natural phenomena. Whether I am entitled to the credit or not, I cannot say. When I wrote, in 'The Tale of a Pony,'

'Bean pods are noisiest when dry,
And you always wink with your weakest eye,'

I did not dream that an eminent Philadelphia ophthalmologist would make this statement, which it appears is true, the subject of an essay before his society. Another eminent scientist who is interested in the elementary conditions of human nature, and the prehensile tendencies of babies' fingers, seriously corroborated my statement about the baby in 'The Luck of Roaring Camp,' which 'wrastled' with Kentuck's finger.

"My stories are true, however, not only in phenomena, but in characters. I do not pretend to say that many of my characters existed exactly as they are described, but I believe there is not one of them who did not have a real human being as a suggesting and starting point. Some of them, indeed, had several. John Oakhurst, for instance, was drawn quite closely from life. On one occasion, however, when a story in which he figures was being discussed, a friend of mine said : 'I know the original of Oakhurst—the man you took him from.'

"'Who?' said I.

"'Young I.——.'

"I was astounded. As a matter of fact, the gambler as portrayed was as good a picture, even to the limp, of young I.——, as of the actual original. The two men, you see, belonged to a class which had strongly marked characteristics, and were generally alike in dress and manner. And so with the others. Perhaps some of my heroes were slightly polished in the setting, and perhaps some of my heroines were somewhat idealized, but they all had an original existence outside of my brain and outside of my books. I know this, though I could not possibly tell you who the originals were or where they were found."

As Mr. Harte talks his hands become eloquent. The gestures are quiet and graceful, but arms, wrist, hands, and fingers come into continuous play. And when he finally lights upon his grievance—like every other man of note, he has a grievance—he becomes particularly earnest, and the gestures are slightly more emphatic.

HOW BRET HARTE WORKS AND DOES NOT WORK.

"I don't object to being written about as I am," he says, "but I particularly dislike being described as I am not. And, for some strange journalistic or human reason, the inventions concerning me seem to have much greater currency and vitality than the truths. Here, for instance," and he examines a pile of newspaper cuttings on the desk, "are two interesting contributions to my public history which came this morning."

The first, from "Galignani's Messenger," read as follows :

"Bret Harte cannot work except in seclusion, and when he is busy on a story he will hide himself away in some suburban retreat known only to his closest friends. Here he will rise just after dawn, be at his desk several hours before breakfast, and remain there, with an interval of an hour for a walk, the whole day."

"I meet this everywhere," said Mr. Harte, "and this," taking up a second cutting in its natural sequence :

"Bret Harte has reached a point where literary work is impossible to him except in absolute solitude. When writing he leaves his own home for suburban lodgings, where no visitor is allowed to trouble him, and where he follows a severe routine of early rising, scant diet, and steady work. It has been generally remarked that one can see this laborious regimen in his latter-day novels." This was from "The Argonaut," San Francisco.

"Now, what is diabolically ingenious in this," continues Mr. Harte, "is that those authoritative statements are untrue in every particular. I never seek seclusion. In fact, I could not work in seclusion. I rise at a civilized hour, about half-past eight o'clock, and eat my breakfast like any other human being. I then go to work, if I have a piece of work in hand, and remain at my desk till noon. I never work after luncheon. I read my proofs with as much interest and, I think, as much care as anybody else, and yet the public is taught to believe that I never see my 'copy' after it once leaves my hands.

"If newspapers were as anxious to print facts about a man as they are to furnish information which their readers will presumably enjoy repeating, it would be different. I won, some years ago, without the slightest effort on my part, the reputation of being the laziest man in America. At first the compliment took the form of an extended paragraph deploring my fatal facility, and telling in deprecating sentences how much I could probably do if I

BRET HARTE.   FROM A DRAWING BY ARTHUR JULE GOODMAN, 1894.

were not so indolent. This grew smaller and smaller, until it took a concise and easily annexable form, viz.: 'Bret Harte is the laziest man in America.' As an interesting adjunct to the personal column I read it, of course with extreme pleasure, in every paper that came habitually under my eye. Denial, of course, was of no earthly use, and the line travelled all over the country, and is doubtless still on its rounds. In the course of time, on a lecturing tour, I reached St. Joe, Missouri. I had been lecturing by night and travelling by day for ten weeks, continuously. A reporter called and desired to know what kind of soap I used—he had heard sinister rumors that it was a highly scented foreign article my opinion of Longfellow, and various other questions of moment. I assured him that I used the soap of the hotel, and concealed nothing from him with regard to Longfellow, but begged him particularly to note the fact of my preternatural activity. He managed these facts correctly in his half-column next morning, but adorned me with a glittering diamond stud of which I had no knowledge. And in the same paper, in another column, I found a pleasant variation from the usual line. There was no allusion to my late labors. It was simply : 'Bret Harte *says* he is not the laziest man in America.' Altogether, therefore, I should perhaps think well of my friend of St. Joe, Missouri.

"Those lectures were an amusing experience," he adds, laughing. "What the people expected in me I do not know. Possibly a six-foot mountaineer, with a voice and lecture in proportion. They always seemed to have mentally confused me with one of my own characters. I am not six feet high, and I do not wear a beard. Whenever I walked out before a strange audience there was a general sense of disappointment, a gasp of astonishment that I could feel, and it always took at least fifteen minutes before they recovered from their surprise sufficiently to listen to what I had to say. I think, even now, that if I had been more herculean in proportions, with a red shirt and top boots, many of those audiences would have felt a deeper thrill from my utterances and a deeper conviction that they had obtained the worth of their money."

A MAN CAREFUL OF DETAILS IN HIS WORK AND HIS PERSON.

The conversation rambles. A polished critic, an epicurean, a man of the world, and carrying everywhere the independence of a distinct literary personality, Bret Harte talks as he writes, like a gentleman. This is a subtile attribute, but one which England never fails to recognize and value, and it is one prime cause of the popularity of his works in the United Kingdom. Continually in evidence also is his distinguishing characteristic, one which is only described by the word "nicety"—nicety in dress, nicety in speech, nicety in thought. This artistic precision and thoughtful attention to details is the most marked attribute of the man, and from it you understand the plane and power of his work. Without it, the most impressive of his stories, "The Luck of Roaring Camp," for instance, could not possibly have been written. It is rather a singular quality to be found in combination with his emotional breadth and dramatic sweep as a writer, but it is the one which finishes and polishes the whole, and it is clearly natural and inherent.

THE CIVIL WAR A GREAT OPPORTUNITY FOR AMERICAN NOVELISTS.

Perhaps the most valuable of all Mr. Harte's ideas are his opinions concerning the literary field of to-day. His views of literature as a profession are now pleasantly optimistic, possibly through the businesslike way in which his interests have long been handled by that most skilful of literary agents, Mr. A. P. Watt. Contemporary life in its highest social aspects he looks upon, however, as most unpromising material for romantic treatment.

"In America," he says, "the great field is the late war. The dramatists have found and utilized it, but the novelists, the romance writers, have in it the richest possible field for works of serious import, and yet, outside of short stories, they seem to have passed it by. If I had time, nothing would please me better than to go over the ground, or portions of it, and make use of it for future work. Our war of the Revolution is not good material for cosmopolitan purposes. This country has never quite forgotten the way in which it ended. But the war of the Rebellion was our own and is our own ; its dramatic and emotional aspects are infinite; and while American writers are coming abroad for scenes to picture, I am in constant fear that some Englishman or Frenchman will go to America and reap the field in romance which we should now, all local feeling having passed away, be utilizing to our own fame and profit."

GEORGE DU MAURIER.

From a photograph by Fradelle & Young, taken for "McClure's Magazine" at Mr. Du Maurier's home.

THE AUTHOR OF "TRILBY."

AN AUTOBIOGRAPHIC INTERVIEW WITH MR. GEORGE DU MAURIER.

The illustrations in this article are from photographs made especially for "McClure's Magazine."

BY ROBERT H. SHERARD

AS I crossed the heath, I passed a group of devout people to whom, standing among them, a Salvation Army girl, with an inspired face, was preaching with great fervor. I did not stay to listen to her, for George du Maurier had appointed me to meet him at his house at three on that Sunday afternoon. But as I went my way, I heard the words: "Never you envy even those who seem most to be envied in this world, for in even the happiest life . . ." and that was all.

Du Maurier's house is in a quiet little street that leads from the open heath down to the township of Hampstead, a street of few houses and of high walls, with trees everywhere, and an air of seclusion and quiet over all. The house stands on the left hand as one walks away from the heath, and is in the angle formed by the quiet street and a lane which leads down to the high road. It is a house of bricks overgrown with ivy, with angles and protrusions, and in the little garden which is to the left of the entrance door stands a large tree. The front door, which opens straight on to the street, is painted white, and is fitted with brass knockers of polished brilliance. As one enters the house, one notices on the wall to the left, just after the threshold is crossed, the original of one of Du Maurier's drawings in "Punch," a drawing concerning two "millionnairesses," with the text written beneath the picture in careful, almost lithographic penmanship.

"That was where I received my training in literature," said Du Maurier. "So Anstey pointed out to me the other day, when I told him how surprised I was at the success of my books, considering that I had never written before. 'Never written!' he cried out. 'Why, my dear Du Maurier, you have been writing all your life, and the best of writing-practice at that. Those little dialogues of yours, which week after week you have fitted to your drawings in 'Punch,' have prepared you admirably. It was *précis* writing, and gave you conciseness and repartee and appositeness, and the best qualities of the writer of fiction.' And," added Du Maurier, "I believe Anstey was quite right, now that I come to think of it."

The waiting-room, or hall, is under an arch, to the right of the passage which leads from the door to the staircase, a cosy corner on which a large model of the Venus of Milo looks down. "There is my great admiration," said Du Maurier in the evening, as he pointed to the armless goddess, and went on to repeat what Heine has said, and mentioned Heine's desire for the Venus's armless embrace.

DU MAURIER IN HIS STUDY.

It was in his study that Du Maurier received me, a large room on the first floor, with a square bay window overlooking the quiet street on the right, and a large window almost reaching to the ceiling, and looking in the direction of the heath, facing the door. It is under this window, the light from which is toned down by brown curtains, that Du Maurier's table stands, comfortably equipped and tidy. On a large blotting-pad lay a thin copy-book, open, and one could see that the right page was covered with large, round-hand writing, whilst on the left page there were, in smaller, more precise penmanship, corrections, emendations, addenda. In a frame stood a large photograph of Du Maurier, and on the other side of the ink-stand was a pile of thin copy-books, blue and red. " A fortnight's work on my new novel," said Du Maurier.

A luxurious room it was, with thick carpets and inviting arm-chairs, the walls covered with stamped leather, and hung with many of the master's drawings in quiet frames. In one corner a water-color portrait, by Du Maurier, of Canon Ainger, and, from the same brush, the picture of a lady with a violin, on the wall to the left of the decorative fireplace, from over which, in the place of honor, another, smaller, model of the armless Venus looks down. To the right is a grand piano, and elsewhere other furniture of noticeable style, and curtains, screens, and ornaments. A beautiful room, in fact, and within it is none of the litter of the man of letters or of the painter.

It was here that I first saw Du Maurier, a quiet man of no great stature, who at the first sight of him impresses one as a man who has suffered greatly, haunted by some evil dream or disturbing apprehension. His welcome is gentle and kindly, but he does not smile, even when he is saying a clever and smile-provoking thing. "You must smoke. One smokes here. It is a studio." Those were amongst the first words that Du Maurier said, and there was hospitality in them and the freemasonry of letters.

DU MAURIER'S FAMILY.

" My full name is George Louis Palmella Busson du Maurier, but we were of very small nobility. My name Palmella was given to me in remembrance of the great friendship between my father's sister and the Duchesse de Palmella, who was the wife of the Portuguese ambassador to France. Our real family name is Busson ; the ' Du Maurier ' comes from the Chateau le Maurier, built some time in the fifteenth century, and still standing in Anjou or Maine, but a brewery to-day. It belonged to our cousins the Auberys, and in the seventeenth century it was the Auberys who wore the title of Du Maurier ; and an Aubery du Maurier who distinguished himself in that century was Louis of that name, who was French ambassador to Holland, and was well liked of the great king. The Auberys and the Bussons married and intermarried, and I cannot quite say without referring to family papers—at present at my bank—when the Bussons assumed the territorial name of Du Maurier ; but my grandfather's name was Robert Mathurin Busson du Maurier, and his name is always followed, in the papers which refer to him, by the title *Gentilhomme verrier*—gentleman glass-blower. For until the Revolution glass-blowing was a monopoly of the *gentilhommes;* that is to say, no commoner might engage in this industry, at that time considered an art. You know the old French saying :

> ' Pour souffler un verre
> Il faut être gentilhomme.' "

" A year or two ago," continued Du Maurier, " I was over in Paris with Burnand and Furniss, and we went into Notre Dame, and as we were examining some of the gravestones with which one of the aisles is in places laid, I came upon a Busson who had been buried there, and on the stone was carved our coat-of-arms, but it was almost all effaced, and there only remained, clearly distinguishable, the black lion, my black lion." It may be added that the Busson genealogy dates from the twelfth century. Du Maurier, though, does not take the subject of descent too seriously. " One is never quite sure," he says, with the shadow of a smile, " about one's descent. So many accidents occur. I made use of many of the names which occur in the papers concerning my family history, in ' Peter Ibbetson.'

" My father was a small *rentier*, whose income was derived from our glass-works in Anjou. He was born in England, for his father had fled to England to escape the guillotine when the Revolution broke out, and they returned to France in 1816. My grandmother was a *bourgeoise*. Her name was Bruaire, and she descended from Jean Bart, the admiral. My grandfather was not a rich man. Indeed, whilst he was in England he had mainly to depend on the liberality of the British Government, which allowed him a pension of twenty

MR. DU MAURIER'S HOUSE ON HAMPSTEAD HEATH.

pounds a year for each member of his family. He died in the post of schoolmaster at Tours.

CHILDHOOD AND YOUTH.

" My mother was an Englishwoman, and was married to my father at the British Embassy in Paris, and I was born in Paris, on March 6, 1834, in a little house in the Champs-Elysées. It bore the number 80. It was afterwards sold by my father, and has since been pulled down. I often look at the spot when I am in Paris and am walking down the Champs-Elysées, and what I most regret at such times are the pine trees which in my childhood used to be there—very different from the miserable, stumpy avenue of to-day. It is a dis-

illusion which comes upon me with equal force at each new visit, for I remember the trees, and the trees only. Indeed, I only lived in the house of my birth for two years, for in 1836 my parents removed to Belgium, and here I remember with peculiar vividness a Belgian man-servant of ours, called Francis. I used to ask him to take me in his arms and to carry me down-stairs to look at some beautiful birds. I used to think that these were real birds each time that I looked at them, although, in fact, they were but painted on the panes, and I had been told so. I remember another childish hallucination. I used to sleep in my parents' room, and when I turned my face to the wall, a door in the wall used to open, and a *charbonnier*, a coal-man, big and black, used to come and take me up and carry me down a long, winding staircase, into a kitchen, where his wife and children were, and treated me very kindly. In truth, there was neither door, nor *charbonnier*, nor kitchen. It was an hallucination; yet it possessed me again and again.

"We stayed three years in Belgium, and when I was five years old I went with my parents to London, where my father took a house—the house which a year later was taken by Charles Dickens—1 Devonshire Terrace, Marylebone Road. Of my life here I best remember that I used to go out riding in the park, on a little pony, escorted by a groom, who led my pony by a strap, and that I did not like to be held in leash this way, and tried to get away. One day when I was grumbling at the groom, he said I was to be a good boy, for there was the Queen surrounded by her lords; and he added : ' Master Georgie, take off your hat to the Queen and all her lords.' And then cantered past a young woman surrounded by horsemen. I waved my hat, and the young woman smiled and kissed her hand to me. It was the Queen and her equerries.

"We only stayed a year in Devonshire Terrace, for my father grew very poor. He was a man of scientific tastes, and lost his money in inventions which never came to anything. So we had to wander forth again, and this time we went to Boulogne, and there we lived in a beautiful house at the top of the Grande Rue. I had sunny hours there, and was very happy. It is a part of my life which I shall describe in one of my books.

"Much of my childhood is related in ' Peter Ibbetson.' My favorite book was the ' Swiss Family Robinson,' and next, ' Robinson Crusoe.' I used to devour these books.

DU MAURIER A LATE SPEAKER.

"I was a late speaker. My parents must have thought me dumb. And one day I surprised them all by coming out with a long sentence. It was, '*Papa est allé chez le boucher pour acheter de la viande pour maman,*' and so astonished everybody."

George du Maurier has recently again astonished everybody in a similar way, coming forth loud and articulate and strong, after a long silence, which one fancied was to be forever prolonged.

"We used to speak both French and English at home, and I was brought up in both languages.

"From Boulogne we went to Paris, to live in an apartment on the first floor of the house No. 108 in the Champs-Elysées. The house still stands, but the ground floor is now a *café*, and the first floor is part of it. I feel sorry when I look up at the windows from which my dear mother's face used to watch for my return from school, and see waiters bustling about and my home invaded.

"I went to school at the age of thirteen, in the Pension Froussard, in the Avenue du Bois de Boulogne. It was kept by a man called Froussard, a splendid fellow, whom I admired immensely and remember with affection and gratitude. He became a deputy after the Revolution of 1848. He was assisted in the school-work by his son, who was also one of the heroes of my youthful days, another splendid fellow. I was a lazy lad, with no particular bent, and may say that I worked really hard for one year. I made a number of friends, of course, but of my comrades at the Pension Froussard, only one distinguished himself in after life. He was a big boy, two years my senior. His name was Louis Becque de Fouquière. He distinguished himself in literature, and edited André Chénier's poems. His life has recently been written by Anatole France.

"Yes, I am ashamed to say that I did not distinguish myself at school. I shall write my school life in my new novel ' The Martians.' At the age of seventeen I went up for my *bachot*, my baccalaureate degree, at the Sorbonne, and was plucked for my written Latin version. It is true that my nose began to bleed during the examination, and that upset me, and, besides, the professor who was in charge of the room had got an idea into his head that I had smuggled a ' crib ' in, and kept watching me so carefully that I got nervous and flurried. My poor mother was very vexed with me for my failure, for we were very poor at that time, and it was important that I should do well. My father was then in England, and shortly after my discomfiture he wrote for me to join him there. We had not informed him of my failure, and I felt very miserable as I crossed, because I thought that he would be very angry with me. He met me at the landing at London Bridge, and, at the sight of my utterly woe-begone face, guessed the truth, and burst out into a roar of laughter. I think that this roar of laughter gave me the greatest pleasure I ever experienced in all my life.

" You see my father was a scientific man, and hated everything that was not science, and despised all books, the classics not less than others, which were not on scientific subjects. I, on the other hand, was fond of books—of some books, at least. When I was quite a boy, I was enthusiastic about Byron, and used to read out 'The Giaour' and 'Don Juan' to my mother for hours together. I knew the shipwreck scene in 'Don Juan' by heart, and recited it again and again ; and though my admiration for Byron has passed, I still greatly delight in that magnificent passage. I can recite every word of it even now. Then came Shelley, for whom my love has lasted, and then Tennyson, for whom my admiration has never wavered, and will last all my life, though now I qualify him with Browning. Swinburne was a revelation to me. When his 'Poems and Ballads' appeared, I was literally frantic about him, but that has worn off.

" My father, then, never reproached me for my failure in the *bachot* examination, indeed, never once alluded to it. He had made up his mind that I was intended for a scientist, and determined to make me one. So he put me as a pupil at the Birkbeck Chemical Laboratory of University College, where I studied chemistry under Dr. Williamson. I am afraid that I was a most unsatisfactory pupil, for I took no interest at all in the work, and spent almost all my time in drawing caricatures. I drew all my life, I may say ; it was my favorite occupation and pastime. Dr. Williamson thought me a very unsatisfactory student at chemistry, but he was greatly amused with my caricatures, and we got on very well together.

" My ambition at that time was to go in for music and singing, but my father objected very strongly to this wish of mine, and invariably discouraged it. My father, I must tell you, possessed himself the sweetest, most beautiful voice that I have ever heard ; and, if he had taken up singing as a profession, would most certainly have been the greatest singer of his time. Indeed, in his youth he had studied music for some time at the Paris Conservatoire,

THE DRAWING-ROOM IN MR. DU MAURIER'S HOUSE.
From a photograph by Fradelle & Young, London.

but his family objected to his following the profession, for they were Legitimists and strong Catholics, and you know in what contempt the stage was held at the beginning of this century. It is a pity, for there were millions in his throat.

"We were all musical in our family: my father, my sister (the sister who married Clement Scott, a most gifted pianiste), and then myself. I was at that time crazy about music, and used to practise my voice wherever and whenever I could, even on the tops of omnibuses. But my father always discouraged me. I remember one night we were crossing Smithfield Market together, and I was talking to my father about music. 'I am sure that I could become a singer,' I said, 'and if you like I will prove it to you. I have my tuning-fork in my pocket. Shall I show you my A?'

"'Yes,' said my father, 'I should like to hear your idea of an A.' So I sang the note. My father laughed. 'Do you call that an A? Let me show you how to sing it.' And then and there rang out a note of music, low and sweet at the onset, and swelling as it went, till it seemed to fill all Smithfield with divine melody. I can never forget that scene, never: the dark night, the lonely place, and that wave of the sweetest sound that my ears have ever heard.

"Sometime later my father relented and gave me a few music lessons. I won him over by showing him a drawing which I had produced in Williamson's class-room, in which I was represented bowing gracefully in acknowledgment of the applause of an audience whom I had electrified with my musical talents. Music has always been a great delight to me, and until recently I could sing well. But I have spoiled my voice by cigarette-smoking.

"My poor father, I may add, as I am speaking of his musical powers, died in my arms—as he was singing one of Count de Ségur's drinking songs. He left this world almost with music on his lips.

"I remained at the Birkbeck Laboratory for two years, that is to say till 1854, when

MR. DU MAURIER AT HIS DRAWING-TABLE.

From a photograph by Fradelle & Young, London.

my father, who was still convinced that I had a great future before me in the pursuit of science, set me up on my account in a chemical laboratory in Bard's Yard, Bucklersbury, in the city. The house is still there; I saw it a few days ago. It was a fine laboratory, for my father being a poor man naturally fitted it up in the most expensive style, with all sorts of instruments. In the midst of my brightly-polished apparatus here I sat, and in the long intervals between business drew and drew.

"The only occasion on which the sage of Bard's Yard was able to render any real service to humanity was when he was engaged by the directors of a company for working certain gold mines in Devonshire which were being greatly 'boomed,' and to which the public was subscribing heavily, to go down to Devonshire to assay the ore. I fancy they expected me to send them a report likely to further tempt the public.

If this was their expectation they were mistaken; for after a few experiments, I went back to town and told them that there was not a vestige of gold in the ore. The directors were of course very dissatisfied with this statement, and insisted on my returning to Devonshire to make further investigation. I went and had a good time of it down in the country, for the miners were very jolly fellows; but I was unable to satisfy my employers, and sent up a report which showed the public that the whole thing was a swindle, and so saved a good many people from loss.

ADOPTS ART AS A PROFESSION—THE LOSS OF HIS EYE.

" My poor father died in 1856, and at the age of twenty-two I returned to Paris and went to live with my mother in the Rue Paradis-Poissonnière. We were very poor, and very dull and dismal it was. However, it was not long before I entered upon what was the best time of my life. That is when, having decided to follow art as a profession, I entered Gleyre's studio to study drawing and painting. Those were my joyous Quartier Latin days, spent in the charming society of Poynter, Whistler, Armstrong, Lamont, and others. I have described Gleyre's studio in 'Trilby.' For Gleyre I had a great admiration, and at that time thought his 'Illusions Perdues' a veritable masterpiece, though I hardly think so now.

"My happy Quartier Latin life lasted only one year, for in 1857 we went to Antwerp, and here I worked at the Antwerp Academy under De Keyser and Van Lerius. And it was on a day in Van Lerius's studio that the great tragedy of my life occurred."

The voice of Du Maurier, who till then had been chatting with animation, suddenly fell, and over the face came an indefinable expression of mingled terror and anger and sorrow.

"I was drawing from a model, when suddenly the girl's head seemed to me to dwindle to the size of a walnut. I clapped my hand over my left eye. Had I been mistaken? I could see as well as ever. But when in its turn I covered my right eye, I learned what had happened. My left eye had failed me; it might be alto-

MR. DU MAURIER'S STUDIO IN HIS HOUSE AT HAMPSTEAD HEATH.
From a photograph by Fradelle & Young, London.

gether lost. It was so sudden a blow that I was as thunderstruck. Seeing my dismay, Van Lerius came up and asked me what might be the matter; and when I told him, he said that it was nothing, that he had had that himself, and so on. And a doctor whom I anxiously consulted that same day comforted me, and said that the accident was a passing one. However, my eye grew worse and worse, and the fear of total blindness beset me constantly."

It was with a movement akin to a shudder that Du Maurier spoke these words, and my mind went back to what I had heard from the girl-preacher as I crossed the heath, as in the same low tones and with the same indefinable expression he continued:

"That was the most tragic event of my life. It has poisoned all my existence."

Du Maurier, as though to shake off a troubling obsession, rose from his chair, and walked about the room, cigarette in hand.

"In the spring of 1859 we heard of a great specialist who lived in Düsseldorf, and we went to see him. He examined my eyes, and he said that though the left eye was certainly lost, I had no reason to fear losing the other, but that I must be very careful, and not drink beer, and not eat cheese, and so on. It was very comforting to know that I was not to be blind, but I have never quite shaken off the terror of that apprehension.

MAKING HIS OWN WAY IN LIFE.

"In the following year I felt that the time had come for me to earn my own living, and so one day I asked my mother to give me ten pounds to enable me to go to London, and told her that I should never ask her for any more money. She did not want me to go, and as to never asking for money, she begged me not to make any such resolution. Poor woman, she would have given me her last penny. But it happened that I never had occasion to ask her assistance; on the contrary, the time came when I was able to add to the comforts of her existence.

"My first lodging in London was in Newman Street, where I shared rooms with Whistler. I afterwards moved to rooms in Earl's Terrace, in the house where Walter Pater died. I began contributing to 'Once a Week' and to 'Punch' very soon after my arrival in London, and shockingly bad my drawing was at the time. My first drawing in 'Punch' appeared in June, 1860, and represented Whistler and myself going into a photographer's studio. The photographer is very angry with us for smoking, and says that his is not an ordinary studio, where one smokes and is disorderly.

"My life was a very prosperous one from the outset in London. I was married in 1863, and my wife and I never once knew financial troubles. My only trouble has been my fear about my eyes. Apart from that I have been very happy."

As Du Maurier was speaking, his second son, Charles, a tall, handsome youth of distinguished manners, entered the room.

"Ah, that is the 'Mummer,' as we call him," said Du Maurier. "Charles is playing in 'Money' at the Garrick, and doing well. He draws three pounds a week, and that's more than my eldest son, who is in the army, is earning."

The conversation turned on the stage. "When I went to consult my old friend John Hare about letting Charles go on the stage," said Du Maurier, "Hare said that provided one can get to the top of the tree, the stage is the most delightful profession; but that for the actor who only succeeds moderately, it is the most miserable, pothouse existence imaginable.

CONNECTION WITH "PUNCH"—A GLIMPSE OF THACKERAY.

"Most of the jokes in 'Punch' are my own, but a good many are sent to me, which I twist and turn into form. But Postlethwaite, Bunthorne, Mrs. Ponsonby Tomkyns, Sir Georgeous Midas, and the other characters associated with my drawings, are all my own creations.

"I have made many interesting friends during my long life in London, and the lecture which I have delivered all over England contains many anecdotes about them. I never met Charles Dickens to speak to him, and only saw him once; that was at Leech's funeral. Thackeray I also met only once, at the house of Mrs. Sartoris. Mrs. Sartoris, who was Adelaide Kemble, and Hamilton Aïdé, who knew of my immense admiration for Thackeray, wanted to introduce me to him, but I refused. I was too diffident. I was so little, and he was so great. But all that evening I remained as close to him as possible, greedily listening to his words. I remember that during the evening an American came up to him—rather a common sort of man—and claimed acquaint-ance. Thackeray received him most cordially, and invited him to dinner. I envied that American. And my admira-tion for Thackeray increased when, as it was getting late, he turned to his two daughters, Minnie and Annie, and said to them, '*Allons, mesdemoiselles, il est temps de s'en aller,*' with the best French accent I have ever heard in an Englishman's mouth.

"Leech was, of course, one of my inti-mates; my mas-ter, I may say, for to some ex-tent my work was modelled on his. I spent the autumn of the year which preceded his death with him at Whitby. He was not very funny, but was kind, amiable, and genial, a delightful man.

"I shall never forget the scene at his funeral. Dean Hole was officiating, and as the first sod fell with a sounding thud on the coffin of our dear, dear friend, Millais, who was stand-ing on the edge of the grave, burst out sob-bing. It was as a signal, for, the moment after, each man in that great concourse of mourners was sobbing also. It was a memorable sight."

AN ALCOVE IN THE DRAWING-ROOM OF DU MAURIER'S HOUSE.
From a photograph by Fradelle & Young, London.

NOVEL-WRITING—THE PLOT OF "TRILBY" OFFERED TO HENRY JAMES.

Then, going on to speak of his literary work, Du Maurier said, "Nobody more than myself was surprised at the great success of my novels. I never expected anything of the sort. I did not know that I could write. I had no idea that I had had any experiences worth recording. The circumstances under which I came to write are curious. I was walking one evening with Henry James up and down the High Street in Bayswater—I had made James's acquaintance much in the same way as I have made yours. James said that he had great difficulty in finding plots for his stories. 'Plots!' I exclaimed, 'I am full of plots;' and I went on to tell him the plot of 'Trilby.' 'But you ought to write that story,' cried James. 'I can't write,' I said, 'I have never writ-ten. If you like the plot so much you may take it.' But James would not take it; he said it was too valuable a pres-ent, and that I must write the story myself.

"Well, on reaching home that night I set to work, and by the next morn-ing I had writ-ten the first two numbers of 'Peter Ibbet-son.' It seemed all to flow from my pen, with-out effort, in a full stream. But I thought it must be poor stuff, and I de-termined to look for an omen to learn whether any success would attend this new departure. So I walked out into the garden, and the very first thing that I saw was a large wheelbarrow, and that comforted me and reassured me; for, as you will remem-ber, there is a wheelbarrow in the first chapter of 'Peter Ibbetson.'

"Some time later I was dining with Osgood, and he said, 'I hear, Du Maurier, that you are writing stories,' and asked me to let him see something. So 'Peter Ibbetson' was sent over to America and was accepted at once. Then 'Trilby' followed, and the 'boom' came, a 'boom' which surprised me immensely, for I never took myself *au sérieux* as a novelist. In-deed, this 'boom' rather distresses me when I reflect that Thackeray never had a 'boom.' And I hold that a 'boom' means nothing as a sign of literary excellence, nothing but money."

Du Maurier writes at irregular intervals, and in such moments as he can snatch from his "Punch" work. "For," he says, "I am taking more pains than ever over my drawing." And so saying, he fetched an album in which he showed me the elaborate preparation, in the way of studies

DU MAURIER'S "SIGNATURE" AS CARVED, ALONG WITH THE SIGNATURES OF OTHER MEMBERS OF THE "PUNCH" STAFF, ON THE TABLE FROM WHICH THE WEEKLY "PUNCH" DINNER IS EATEN.

and sketches, for a cartoon which was to appear in a week or two in his paper. One figure, from a female model, had been drawn several times. There was here the infinite capacity for taking pains. "I usually write on the top of the piano, standing, and I never look at my manuscript as I write, partly to spare my eyes, and partly because the writing seems literally to flow from my pen. My best time is just after lunch. My writing is frequently interrupted, and I walk about the studio and smoke, and then back to the manuscript once more. Afterwards I revise, very carefully now, for I am taking great pains with my new book. 'The Martians' is to be a very long book, and I cannot say when it will be finished."

A summons from Mrs. du Maurier to the drawing-room, where tea was served, here interrupted the conversation. A comfortable room, with amiable people whom one seemed to recognize. Over the mantel three portraits of Du Maurier's children, by himself. "*Les voilà*," he said, not without pride. Above these a water-color picture of the character of the drawings in "Punch." "It has been hawked round all over America and England," said Du Maurier of this picture, "at exhibitions and places, but nobody would buy it."

A MAN AT HIS BEST AFTER FORTY.

Over the fire in the comfortable room the conversation touched on many things.

"Every book which is worth anything," said Du Maurier, "has had its original life." And again, "I think that the best years in a man's life are after he is forty. So Trollope used to say. Does Daudet say so too? A man at forty has ceased to hunt the moon. I would add that in order to enjoy life after forty, it is perhaps necessary to have achieved, before reaching that age, at least some success." He spoke of the letters he has been receiving since the "boom," and said that on an average he received five letters a day from America, of a most flattering description. "Some of my correspondents, however, don't give a man his 'du'," he remarked, with a shadow of a smile.

Du Maurier speaks willingly and enthusiastically about literature. He is an ardent admirer of Stevenson, and quoted with gusto the passage in "Kidnapped" where the scene between David Balfour and Cluny is described. "One would have to look at one's guests," he said, "before inviting them, if not precisely satisfied with one's hospitality, to step outside and take their measure. Imagine me proposing such an arrangement to a giant like Val Prinsep."

The day on which he is able to devote most time to writing is Thursday. "*C'est mon grand jour.*" On Wednesdays he is engaged with a model; a female model comes every Friday.

It is characteristic of the man that he should work with such renewed application at his old craft, in spite of the fact that circumstances have thrown wide open to him the gates of a new career.

He reminds one as to physique, and in certain manifestations of a very nervous temperament, of another giant worker, whose name is Émile Zola.

But he is altogether original and himself, a strong and striking individuality, a man altogether deserving of his past and present good fortune.

A. CONAN DOYLE AND ROBERT BARR.

REAL CONVERSATION BETWEEN THEM.

RECORDED BY MR. BARR.

IN the very beginning I wish to set down the fact that I am not a professional interviewer, but that I have some acquaintance with the principles of the art. The observant reader will notice that I understand the business, because I have managed to run in five capital "I's" in the first few lines of this article. There you have the whole secret of interviewing as practiced A.D. 1894, in England. The successful interviewer blazons forth as much of his own personality as possible, using his vic-

BARR AND DOYLE AT DR. DOYLE'S HOUSE, SOUTH NORWOOD. FROM A PHOTOGRAPH BY FRADELLE & YOUNG, 246 REGENT STREET, LONDON, W.

tim as a peg on which to hang his own opinions. If the interviewer could be induced to hang himself as well as his opinions, the world would be brighter and better. I loathe the English pompous interview.

But the interview in England is an imported article; it is not native to the soil. In America you get the real thing, and even the youngest newspaper man understands how it should be done. An interviewer should be like a clear sheet of plate glass that forms the front window of an attractive store, through which you can see the articles displayed, scarcely suspecting that anything stands between you and the interesting collection.

Yet some people are never satisfied, and there arose a man in the United States who resolved to invent a new kind of interview. His name is S. S. McClure, and he is the owner and editor of this Magazine. I hope 1 may be allowed to praise or abuse a man in his own magazine, and I hereby give him warning that if he cuts out or changes a line of my copy I will never write another word for him. He may disclaim what I say in any other portion of this periodical, if he likes, but I alone am responsible for this section. He would have no hesitation in asking Gabriel to write him an article on the latest thing in trumpets, and the remarkable thing is, he would actually get the manuscript.

So one day S. S. McClure invented what he thought was a new style of interview, which he patented under the title of "Real Conversations." The almanac of the future, which sprinkles choice bits of information among weather predictions and signs of the zodiac, will have this line: "April 14, 1893—Real Conversations invented by S. S. McClure."

Yet the idea was not new; we all have practiced it as boys. We got two dogs together who held different opinions on social matters, and urged them to discuss the question, while we stood by and enjoyed the argument. This is what McClure now does with two writers, and the weapon in the Real Conversation, as in the dog-fight, is the jaw.

The only fault that I have to find with these Real Conversations is that they are not conversations, and that they cannot be real. Try to imagine two sane men sitting down deliberately to talk for publication! Only a master mind could have conceived such a situation—a mind like that of Mr. McClure, accustomed to accomplishing the impossible. Now, if he were to station a

shorthand reporter behind a screen, as Louis XI. placed Quentin Durward when the king interviewed the Count of Crevecœur, he might perhaps get a Real Conversation, but otherwise I don't see how it is to be done.

To show the practical difficulties that meet a Real Conversationalist at the very beginning, I pulled out my note-book and pencil, and, looking across at my victim, solemnly said:

"Now, Conan Doyle, talk."

Instead of complying with my most reasonable request, the novelist threw back his head and laughed, and, impressed as I was with the momentousness of the occasion, so hearty and infectious is his laugh that after a few moments I was compelled to join him.

We had looted two comfortable wicker chairs from the house, and were seated at the farther end of the long lawn that stretches from the Doyle residence towards the city of London. It is one of those smooth, exceedingly green, velvety lawns to be found only in England, yet easy of manufacture there; for, as the Oxford gardener said to the American visitor, all you have to do is to leave the lawn outdoors for five hundred years or so, cutting and rolling it frequently, and there you are. Little, white, hard rubber golf balls lay about on the grass, like croquet balls that had shrunk from exposure to the weather. Mr. Doyle is a golf inebriate, and practices on this lawn, landing the balls in a tub when he makes the right sort of a hit, and generally breaking a window when he doesn't.

I put away my note-book and pencil.

"I have a proposal to make," I said. "You and I have frequently set the world right, and solved all the problems, with no magazine editor to make us afraid. We have talked in your garden and in mine, at your hospitable board and at mine, at your club and at mine, on your golf ground and —yes, I remember now, I haven't one of my own; now I know your views on things pretty well, so I will 'fake' a Real Conversation, as we say in the States."

"But that wouldn't be quite fair to McClure's readers, would it?" objected Doyle, who is an honest man and has never had the advantage of a newspaper training. "I read all of those Real Conversations in the magazine, and I thought them most interesting. The idea seems to me a good one."

"Now that ought to show you how easy it will be for me to make up a Real Conversation with you. Your opinion and mine are always the opposite of each other. All I would have to do would be to remember what I thought on any subject, then write something entirely different, and I would have Conan Doyle. That proves to me the hollowness of the other interviews McClure has published. Howells agreed with Boyesen, Hamlin Garland agreed with James Whitcomb Riley, and so on all along the line. This isn't natural. No literary man ever agrees with any other literary man. He sometimes pretends to to attain; his criticism, even if severe, would be helpful and intelligent. A schoolboy, on the other hand, seems to give his verdict on a book by intuition, but he rarely makes a mistake. See how the schoolboys of the world have made "Treasure Island" their own. Of course, I would not expect an accurate estimate of "Robert Elsmere" from a schoolboy.

Barr. I suppose an author would hardly like to slate another author's work—publicly. Besides, he would be compelled, as

A CORNER OF DR. DOYLE'S DRAWING ROOM. FROM A PHOTOGRAPH BY ELLIOTT & FRY, BAKER STREET, LONDON, W.

like the books another fellow has written, but that is all humbug. He doesn't in his heart; he knows he could have done them better himself."

"Oh, you're all wrong there; all wrong —entirely wrong! Now, if I had to choose my critics, I would choose my fellow-workers, or schoolboys."

"Just what I said. You are placing the other authors on a level with schoolboys! That is worse than——"

Doyle. Listen to me. A fellow-author knows the difficulties I have to contend with; he appreciates the effect I am trying a matter of self-protection, to keep up the pretence that there is such a thing as literature in England at the present moment. But there is Mr. Howells, who has no English axe to grind, and he, from the calm, serene, unprejudiced atmosphere of New York, frankly admits that literature in England is a thing of the past, and that the authors of to-day do not understand even the rudiments of their business. Of course you agree with him?

Doyle. I think there never was a time when there was a better promise. There are at least a dozen men and women who have made a deep mark, and who are still young. No one can say how far they may go. Some of them are sure to develop, for the past shows us that fiction is an art which improves up to the age of fifty or so. With fuller knowledge of life comes greater power in describing it.

Barr. A dozen! You always were a generous man, Doyle. Who are the talented twelve, so that I may cable to Howells?

Doyle. There are more than a dozen —Barrie, Kipling, Mrs. Olive Schreiner, Sarah Grand, Miss Harraden, Gilbert Parker, Quiller-Couch, Hall Caine, Stevenson, Stanley Weyman, Anthony Hope, Crockett, Rider Haggard, Jerome, Zangwill, Clark Russell, George Moore—many of them under thirty and few of them much over it. There are others, of course. These names just happen to occur to me.

DR. JOSEPH BELL, THE ORIGINAL OF SHERLOCK HOLMES. FROM A PHOTOGRAPH BY A. SWAN WATSON, EDINBURGH.

Barr. You think a man improves up to fifty?

Doyle. Certainly, if he keeps out of a groove and refuses to do his work in a mechanical way. Why, many of the greatest writers in our fiction did not begin until after forty. Thackeray was about forty. Scott was past forty. Charles Reade and George Eliot were as much. Richardson was fifty. To draw life, one must know it.

Barr. My experience is that when a man is fifty he knows he will improve until he is sixty, and when he is sixty he feels that improvement will keep right on until he is seventy; whereas, when he is twenty he *thinks* that perhaps he will know more when he is thirty, but is not sure. Man is an amusing animal. Now I would like an American dozen, if you don't mind.

Doyle. I have not read a book for a long time that has stirred me as much as Miss Wilkins's "Pembroke." I think she is a very great writer. It is always

SHERLOCK HOLMES. FROM A PHOTOGRAPH OF A BUST BY WILKINS.

risky to call a recent book a classic, but this one really seems to me to have every characteristic of one.

Barr. Well?

Doyle. Well!

Barr. That is only one. Don't you read American fiction?

Doyle. Not as much as I should wish, very superficial things, and good old human nature is always there under a coat of varnish. When one hears of a literature of the West or of the South, it sounds aggressively sectional.

Barr. Sectional? If it comes to that, who could be more sectional than Hardy or Barrie—the one giving us the literature of

DR. DOYLE IN HIS STUDY. FROM A PHOTOGRAPH BY FRADELLE & YOUNG, 246 REGENT STREET, LONDON, W.

but what I have read has, I hope, been fairly representative. I know Cable's work and Eugene Field's and Hamlin Garland's and Edgar Fawcett's and Richard Harding Davis's. I think Harold Frederic's "In the Valley" is one of the best of recent historical romances. The danger for American fiction is, I think, that it should run in many brooks instead of one broad stream. There is a tendency to overaccentuate local peculiarities; differences, after all, are a county and the other of a village? You know that a person in a neighboring village said of Barrie, that he was "no sae bad fur a Kerrimuer man." When you speak of a section in America, you must not forget it may be a bit of land as big as France.

Doyle. Barrie and Hardy have gained success by showing how the Scotch or Wessex peasant shares our common human nature, not by accentuating the points in which they differ from us.

DR. DOYLE'S ICELAND FALCON.

Barr. Well, I think Howells is demolished. What do you think of him and of James?

Doyle. James, I think, has had a great and permanent influence upon fiction. His beautiful clear-cut style and his artistic restraint must affect every one who reads him. I'm sure his "Portrait of a Lady" was an education to me, though one has not always the wit to profit by one's education.

Barr. Yes; James is a writer of whom you English people ought to be proud. I wish we had an American like him. Still, thank goodness, we have our William Dean Howells. I love Howells so much that I feel sure you must have something to say against him; what is it?

Doyle. I admire his honest, earnest work, but I do not admire his attitude towards all writers and critics who happen to differ

from his school. One can like Valdes and Bourget and Miss Austen without throwing stones at Scott and Thackeray and Dickens. There is plenty of room for all.

Barr. But there is the question of art.

Doyle. We talk so much about art, that we tend to forget what this art was ever invented for. It was to amuse mankind—to help the sick and the dull and the weary. If Scott and Dickens have done this for millions, they have done well by their art.

Barr. You don't think, then, that the object of all fiction is to draw life as it is?

Doyle. Where would Gulliver and Don Quixote and Dante and Goethe be, if that were so? No; the object of fiction is to interest, and the best fiction is that which interests most. If you can interest by drawing life as it is, by all means do so. But there is no reason why you should object to your neighbor using other means.

Barr. You do not approve of the theological novel then?

Doyle. Oh yes, I do, if it is made interesting. I think the age of fiction is coming—the age when religious and social and political changes will all be effected by means of the novelist. Look, within recent years, how much has been done by such books as "Looking Backward" or "Robert Elsmere." Everybody is educated now, but comparatively few are very educated. To get an idea to penetrate to the masses of the people, you must put fiction round it, like sugar round a pill. No statesman and no ecclesiastic will have the influence on public opinion which the novelist of the future will have. If he has strong convictions, he will have wonderful facilities for impressing them on others. Still his first business will always be to interest. If he can't get his sugar right, people will refuse his pill.

At this point nature revolted. She thought the subject too dry, and she proceeded to wet it down. A black thundercloud came up over the Crystal Palace, and the first thing we knew the shower was upon us. Both of us, luckily, knew enough to come in out of the rain. Two men hastily grasped two wicker chairs and bolted for the house, leaving literature to take care of itself in the back garden.

Conan Doyle's study, workshop, and smoking-room is a nice place in a downpour, and I can recommend the novelist's brand of cigarettes. Show me the room in which a man works, and I'll show you —how to smoke his cigarettes. The workbench stands in the corner—one of those flat-topped desks so prevalent in England. The English author does not seem to take kindly to the haughty, roller-top American desk, covered with transparent varnish and twenty-three patents.

There is a bookcase, filled with solid historical volumes for the most part. The most remarkable feature of the room is a series of water-color drawings done by Conan Doyle's father. The Doyle family has always been a family of artists, and the celebrated cover of "Punch" is, as everybody knows, the work of Dicky Doyle.

ROBERT BARR AT HIS DESK IN THE "IDLER" OFFICE. FROM A PHOTOGRAPH BY FRADELLE & YOUNG, 246 REGENT STREET, LONDON, W.

The drawings by Mr. Doyle's father are most weird and imaginative, being in art something like what Edgar Allan Poe's stories are in fiction.

There are harpoons on the wall, for Doyle has been a whale fisher in his time, and has the skull of a polar bear and the stuffed body of an Iceland falcon to show that his aim was accurate. There are but two other Iceland falcons in England. The novelist came nearer to the North Pole than New York is to Chicago, and it has always struck me as strange that he did not take a sleeping-car and go through to the Pole and spend a night there. But he was young then and let opportunities slip. He spent his twenty-first birthday within the Arctic Circle.

Here are three stories of his Arctic experiences. You see, I am going to sugar-coat the Real Conversation.

The whaler sailed from Peterhead, and the crew were Scotsmen with one exception. Doyle was supposed to be the surgeon of the craft. He brought two pairs of boxing-gloves with him, and one of the men, who was handy with his fists, was ambitious to have a bout. Doyle accommodated him. The man was strong, but had no science. Finding himself hard pressed, Doyle struck out, and the cabin table being fastened to the floor with no give to it, the sailor, when he struck it after the blow, found his feet in the air and his head on the floor behind the table.

The man was heard afterwards to say to a companion in tones of great admiration: "Man! McAlpine, yon's the best surgeon we've ever had. He knocked me clean ower th' table an' blacked ma e'e."

Few men have had such a compliment paid to their medical qualifications.

The man who was not a Scotsman was a gloomy, taciturn person, popularly supposed to be a fugitive from justice, and held in deep respect on that account. He went on the principle that deeds speak louder than words. On one occasion the cook took the liberty of being drunk for three days. On the third day the murderer thought this had gone far, just far, enough. The cooking was something awful. He rose without a word, seized a long-handled saucepan and brought it down on the cook's head. The bottom of the pan broke like glass, and the iron rim remained around the astonished cook's neck like a collar. The man, still without a word, walked gloomily to his seat. There was no more bad cooking on that voyage.

They used to throw an ice-anchor on a berg when they lay for some hours beside an ice-field, and then was the time to take a rise out of the innocent polar bear, who is not accustomed to the Peterhead brand of humor. They would put all the grease, bones, and galley refuse into the furnace, and the scent of the burning spread along the Arctic Circle for miles. In a few hours all the bears between there and the Pole would come trooping along with noses high in the air, wondering where the banquet was. When they read the signal, "April Fool," flagged from the mast-head, the bears grunted and trudged off home again.

Conan Doyle is not a man who goes to extremes, but it seems to me that he did in the matter of his voyaging. He came home from the Arctic Circle, took his degree at Edinburgh, and at once shipped for the west African coast.

Here is a tragedy of the sea which occurred when Doyle was a boy. He read an account of it at the time, and it made a powerful impression on his young mind. An American ship called the "Marie Celeste" was found abandoned off the west coast. Nothing on her was disturbed, and there were no signs of a struggle. Her cargo was untouched, and there was no evidence that she had come through a storm. On the cabin table was screwed a sewing machine, and on the arm of the sewing machine was a spool of silk thread, which would have fallen off if there had been any motion of the vessel. She was loaded with clocks, and her papers showed that she left Baltimore for Lisbon. She was taken to Gibraltar, but from that day to this no one knows what became of the captain and crew of the "Marie Celeste."

This mystery of the sea set the future Sherlock Holmes at work trying to find a solution for it. There was no clew to go on, except an old Spanish sword found in the forecastle, which showed signs of having been recently cleaned. Doyle's solution of the problem appeared in the form of a story for the "Cornhill Magazine," entitled, "J. Habbakuk Jephson's Statement." Jephson was supposed to be an American doctor who had taken passage on the ship for his health. Shortly after the story appeared, the following telegram was printed in all the London papers:

"Solly Flood, Her Majesty's advocate-general at Gibraltar, telegraphs that the statement of J. Habbakuk Jephson is nothing less than a fabrication."

Which indeed it was; but the telegram was a compliment to the realism of the story, to say the least.

On the bookcase in the study there stands a bust of a man with a keen, shrewd face.

"Who is the statesman?" I asked.

"Oh, that is Sherlock Holmes," said Doyle. "A young sculptor named Wilkins, from Birmingham, sent it to me. Isn't it good?"

"Excellent. By the way, is Sherlock Holmes really dead?"

"Doyle, I have known you now for seven years, and I know you thoroughly. I am going to say something to you that you will remember in after life. Doyle, you will never come to any good!"

The making of an historical novel involves much hard reading. The results of this hard reading, Doyle sets down in a note-book. Sometimes all he gets out of several volumes is represented by a couple

Robert Barr.   Miss Doyle.   Conan Doyle.   Mrs Doyle.   Robert McClure.

A GROUP IN DR. DOYLE'S GARDEN.

"Yes; I shall never write another Holmes story."

Dr. Conan Doyle is a methodical worker, and a hard worker. He pastes up over his mantel-shelf a list of the things he intends to do in the coming six months, and he sticks to his task until it is done. He must be a great disappointment to his old teacher. When he had finished school the teacher called the boy up before him and said solemnly:

of pages in this book. In turning over the most recent pages I saw much about Napoleon, and I knew that some marvellously good short stories which Doyle has recently written, are set in the stormy period of Napoleon's time.

"I suppose you are an admirer of that unscrupulous ruffian?" I said gently.

"He was a wonderful man—perhaps the most wonderful man who ever lived. What strikes me is the lack of finality in his

CONAN DOYLE AT 4 YEARS OF AGE.

CONAN DOYLE AT 14.

CONAN DOYLE AT 22.

CONAN DOYLE AT 28.

character. When you make up your mind that he is a complete villain, you come on some noble trait; and then your admiration of this is lost in some act of incredible meanness. But just think of it! Here was a young fellow of thirty, a man who had had no social advantages and but slight educational training, a member of a poverty stricken family, entering a room with a troop of kings at his heels, and all the rest of them jealous if he spoke a moment longer to one than to the

CONAN DOYLE AT THE PRESENT TIME.

others. Then, there must have been a great personal charm about the man, for some of those intimate with him loved him. His secretary, Méneval, writes of him with almost doting affection."

"Yes; and then a dealer in fiction must bow down to Napoleon as the most accomplished liar that ever lived."

"Oh, no one could ever compete with him in that line. If he intended to invade Africa, he would give out that he was going to Russia; then he would tell his inti-mates in strict confidence that Germany was the spot he had his eye on; and finally he would whisper in the ear of his most confidential secretary that Spain was the point of attack. He was certainly an amazing and talented liar."

"Do you think his power in this direction was the secret of his success, and is lying a virtue you would advise us all to cultivate?"

"The secret of his success seems to me to have been his ability to originate gigantic schemes that seemed fantas-tic and impossible, while his mastery of detail enabled him to bring his projects to completion where any other man would have failed."

At the time this appears in print, Dr. Conan Doyle will be in America. He goes there ostensibly to deliver the series of lectures that has been so successful in England, but the real object of his visit is to see the country. This is a laudable ambition, and I hope the United States and Conan Doyle will mutually like each other.

Cordially yours,

Eugene Field.

Chicago, June 26, 1893.

EUGENE FIELD AND HAMLIN GARLAND.

A CONVERSATION.

RECORDED BY HAMLIN GARLAND.

ONE afternoon quite recently two men sat in an attic study in one of the most interesting homes in the city of Chicago,—a home that was a museum of old books, rare books, Indian relics, dramatic souvenirs and bric-a-brac indescribable, but each piece with a history.

It was a beautiful June day, and the study window looked out upon a lawn of large trees where children were rioting. It was a part of Chicago which the traveller never sees, green and restful and dignified, the lake not far off.

The host was a tall, thin-haired man with a New England face of the Scotch type, rugged, smoothly shaven, and generally very solemn—suspiciously solemn in expression. His infrequent smile curled his wide, expressive mouth in fantastic grimaces which seemed not to affect the steady gravity of the blue-gray eyes. He was stripped to his shirt-sleeves and sat with feet on a small stand. He chewed reflectively upon a cigar during the opening of the talk. His voice was deep, but rather dry in quality.

The other man was a rather heavily built man, with brown hair and beard cut rather close. He listened, mainly, going off into gusts of laughter occasionally as the other man gave a quaint turn to some very frank phrase. The tall host was Eugene Field, the interviewer a Western writer by the name of Garland.

"Well, now, brother Field," said Garland, interrupting his host as he was about to open another case of rare books, "you remember I'm to interview you to-day."

Field scowled savagely.

"Oh, say, Garland, can't we put that thing off?"

"No. Must be did," replied his friend decisively. "Now, there are two ways to do this thing. We can be as literary and as deliciously select in our dialogue as Mr. Howells and Professor Boyesen were, or we can be wild and woolly. How would it do to be as wild and

woolly as those Eastern fellers expect us to be?"

"All right," said Field, taking his seat well up on the small of his back. "What does it all mean, anyway? What you goin' to do?"

"I'm goin' to take notes while we talk, and I'm goin' to put this thing down pretty close to the fact, now, you bet," said Garland, sharpening a pencil.

"Where you wan' to begin?"

"Oh, we'll have to begin with your ancestry, though it's a good deal like the introductory chapter to the old-fashioned novels. We'll start early; with your birth, for instance."

"Well, I was born in St. Louis."

"Is that so?" The interviewer showed an unprofessional surprise. "Why, I thought you were born in Massachusetts."

"No," said Field, reflectively. "No. I'm sorry, of course, but I was born in St. Louis; but my parents were Vermont people." He mentioned this as an extenuating circumstance, evidently. "My father was a lawyer. He was a precocious boy,—graduated from Middlebury College when he was fifteen, and when he was nineteen was made State's Attorney by special act of the legislature; without that he would have had to wait until he was twenty-one. He married and came West, and I was born in 1850."

"So you're forty-three? Where does the New England life come in?"

THE FIELD HOMESTEAD AT FAYETTEVILLE, VERMONT.

14

"When I was seven years old my mother died, and father packed us boys right off to Massachusetts and put us under the care of a maiden cousin, a Miss French,—she was a fine woman, too."

Garland looked up from his scratch-pad to ask, "This was at Amherst?"

"Yes. I stayed there until I was nineteen, and they were the sweetest and finest days of my life. I like old Amherst." He paused a moment, and his long face slowly lightened up. "By the way, here's something you'll like. When I was nine years old father sent us up to Fayetteville, Vermont, to the old homestead where my grandmother lived. We stayed there seven months," he said with a grim curl of his lips, "and the old lady got all the grandson she wanted. She didn't want the visit repeated."

He sat a moment in silence, and his face softened and his eyes grew tender. "I tell you, Garland, a man's got to have a year of country experience somewhere in him. My love for nature dates from that visit, because I had never lived in the country before. Sooner or later a man rots if he lives too far away from the grass and the trees."

"You're right there, Field, only I didn't know you felt it so deeply. I supposed you hated farm life."

"I do; but farm life is not nature. I'd like to live in the country without the effects of work and dirt and flies."

The word "flies" started him off on a side-track. "Say! You should see my boys. I go up to a farm near Fox Lake and stay a week every year, suffering all sorts of tortures, in order to give my boys a chance to see farm life. I sit there nights trying to read by a vile-smelling old kerosene lamp, the flies trooping in so that you can't keep the window down, you know, and those boys lying there all the time on a hot husk bed, faces spattered with mosquito bites, and sweating like pigs—and happy as angels. The roar of the flies and mosquitoes is sweetest lullaby to a tired boy."

"Well, now, going back to that visit," said the interviewer with persistency to his plan.

"Oh, yes. Well, my grandmother was a regular old New England Congregationalist. Say, I've got a sermon I wrote when I was nine. The old lady used to give me ten cents for every sermon I'd write. Like to see it?"

"Well, I should say. A sermon at nine years! Field, you started in well."

"Didn't I?" he replied, while getting the book. "And you bet it's a corker." He produced the volume, which was a small bundle of note-paper bound beautifully. It was written in a boy's formal hand. He sat down to read it:

"I would remark secondly that conscience makes the way of transgressors hard; for every act of pleasure, every act of Guilt his conscience smites him. The last of his stay on earth will appear horrible to the beholder. Some times, however, he will be stayed in his guilt. A death in a family of some favorite object or be attacked by Some disease himself is brought to the portals of the grave. Then for a little time perhaps he is stayed in his wickedness, but before long he returns to his worldly lust. Oh, it is indeed bad for sinners to go down into perdition over all the obstacles which God has placed in his path. But many I am afraid do go down into perdition, for wide gate and broad is the way that leadeth to destruction and many there be that go in thereat."

He stopped occasionally to look at Garland gravely, as he read some particularly comical phrase: "'I secondly remark'—ain't that great?—'that the wise man remembers even how near he is to the portals of death.' 'Portals of death' is good. 'One should strive to walk the narrow way and not the one which leads to perdition.' I was heavy on quotations, you notice."

"Is this the first and last of your sermons?" queried Garland, with an amused smile.

"The first and last. Grandmother soon gave me up as bad material for a preacher. She paid me five dollars for learning the Ten Commandments. I used to be very slow at 'committing to memory.' I recall that while I was thus committing the book of Acts, my brother committed that book and the Gospel of Matthew, part of John, the thirteenth chapter of First Corinthians, and the Westminster Catechism. I would not now exchange for any amount of money the acquaintance with the Bible that was drummed into me when I was a boy. At learning 'pieces to speak' I was, however, unusually quick, and my favorites were: 'Marco Bozzaris,' 'Psalm of Life,' Drake's 'American Flag,' Longfellow's 'Launching of the Ship,' Webster's 'Action,' Shakespeare's 'Clarence's Dream' (Richard III.), and 'Wolsey to Cromwell,' 'Death of Virginia,' 'Horatius at the Bridge,' 'Hymn of the Moravian Nuns,' 'Absalom,' 'Lochiel's Warning,' 'Maclean's Revenge,' Bulwer's translation of Schiller's 'The Diver,' 'Landing of the Pilgrims,' Bryant's 'Melancholy Days,' 'Burial of Sir John Moore,' and 'Hohenlinden,'

"I remember when I was thirteen our

EUGENE FIELD'S HOME AT BUENA PARK, CHICAGO.

cousin said she'd give us a Christmas tree. So we went down into Patrick's swamp—I suppose the names are all changed now—and dug up a little pine tree about as tall as we were, and planted it in a tub. On the night of Christmas Day, just when we were dancing around the tree, making merry and having a high-old-jinks of a time, the way children will, grandma came in and looked at us. 'Will this popery never cease?' was all she said, and out she flounced."

"Yes, that was the old Puritan idea of it. But did live——"

"Now, hold on," he interrupted. "I want to finish. We planted that tree near the corner of Sunset Avenue and Amity Street, and it's there now, a magnificent tree. Some time when I'm East I'm going to go up there with my brother and put a tablet on it—'Pause, busy traveller, and give a thought to the happy days of two Western boys who lived in old New England, and make resolve to render the boyhood near you happier and brighter,' or something like that."

"That's a pretty idea," Garland agreed. He felt something fine and tender in the man's voice, which was generally hard and dry, but wonderfully expressive.

"Now, this sermon I had bound just for the sake of old times. If I didn't have it right here, I wouldn't believe I ever wrote such stuff. I tell you, a boy's a queer combination," he ended, referring to the book again.

"You'll see that I signed my name, those days, 'E. P. Field.' The 'P.' stands for Phillips.

"As I grew old enough to realize it, I was much chagrined to find I had no middle name like the rest of the boys, so I took the name of Phillips. I was a great admirer of Wendell Phillips,—am yet,—though I'm not a reformer. You'll see here,"—he pointed at the top of the pages,—"I wrote the word 'sensual.' Evidently I was struck with the word, and was seeking a chance to ring it in somewhere, but failed." They both laughed over the matter while Field put the book back.

"Are you a college man?" asked Garland. "I've noticed your deplorable tendency toward the classics."

"I fitted for college when I was sixteen. My health was bad, or I should have entered right off. I had pretty nearly everything that was going in the way of diseases,"—this was said with a comical twist of the voice—"so I didn't get to Williams till I was eighteen. My health improved right along, but I'm sorry to say that of the college did not." He smiled again, a smile that meant a very great deal.

"What happened then?"

"Well, my father died, and I returned West. I went to live with my guardian, Professor Burgess of Knox College. This college is situated at Galesburg, Illinois. This is the college that has lately conferred A. M. upon me. The professor's guardianship was merely nominal, however. I did about as I pleased.

"I next went to the State University at Columbia, Missouri. It was an old slaveholding town, but I liked it. I've got a streak of Southern feeling in me." He said abruptly, "I'm an aristocrat. I'm looking for a Mæcenas. I have mighty little in common with most of the wealthy, but I like the idea of wealth in the abstract." He failed to make the distinction quite clear, but he went on as if realizing that this might be a thin spot of ice.

"At twenty-one I came into sixty thousand dollars, and I went to Europe, taking a friend, a young fellow of about my own age, with me. I had a lovely time !" he added, and again the smile conveyed vast meaning.

Garland looked up from his pad.

"You must have had. Did you 'blow in the whole business'?"

"Pretty near. I *swatted* the money around. Just think of it !" he exclaimed, warming with the recollection. "A boy of twenty-one, without father or mother, and sixty thousand dollars. Oh, it was a lovely combination ! I saw more things and did more things than are dreamt of in your philosophy, Horatio," he paraphrased, looking at his friend with a strange expression of amusement and pleasure and regret. "I had money. I paid it out for experience—it was plenty. Experience was lying around loose."

"Came home when the money gave out, I reckon?"

"Yes. Came back to St. Louis, and went to work on the 'Journal.' I had previously tried to 'enter journalism,' as I called it then. About the time I was twenty-one I went to Stilson Hutchins, and told him who I was, and he said :

"'All right. I'll give you a chance, but we don't pay much.' Of course I told him pay didn't matter.

"'Well !' he said, 'go down to the Olympia, and write up the play there to-night.' I went down, and I brought most of my critical acumen to bear upon an actor by the name of Charley Pope, who was playing Mercutio for Mrs. D. P. Bowers. His wig didn't fit, and all my best writing centred about that wig. I sent the critique in, blame fine as I thought, with illuminated initial letters, and all that. Oh, it was lovely ! and the next morning I was deeply pained and disgusted to find it mutilated,—all that about the wig, the choicest part, was cut out. I thought I'd quit journalism forever. I don't suppose Hutchins connects Eugene Field with the —— fool that wrote that critique. I don't myself," he added with a quick half-smile lifting again the corner

of his solemn mouth. It was like a ripple on a still pool.

"Well, when did you really get into the work?" his friend asked, for he seemed about to go off into another by-path.

"Oh, after I came back from Europe I was 'busted,' and had to go to work. I met Stanley Waterloo about that time, and his talk induced me to go to work for the 'Journal' as a reporter. I soon got to be city editor, but I didn't like it. I liked to have fun with people. I liked to have my fun as I went along. About this time I married the sister of the friend who went

THE HALL.

with me to Europe, and, feeling my new responsibilities, I went up to St. Joseph as city editor." He mused for a moment in silence. "It was terrific hard work, but I wouldn't give a good deal for those two years."

"Have you ever drawn upon them for material?" asked Garland with a novelist's perception of their possibilities.

"No, but I may some time. Things have to get pretty misty before I can use 'em. I'm not like you fellows," he said, referring to the realists. "I got thirty dollars a week ; wasn't that princely?"

"Nothing else ; but you earned it, no doubt."

"Earned it ? Why, Great Scott ! I did

the whole business, except turning the handle of the press.

"Well, in 1877 I was called back to the 'Journal' in St. Louis as editorial writer of paragraphs. That was the beginning of my own line of work."

"When did you do your first work in verse?" asked Garland.

The tall man brought his feet down to the floor with a bang, and thrust his hand out toward his friend. "*There!* I'm glad you said *verse*. For heaven's sake don't ever say I call my stuff poetry. I never do. I don't pass judgment on it like that." After a little he resumed: "The first that I wrote was 'Christmas Treasures.' I wrote that one night to fill in a chink in the paper."

"Give me a touch of it?" asked his friend.

He chewed his cigar in the effort to remember. "I don't read it much. I put it with the collection for the sake of old times." He read a few lines of it, and read it extremely well, before returning to his history.

CHRISTMAS TREASURES.

I count my treasures o'er with care,—
  The little toy my darling knew,
  A little sock of faded hue,
A little lock of golden hair.

Long years ago this holy time,
  My little one—my all to me—
  Sat robed in white upon my knee,
And heard the merry Christmas chime.

"Tell me, my little golden-head,
  If Santa Claus should come to-night,
  What shall he bring my baby bright,—
What treasure for my boy?" I said.

THE DINING-ROOM.

A CORNER IN THE LIBRARY.

Then he named this little toy,
  While in his round and mournful eyes
  There came a look of sweet surprise
That spake his quiet, trustful joy.

And as he lisped his evening prayer,
  He asked the boon with childish grace,
  Then, toddling to the chimney-place,
He hung this little stocking there.

That night, while lengthening shadows crept,
  I saw the white-winged angels come
  With singing to our lowly home,
And kiss my darling as he slept.

They must have heard his little prayer,
  For in the morn, with rapturous face
  He toddled to the chimney-place,
And found this little treasure there.

They came again one Christmas-tide,—
  That angel host so fair and white!
  And, singing all that glorious night,
They lured my darling from my side.

A little sock, a little toy,
  A little lock of golden hair,
  The Christmas music on the air,
A watching for my baby boy.

But if again that angel train
  And golden head come back to me,
  To bear me to Eternity,
My watching will not be in vain.

"I went next to the Kansas City 'Times' as managing editor. I wrote there that 'Little Peach,' which still chases me around the country."

THE LITTLE PEACH.

A little peach in the orchard grew,
A little peach of emerald hue;
Warmed by the sun and wet by the dew,
  It grew.

One day, passing that orchard through,
That little peach dawned on the view
Of Johnny Jones and his sister Sue,
  Them two.

Up at that peach a club they threw,
Down from the stem on which it grew
Fell that peach of emerald hue.
　　Mon Dieu!

John took a bite and Sue a chew,
And then the trouble began to brew,
Trouble the doctor couldn't subdue.
　　Too true!

Under the turf where the daisies grew
They planted John and his sister Sue,
And their little souls to the angels flew,
　　Boo hoo!

What of that peach of the emerald hue,
Warmed by the sun and wet by the dew?
Ah, well, its mission on earth is through.
　　Adieu!

"I went to the Denver 'Tribune' next, and stayed there till 1883. The most conspicuous thing I did there was the burlesque primer series. 'See the po-lice-man. Has he a club? Yes, he has a club,' etc. These were so widely copied and pirated that I put them into a little book which is very rare, thank heaven! I hope I have the only copy of it. The other thing which rose above the level of my ordinary work was a bit of verse, 'The Wanderer,' which I credited to Modjeska, and which has given her no little annoyance."

THE WANDERER.

Upon a mountain height, far from the sea,
　I found a shell;
And to my listening ear the lonely thing
Ever a song of ocean seemed to sing,
　Ever a tale of ocean seemed to tell.

How came the shell upon that mountain height?
　Ah, who can say
Whether there dropped by some too careless hand,
Or whether there cast when ocean swept the land,
　Ere the Eternal had ordained the day?

Strange, was it not? Far from its native deep,
　One song it sang—
Sang of the awful mysteries of the tide,
Sang of the misty sea, profound and wide,
　Ever with echoes of the ocean rang.

And as the shell upon the mountain height
　Sings of the sea,
So do I ever, leagues and leagues away,
So do I ever, wandering where I may,
　Sing, O my home! sing, O my home! of thee.

"That brings you up to Chicago, doesn't it?"

"In 1883 Melville Stone asked me to join him on the 'News,' and I did. Since then my life has been uneventful."

"I might not think so. Did you establish the column 'Sharps and Flats' at once?"

"Yes. I told Stone I'd write a good deal of musical matter, and the name seemed appropriate. We tried to change it several times, but no go."

"I first saw your work in the 'News.' I was attracted by your satirical studies of Chicago. I don't always like what you write, but I liked your war against sham."

Field became serious at once, and leaned towards the other man in an attitude of great earnestness. The deepest note in the man's voice came out. "I hate a sham or a fraud; not so much a fraud, for a fraud means brains very often, but a sham makes me mad clear through," he said savagely. His fighting quality came out in the thrust of the chin. Here was the man whom the frauds and shams fear.

"That is evident. But I don't think the people make the broadest application of your satires. They apply them to Chicago. There is quite a feeling. I suppose you know about this. They say you've hurt Chicago art."

"I hope I have, so far as the bogus art and imitation culture of my city is concerned. As a matter of fact the same kind of thing exists in Boston and New York, only they're used to it there. I've jumped on that crowd of faddists, I'll admit, as hard as I could; but I don't think any one can say I've ever willingly done any real man or woman an injury. If I have, I've always tried to square the thing up." Here was the man's fairness, kindliness of heart, coming to the surface in good simple way.

The other man was visibly impressed with his friend's earnestness, but he pursued his course. "You've had offers to go East, according to the papers."

"Yes, but I'm not going—why should I? I'm in my element here. They haven't any element there. They've got atmosphere there, and it's pretty thin sometimes. I call it." He uttered "atmosphere" with a drawling, attenuated nasal, to express his contempt. "I don't want literary atmosphere. I want to be in an *element* where I can tumble around and yell without falling in a fit for lack of breath."

The interviewer was scratching away like mad—this was his chance.

Field's mind took a sudden turn now, and he said emphatically: "Garland, I'm a newspaper man. I don't claim to be anything else. I've never written a thing for the magazines, and I never was asked to, till about four years ago. I never have put a high estimate upon my verse. That it's popular is because my sympathies and the public's happen to run on parallel lines just now. That's all. Not much of it will live."

"I don't know about that, brother Field," said Garland, pausing to rest. "I think you underestimate some of that work. Your reminiscent boy-life poems and your songs of childhood are thoroughly American, and fine and tender. They'll take care of themselves."

"Yes, but my best work has been along lines of satire. I've consistently made war upon shams. I've stood always in my work for decency and manliness and honesty. I think that'll remain true, you'll find. I'm not much physically, but morally I'm not a coward. I don't pretend to be a reformer; I leave that to others. I hate logarithms.

life," pursued Garland, who called himself a veritist, and enjoyed getting his friend as nearly on his ground as possible.

"Yes, that's so, but that's in the far past," Field admitted. Garland took the thought up.

"Time helps you, then. Time is a romancer. He halves the fact, but we veritists find the *present* fact haloed with significance, if not beauty."

Field dodged the point.

"Yes, I like to do those boy-life verses. I like to live over the joys and tragedies —because we had our tragedies."

"Didn't we! Weeding the onion-bed on circus day, for example."

"Yes, or gettin' a terrible strappin' for

THE DRAWING-ROOM.

I like speculative astronomy. I am naturally a lover of romance. My mind turns towards the far past or future. I like to illustrate the foolery of these society folks by stories which I invent. The present don't interest me—at least not taken as it is. Possibilities interest me."

"That's a good way to put it," said the other man. "It's a question of the impossible, the possible, and the probable. I like the probable. I like the near-at-hand. I feel the most vital interest in the average fact."

'I know you do; and I like it after you get through with it, but I don't care to deal with the raw material myself. I like the archaic."

"Yet some of your finest things, I repeat, are your reminiscent verses of boy-

goin' swimming without permission. Oh, it all comes back to me, all sweet and fine, somehow. I've forgotten all the unpleasant things. I remember only the best of it all. I like boy-life. I like children. I like young men. I like the buoyancy of youth and its freshness. It's a God's pity that every young child can't get a taste of country life at some time. It's a fund of inspiration to a man." Again the finer quality in the man came out in his face and voice.

"Your life in New England and the South, and also in the West, has been of great help to you, I think."

"Yes, and a big disadvantage. When I go East Stedman calls me a typical Westerner, and when I come West they call me a Yankee—so there I am!"

"Now you touch a great theme. You're right, Field. The next ten years will see literary horizons change mightily. The West is dead sure to be in the game from this time on. A man can't be out here a week without feeling the thrill of latent powers. The West is coming to its manhood. The West is the place for enthusiasm. Her history is making."

Field took up the note. "I've got faith in it. I love New England for her heritage to me. I like her old stone walls and meadows, but when I get back West—well, I'm home, that's all. My love for the West has got blood in it."

Garland laughed in sudden perception of their earnestness. "We're both talking like a couple of 'boomers.' It might be characteristic, however, to apply the methods of the 'boomers' of town lots to the development of art and literature. What say?"

"It can be done. It will come in the course of events."

"In our enthusiasm we have skated away from the subject. You are forty-

MR. FIELD'S TREASURES: THE GLADSTONE AXE, C. A. DANA'S SHEARS, THE HORACES.

"There's no doubt of your being a Westerner."

"I hope not. I believe in the West. I tell you, brother Garland, the West is the coming country. We ought to have a big magazine to develop the West. It's absurd to suppose we're going on always being tributary to the East!"

Garland laid down his pad and lifted his big fist in the air like a maul. His enthusiasm rose like a flood.

three, then; you realize there's a lot of work before you, I hope."

"Yes, yes, my serious work is just begun. I'm a man of slow development. I feel that. I know my faults and my weaknesses. I'm getting myself in hand. Now, Garland, I'm with you in your purposes, but I go a different way. You go into things direct. I'm naturally allusive. My work is almost always allusive, if you've noticed."

" Do you write rapidly ? "

" I write my verse easily, but my prose I sweat over. Don't you ? "

" I toil in revision, even when I have what the other fellows call an inspiration."

" I tell you, Garland, genius is not in it. It's work and patience, and staying with a thing. Inspiration is all right and pretty and a suggestion, but it's when a man gets a pen in his hand and sweats blood that inspiration begins to enter in."

" Well, what are your plans for the future? Your readers want to know that. "

His face glowed as he replied : " I'm going to write a sentimental life of Horace. We know mighty little of him, but what I don't know I'll make up. I'll write such a life as he *must* have lived ; the life we all live when boys."

The younger man put up his notes, and they walked down and out under the trees, with the gibbous moon shining through the gently moving leaves. They passed a couple of young people walking slow—his voice a murmur, hers a whisper.

" There they go. Youth ! Youth ! " said Field.

PORTRAITS OF EUGENE FIELD.

AGE SIX MONTHS.

AGE 12.

AGE 20.

AGE 23.

AGE 31.

AGE 34.

AGE 42.

PORTRAITS OF DWIGHT LYMAN MOODY.

1854. AGE 17. MR. MOODY AS HE APPEARED
AT THE TIME HE REMOVED FROM THE
FAMILY FARM TO BOSTON.

1863. AGE 26.

MR. MOODY IN 1882. AGE 45. FROM A PHOTOGRAPH BY PIERRE PETIT, PARIS.

MR. MOODY: SOME IMPRESSIONS AND FACTS.

By HENRY DRUMMOND, LL.D., F.R.S.E., F.G.S.

Author of "Natural Law in the Spiritual World," "The Greatest Thing in the World," "The Ascent of Man," etc.

TO gain just the right impression of Mr. Moody you must make a pilgrimage to Northfield. Take the train to the way-side depot in Massachusetts which bears that name, or, better still, to South Vernon, where the fast trains stop. Northfield, his birthplace and his present home, is distant about a couple of miles, but at certain seasons of the year you will find awaiting trains a two-horse buggy, not conspicuous for varnish, but famous for pace, driven by a stout farmer-like person in a slouch hat. As he drives you to the spacious hotel—a creation of Mr. Moody's—he will answer your questions about the place in a brusque, business-like way; indulge, probably, in a few laconic witticisms, or discuss the political situation or the last strike with a shrewdness which convinces you that, if the Northfield people are of this level-headed type, they are at least a worthy field for the great preacher's energies. Presently, on the other side of the river, on one of those luscious, grassy slopes, framed in with forest and bounded with the blue receding hills, which give the Connecticut Valley its dream-like beauty, the great halls and colleges of the new Northfield which Mr. Moody has built, begin to appear. Your astonishment is great, not so much to find a New England hamlet possessing a dozen of the finest educational buildings in America—for the neighboring townships of Amherst and Northampton are already famous for their collegiate institutions—but to discover that these owe their existence to a man whose name is, perhaps, associated in the minds of three-fourths of his countrymen, not with education, but with the want of it. But presently, when you are deposited at the door of the hotel, a more astounding discovery greets you. For when you ask the clerk whether the great man himself is at home, and where you can see him, he will point to your coachman, now disappearing like lightning down the drive, and—too much accustomed to Mr. Moody's humor to smile at his latest jest—whisper, "That's him."

If this **does** not actually happen in your

HENRY DRUMMOND.

case, it is certain it has happened;[*] and nothing could more fittingly introduce you to the man, or make you realize the naturalness, the simplicity, the genuine and unaffected humanity of this great unspoilt and unspoilable personality.

MR. MOODY MUCH MISUNDERSTOOD.

Simple as this man is, and homely as are his surroundings, probably America possesses at this moment no more extraordinary personage; nor even amongst the most brilliant of her sons has any

* At the beginning of each of the terms, hundreds of students, many of them strangers, arrive to attend those seminaries. At such times Mr. Moody literally haunts the depots, to meet them the moment they most need a friend, and give them that personal welcome which is more to many of them than half their education. When casual visitors, mistaking perhaps the only vehicle in waiting for a public conveyance, have taken possession for themselves and their luggage, the driver, circumstances permitting, has duly risen to the occasion. The fact, by the way, that he so escapes recognition, illustrates a peculiarity. Mr. Moody, owing to a life-long resistance to the self-advertisement of the camera, is probably less known by photographs than any public man.

rendered more stupendous or more enduring service to his country or his time. No
public man is less understood, especially
by the thinking world, than D. L. Moody.
It is not that it is unaware of his existence,
or even that it does not respect him. But
his line is so special, his work has lain so
apart from what it conceives to be the
rational channels of progress, that it has
never felt called upon to take him seriously. So little, indeed, is the true stature
of this man known to the mass of his
generation, that the preliminary estimate
recorded here must seem both extravagant
and ill-considered. To whole sections of
the community the mere word evangelical
is a synonym for whatever is narrow,
strained, superficial, and unreal. Assumed
to be heir to all that is hectic in religion,
and sensational in the methods of propa-
gating it, men who, like Mr. Moody, earn
this name are unconsciously credited with
the worst traditions of their class. It will
surprise many to know that Mr. Moody is
as different from the supposed type of his
class as light is from dark ; that while he
would be the last to repudiate the name,
indeed, while glorying more and more each
day he lives in the work of the evangelist, he
sees the weaknesses, the narrownesses, and
the limitations of that order with as clear
an eye as the most unsparing of its critics.
But especially will it surprise many to
know that while preaching to the masses
has been the main outward work of Mr.
Moody's life, he has, perhaps, more, and
more varied, irons in the fire—educational,

philanthropic, religious—than almost any
living man ; and that vast as has been his
public service as a preacher to the masses,
it is probably true that his personal influence and private character have done as
much as his preaching to affect his day
and generation.

Discussion has abounded lately as to the
standards by which a country shall judge
its great men. And the verdict has been
given unanimously on behalf of moral influence. Whether estimated by the moral
qualities which go to the making up of his
personal character, or the extent to which
he has impressed these upon whole com-
munities of men on both sides of the
Atlantic, there is, perhaps, no more truly
great man living than D. L. Moody. By
moral influences in this connection I do not
mean in any restricted sense religious influence. I mean the influence which, with
whatever doctrinal accompaniments, or
under whatever ecclesiastical flag, leads
men to better lives and higher ideals ; the
influence which makes for noble character,
personal enthusiasm, social well-being, and
national righteousness. I have never heard
Mr. Moody defend any particular church ;
I have never heard him quoted as a theo-
logian. But I have met multitudes, and
personally know, in large numbers, men
and women of all churches and creeds,
of many countries and ranks, from the
poorest to the richest, and from the most
ignorant to the most wise, upon whom he
has placed an ineffaceable moral mark.
There is no large town in Great Britain or

THE MOODY HOMESTEAD AT NORTHFIELD, MASSACHUSETTS, WHERE D. L. MOODY WAS BORN.

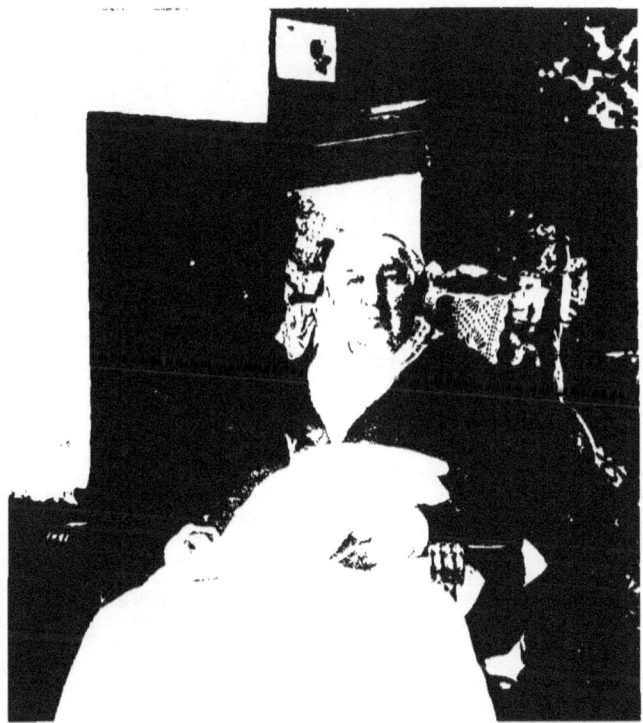

MRS. BETSEY MOODY, MOTHER OF D. L. MOODY.

Ireland, and I perceive there are few in America, where this man has not gone, where he has not lived for days, weeks, or months, and where he has not left behind him personal inspirations which live to this day; inspirations which, from the moment of their birth, have not ceased to evidence themselves in practical ways—in furthering domestic happiness and peace; in charities and philanthropies; in social, religious, and even municipal and national service.

It is no part of the present object to give a detailed account of Mr. Moody's career, still less of his private life. The sacred character of much of his work also forbids allusion in this brief sketch to much that those more deeply interested in him, and in the message which he proclaims, would like to have expressed or analyzed. All that is designed is to give the outside reader some few particulars to introduce him to, and interest him in, the man.

BOYHOOD ON A NEW ENGLAND FARM.

Fifty-seven years ago (February 5, 1837) Dwight Lyman Moody was born in the same New England valley where, as already said, he lives to-day. Four years later his father died, leaving a widow, nine children—the eldest but thirteen years of age—a little home on the mountain side, and an acre or two of mortgaged land. How this widow shouldered her burden of poverty, debt, and care; how she brought up her helpless flock, keeping all together in the old home, educating them, and sending them out into life stamped with her own indomitable courage and lofty principle, is one of those unrecorded histories whose page, when time unfolds it, will be found to contain the secret of nearly all that is greatest in the world's past. It is delightful to think that this mother has survived to see her labors crowned, and still lives, a venerable and beautiful figure, near the scene of her early

battles. There, in a sunny room of the little farm, she sits with faculties unimpaired, cherished by an entire community, and surrounded with all the love and gratitude which her children and her children's children can heap upon her. One has only to look at the strong, wise face, or listen to the firm yet gentle tones, to behold the source of those qualities of sagacity, energy, self-unconsciousness, and faith which have made the greatest of her sons what he is.

Until his seventeenth year Mr. Moody's boyhood was spent at home. What a merry, adventurous, rough-and-tumble boyhood it must have been, how much fuller of escapade than of education, those who know Mr. Moody's irrepressible temperament and buoyant humor will not require the traditions of his Northfield schoolmates to recall. The village school was the only seminary he ever attended, and his course was constantly interrupted by the duties of the home and of the farm. He learned little about books, but much about horses, crops, and men; his mind ran wild, and his memory stored up nothing but the alphabet of knowledge. But in these early country days his bodily form strengthened to iron, and he built up that constitution which in after life enabled him not only to do the work of ten, but to sustain without a break through four decades as arduous and exhausting work as was ever given to man to do. Innocent at this stage of "religion," he was known in the neighborhood simply as a raw lad, high-spirited, generous, daring, with a will of his own, and a certain audacious originality which, added to the fiery energy of

his disposition, foreboded a probable future either in the ranks of the incorrigibles or, if fate were kind, perchance of the immortals.

Somewhere about his eighteenth year the turning point came. Vast as were the issues, the circumstances were in no way eventful. Leaving school, the boy had set out for Boston, where he had an uncle, to push his fortune. His uncle, with some trepidation, offered him a place in his store; but, seeing the kind of nature he had to deal with, laid down certain conditions which the astute man thought might at least minimize explosions. One of these conditions was, that the lad should attend church and Sunday school. These influences—and it is interesting to note that they are simply the normal influences of a Christian society—did their work. On the surface what appears is this: that he attended church—to order, and listened with more or less attention; that he went to Sunday school, and, when he recovered his breath, asked awkward questions of his teacher; that, by and by, when he applied for membership in the congregation, he was summarily rejected, and told to wait six months until he learned a little more about it; and, lastly, that said period of probation having expired, he was duly received into communion. The decisive instrument during this period seems to have been his Sunday-school teacher, Mr. Edward Kimball, whose influence upon his charge was not merely professional, but personal and direct. In private friendship he urged young Moody to the supreme decision, and Mr. Moody never ceased to express his gratitude to the layman who met him at the parting of the ways, and led his thoughts and energies in the direction in which they have done such service to the world.

REMOVAL TO CHICAGO—RARE GIFT FOR BUSINESS.

The immediate fruit of this change was not specially apparent. The ambitions of the lad chiefly lay in the line of mercantile success; and his next move was to find a larger and freer field for the abilities for business which he began to discover in himself. This he found in the then new world of Chicago. Arriving there, with due introductions, he was soon engaged as salesman in a large and busy store, with possibilities of work and promotion which suited his taste. That he distinguished himself almost at once, goes without saying. In a year or two he was earning a salary considerable for one of his years, and his business capacity became speedily so proved that his future prosperity was assured. "He would never sit down in the store," writes one of his fellows, "to chat or read the paper, as the other clerks did when there were no customers; but as soon as he had served one buyer, he was on the lookout for another. If none appeared, he would start off to the hotels or depots, or walk the streets in search of one. He would sometimes stand on the sidewalk in front of his place of business, looking eagerly up and down for a man who had the appearance of a merchant from the country, and some of his fellow-clerks were accustomed laughingly to say: 'There is the spider again, watching for a fly.'"

The taunt is sometimes levelled at religion, that mainly those become religious teachers who are not fit for anything else. The charge is not worth answering; but it is worth recording that in the case of Mr. Moody the very reverse is the case. If Mr. Moody had remained in business, there is almost no question that he would have been to-day one of the wealthiest men in the United States. His enterprise, his organizing power, his knowledge and management of men are admitted by friend and foe to be of the highest order; while such is his generalship—as proved, for example, in the great religious campaign in Great Britain in 1873–75—that, had he

VIEW FROM THE PORCH OF MR. MOODY'S HOUSE AT NORTHFIELD.

MR. MOODY'S HOUSE AT NORTHFIELD IN WINTER, LOOKING EAST.

chosen a military career, he would have risen to the first rank among leaders. One of the merchant princes of Britain, the well-known director of one of the largest steamship companies in the world, assured the writer lately that in the course of a life-long commercial experience he had never met a man with more business capacity and sheer executive ability than D. L. Moody. Let any one visit Northfield, with its noble piles of institutions, or study the history of the work conceived, directed, financed, and carried out on such a colossal scale by Mr. Moody during the time of the World's Fair at Chicago, and he will discover for himself the size, the mere intellectual quality, creative power, and organizing skill of the brain behind them.

Undiverted, however, from a deeper purpose even by the glamor of a successful business life, Mr. Moody's moral and religious instincts led him almost from the day of his arrival in Chicago to devote what spare time he had to the work of the Church. He began by hiring four pews in the church to which he had attached himself, and these he attempted to fill every Sunday with young men like himself. This work for a temperament like his soon proved too slow, and he sought fuller outlets for his enthusiasm. Applying for the post of teacher in an obscure Sunday school, he was told by the superintendent that it was scholars he wanted, not teachers, but that he would let him try his hand if he could find the scholars. Next Sun-

day the new candidate appeared with a procession of eighteen urchins, ragged, rowdy, and barefooted, on whom he straightway proceeded to operate. Hunting up children and general recruiting for mission halls remained favorite pursuits for years to come, and his success was signal. In all this class of work he was a natural adept, and his early experiences as a scout were full of adventure. This was probably the most picturesque period of Mr. Moody's life, and not the least useful. Now we find him tract-distributing in the slums; again, visiting among the docks; and, finally, he started a mission of his own in one of the lowest haunts of the city. There he saw life in all its phases; he learned what practical religion was; he tried in succession every known method of Christian work; and when any of the conventional methods failed, invented new ones. Opposition, discouragement, failure, lay met at every turn and in every form; but one thing he never learned—how to give up man or scheme he had once set his heart on. For years this guerilla work, hand to hand, and heart to heart, went on. He ran through the whole gamut of mission experience, tackling the most difficult districts and the most adverse circumstances, doing all the odd jobs and menial work himself, never attempting much in the way of public speaking, but employing others whom he thought more fit; making friends especially with children, and through them with their dissolute fathers and starving mothers.

Great as was his success, the main reward achieved was to the worker himself. Here he was broken in, moulded, toned down, disciplined, in a dozen needed directions, and in this long and severe apprenticeship he unconsciously qualified himself to become the teacher of the Church in all methods of reaching the masses and winning men. He found out where his strength lay, and where his weakness; he learned that saving men was no child's play, but meant practically giving a life for a life; that regeneration was no milk and water experience; that, as Mrs. Browning says:

" It takes a high-soul'd man
To move the masses—even to a cleaner sty,"

But for this personal discipline it is doubtful if Mr. Moody would ever have been heard of outside the purlieus of Chicago. The clergy, bewildered by his eccentric genius, and suspicious of his unconventional ways, looked askance at him; and it was only as time mellowed his headstrong youth into a soberer, yet not less zealous, manhood that the solitary worker found influential friends to countenance and guide him. His activity, especially during the years of the war, when he served with almost superhuman devotion in the Christian Commission, led many of his fellow-laborers to know his worth; and the war over, he became at last a recognized factor in the religious life of Chicago. The mission which he had slowly built up was elevated to the rank of a church, with Mr. Moody, who had long since given up business in order to devote his entire time to what lay nearer his heart, as its pastor.

MR. MOODY'S SLOW DEVELOPMENT AS A PUBLIC SPEAKER.

As a public speaker up to this time Mr. Moody was the reverse of celebrated. When he first attempted speaking, in Boston, he was promptly told to hold his tongue, and further efforts in Chicago were not less discouraging. " He had never heard," writes Mr. Daniells, in his well-known biography, " of Talleyrand's famous doctrine, that speech is useful for concealing one's thoughts. Like Antony, he only spoke ' right on.' There was frequently a pungency in his exhortation which his brethren did not altogether relish. Sometimes in his prayers he would express opinions to the Lord concerning them which were by no means flattering; and it was not long before he received the same fatherly advice which had been given him at Boston—to the effect that he should keep his four pews full of young men, and leave the speaking and praying to those who could do it better." Undaunted by such pleasantries, Mr. Moody did, on occasion, continue to use his tongue—no doubt much ashamed of himself. He spoke not because he thought

DINING-ROOM, MR. MOODY'S HOUSE AT NORTHFIELD.

he could speak, but because he could not be silent. The ragged children whom he gathered round him in the empty saloon near the North Side Market, had to be talked to somehow, and among such audiences, with neither premeditation nor preparation, he laid the foundations of that amazingly direct anecdotal style and explosive delivery which became such a splendid instrument of his future service. Training for the public platform, this man, who has done more platform work than any man of his generation, had none. He knew only two books, the Bible and Human Nature. Out of these he spoke; and because both are books of life, his words were afire with life; and the people to whom he spoke, being real people, listened and understood. When Mr. Moody first began to be in demand on public platforms, it was not because he could speak. It was his experience that was wanted, not his eloquence. As a practical man in work among the masses, his advice and enthusiasm were called for at Sunday school and other conventions, and he soon became known in this connection throughout the surrounding States. It was at one of these conventions that he had the good fortune to meet Mr. Ira D. Sankey, whose name must ever be associated with his, and who henceforth shared his labors at home and abroad, and contributed, in ways the value of which it is impossible to exaggerate, to the success of his after work.

Were one asked what, on the human side, were the effective ingredients in Mr. Moody's sermons, one would find the answer difficult. Probably the foremost is the tremendous conviction with which they are uttered. Next to that is their point and direction. Every blow is straight from the shoulder, and every stroke tells. Whatever canons they violate, whatever fault the critics may find with their art, their rhetoric, or even with their theology, as appeals to the people they do their work, and with extraordinary

power. If eloquence is measured by its effects upon an audience, and not by its balanced sentences and cumulative periods, then here is eloquence of the highest order. In sheer persuasiveness Mr. Moody has few equals, and rugged as his preaching may seem to some, there is in it a pathos of a quality which few orators have ever reached, an appealing tenderness which not only wholly redeems it, but raises it, not unseldom almost to sublimity. No report can do the faintest justice to this or to the other most characteristic qualities of his public speech, but here is a specimen taken almost at random: "I can imagine when Christ said to the little band around Him, 'Go ye into all the world and preach the gospel,' Peter said, 'Lord, do you really mean that we are to go back to Jerusalem and preach the gospel to those men that murdered you?' 'Yes,' said Christ, 'go, hunt up that man that spat in my face, tell him he may have a seat in my kingdom yet. Yes, Peter, go find that man that made that cruel crown of thorns and placed it on my brow, and tell him I will have a crown ready for him when he comes into my kingdom, and there will be no thorns in it. Hunt up that man that took a reed and brought it down over the cruel thorns, driving them into my brow, and tell him I will put a sceptre in his hand, and he shall rule over the nations of the earth, if he will accept salvation. Search for the man that drove the spear into my side, and tell him there is a nearer way to my heart than that. Tell him I forgive

MR. MOODY'S STUDY.

Buildings and Grounds of the Young Ladies' Seminary.

A VIEW FROM THE WEST SIDE OF THE CONNECTICUT RIVER, AT NORTHFIELD, MASSACHUSETTS.

Mr. Moody's House.

him freely, and that he can be saved if he will accept salvation as a gift.'" *Tell him there is a nearer way to my heart than that* —prepared or impromptu, what dramatist could surpass the touch?

MR. MOODY'S MANNER OF PREPARING A SERMON.

His method of sermon-making is original. In reality his sermons are never made, they are always still in the making. Suppose the subject is Paul : he takes a monstrous envelope capable of holding some hundreds of slips of paper, labels it " Paul," and slowly stocks it with original notes, cuttings from papers, extracts from books, illustrations, scraps of all kinds, nearly or remotely referring to the subject. After accumulating these, it may be for years, he wades

novelty both in the subject matter and in the arrangement, for the particular seventy varies with each time of delivery. No greater mistake could be made than to imagine that Mr. Moody does not study for his sermons. On the contrary he is always studying. When in the evangelistic field, the batch of envelopes, bursting with fatness, appears the moment breakfast is over ; and the stranger who enters at almost any time of the day, except at the hours of platform work, will find him with his litter of notes, either stuffing himself or his portfolios with the new " points " he has picked up through the day. His search for these " points," and especially for light upon texts, Bible ideas, or characters, is ceaseless, and he has an eye like an eagle for anything really good. Possessing a considerable library, he browses over it when at home ; but his books are chiefly

HOTEL NORTHFIELD ; OCCUPIED FROM OCTOBER TO MARCH BY THE NORTHFIELD TRAINING SCHOOL.

through the mass, selects a number of the most striking points, arranges them, and, finally, makes a few jottings in a large hand, and these he carries with him to the platform. The process of looking through the whole envelope is repeated each time the sermon is preached. Partly on this account, and partly because in delivery he forgets some points, or disproportionately amplifies others, no two sermons are ever exactly the same. By this method also—a matter of much more importance—the delivery is always fresh to himself. Thus, to make this clearer, suppose that after a thorough sifting, one hundred eligible points remain in the envelope. Every time the sermon is preached, these hundred are overhauled. But no single sermon, by a mere limitation of time, can contain, say, more than seventy. Hence, though the general scheme is the same, there is always

men, and no student ever read the everopen page more diligently, more intelligently, or to more immediate practical purpose.

To Mr. Moody himself, it has always been a standing marvel that people should come to hear him. He honestly believes that ten thousand sermons are made every week, in obscure towns, and by unknown men, vastly better than anything he can do. All he knows about his own productions is that somehow they achieve the result intended. No man is more willing to stand aside and let others speak. His search for men to whom the people will listen, for men who, whatever the meagreness of their message, can yet hold an audience, has been life-long, and whenever and wherever he finds such men he instantly seeks to employ them. The word jealousy he has never heard. At one of his own conventions at Northfield, he has been known to keep silent—but for the exercise of the duties of chairman — during almost the whole ten days' sederunt, while mediocre men—I speak comparatively, not disrespectfully — were pushed to the front.

It is at such conferences, by the way, no matter in what part of the world they are held, that one discovers Mr. Moody's size. He gathers round him the best men he can find, and very good men most of them are ; but when one comes away it is always Mr. Moody that one remembers. It is he who leaves the impress upon us ; his word and spirit live ; the rest of us are forgotten and forget one another. It is the same story when on the evangelistic round. In every city the prominent workers in that field for leagues around are all in evidence. They crowd round the central figure like bees ; you can review the whole army at once. And it is no disparagement to the others to say—what each probably feels for himself—that so high is the stature and commanding personality of Mr. Moody that there seems to be but one real man among them, one character untarnished by intolerance or pettiness, pretentiousness, or self-seeking. The man who should judge Mr. Moody by the rest of us who support his cause would do a great injustice. He makes mistakes like other men ; but in largeness of heart, in breadth of view, in single-eyedness and humility, in teachableness and self-obliteration, in sheer goodness and love, none can stand beside him.

MR. MOODY'S FIRST VISIT TO GREAT BRITAIN.

After the early Chicago days the most remarkable episode in Mr. Moody's career was his preaching tour in Great Britain. The burning down of his church in Chicago severed the tie which bound him to the city, and though he still retained a connection with it, his ministry henceforth belonged to the world. Leaving his mark on Chicago, in many directions—on missions, churches, and, not least, on the Young Men's Christian Association—and already famous in the West for his success in evangelical work, he arrived in England, with his colleague Mr. Sankey, in June, 1873. The opening of their work there was not auspicious. Two of the friends who had invited them had died, and the strangers had an uphill fight. No one had heard of them ; the clergy received them coldly ; Mr. Moody's so-called Americanisms prejudiced the super-refined against him ; the organ and the solos of Mr. Sankey were an innovation sufficient to ruin almost any cause. For some time the prospect was bleak enough. In the town of Newcastle finally some faint show of public interest was awakened. One or two earnest ministers in Edinburgh went to see for themselves. On returning they reported cautiously, but on the whole favorably, to their brethren. The immediate result was an invitation to visit the capital of Scotland ; and the final result was the starting of a religious movement, quiet, deep, and

THE NORTHFIELD AUDITORIUM : COMPLETED DURING THE PRESENT YEAR, AND THE NEWEST IN THE GROUP OF SEMINARY BUILDINGS. IT HAS A SEATING CAPACITY OF THREE THOUSAND.

lasting, which moved the country from shore to shore, spread to England, Wales, and Ireland, and reached a climax two years later in London itself.

This is not the place, as already said, to enter either into criticism or into details of such a work. Like all popular movements, it had its mistakes, its exaggerations, even its grave dangers; but these were probably never less in any equally wide-spread movement of history, nor was the balance of good upon the whole ever greater, more solid, or more enduring. People who understand by a religious movement only a promiscuous carnival of hysterical natures, beginning in excitement and ending in moral exhaustion and fanaticism, will probably be assured in vain that whatever were the lasting characteristics of this movement, these were not. That such elements were wholly absent may not be asserted; human nature is human nature; but always the first to fight them, on the rare occasions when they appeared, was Mr. Moody himself. He, above all popular preachers, worked for solid results. Even the mere harvesting—his own special department—was a secondary thing to him compared with the garnering of the fruits by the Church and their subsequent growth and further fruitfulness. It was the writer's privilege as a humble camp-follower to follow the fortunes of this campaign personally from town to town, and from city to city, throughout the three kingdoms, for over a year. And time has only deepened the impression not only of the magnitude of the results immediately secured, but equally of the permanence of the after effects upon every field of social, philanthropic, and religious activity. It is not too much to say that Scotland—one can speak with less knowledge of England and Ireland—would not have been the same to-day but for the visit of Mr. Moody and Mr. Sankey; and that so far-reaching was, and is, the influence of their work, that any one who knows the inner religious history of the country must regard this time as nothing short of a national epoch. If this is a specimen of what has been effected even in less degree elsewhere, it represents a fact of commanding importance. Those who can speak with authority of the long series of campaigns which succeeded this in America, testify in many cases with almost equal assurance of the results achieved both throughout the United States and Canada.

After his return from Great Britain, in 1875, Mr. Moody made his home at North-field, his house in Chicago having been swept away by the fire. And from this point onward his activity assumed a new and extraordinary development. Continuing his evangelistic work in America, and even on one occasion revisiting England, he spent his intervals of repose in planning and founding the great educational institutions of which Northfield is now the centre.

MR. MOODY'S SCHOOLS AT NORTHFIELD.

There is no stronger proof of Mr. Moody's breadth of mind than that he should have inaugurated this work. For an evangelist seriously to concern himself with such matters is unusual; but that the greatest evangelist of his day, not when his powers were failing, but in the prime of life, and in the zenith of his success, should divert so great a measure of his strength into educational channels, is a phenomenal circumstance. The explanation is manifold. No man sees so much slip-shod, unsatisfactory and half-done work as the evangelist; no man so learns the worth of solidity, the necessity for a firm basis for religion to work upon, the importance to the Kingdom of God of men who "weigh." The value, above all things, of character, of the sound mind and disciplined judgment, are borne in upon him every day he lives. Converts without these are weak-kneed and useless; Christian workers inefficient, if not dangerous. Mr. Moody saw that the object of Christianity was to make good men and good women; good men and good women who would serve their God and their country not only with all their heart, but with all their mind and all their strength. Hence he would found institutions for turning out such characters. His pupils should be committed to nothing as regards a future profession. They might become ministers or missionaries, evangelists or teachers, farmers or politicians, business men or lawyers. All that he would secure would be that they should have a chance, a chance of becoming useful, educated, God-fearing men. A favorite aphorism with him is, that "it is better to set ten men to work than to do the work of ten men." His institutions were founded to equip other men to work, not in the precise line, but in the same broad interest as himself. He himself had had the scantiest equipment for his life-work, and he daily lamented—though perhaps no one else ever did—the deficiency. In his journeys he constantly met young men and young women of earnest spirit,

MR. MOODY HOLDING A SERVICE ON THE HILL CALLED "NEW CALVARY," NEAR JERUSALEM, SUNDAY AFTERNOON, APRIL 28, 1892.   MR. MOODY STANDS WHERE LINES DRAWN FROM THE TWO STARS AT THE MARGIN OF THE PICTURE WOULD CROSS EACH OTHER.

with circumstances against them, who were in danger of being lost to themselves and to the community. These especially it was his desire to help, and afford a chance in life. "The motive," says the "Official Handbook," "presented for the pursuit of an education is the power it confers for Christian life and usefulness, not the means it affords to social distinction, or the gratification of selfish ambition. It is designed to combine, with other instruction, an unusual amount of instruction in the Bible, and it is intended that all the training given shall exhibit a thoroughly Christian spirit. . . . No constraint is placed on the religious views of any one. . . . The chief emphasis of the instruction given is placed upon the life."

The plan, of course, developed by degrees, but once resolved upon, the beginning was made with characteristic decision; for the years other men spend in criticising a project, Mr. Moody spends in executing it. One day in his own house, talking with Mr. H. N. F. Marshall about the advisability of immediately securing a piece of property—some sixteen acres close to his door—his friend expressed his assent. The words were scarcely uttered when the owner of the land was seen walking along the road. He was invited in, the price fixed, and, to the astonishment of the owner, the papers made out on the spot. Next winter a second lot was bought, the building of a seminary for female students commenced, and at the present moment the land in connection with this one institution amounts to over two hundred and seventy acres. The current expense of this one school per annum is over fifty-one thousand dollars, thirty thousand dollars of which comes from the students themselves; and the existing endowment, the most of which, however, is not yet available, reaches one hundred and four thousand dollars. Dotted over the noble campus thus secured, and clustered especially near Mr. Moody's home, stand ten spacious buildings and a number of smaller size, all connected with the Ladies' Seminary. The education, up to the standard aimed at, is of first-rate quality, and prepares students for entrance into Wellesley and other institutions of similar high rank.

Four miles distant from the Ladies' Seminary, on the rising ground on the opposite side of the river, are the no less imposing buildings of the Mount Hermon School for Young Men. Conceived earlier than the former, but carried out later, this institu-

tion is similar in character, though many of the details are different. Its three or four hundred students are housed in ten fine buildings, with a score of smaller ones. Surrounding the whole is a great farm of two hundred and seventy acres, farmed by the pupils themselves. This economic addition to the educational training of the students is an inspiration of Mr. Moody's. Nearly every pupil is required to do from an hour and a half to two hours and a half of farm or industrial work each day, and much of the domestic work is similarly distributed. The lads work on the roads, in the fields, in the woods; in the refectory, laundry, and kitchen; they take charge of the horses, the cattle, the hogs, and the hens—for the advantage of all which the sceptical may be referred to Mr. Ruskin. Once or twice a year nearly everyone's work is changed; the indoor lads go out, the farm lads come in. Those who before entering the school had already learned trades, have the opportunity of pursuing them in leisure hours, and though the industrial department is strongly subordinated to the educational, many in this way help to pay the fee of one hundred dollars exacted annually from each pupil, which pays for tuition, board, rooms, etc.*

THE LARGE PROFITS OF THE MOODY AND SANKEY HYMN-BOOK.

The mention of this fee—which, it may be said in passing, only covers half the cost—suggests the question as to how the vast expenses of these and other institutions, such as the new Bible Institute in Chicago, and the Bible, sewing and cooking school into which the Northfield Hotel is converted in winter, are defrayed. The buildings themselves and the land have been largely the gift of friends, but much of the cost of maintenance is paid out of Mr. Moody's own pocket. The fact that Mr. Moody has a pocket has been largely dwelt upon by his enemies, and the amount and source of its contents are subjects of curious speculation. I shall suppose the critic to be honest, and divulge to him a fact which the world has been slow to learn—the secret of Mr. Moody's pocket. It is, briefly, that Mr. Moody is the owner of one of the most paying literary properties in existence. It is the hymn-book

* An extensive literature, up to date and fully describing all the Northfield institutions, splendidly edited by Mr. Henry W. Rankin, one of Mr. Moody's most wise and accomplished coadjutors, may be had at Revell's, 112 Fifth Avenue, New York.

which, first used at his meetings in conjunction with Mr. Sankey, whose genius created it, is now in universal use throughout the civilized world. Twenty years ago he offered it for nothing to a dozen different publishers, but none of them would look at it. Failing to find a publisher, Mr. Moody, with almost the last few dollars he possessed, had it printed in London in 1873. The copyright stood in his name ; any loss that might have been suffered was his ; and to any gain, by all the laws of business, he was justly entitled. The success, slow at first, presently became gigantic. The two evangelists saw a fortune in their hymn-book. But they saw something which was more vital to them than a fortune—that the busybody and the evil tongue would accuse them, if they but touched one cent of it, of preaching the gospel for gain. What did they do? They refused to touch it—literally even to touch it. The royalty was handed direct from the publishers to a committee of well-known business men in London, who distributed it to various charities. When the evangelists left London, a similar committee, with Mr. W. E. Dodge at its head, was formed in New York. For many years this committee faithfully disbursed the trust, and finally handed over its responsibility to a committee of no less weight and honor—the trustees of the Northfield seminaries, to be used henceforth in their behalf. Such is the history of Mr. Moody's pocket.

In the year 1889 Mr. Moody broke out in a new place. Not content with having founded two great schools at Northfield, he turned his attention to Chicago, and inaugurated there one of his most successful enterprises—the Bible Institute. This scheme grew out of many years' thought. The general idea was to equip lay workers —men and women—for work among the poor, the outcast, the churchless, and the illiterate. In every centre of population there is a call for such help. The demand for city missionaries, Bible readers, evangelists, superintendents of Christian and philanthropic institutions, is unlimited. In the foreign field it is equally claimant. Mr. Moody saw that all over the country were those who, with a little special training, might become effective workers in these various spheres—some whose early opportunities had been neglected ; some who were too old or too poor to go to college ; and others who, half their time, had to earn their living. To meet such workers and such work the Institute was conceived. The heart of Chicago, both morally and

physically, offered a suitable site ; and here, adjoining the Chicago Avenue Church, a preliminary purchase of land was made at a cost of fifty-five thousand dollars. On part of this land, for a similar sum, a three-storied building was put up to accommodate male students, while three houses, already standing on the property, were transformed into a ladies' department. No sooner were the doors opened than some ninety men and fifty women began work. So immediate was the response that all the available accommodation was used up, and important enlargements have had to be made since. The mornings at the Institute are largely given up to Bible study and music, the afternoons to private study and visitation, and the evenings to evangelistic work. In the second year of its existence no fewer than two hundred and forty-eight students were on the roll-book. In addition to private study, these conducted over three thousand meetings, large and small, in the city and neighborhood, paid ten thousand visits to the homes of the poor, and "called in" at more than a thousand saloons.

As to the ultimate destination of the workers, the statistics for this same year record the following :

At work in India are three, one man and two women ; in China, three men and one woman, with four more (sexes equally divided) waiting appointment there ; in Africa, two men and two women, with two men and one woman waiting appointment ; in Turkey, one man and five women ; in South America, one man and one woman ; in Bulgaria, Persia, Burma, and Japan, one woman to each ; among the North American Indians, three women and one man. In the home field, in America, are thirty-seven men and nine women employed in evangelistic work, thirty-one in pastoral work (including many ministers who had come for further study), and twenty-nine in other schools and colleges. Sunday-school missions employ five men ; home missions, two ; the Young Men's Christian Association, seven ; the Young Women's Christian Association, two. Five men and one woman are "singing evangelists." Several have positions in charitable institutions, others are evangelists, and twenty are teachers. This is a pretty fair record for a two years old institute.

Not quite on the same lines, but with certain features in common, is still a fourth institution founded by the evangelist at Northfield about the same time. This is, perhaps, one of his most original developments—the Northfield Training School for Women. In his own work at Chicago, and in his evangelistic rounds among the churches, he had learned to appreciate the exceptional value of women in ministering to the poor. He saw, however, that women of the right stamp were not always to be found where they were needed most, and in many cases where they were to be found, their work was marred by inexperience and lack of training. He determined, therefore, to start a novel species of training school, which city churches and mission fields could draw upon, not for highly educated missionaries, but for Christian women who had undergone a measure of special instruction, especially in Bible knowledge and *domestic economy*—the latter being the special feature. The initial obstacle of a building in which to start his institute was no difficulty to Mr. Moody. Among the many great buildings of Northfield there was one which, every winter, was an eyesore to him. It was the Northfield Hotel, and it was an eye-sore because it was empty. After the busy season in summer, it was shut up from October till the end of March, and Mr. Moody resolved that he would turn its halls into lecture rooms, its bedrooms into dormitories, stock the first with teachers and the second with scholars, and start the work of the Training School as soon as the last guest was off the premises.

In October, 1890, the first term opened. Six instructors were provided, and fifty-six students took up residence at once. Next year the numbers were almost doubled, and the hotel college to-day is in a fair way to become a large and important institution. In addition to systematic Bible study, which forms the backbone of the curriculum, the pupils are taught those branches of domestic economy which are most likely to be useful in their work among the homes of the poor. Much stress is laid upon cooking, especially the preparation of foods for the sick, and a distinct department is also devoted to dressmaking. An objection was raised at the outset that the students, during their term of residence, were isolated from the active Christian work in which their lives were to be spent, and that hence the most important part of their training must be merely theoretical. But this difficulty has solved itself. Though not contemplated at the founding of the school, the living energy and enthusiasm of the students have sought their own outlets; and now, all through the winter, flying columns may be found scouring the country-side in all directions, visiting the homesteads, and holding services in hamlets, cottages, and schoolhouses.

MR. MOODY UNDENOMINATIONAL AND UNSECTARIAN IN HIS WORKS.

Like all Mr. Moody's institutions, the winter Training Home is undenominational and unsectarian. It is a peculiarity of Northfield, that every door is open not only to the Church Universal, but to the world. Every State in the Union is represented among the students of his two great colleges, and almost every nation and race. On the college books are, or have been, Africans, Armenians, Turks, Syrians, Austrians, Hungarians, Canadians, Danes, Dutch, English, French, German, Indian, Irish, Japanese, Chinese, Norwegians, Russians, Scotch, Swedish, Alaskans, and Bulgarians. These include every type of Christianity, members of every Christian denomination, and disciples of every Christian creed. Twenty-two denominations, at least, have shared the hospitality of the schools. This, for a religious educational institution, is itself a liberal education; and that Mr. Moody should not only have permitted, but encouraged, this cosmopolitan and unsectarian character, is a witness at once to his sagacity and to his breadth.

With everything in his special career, in his habitual environment, and in the traditions of his special work, to make him intolerant, Mr. Moody's sympathies have only broadened with time. Some years ago the Roman Catholics in Northfield determined to build a church. They went round the township collecting subscriptions, and by and by approached Mr. Moody's door. How did he receive them? The narrower evangelical would have shut the door in their faces, or opened it only to give them a lecture on the blasphemies of the Pope or the iniquities of the Scarlet Woman. Mr. Moody gave them one of the handsomest subscriptions on their list. Not content with that, when their little chapel was finished, he presented them with an organ. "Why," he exclaimed, when some one challenged the action, "if they are Roman Catholics, it is better they should be good Roman Catholics than bad. It is surely better to have a Catholic Church than none; and as for the organ, if they are to have music in their church, it is better to have good music. Besides," he added, "these are my own townspeople. If ever I am to be of the least use to them, surely I must help them." What the kindly feeling did for them, it is difficult to say ; but what it did for Mr. Moody, is matter of local history. For, a short time after, it was rumored that he was going to build a church, and the site was pointed out by the villagers—a rocky knoll close by the present hotel. One day Mr. Moody found the summit of this knoll covered with great piles of stones. The Roman Catholics had taken their teams up the mountain, and brought down, as a return present, enough building-stone to form the foundations of his church.

Mr. Moody's relations with the Northfield people and with all the people for miles and miles around are of the same type. So far from being without honor in his own country, it is there he is honored most. This fact—and nothing more truly decisive of character can be said—may be verified even by the stranger on the cars. The nearer he approaches Northfield, the more thorough and genuine will find the appreciation of Mr. Moody ; and when he passes under Mr. Moody's own roof, he will find it truest, surest, and most affectionate of all. It is forbidden here to invade the privacy of Mr. Moody's home. Suffice it to say that no more perfect home-life exists in the world, and that one only begins to know the greatness, the tenderness, and the simple beauty of this man's character when one sees him at his own fireside. One evidence of this greatness it is difficult to omit recording. If you were to ask Mr. Moody—which it would never occur to you to do—what, apart from the inspirations of his personal faith, was the secret of his success, of his happiness and usefulness in life, he would assuredly answer, "Mrs. Moody."

THE WIDE REACH OF MR. MOODY'S LABORS.

When one has recorded the rise and progress of the four institutions which have been named, one but stands on the threshold of the history of the tangible memorials of Mr. Moody's career. To realize even partially the intangible results of his life, is not within the compass of man's power ; but even the tangible results—the results which have definite visible outcome, which are capable of statistical expression, which can be seen in action in different parts of the world to-day—it would tax a diligent historian to tabulate. The sympathies and activities of men like D. L. Moody are supposed by many to be wasted on the empty air. It will surprise

them to be told that he is probably responsible for more actual stone and lime than almost any man in the world. There is scarcely a great city in England where he has not left behind him some visible memorial. His progress through Great Britain and Ireland, now nearly twenty years ago, is marked to-day by halls, churches, institutes, and other buildings which owe their existence directly to his influence. In the capital of each of these countries—in London, Edinburgh, and Dublin—great buildings stand to-day which, but for him, had had no existence. In the city where these words are written, at least three important institutions, each the centre of much work and of a multitude of workers, Christian philanthropy owes to him. Young Men's Christian Associations all over the land have been housed, and in many cases sumptuously housed, not only largely by his initiative, but by his personal actions in raising funds. Mr. Moody is the most magnificent beggar Great Britain has ever known. He will talk over a millionnaire in less time than it takes other men to apologize for intruding upon his time. His gift for extracting money amounts to genius. The hard, the sordid, the miserly, positively melt before him. But his power to deal with refractory ones is not the best of it. His supreme success is with the already liberal, with those who give, or think they give, handsomely already. These he somehow convinces that their givings are nothing at all ; and there are multitudes of rich men in the world who would confess that Mr. Moody inaugurated for them, and for their churches and cities, the day of large subscriptions. The process by which he works is, of course, a secret, but one half of it probably depends upon two things. In the first place, his appeals are wholly for others ; for places—I am speaking of England—in which he would never set foot again; for causes in which he had no personal stake. In the second place, he always knew the right moment to strike.

HOW MR. MOODY ORGANIZED A GREAT CHARITY IN TEN MINUTES.

On one occasion, to recall an illustration of the last he had convened a great conference in Liverpool. The theme for discussion was a favorite one—"How to reach the masses." One of the speakers, the Rev. Charles Garrett, in a powerful speech, expressed his conviction that the chief want of the masses in Liverpool was the institution of cheap houses of refreshment to counteract the saloons. When he had finished, Mr. Moody called upon him to speak for ten minutes more. That ten minutes might almost be said to have been a crisis in the social history of Liverpool. Mr. Moody spent it in whispered conversation with gentlemen on the platform. No sooner was the speaker done than Mr. Moody sprang to his feet and announced that a company had been formed to carry out the objects Mr. Garrett had advocated; that various gentlemen, whom he named (Mr. Alexander Balfour, Mr. Samuel Smith, M. P., Mr. Lockhart, and others), had each taken one thousand shares of five dollars each, and that the subscription list would be open till the end of the meeting. The capital was gathered almost before the adjournment, and a company floated under the name of the "British Workman Company, Limited," which has not only worked a small revolution in Liverpool, but—what was not contemplated or wished for, except as an index of healthy business—paid a handsome dividend to the shareholders. For twenty years this company has gone on increasing; its ramifications are in every quarter of the city; it has returned ten per cent. throughout the whole period, except for one (strike) year, when it returned seven; and, above all, it has been copied by cities and towns innumerable all over Great Britain. To Mr. Garrett, who unconsciously set the ball a-rolling, the personal consequences were as curious as they were unexpected. "You must take charge of this thing," said Mr. Moody to him, "or at least you must keep your eye on it." "That cannot be," was the reply. "I am a Wesleyan; my three years in Liverpool have expired; I must pass to another circuit." "No," said Mr. Moody, "you must stay here." Mr. Garrett assured him it was quite impossible, the Methodist Conference made no exceptions. But Mr. Moody would not be beaten. He got up a petition to the Conference. It was granted—an almost unheard-of thing—and Mr. Garrett remains in his Liverpool church to this day. This last incident proves at least one thing—that Mr. Moody's audacity is at least equalled by his influence.

THE CHARACTER OF MR. MOODY'S GREATNESS.

That I have not told one tithe that is due to the subject of this sketch, I painfully realize now that my space has narrowed to its close. It is of small significance that one should make out this or the other man to be numbered among the world's great. But it is of importance to national ideals, that standards of worthiness should be truly drawn, and, when those who answer to them in real life appear, that they should be held up for the world's instruction. Mr. Moody himself has never asked for justice, and never for homage. The criticism which sours, and the adulation—an adulation at epochs in his life amounting to worship—which spoils, have left him alike untouched. The way he turned aside from applause in England struck multitudes with wonder. To be courted was to him not merely a thing to be discouraged on general principles; it simply made him miserable. At the close of a great meeting, when crowds, not of the base, but of the worthy, thronged the platform to press his hand, somehow he had always disappeared. When they followed him to his hotel, its doors were barred. When they wrote him, as they did in thousands, they got no response. This man would not be praised. Yet, partly for this very reason, those who love him love to praise him. And I may as well confess what has induced me, against keen personal dislike to all that is personal, to write these articles. One day, travelling in America last summer, a high dignitary of the Church in my presence made a contemptuous reference to Mr. Moody. A score of times in my life I have sailed in on such occasions, and at least taught the detractor some facts. On this occasion, with due humility, I asked the speaker if he had ever met him? He had not; and the reply elicited that the name which he had used so lightly was to him no more than an echo. I determined that, time being then denied, I would take the first opportunity of bringing that echo nearer him. It is for him these words were written.

WHITTIER'S OPINION OF MR. MOODY.

In the Life of Whittier, just published, the patronizing reference to Mr. Moody but too plainly confirms the statement with which the first article opened—that few men were less known to their contemporaries.

"Moody and Sankey," writes the poet, "are busy in Boston. The papers give the discourses of Mr. Moody, which seem rather commonplace and poor, but the man is in earnest. . . . I hope he will do good, and believe that he will reach and move some who could not be touched by James Freeman Clarke or Phillips Brooks. I cannot accept his theology, or part of it at least, and his methods are not to my taste. But if he can make the drunkard, the gambler, and the debauchee into decent men, and make the lot of their weariful wives and children less bitter, I bid him God-speed."

I have called these words patronizing, but the expression should be withdrawn. Whittier was incapable of that. They are broad, large-hearted, even kind. But they are not the right words. They are the stereotyped charities which sweet natures apply to anything not absolutely harmful, and contain no more impression of the tremendous intellectual and moral force of *the man behind* than if the reference were to the obscurest Salvation Army zealot. I shall not indorse, for it could only give offence, the remark of a certain author of world-wide repute when he read the words : " Moody ! Why, he could have put half a dozen Whittiers in his pocket, and they would never have been noticed ; " but I shall indorse, and with hearty good-will, a judgment which he further added. " I have always held," he said—and he is a man who has met every great contemporary thinker from Carlyle downward— " that in sheer brain-size, in the mere raw material of intellect, Moody stands among the first three or four great men I have ever known." I believe Great Britain is credited with having " discovered " Mr. Moody. It may or may not be ; but if it be, it was men of the quality and the experience of my friend who made the discovery ; and that so many distinguished men in America have failed to appreciate

him is a circumstance which has only one explanation—that they have never had the opportunity.

An American estimate, nevertheless, meets my eye as I lay down the pen, which I gladly plead space for, as it proves that in Mr. Moody's own country there are not wanting those who discern how much he stands for. They are the notes, slightly condensed, of one whose opportunities for judging of his life and work have been exceptionally wide. In his opinion :

1. " No other living man has done so much directly in the way of uniting man to God, and in restoring men to their true centre.

2. " No other living man has done so much to unite man with man, to break down personal grudges and ecclesiastical barriers, bringing into united worship and harmonious coöperation men of diverse views and dispositions.

3. " No other living man has set so many other people to work, and developed, by awakening the sense of responsibility, latent talents and powers which would otherwise have lain dormant.

4. " No other living man, by precept and example, has so vindicated the rights, privileges, and duties of laymen.

5. " No other living man has raised more money for other people's enterprises.

6. " No other evangelist has kept himself so aloof from fads, religious or otherwise ; from isms, from special reforms, from running specific doctrines, or attacking specific sins ; has so concentrated his life upon the one supreme endeavor."

If one-fourth of this be true, it is a unique and noble record ; if all be true, which of us is worthy even to characterize it ?

PORTRAITS OF PROFESSOR HENRY DRUMMOND.

Born at Stirling, Scotland, 1851.

FROM AN EARLY MINIATURE.

WHEN A FRESHMAN IN COLLEGE, FROM A PHOTOGRAPH
BY CROWE AND RODGERS, STIRLING.

AS A TRAVELLER IN CENTRAL AFRICA. AGE 35 OR 36.

AGE 37. 1888. FROM A PHOTOGRAPH BY LAFAYETTE, DUBLIN.

AGE 39. 1890.

IN 1893. FROM A SNAP SHOT IN QUEBEC.

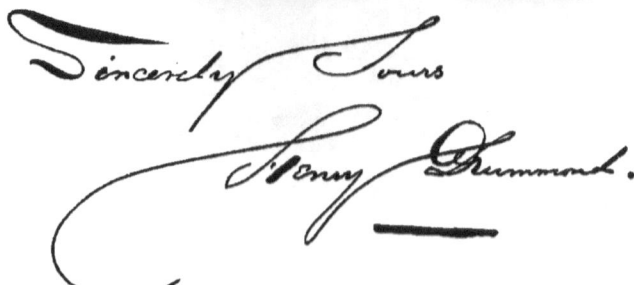

PORTRAITS OF GEORGE W. CABLE.

Born at New Orleans October 12, 1844.

AGE 9. 1853.

1874. FIRST SKETCHES OF CREOLE LIFE.

AGE 19. 1863.

1882. "DOCTOR SEVIER."

AGE 24. 1853.

AGE 40. 1885. "BONAVENTURE."

MR. CAULE IN 1892.

AGE 21, PARIS, 1861. "LETTERS FROM MY MILL."

AGE 30, PARIS, 1870.

AGE 35, PARIS, 1875. "FROMONT JEUNE ET RISLER
AINÉ."

DAUDET AT THE PRESENT DAY.

ALPHONSE DAUDET AT HOME.

HIS OWN ACCOUNT OF HIS LIFE AND WORK

REPORTED BY R. H. SHERARD.

THOUGH now grown wealthy, and one of the first personages in Parisian society, being the most welcome guest in such exclusive drawing-rooms as that of the Princess Mathilde, the simple and good-hearted Alphonse Daudet is the most accessible man in Paris. I don't believe that any one is ever turned away from his door.

He lives in the fashionable Faubourg St. Germain quarter, on the fourth floor of a house in the Rue de Bellechasse which is reputed to possess the most elegant staircase of any apartment house in Paris. His apartment is simply furnished, and is in great contrast to that of Zola or of Dumas. Still there are not wanting for its decoration objects of art, and especially may be mentioned some fine old oak furniture. To the right of the table on which he writes is a Normandy farmhouse cupboard of carved oak which is a treasure in itself. The table, like that of many other successful men of letters in Paris, is a very large and highly ornamental one, reminding one of an altar; while the chair which is set against it, though less throne-like than that of Emile Zola, is stately and decorative. Daudet's study is the most comfortable room in the house. The three windows look out on a pleasant garden, and, as they face the south, the sun streams through the red-embroidered lace curtains nearly all the day. The doors are draped with Oriental portières; a heavy carpet covers the floor, and the furniture, apart from the work-table and chair, is for comfort and not for show. Daudet's favorite place, when not writing, is on a little sofa which stands by the fireplace. When the master is seated here, his back is to the light. His visitor sits opposite to him on another couch, and between them is a small round table, on which may usually be seen the latest book of the day, and—for Daudet is a great smoker—cigars and cigarettes. There are few pictures in the room, but there is a fine portrait of Flaubert to be noticed, whilst over the bookshelf which lines the wall behind the writing-table is a portrait of the lady to whom Daudet confesses that he owes all the success as well as all the happiness of his life, the portrait of Madame Daudet.

Nothing can be more charming than the welcome which the master of the house extends to even the stranger who calls upon him for the first time. The free-masonry of letters or of Bohemia is nowhere in Paris so graciously encouraged as here. His intimates he calls "my sons," and it is this term that he applies also to his secretary and confidant, the excellent Monsieur Hebner. His good humor and unvarying kindness to one and all are the more admirable that, always a nervous sufferer, he has of late years been almost a confirmed invalid. He cannot move about the room but with the help of his stick; he has many nights when, racked with pain, he is unable to sleep; and it is consequently with surprise that those who know him see that he never lets an impatient word or gesture escape him, even under circumstances when one or the other would be perfectly justifiable. The consequence is, that Daudet has not a single enemy in the world. There are many who do not admire his work; but none who do not love the man for his sweetness, just as all are fascinated with his brilliant wit. It is one of the rarest of intellectual treats to hear Daudet talk as he talks at his table, or at his wife's "at-

homes" on Wednesday evenings, or on Sunday mornings, when from ten to twelve he receives his literary friends. He has a very free way of speech, and when alone with men uses whatever expressions best suit his purpose ; but every sentence is an epigram or an anecdote, a souvenir or a criticism. It is a sight that one must remember who has seen Alphonse Daudet sitting at his table, or on the couch by the fireside, in an attitude which always betrays how ill at ease he is, and yet showing himself superior to this, and with eyes fixed, rarely on the person whom he is addressing, but on something, pen or cigarette, which he turns and turns in his nervous fingers, conversing on whatever may be the topic of the day. He takes a keen interest in politics, and, indeed, seems to prefer to speak on these rather than on any other topic except literature.

HARDSHIPS OF CHILDHOOD AND YOUTH.

When, the other day, I asked him to tell me of his life, he said, speaking of his early youth, "I have often tried to collect the memories of my childhood, to write them out in Provençal, the language of my native land ; but my youth was such a sad one that these are all résuméd in the title of a book of my *souvenirs de jeunesse*, 'Mi Poou,' which means, in Provençal, 'My Fears.' Yes, fears and tears ; that is what my youth consisted of. I was born at Nîmes, where my father was a small tradesman. My youth at home was a lamentable one. I have no recollection of home which is not a sorrowful one, a recollection of tears. The baker who refuses bread ; the servant whose wages could not be paid, and who declares that she will stay on without wages, and becomes familiar in consequence, and says 'thou' to her master ; the mother always in tears ; the father always scolding. My country is a country of monuments. I played at marbles in the ruins of the temple of Diana, and raced with my little comrades in the devastated Roman arena. It is a beautiful country, however, and I am proud of my relation to it. My name seems to indicate that I descend from the Moorish settlers of Provence ; for, as you know, the Provençal people is largely of Moorish extraction. Indeed, it is from that circumstance that I have drawn much of the humor of my books, such as 'Tartarin.' It is funny, you know, to hear of men with bushy black hair and flaring eyes, like bandits and wild warriors, who are, the one a peaceful baker,

the other the least offensive of apothecaries. I myself have the Moorish type, and my name Daudet, according to the version which I like best, is the Moorish for David. Half my family is called David. Others say that Daudet means 'Deodat,' which is a very common name in Provence, and which, derived from *Deo datus*, means 'Given by God.'

"I know little of my predecessors, except that in 1720 there was a Chevalier Daudet, who wrote poetry and had a decade of celebrity in the South. But my brother Ernest, who used to be ambitious, in his book 'Mon Frère et Moi,' has tried to trace our genealogy from a noble family. Whatever we were at one time, we had come very low down in the world when I came into existence, and my childhood was as miserable a one as can be fancied. I have to some extent related its unhappiness in my book 'Le Petit Chose.' Oh! and apropos of 'Le Petit Chose,' let me declare, on my word of honor, that I had never read a line of Dickens when I wrote that book. People have said that I was inspired by Dickens, but that is not true. It was an English friend of mine, whom I had at Nîmes, a boy called Benasset, who first told me that I was very like Dickens in personal appearance. Perhaps that is the reason why people trace a resemblance in our work also."

"My most vivid recollection of youth is the terrible fear that I had of the mad dog. I was brought up at nurse in a village called Fons, which must have been called so because there was no fountain, and indeed no water, within eight miles. It was the most arid of places, and doubtless this was to some extent the reason why there were so many mad dogs in the district. I remember that the washerwomen of the village used to take tram to the Rhone to wash their linen, and that, when they returned in the evenings, all the people of the village used to line the road, as they passed with their wet clothes, to get a whiff of cool air and the scent of the water. Perhaps it was because there was no water anywhere that, when I was a child, I so longed for the sea ; and that, when I did not wish to be a poet, I prayed that I might become a sailor. But to tell you of the mad dogs that haunted my earliest days. My foster-father was an innkeeper. His name was Garrimon, which is Provençal for 'Mountain Rat.' Is not that a splendid name—Garrimon ? Why have I never used it in any of my books! Well, Garrimon's tavern was the rendezvous of the village. The *café* was on the first floor, and I can remember how, at nightfall, the black-bearded, dark-eyed men of the village, armed to the teeth, one with a sword, another with a gun, and most with scythes, used to come in from all parts of the district, talking of nothing but the *Chin Foü*, the mad dog, that was scouring the land, and against whom they had armed themselves. Then I ran to Néno, my foster-mother, and clung to her skirts, and lay awake at nights, trembling, as I thought of the *Chin Foü* and of the terrible weapons that the men carried because they, strong, black-bearded men, were as frightened at him as the quaking little wretch who started at every sound

that the wind made in the eaves of the old house. Where I lay in bed, I could hear rough voices, as they sat round the inn-tables, drinking lemonade—for the Provençal is so excitable by nature that mere lemonade acts upon him like strong drink —and it was the *Chin Foü*, and nothing but the *Chin Foü*, which they talked about. But what brought my horror to a climax, and left an ineffaceable impression on me, was, that one day I nearly met the mad dog. It was a summer evening, I remember, and I was walking home, carrying a little basket, along a path white with dust, through thick vines. Suddenly I heard wild cries, '*Aou Chin Foü! Aou Chin Foü!*' Then came a discharge of

DAUDET AND HIS ELDEST SON, LÉON, IN DAUDET'S STUDY.

From a photograph taken especially for McClure's Magazine.

guns. Mad with terror I jumped into the vines, rolling head over ears; and, as I lay there, unable to stir a finger, I heard the dog go by as if a hurricane were passing; heard his fierce breath, and the thunder of the stones that in his mad course he rolled before him; and my heart stopped beating, in a paroxysm of terror, which is the strongest emotion that I have ever felt in all my life. Since then I have an absolute horror of dogs, and, by extension, indeed, of all animals. People have reproached me for this, and say that a poet cannot dislike animals. I can't help it. I hate them all. I think that they are what is ugly and vile in nature. They are caricatures of all that is most loathsome and base in man; they are the latrines of humanity. And, curiously enough, all my children have inherited this same horror of dogs.

"I remember that at nineteen, when I was down in the valley of Chevreuse, not far from Madame Adam's place at Gif, the recollection of that afternoon came upon me so strongly, that, borrowing Victor Hugo's title, I wrote the 'Forty Days of a Condemned Man,' in which I essayed to depict, day by day, the sensations of a man who has been bitten by a mad dog. This work made me ill, a neuropath. Before I had finished writing it, I had grown to believe that I had indeed been bitten, and the result was that my horror and dread were confirmed. The sight of a dog is to-day still enough to distress me exceedingly. This phenomenon makes me think, what I have noticed before and repeatedly, that, comparing man to a book, he is set up in type at a very early age, and, in after life, it is only new editions of him that are printed; by which I mean that a man's character and habits are crystallized whilst he is still a very young man, and in after life he only goes through the same phases of emotion over and over again.

"Other memories of my youth? Well, the Homeric battles that we children of the town used to have. Nîmes is divided into Huguenots and Roman Catholics, and each party hated the other as keenly as they did in France on the day of Saint Bartholomew, which dawned on that sanguinary eve. The feud was as keen between the children of the town, and many were the battles with stones that we fought in the streets. I have on my forehead to

MADAME DAUDET AND HER DAUGHTER.

this day the cicatrice of a wound which I received from a Huguenot stone in one of those fights. I have described these fights in 'Numa Roumestan;' and here let me tell you that Numa Roumestan is Alphonse Daudet. It was said that he was Gambetta. Nothing of the sort. Numa Roumestan is Alphonse Daudet, with all his foibles and what strength he may have.

"My father had seventeen children, but only three lived to grow up: Ernest, a sister who married the brother of my wife, and myself. I knew only one of the others, being myself one of the younger. That was my brother Henri. I shall never forget the day when the news of his death reached home. It

came by telegram: 'He is dead. Pray God for him.' My father rose from the table, and cried, 'He is dead! He is dead! He is dead!' His gesture, his intonation, which had something of ancient tragedy about it, impressed me profoundly, and I remember that all that night I lay awake, trying to imitate my father's voice, to find the tragic ring of his voice, repeating 'He is dead! He is dead!' over and over again until I found it.

"I have told you that I longed for the sea. How I devoured the first novels that I read, 'Midshipman Easy,' by Marryat, 'Robinson Crusoe,' and 'The Pilot'! How I used to dream of all that water, and of the cold winds blowing across the brine! I dare say it was from this love of the water that I felt quite happy when I was sent to Lyons to school, because there I saw water and boats, and it was in some way a realization of my longings. I was ten when I was sent to school, and I remained at school until I was fifteen and a half. I delighted in Latin, and became a good Latin scholar, so that I was afterwards able to help my son Léon in his studies, going over all his books with him. I loved Tacitus; disliked Cicero. Tacitus has had a great influence on French literature since Chateaubriand. What I best remember of my school-days is the handwriting of every one of my little comrades. Often, in my nights of fever, lying awake, I have seen, as in hieroglyphs upon a huge wall, the writings of all those boys, and have passed hours, as it seemed, in attributing to its author each varied piece of penmanship. I made only one friend, whose name was Garrison, a man of the most extraordinary inconsequentiality. He called on me not long ago, for the first time since we parted at school, and I then heard that, though he had been in Paris almost as long as I had, he had never ventured to come near me. He told me, after much hesitation, that he was a manufacturer of dolls' boots, in a street near La Roquette; but that business was bad, and he wanted me to help him to do something else. I also learned that he had a son, who, he told me, was a comic actor at the Beaumarchais Theatre.

"It was on leaving the Lycée at Lyons that I entered upon what was the worst year of my life. It was only during that horrible period that I ever thought of suicide. But I had not the courage to finish with existence. It requires a great deal of courage to be a suicide. From the age of fifteen and a half to the age of sixteen and a half I was an usher in a school at Alais. The children at the school were very cruel to me. They laughed at me for

DAUDET'S SECOND SON.

my short-sightedness. They played impish tricks upon me because I was short-sighted. Yet I tried to conciliate them. I remember that I used to tell them stories, which I made up as I went along. The misery that I afterwards suffered in Paris was nothing compared to that year. I was free in Paris. There I was a slave, a butt. How horrible it was, and I was so sensitive a lad! I have told of this in the preface to 'Petit Chose,' which, by the way, I wrote too early. There was a child to whom I had been especially attentive, and who had promised me that he would take me to his parents' house during the vacation. I was so pleased, and did so look forward to this treat! Well, on the day of the prizes, in the distribution of which my young friend had received quite a number, which he owed to my coaching, he led me up to his parents, who were standing, waiting for him, by a grand landau, and said: 'Papa, mamma, here is Monsieur Daudet, who has been so good to me, and to whom I owe all these books.' Well, papa and mamma, stout bourgeois people in Sunday clothes, simply turned their backs on me, and drove off with my young pupil, without a single word. And I had so looked forward to a holiday in the country with the lad, whom I loved sincerely. I could not stand the life more than a year, and at the age of seventeen went to Paris, without prospects of any kind, determined to starve rather than to continue a life of suffering drudgery. My brother Ernest was in Paris at the time as secretary to an old gentleman, and he gave me a shelter. I had two francs in my pocket when I arrived in Paris, and I had to share my brother's bed. I brought some rubbishy manuscripts with me, poetry, chiefly of a religious character.

LITERARY LIFE IN PARIS.

"My first poem, indeed the first thing of mine that was printed, was published in the 'Gazette de Lyon,' in 1855. I was at that time fifteen years old. It was not long after my arrival in Paris that I was left entirely to my own resources; for my brother, losing his place as secretary, was forced to leave the capital, going into the country to edit a provincial paper. I then entered upon a period of the blackest misery, of the most doleful Bohemianism. I have suffered in the way of privation all that a man could suffer. I have known days without bread; I have spent days in bed because I had no boots to go out in.

I have had boots which made a squashy sound each step that I took. But what made me suffer most was, that I had often to wear dirty linen, because I could not pay a washerwoman. Often I had to fail to keep appointments given me by the fair—I was a handsome lad and liked by ladies—because I was too dirty and shabby to go. I spent three years of my life in this way—from the age of eighteen, when my brother left Paris, to twenty-one.

"At that moment Duc de Morny offered me employment. His offer came to me in the midst of horror, shame, and distress. He had heard of me in this way: Some time before, I had published my first book of poems, a small volume of eighty pages, entitled 'Les Amoureuses.' This book made my fortune. De Morny had heard the brothers Lyonnet reciting one of my poems out of this book, a poem called 'Les Prunes,' at the empress's, and I believe the empress asked him to make some inquiries about the poet. He sent to ask me what I needed to live on, and, accepting his patronage, I entered his service as *attaché de cabinet.* I passed at once from the most dingy Bohemianism to a butterfly life, learning all that there is of pleasure and luxury in existence. But somehow the legend of my Bohemianism clung to me, as it has clung to me all my life. Some people could never take me *au sérieux.* I remember that I once dined with the Duc Decazes for the purpose of one of my novels. I had written to tell him that I wanted to make use of his experiences, and he had asked me to dinner. Well, during the whole meal he related anecdotes of his career; but, thinking that he had to deal with a Bohemian, he arranged his anecdotes, as he thought, to interest me most. Thus he always began each story with 'I was taking a bock.' I suppose he thought that my idea of life was of beer-drinking in a *café.* At last I said : 'Your Excellency seems to be very fond of beer,' and afterwards added : 'It is a drink that I have never been able to support.' He seemed to understand what I meant, and changed his tone. But just as I left him—it was at two o'clock in the morning, and the lackeys, I remember, were all half dead with fatigue—he said : 'And now let us go and lay traps for Bismarck.' I went away thinking what an ass the man was to think that I should believe that he was going to do anything but go up-stairs to his wife ; and he, no doubt, went up-stairs to his wife thinking what an ass I must be to believe what he

had said. From the age of twenty-one I had only happiness. I may say that I was too happy. I am paying for it now. I believe that people always have to pay for what they have done and what they have enjoyed, and that therein lie justice and compensation for all, even on earth. Everybody's account is settled in this life. Of that I am sure.

"As to my success : About, writing for the 'Athenæum,' came to see me in 1872, to ask me what I was earning. He was writing something about the incomes of various men of letters, and, making up my accounts, I found that the amount of my average earnings at that time from literature was five thousand francs a year. Two years later, that is to say in 1874, I published 'Froment jeune et Risler aîné,' which brought me a great reputation, and greatly increased my income. Since 1878 I never made less than a hundred thousand francs a year, including my plays and novels. The book which gave me the most trouble was 'L'Évangéliste,' because my turn of mind is not in the least religious. It was 'L'Évangéliste,' also, that provoked the bitterest criticism, a book which made me numerous enemies. After its publication I was flooded with anonymous letters, some of the most offensive character. I remember receiving one which was so abominable that I took it to Pailleron to show it to him, and all who saw it said that it was the worst thing of its kind that they had ever seen.

HABITS OF WORK.

"My way of working is irregularity itself. Sometimes I work for eighteen hours a day, and day after day. At other times I pass months without touching a pen. I write very slowly, and revise and revise. I am never satisfied with my work. My novels I always write myself. I never could dictate a novel. As to my plays, I used formerly to dictate them. That was when I could walk. I had a certain talent in my legs. Since my illness I have had to abandon that mode of work, and I regret it. I am an improvisator, and in this respect differ from Zola. I am now writing a novel about youth, called 'Soutien de Famille,' and these note-books of mine will show you my way of work. This is the first book. It contains, as you see, nothing but notes and suggestions. The passages which are scratched out with red or blue pencil are passages of which I have already made use. This is the second stage. You see only one page is written upon, the opposite one being left blank. Opposite each first composition I write the amended copy. The page on the right is the improved copy of the page on the left. After that I shall rewrite the whole. So that, leaving the notes out of consideration, I write each manuscript three times running, and, if I could, would write it as many times more; for, as I have said, I am never satisfied with my work.

"I am a feverish and a spasmodic worker, but when in the mood can work very hard. When the fit is upon me I allow nothing to interrupt me, not even leaving my writing table for meals. I have my food brought to my desk, eat hurriedly, and set to work before digestion begins. Thus I anticipate the drowsiness that digestion always brings with it, and escape its consequences. Now that I am ill, however, I do not often have those periods of splendid energy. I can produce only very slowly, and I feel quite nervous about 'Soutien de Famille' when I think that it is already expected by the public and announced by the publishers. As to my literary creed, it is one of absolute independence for the writer. I have always rebelled against the three classic traditions of French literature; that is to say, the French Academy, the Théâtre Français, and the 'Revue des Deux Mondes.' I consider the Academy a collection of mediocrities, and would hold myself dishonored to be one of them.

"I am very, very nervous. There are times when I feel that, if a light were set to me, I should blaze up in red flame. Sometimes this nervousness of mine plays me bad tricks. I remember that it cost me a large sum of money one morning recently. A kind of dramatic agent, accompanied by his wife, came to see me, to ask me to sell them the rights of translation of my play, 'Lutte Pour la Vie;' and they bothered and irritated me so, that, in order to get rid of them, I sold them this right for four thousand francs. The woman told me how handsome I was, and said that the ladies must have been very fond

A CORNER IN DAUDET'S DRAWING-ROOM.

of me when I was a young man. She had a hat with feathers in it, and was altogether a most extraordinary person. An hour later I heard that these people had sold a part of the right I had ceded to them for thirty thousand francs; so that my nervousness that morning cost me about one thousand pounds.

"I must say that in my literary work I owe nearly all to my wife. She rereads all my books, and advises me on every point. She is all that is most charming, and has a wonderful mind, entirely opposed to mine, a synthetic spirit. I married at the age of twenty-six, and, strangely enough, I had always vowed that I never would marry a woman with literary tastes. The very first time that I met my wife was at a party at Ville d'Avray, where she recited a piece of poetry called 'Le Tremble.' She was dressed in white, and her appearance, as well as the way she declaimed those verses, produced an immense effect upon me. As we were leaving the house, my sister, who was with me, and who knew my aversion for women who dabble in literature, said to me, 'Well, Alphonse, that is not your style, is it?' I confessed, stammeringly, that I had no other hope then than that that girl should become my wife. I was fortunate enough to win her, and it was the greatest blessing that has been accorded to me in the course of a most happy and successful life. She is very different from me, practical and logical. Now, I am thoroughly superstitious. Thus I have a horror of the number thirteen, and would not walk under a ladder, or travel on a Friday, for any consideration. Our two characters are entirely opposed, and so are our ways of thinking. That is perhaps why we are such excellent friends.

"I have been very happy. There is my son Léon. I think that in him, Maurice Barrés, and in some other young men, lies the future of French literature. And then my other children. There is my little daughter Edmée, the godchild of De Goncourt. What can make a man happier than to have a ray of sunlight, like my little Edmée, charming, dainty, little six-year-old Parisienne that she is, about the house? There is a life of happiness in her presence alone."

As Daudet spoke, little Edmée ran into the room, just returned from a walk, and clambered upon the master's knees, and kissed him again and again; and it was a pretty sight to see the two. Daudet had some chocolate cigarettes in a drawer, and gave them to his daughter; and she said, "I shall die of happiness," when he gave them. It was emotional and Provençal, but sincere and pretty.

"The part of my success," continued Daudet, "which gave me the least pleasure, perhaps, was my advancement in the Legion of Honor to the degree of officer. I remember well, it was seven years ago, and I was in a box at the Théâtre Français, watching Mounet-Sully playing the part of Hamlet; and just when the curtain fell on the first act, and I had risen, saying, 'I must go and embrace Mounet: he has been sublime,' I felt myself plucked by the sleeve, and looking around saw Floquet. He seemed much excited, and said, 'I have a good piece of news for you, Daudet. It is settled. Your nomination as officer of the Legion of Honor will appear in to-morrow's "Gazette."' And I said, 'Oh, I can't stop to

talk about that now! I must go and kiss Mounet, who has been magnificent.' And I remember reading in Floquet's eyes that he didn't believe that my indifference was sincere. These people who decorate us against our will—I am sure that I never solicited or asked for any such honor; and if I did not refuse it, it was only because it is priggish to refuse, because it gets you talked about—these people, I say, are all people who themselves are not decorated; who seem to despise the reward which they dangle before our eyes, saying, 'If you are good boys and write properly, you shall have this pretty cross.' They treat us like children, despising themselves what they hold out to us as such a great inducement. Floquet wouldn't believe that I didn't care a snap of the fingers for his cross, and that all I wanted was to get away behind the scenes to compliment Mounet on his performance. When I saw the news officially announced next day, I felt sorry because I had received this distinction above the head of De Goncourt; and I feared lest De Goncourt, for whom I have the greatest reverence, would feel hurt at my having been preferred.

"Speaking of actors and of theatres, it may be of interest to relate that I never am present at any of the first productions of my plays. I am much too nervous, and always go away as far from the theatre as I can contrive, when a play of mine is being produced for the first time. It is only on the following morning that I learn whether it has been a success or not, and this generally from the manner of my *concierge*. If it has been a success, she is most respectful. If the papers have told her that her lodger has scored a failure, there is pity blended with contempt in the way in which

CHAMP ROSAY, DAUDET'S COUNTRY RESIDENCE.

she hands me my letters. It is an amusing insight into human character that is afforded to a dramatic writer by the conduct of his friends and of acquaintances on the morrow of a failure. Some pretend not to see him, not knowing what to say. Others come and try to console him, literally try to rub in lotion on the wounded heart. The servants grow familiar, and it is when your porter asks you for a box, or a pair of stalls in the dress circle, that you know that your work is definitely condemned.

MADAME DAUDET IN THE FLOWER GARDEN AT CHAMP ROSAY.

But I have been so fortunate in life—I am paying for it now—that I have very rarely had these experiences."

HIS RETIRED LIFE.

Speaking of his friends, Daudet said that since his illness he has rarely gone out. He is a frequent visitor to the house of the Princess Mathilde, and rarely a week passes without his visiting De Goncourt, for whom he has the greatest affection. But the most part of his time is spent at home. On Sunday mornings his friends call on him, and often as many as twenty people are sitting round his chair, listening to his talk. He has been particularly spirited on the abominable scandals that have been disgusting France of late, and those who heard it will not easily forget the diatribe which he pronounced against Soinoury for his treatment of Madame Cottu. "I can see him," cried Daudet, "this police official, full of his own importance, with his stupid disdain of women, proceeding from his ignorance of anything like a real woman, stroking his whiskers, and saying, 'I'll soon get the little woman to say all that she knows.'

"If the people haven't revolted," he said, "and if there has been no revolution caused by abominations which only a few years ago would have caused barricades to rise in every street of Paris, it is because, as I have noticed, a complete transformation has been effected in the character of the French people, during the last ten or fifteen years, by the militarism to which the country has been subjected since the enforcement of the new army laws. The fear of the corporal is upon every Frenchman, and it is discipline that keeps quiet the men who, fifteen years ago, would have protested at the point of the bayonet against the abominable scoundrels who are plundering France."

Daudet, it may be remarked, says what he has to say without fear or reticence. The other day, in some *salon*, he was sitting next to an advocate-general who began a panegyric on a certain procureur-general, at that time the most powerful man in France. "I don't want to hear a word about him," cried Daudet. "He is the most abominable scoundrel that I have ever heard of."

It is strange that with such frank outspokenness he should have so few enemies, but the reason of this is, no doubt, the inexpressible charm of his manner. One cannot approach Daudet without loving him—loving him for his handsome face, his large heart, and the entire simplicity of a man who has been petted, but not spoiled, for so many years by Fortune and Fortune's favorites. Amongst men of letters, though many criticise his work, he is a universal favorite. I have seen him embraced like a father by those whom he has befriended. His charity is immense.

DAUDET ON THE BANKS OF THE SEINE AT CHAMP ROSAY.

"In reviewing my past life," said Daudet, "I find that no period has remained more vividly impressed on my memory than the period of the war. My memory betrays me in many respects, so that I have compared it to a forest in which large patches burned up by the sun are quite dead. But 1870 is as clear in my mind as if it were yesterday. I can see the streets without light, the slouching shadows of the streets. I remember, as if they had just crossed my lips, the infamous fricassees that we ate. I was a soldier at the time, and oh, so energetic and full of life! It was the most active period of my life. I was always a *batailleur*, fond of sword-play and the hazards of combat, and I think that that period was the most intense of my existence. One date that I remember most vividly was that of the 31st of October, when the news of the surrender of Metz reached Paris. I was then in the ninety-seventh *de marche*, and was sent to communicate the news, on a winter's morning, to Myre de Villiers, who took me with him

Nobody applies to him for help or assistance in vain. It was amusing, and yet pathetic, to hear him the other day describing the interview he had had with a poor *confrère*, who came in rags, and who stood tearing at his straggling beard, hesitating to tell the real reason of his visit, which was to ask Daudet for the means to pay three terms of rent. Unless he paid at once, he and his family would be cast into the street. He went away a happy man, with Daudet's promise that his need would be met.

to communicate it to the soldiers at the different forts around Paris. What a poignant day that was! At each fort the general was surrounded by men. 'Metz is surrendered! We have been betrayed! Bazaine has turned traitor!' was what he had to say. I can remember some who burst into tears, others who threw down their guns and swore horribly. It was a great and a terrible experience. Still I prefer to think of that than of my horrible childhood. Is it possible," cried he, "that a child can be so unhappy as I was?"

www.ingramcontent.com/pod-product-compliance
Lightning Source LLC
Chambersburg PA
CBHW031429020726
47499CB00005B/1655